A Conjuring of Assassins

A
CONJURING
of
ASSASSINS

Cate Glass

A TOM DOHERTY ASSOCIATES BOOK

NEW YORK

A CONJURING OF ASSASSINS

Copyright © 2020 by Carol Berg

All rights reserved.

Maps by Rhys Davies

A Tor Book
Published by Tom Doherty Associates
120 Broadway
New York, NY 10271

www.tor-forge.com

Tor® is a registered trademark of Macmillan Publishing Group, LLC.

Library of Congress Cataloging-in-Publication Data

Names: Glass, Cate, author.
Title: A conjuring of assassins / Cate Glass.
Description: First edition. | New York : Tor, 2020. | Series: Chimera; 2 |
"A Tom Doherty Associates book."
Identifiers: LCCN 2019042694 (print) | LCCN 2019042695 (ebook) |
ISBN 9781250311023 (trade paperback) | ISBN 9781250311016 (ebook)
Subjects: GSAFD: Fantasy fiction.
Classification: LCC PS3607.L3645 C66 2020 (print) | LCC PS3607.L3645
(ebook) | DDC 813/.6—dc23
LC record available at https://lccn.loc.gov/2019042694
LC ebook record available at https://lccn.loc.gov/2019042695

Our books may be purchased in bulk for promotional, educational,
or business use. Please contact your local bookseller or
the Macmillan Corporate and Premium Sales Department
at 1-800-221-7945, extension 5442, or by email at
MacmillanSpecialMarkets@macmillan.com.

First Edition: February 2020

Printed in the United States of America

0 9 8 7 6 5 4 3 2 1

For Kylie, Madeline, Ethan, and Sara.
May your delight in books and stories and words
take you places you cannot imagine.

to Eide

Invidia

Argento

Kairys

Cantagna

Tibernia

Cuarona

Mercediare

To Empyria, Lhampur,
and Paolin

Il Corsia

Riccia-by-the-sea

Mare di
Ossa

Varela

Hylides

Mare
di Lacrime

Isles of
Lesh

Rhys Da.

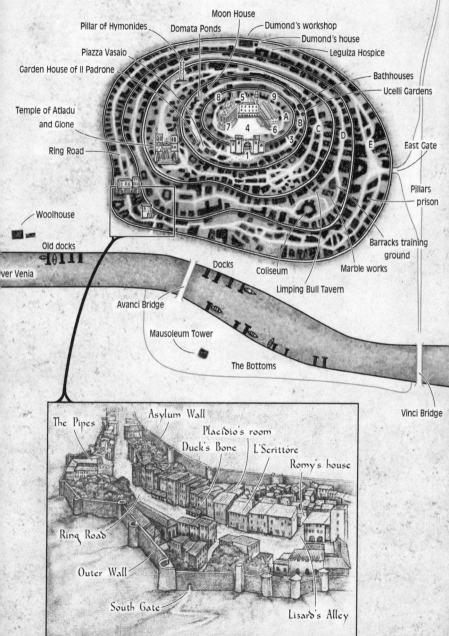

City of CANTAGNA

A. The Heights
B. Merchant Ring
C. Market Ring
D. Asylum Ring
E. Beggars Ring

1. Cambio Gate
2. Piazza Cambio
3. Via Mortua
4. Piazza Livello and Statue of Atladu's Leviathan

5. Palazzo Segnori
6. Gallanos bank
7. Philosophic Academie
8. Palazzo Fermi
9. Palazzo Ignazio

Moon House
Pillar of Hymonides
Domata Ponds
Dumond's workshop
Dumond's house
Piazza Vasaio
Leguiza Hospice
Garden House of Il Padrone
Bathhouses
Ucelli Gardens
Temple of Atladu and Gione
Ring Road
East Gate
Pillars prison
Woolhouse
Old docks
River Venia
Docks
Barracks training ground
Marble works
Coliseum
Limping Bull Tavern
Avanci Bridge
Mausoleum Tower
The Bottoms
Vinci Bridge

The Pipes
Asylum Wall
Placidio's room
Duck's Bone
L'Scrittóre
Romy's house
Ring Road
Outer Wall
South Gate
Lisard's Alley

Rhys Davies

A Conjuring of Assassins

Nature plays a clever trick on us at our birth. In the moment we are given a name, nature embeds that little scrap of language in our souls, where it remains inexorably attached until our death. Its utterance forever elicits a firework of pleasure, pride, disgust, or simple familiarity, no matter what titles or false names we assemble through the years.

The Shadow Lord, in the years of our companionship, would have smiled at this earnest pronouncement, even while expressing doubts that such was always so. He was ever skeptical of matters regarding the soul or eternity. Yet my own experience served as a prime exemplar of my premise.

I was born Romy, eldest of thirteen children my parents could not afford to feed. One brother and I, out of those thirteen, were born cursed with the taint of magic in this world that believes sorcerers are a monster's get and must be eradicated.

From an ignorant, filthy child of ten, procurers at the Moon

House groomed, whipped, and educated me into a person they named Cataline, a courtesan of impeccable wit, taste, and manners. But inside I was always scrawny, starving Romy, terrified that either my tutors or the fearsome man to whom I was gifted five years later would discover the corruption I spent every hour hiding.

After nine years, when I fell from the Shadow Lord's grace and was banished from his house, it was pitifully easy to become Romy again. But Romy became smart, tough, and practical. Romy survived, even amid such ruin.

Only when events forced me to become something new, a confidential agent who used her perverse gift for magical impersonation to serve her onetime master's better purposes, did I discover that my magic could actually break that tether between name and soul, leaving me stranded in my own body bearing someone else's name and memories. Which is why the threads of the Chimera's second adventure began to weave themselves together in a grimy alehouse I had never visited before . . .

I

T he air in the noisy alehouse blurred with more than greasy smoke. The slim, pearl-handled dagger laid out on the plank table shimmered around its edges. And it wasn't simply the thump of boots or the raucous rattle of the tabor that made the world quiver. Something wasn't right.

The dagger certainly wasn't right. *I* wasn't right. An important answer sat at the tip of my tongue, so very close . . . but I couldn't even recall the question.

"Enough is enough," said the black-eyed youth sitting across the table from me. "She can't do it."

I knew the youth. His new red shirt was made of— Why couldn't I remember?

"Pull her out." The big man seated next to the youth was almost invisible in the shadowed corner of the bench.

"Out of what?" I snapped behind my teeth. I kept my voice down, even though the Quarter Day holidaymakers made it near impossible to hear anything. "What are you talking about?"

Lady Fortune's dam, what was wrong with me?

The youth reached across the table and grabbed my wrist. "Guess you have to try again another day, *Romy*. Some of us have things to do. Like eat."

In the instant he spoke that name, the entirety of my identity—name, parentage, occupation, reasons for being in this nasty place—sloughed away like a false skin. As it was.

My true name was Romy. Sorceress. Scribe. Once a very expensive whore. A woman who had, over her five-and-twenty years, acquired a broad education in culture, languages, history, art, politics, pain, fear, self-control, and the habits of wealthy Cantagnans. Of late, a confidential agent employed by the Shadow Lord of Cantagna. An *incompetent* sorceress who couldn't release herself from her own spellwork.

"By the Sisters! How many trials does that make?"

"I'm thinking a hundred," said my brother Neri with an annoying smirk. He shot up from his seat and shoved the pearl-handled dagger toward me. "I believe I've just enough time for a bowl of rabbit pie before I head for the Duck's Bone. Fesci's backside will boil if I'm late for my shift."

He vanished into the smoke and noise.

Shivering with the aftermath of magic-working, I closed my fingers about the dagger's cool hilt and thumped the heel of my fist on my aching head. I'd been certain the elegant little weapon I'd owned for more than a decade, a reminder of both the worst and the best years of my life, could enable me to remember my own damnable name.

My particular variety of Dragonis's taint allowed me to impersonate whomever I chose to be. When I invoked my magic, my body did not change. I remained a dark-eyed woman of moderate height, shaped in ways both men and women named comely. It was the magic that laid a mask over me, making me believe I was the other so completely that the Shadow Lord himself, who knew me as intimately as any human could know another, had not recognized me when I stood before him. It was a formidable and most useful talent—with the one draw-back. Once I left Romy behind, only someone speaking my true name while touching my skin could get me back to her. Wholly impractical.

"You needs must ink the hints on your ass, lady scribe, so's when you go topsy-turvy you can find yourself again," said the man in the corner.

Someone opened the alehouse door, letting in the mid-afternoon glare. The dueling scar that creased my companion's left cheek from brow to unruly black beard gleamed faintly red in a stray sunbeam. He planted his boots on the bench, settled lower in the corner, and clapped his shabby, flat-brimmed hat entirely over his face, as if ready for a nap.

Placidio di Vasil was a professional duelist, Neri's sword-master, and my tutor in the field of combat. He made me run up cliffs, slam fists and feet into the heavy leather bolsters that hung in the deserted warehouse where we trained, and wield a variety of blades with more general effectiveness than the de-fensive knifework I'd learned as a girl. Placidio was a demon-tainted sorcerer, as well, and a man I trusted with our lives.

"How will the Chimera ever be an effective partnership if I must have a minder every time I do an impersonation?"

He gave no answer. Probably because there was none. But

this was his problem as much as my own. My partners and I were poised on the brink of our second dangerous venture in as many months, and if my magic was to be at all useful, I had to be able to disentangle myself from it.

"I was closer this time," I said, propping my chin on my fist. "The world went blurry, and I wasn't thinking as Monette the cloth merchant's daughter anymore. Certain, I wasn't thinking of you as my father. But I wasn't thinking as me, either."

I'd hoped that using the magic among strangers, instead of in my house or our training ground, would force me to keep Romy closer to the surface. One magic sniffer pointing a finger at me could get us all dead.

My plan had worked. Just not well enough.

"If you require a parent for your next practice session, get Dumond to play him. None'd b'lieve a spiff dandy like me old enough to sire a witchy female like you . . ." The slurred jibe faded into heavy breathing.

Placidio's somnolence was not to be mistaken for sleep. I'd come to think he never truly slept, which explained, in part, why he sucked down enough wine, ale, and mead in a day to supply a small village. Despite his duelist's fitness and his modest age of four-and-thirty, old wounds and old griefs weighed heavy on him.

"If I can immerse myself deep enough in an impersonation to believe *you* to be my father, Segno di Vasil, and then get myself out again, it will give an inestimable boost to my confidence. Besides, Dumond shudders at the thought of masquerades."

A scheme of impersonation and forgery to foil a threat to Cantagna's peace had brought the four of us together—Placidio,

Dumond the metalsmith, my brother Neri, and me, demon-tainted sorcerers all—and given us the rare satisfaction of using our talents for a cause other than preserving our own lives. We called ourselves the Chimera, a fantastical beast of many parts, the impossible made flesh.

Like giddy fools, we had taken on another such worthy effort within a day of finishing the first. It should be simple enough—find a dangerous document and destroy it. The prisoner who had hidden the document was being transported to Cantagna. We were awaiting only the Shadow Lord's signal that he had arrived.

Unlike me, our employer was not disturbed by his multiplicity of names. He was equally comfortable as *il Padroné*, benevolent patron of the arts and advocate for the rule of law, and the Shadow Lord, the ruthless manipulator whose will was crossed only with peril. Both were true aspects of the man born Alessandro di Gallanos, the wealthiest and most powerful man in wealthy, powerful Cantagna. For nine years I had called him Sandro.

"Maybe I won't need to use my magic at all in the new venture," I said. "Getting inside a prison cell is more up Dumond's alley—or Neri's. I wonder—"

Neri emerged from the crowd like a thunderclap from a clear sky. "Swordmaster, someone's come looking for you!"

A scrawny fellow with wispy red hair, peeling skin, and bad teeth shoved Neri aside and slapped a dirty woven badge on the table. The stink of sour flesh and moldy garlic wafted from him.

"Placidio di Vasil, I bring answer for the insulting challenge you threw at my uncle yesternight in front of twenty witnesses.

My own self will stand for him at Bawds Field in one hour. Be there or be deemed coward forever more."

"What?" Placidio threw off his hat and snatched up the badge. "Come back here, Buto! Does your uncle know about this?"

Placidio's outrage could have been heard clear up to the Piazza Livello at the heart and height of the city. But the scrawny man had already vanished through the silenced crowd.

"Damnable idiot. An hour?" Placidio scraped fingers through his matted hair.

"You challenged someone for yourself!" Neri gawped after the man. "Who is it? What did he do?"

Professional duelists fought other people's battles. Only the stupid ones risked injury by fighting for free—for themselves—or so Placidio always claimed.

"One wrong, cursed, confusticated word." He slammed his hat back on his head and shoved the table away, trapping me on my own bench. "Another lesson for you two. Never exchange insults with a pox-raddled moron in the middle of a card game."

The tapgirl yanked another bung, and like a spark near nitre powder, it reignited the clamor of drinkers and the whistle and rattle of the musicians.

"Another match?" I said, in quiet frustration. "We could get the Shadow Lord's signal at any moment. And no referees, I'm guessing."

"Told you before, lady scribe, my matches are naught for you to worry on. But if it eases you, the only difficulty here is how *not* to kill this maggot."

"But for someone unsavory like this fellow, you need a second. A witness, at least," said Neri, bolder than I in the face of

Placidio's unyielding personal boundaries . . . or at the *backside* of them. Placidio was already three steps from the table.

Neri persisted. "No time to fetch a neutral."

Placidio whirled around, his cinder-gray eyes picking at Neri. After a moment, he spoke grudgingly. "Witness, aye. That could be useful. Mostly it would do you good to see how an overeager idiot like Buto conducts himself, lest you start thinking you've learned enough from your lessons. But you are *not* my second. I alone do the talking. You will stay where I tell you—at the split-trunk nettle tree west of the path from the prison. Well hid. Neither toe nor eyelash to be seen. And you stay exactly there till the end."

Placidio didn't need to add what dire consequence would follow disobedience. Nonetheless, Neri hurried after him like a hound after its hunter. As he had abandoned his bowl of rabbit pie, I was not inordinately surprised when he darted back to the table before reaching the door to the street.

"Romy, talk to Fesci for me. Tell her I've dueling business with Placidio and will be late. She always fusses over him, so she won't be all bent when I get there."

He didn't linger to finish the pie, nor to hear my answer. He knew he'd get a lecture.

Neri had come a long way from the angry, ignorant youth who used his magic to steal three rubies, getting our family exiled and the two of us very nearly executed. But he was still rash and headstrong, and forever assumed one or the other of the Chimera would pull him out of the fire if he danced too close.

Since the dawn of the world, the First Law of Creation had mandated death for anyone tainted with the monster Dragonis's magic, lest they use their fiendish talents to set the beast free to wreak the world's end. The earth's shudders that flattened villages, and the mountains' yearly spews of ash, smoke, and scalding rock, provided clear reminders of the malignancy imprisoned beneath the Costa Drago. But whether one believed or not—and after nine years' immersion in history, reason, and philosophy I was skeptical—the First Law made no distinction between those who *worked* magic and those corrupted by association with it. A careless mistake could pose a real and mortal danger to Placidio, Dumond and his family, and me, as well as to Neri himself.

I shoved the table back to its place and set out for Bawds Field. When Neri saw I'd not done his bidding, he could decide for himself if he wanted to risk a reckoning with Taverner Fesci.

· · ·

Bawds Field, shielded from public view by the bleak bulk of the prison, a few nettle trees, and a tall bordering scrub of firethorn and prickly juniper, was often used for grudge fights, including duels *not* registered with the referees who maintained the city's professional Dueling List. The place had gotten its name back when Cantagna was governed by a hereditary grand duc instead of our elected Sestorale. The nobleman had taken a young wife who was horrified to learn that bawdy houses were legal in her husband's demesne. Even worse, the grand duc required their prices stay low as a way to make whores accessible to every citizen who desired to partake of their services.

The ducessa must have had the charms of a goddess, a will of forged steel, and no conscience to speak of, as within a month of the noble marriage, every bawd, pimp, whore, and catamite in Cantagna had been marched into a wasteland behind the

Pillars Prison and hanged. Tutors at the Moon House had used that story to remind us students how fortunate we were that not only were we not criminals, but that our beauty and skills would command a price that only someone like a grand duc— or a wealthy banker—could afford. At age ten, I had not felt comforted.

In the center of the pounded dirt and gravel, the scrawny man called Buto donned a mail shirt. Two equally disreputable comrades marked out a large, slightly lopsided circle with stones and bits of rubble, planting sticks in the ground at four quarter points.

Placidio stood to one side in his dueling leathers, hands clasped behind his back, his favored dueling sword at his side. His relaxed but wary posture should be intimidating to anyone who had ever watched him fight.

And Neri? I stood between the twin trunks of the giant nettle tree on the west side of the field—exactly where Placidio had told Neri to hide. Neri wasn't there. Nor was he out of sight. His red shirt shone like a signal flag from a thicket on the opposite side of the field.

Using the path behind the scrub, I headed for Neri.

"You are familiar with Cantagna's Code Duello, young Buto?" Placidio's booming query drew me to a gap in the stand of firethorn.

I'd never watched one of Placidio's duels. For one, I saw enough of his skills when I trained with him. For another, I assumed he had reasons for saying so little of when, where, or whom he was fighting; his privacies were very important to him. And, in truth, it made good sense for Placidio, Dumond, and Neri and me to keep our non-Chimera lives separate.

"We're to stand opposite each other on the circle." The scrawny man puffed out his chest. "We salute, then take our stance. A third party—Minque—drops the ribbon and we fight. First man steps out of the circle forfeits the challenge. In our case, he must stand on a table at the Kettle and Stoke tonight and apologize to my uncle."

"'Tis gratifying you've studied the Code, segno," said Placidio, his baritone clear and calm. "So, your uncle is not one of these fellows?"

"Certain, you know they're not my uncle!"

"Then alas, despite your courage and stalwart bearing, we cannot proceed. You've not yet come of age, and the verisame Code you've quoted so accurately states that an underage combatant cannot stand for a partisan without that partisan's presence. Were we to go ahead, I would be in dreadful difficulty with the Dueling Commission."

"You're just trying to get out of this," snarled the young man. "Cowardly! You're a broke-down drunk with the shakes! Everyone says so."

The insult wouldn't ruffle Placidio, as he cultivated that reputation. But then, neither would it induce any inclination to benevolence.

"I'll not deny that I was in a less than cogent state when I threw the challenge. And I am willing to pay the price for my folly. I will even add the condition that the first one driven out of the circle must not only apologize to your uncle, but crow like rooster at the same time. That would ensure I never forget to mind my manners when drunk. But I must insist that your uncle be present. I'll wait right here while he is summoned. You may accuse me as a drunkard, but you'll not have me up on charges for dueling a pup when its handler is away."

The young man spluttered, then whipped around and beckoned one of his henchmen. As they did not bellow their energetic consultation, I didn't hear what was said. But one of the lads took off, and scrawny Buto looked as if he'd swallowed a pig entire. Not near as awful as he would when Placidio was done with him, I'd guess. I couldn't imagine my swordmaster allowing this pompous little twit to win.

Placidio was a brilliant swordsman even without the astonishing magical gift that allowed him to anticipate an opponent's moves. Sadly, to avoid notice, he had to take a pounding on a regular basis, which kept him poor, bruised, and settled in the middle ranks of the Dueling List. Certain, he was an invaluable partner. Not only was he strong, skilled, and inured to fear, he was the most observant person I had ever known. He would know Neri was out of position.

I returned to my own objective—informing my brother that I'd not carry his excuses. Just as I reached the spot where the path from the Pillars Prison met the fainter track that circled the haunted field, more noise reached me from the dueling ground. I couldn't resist stopping to watch through the tangled scrub.

The uncle must have been awaiting his justification in the aforementioned Kettle and Stoke—a close-by alehouse. Placidio acknowledged one man from a group of three new arrivals, better dressed than Buto, but not by much. A slouched hat with a plume of desiccated feathers prevented any chance of me recognizing the man.

Buto returned to the boundary of the ring. Placidio did the same and drew his sword.

The scrawny Buto—perhaps noticing that Placidio's hands were perfectly steady—fumbled his own weapon out of its silver-banded sheath. Who were these people? Grimy, but not impoverished. Even from here I could see Buto's sword was of good quality.

"Who the devil have we here?" The man was just behind me.

"The little pustule has a fetching audience, Lonzo! Mayhap we can do a little dueling right here!"

The voices—oily with innuendo—spun me around, on my guard.

One glimpse had me dipping a knee and ducking my head—horrified. It was impossible to mistake Lawyer Cinnetti's grand moustaches above the wide fleshy lips, the overpadded doublet, the soiled neck ruff, unchanged since the day half a year ago when I'd applied to him for writing work. The day he'd tried to force himself on me.

Cinnetti and his companion reeked of wine and lust. Their position blocked any escape except through the impossibly firethorn scrub.

"I'm Druda, noble segnoré," I said, tasting bile as I spoke. "Segno Buto's friend. I've come to see how he takes this drunkard bully down."

On that awful day, I'd used a stunted offshoot of my magic to remove my name and the circumstance of our meeting from Cinnetti's mind. But I'd been so rattled . . . so terrified . . . and I'd no idea how to tie off all threads of a memory when I used magic to destroy it. If he saw me . . . as Romy . . . he might well recall my face and how I had kicked him in the balls and threatened to cut off his prick. Such a man did not forget insults.

Cinnetti's lizard-skin boots stepped close. His fingers twined my hair, gripping it tight as they had on that vile afternoon when he'd so nearly had his way. His other hand traced the line of my neck across my breasts and back up to my chin.

"Don't be shy, Damizella Druda. We'll just have a friendly romp, mmm?" His insistent knuckle commanded me to look up.

"You didn't tell me there'd be sweetmeats at this scuffle, Lonzo." The other man's bulk moved in close, his shadow blocking the sun. Sharp thorns pricked my back. "You must share."

Never in this life would I forget those lips smothering my face. That greasy moustache. The spidery hands. The murderous look on his face when he had sworn to teach me of his needs next time he saw me.

I knew only one way to be sure Cinnetti wouldn't recognize me. Neri was close. As soon as she could shed these two, Druda must head straight for him. He would pull me out.

Reaching deep for magic, I grabbed at a story, drew all of my will, and let go of my own self . . .

I lifted my chin. "Oh, good gentlemen . . . you flatter me. Buto is not half one of you. And you are two! What is a modest girl to do?"

Fluttering my lashes, I gazed from one to the other—not the worst rakes I'd ever pleasured—even as I reached for the roaming hand and nibbled at the fleshy pad beneath his thumb. Old Merle, my bawd, had taught me how to *deflect* without *discouraging*.

The tall man reached for the laces at my bodice.

I nipped the moustached man's hand and twirled to his side. He tried to plant a kiss, but missed. His breath was sour. Good wine could cover that.

"Witch!" said the tall man, whose beard had threads of gray. The tease unsettled me, but I rubbed my hip against his backside, making promises I might or might not keep.

The moustached man stroked my neck. Not a pleasurable touch. But these two had fat purses on their belts. Perhaps I could lure them to the alehouse where I'd met Buto. It had private rooms up the stair, where I could set my own price and keep Old Merle's share for myself. That could be worth the beating when she found out. She always found out . . .

"Saluto!"

"Fight's starting," I said, taking advantage of the distraction to loose the men's hold on me. I stepped to the side and pointed through the scrub. "Got to watch this before seeing to our fun. Promised him."

Buto was a scabby little nuisance . . . but rich. He wanted me to witness his triumph.

"En garde!"

Buto and the other man—he was tall and broad in the back, and didn't look at all drunk—struck a ready pose. Buto's squirrely friend Minque held up a blue kerchief halfway between. A moment's pause and he dropped it.

The big man stepped forward, sword at the ready, but he didn't strike or lunge. Buto ran at him yelling, pulling up short just when the big man stepped to the side and crashed the hilt of his blade against Buto's head. Buto staggered but stayed on his feet.

I knew what that blow felt like. The piercing light behind the eyes. The world dropping out from under. The stomach churning. Old Merle had a way with her broke-off broom handle . . .

"Enough of Buto's folly." One of the moustached man's busy hands found my hair again. He pulled me to him and reached between my legs, squeezing my thigh. "What's this?"

As an answer, I giggled and grabbed his hand in my hair, pinched it hard to make him let go, and twisted away before he could get a firmer grip. Before he could anger, I kissed those dirty fingers, laughing as I did so. Teasing him. Pulling away all the while.

Old Merle always found out when I cheated her. No purse was worth another month of headaches and half rations.

Tugging at his codpiece, I danced around behind the tall one. "You fellas gonna duel over me? 'Twill be more fun than Buto's having, I'll say. I'll pleasure the winner of *your* match till his eyeballs roll back in his head."

"There's enough of you for two. Don't need any dueling." Growling, the moustache man shoved his friend aside and lunged, but I ran. Back to the path and around Bawds Field.

The two chased me, boots pounding, the moustache man cursing, the tall man chortling. I ran to where I'd seen a man in a red shirt. Certain, he would help me escape these two. But I saw naught of him as I raced past the sprinkle of onlookers, back to the streets, up to the Ring Road. The red shirt man was likely just another of Buto's posturing friends with filthy minds.

Once on the Ring Road, I ducked behind noodle stalls, into a weaver's shop, and out again from the back. Into alleys and through squeezes that folk bigger than me couldn't fit. Through more stalls. Some were half-familiar places, where folk made as if they knew me, but then said I wasn't who they thought.

By the time I lost the two men, I was lost, too. No matter that the market streets and the Ring Road were familiar, I couldn't find the turning to Old Merle's. She'd beat the life out of me if I didn't get back for the evening. It was Quarter Day and folk had sorrows to drown and coin to spend, and I'd have twenty or more through my crib before next dawn.

I tried asking, but no one in this part of the Beggars Ring had heard of Old Merle. And I couldn't remember the name of the quartiere . . . nor the street . . . nor what else was close to her house. I kept going . . . on and on. What was the alehouse where they had private rooms upstairs? Why couldn't I remember? I'd been with Merle for years, since— Since I was ten and the man took me to the yellow house where they stripped and washed me, cut my hair, and put me in a closet.

No, that couldn't be right. Old Merle had got me off a pimp. She'd gave me the crib with a bed and a washstand. But I couldn't see it in my head, nor where I kept my things. Surely I had things there.

Atremble, I stumbled into an old stone ruin, long collapsed, and sank into a corner overgrown with weeds. *Think, Druda.* Even my name sounded wrong. My head pounded, every thought twisted into knots as I went over all that had happened since I glimpsed the moustache man. Had he slipped me mysenthe? Certain, I wasn't drowsy or pleasured by it. Maybe he had poison on those dirty fingers. My gut rebelled and I vomited out whatever I'd eaten or drunk that morning, but I couldn't even recall what that had been.

When the sun settled low to the west, fear crawled into me

like black mold, coating my spirit, my heart. Old Merle . . . I couldn't recall her face neither, only the rules, the beatings. I would welcome a slap from her just now. She knew me.

Night brought a quiet mumbling from the other side of the wall. I huddled deeper in the corner. My hand found its own way into a pocket in my black skirt and pulled out a slim dagger with a white handle. I peered around the stone.

A hunchbacked woman trudged slowly through the rubble, herding a pair of geese. Whether the mumble was hers or the birds', I didn't know.

The knife must have been what the moustache man remarked when he was groping. Impossible that I could have such a fine thing and not recall how I'd come to have it. My *hand* remembered—not just where it was kept in a sheath strapped to my thigh, but how to hold it. How to kill with it. The object itself, though . . . strange how it pained my heart till I thought it must crack. Crazy.

The city bells tolled hour after hour as I huddled there. Empty. Lost. Best move or I'd lose my mind entire. I'd best go back to Bawds Field, behind the prison down near the East Gate. That was the only place I'd been that I could see in my mind's eye. I would search for nearby alehouses and ask after Buto. *He* could surely tell me what I needed to know. Unless he was dead. Unless I had forgotten how to speak. Unless there was a demon slithering through my veins, eating my brain.

Full panicked, I jumped up and ran, clutching the dagger in my right hand as if it were a lodestone to guide me. My left hand I held outspread with ring finger and smallest finger curled tight to ward me from demons.

The last glow of sunset proved the Bawds Field deserted.

I circled aimlessly as the light faded, looking for signs that anyone had truly been here or if the whole day had been but a terrible dream. When I found a rag stiff with dried blood, I dropped to my knees weeping. Clutching it to my breast, I prayed to the Unseeable Gods that Buto lived, so that I could find him and ask where he'd met me.

"Romy? Is that you?" The voice seemed to come from everywhere at once. That name was what those Beggars Ring folk had called me by mistake.

"Not her," I whispered, though I wished I were. Old Merle wouldn't send after me, unless she heard I'd took a crib with some other bawd. Then she'd send someone to cut my face. I gripped the dagger, ready to plunge it into any who thought to touch me.

An ivory light shone out, glaring in my eyes. "She's over here. I'm sure of it. Black skirt, white chemise, blue kirtle. Wasn't that what she was wearing?"

I scrambled to my feet and backed away, ready to run.

"Romy, it's me! Wait, wait . . ."

He was a comely youth with black hair and black eyes. What if he worked for the moustache man or his tall friend?

"Don't know who you're looking for," I said, "but it ain't me. Get away. I've a weapon, and I can hurt you with it."

"Certain, you can. You taught me how to use it. The Santorini Thrust. Remember? That's your dagger with the pearl handle you got from the Moon House. Then *he* gifted it back to you. You know who. The one we don't speak of out in places like this."

Footsteps approached on every side of me. I thought my skull would burst.

"A good guess that she'd be here, Dumond." This from a big man come into the light, the very one who'd fought Buto.

"Did you kill him?" I yelled, squeezing the bloody rag. "Great Mother of us all, tell me you didn't kill Buto." Maybe the only person in the world who knew me.

"Didn't," the big man said softly. "His scabby complexion has taken another ill turn, but I didn't even make him crow like a rooster."

"Romy." A woman's voice this time. On my left. She was small, foreign. Not young, but such beautiful skin. And eyes so kind as I'd never seen. Hands open. "May I come near? I'm so glad we found you. Your brother was so worried. Some in the neighborhood thought they recognized you, but you look . . . different . . . tonight. Astonishing how you do that."

"What brother? Who are you all?" I brandished the knife. "Did Old Merle send you?"

I was shaking again. Cold. Everything I knew of the world— little as it was—was thin and wavering like the youth's lamp- light.

"We're your partners." This dry, cool voice came from behind.

Before I could spin to see him, a pair of thick, comfortable arms grabbed me around the middle. I struggled and yelled, and struck at him with the knife, but the woman's slim fingers gently touched my cheek. "Romy. Come back."

The world came rushing back, and like the delicate-flower kind of woman I had ever despised, I collapsed, quivering like a birch leaf, breathless, angry, and awash in tears.

2

L awyer Cinnetti!" said Neri. "He's the one that almost—
Gods' balls, Romy. If he'd recognized you, he'd have cut
your throat. I saw his face that day."

"I couldn't take the risk, not with the two of them so determined. I'd no time to plan, no time to invent a complete person,
no time to let you or Placidio know." But I'd counted on Neri being where I'd seen him so he could release me from the magic,
and he wasn't there. "All of you came looking for me. I can't
even begin—"

Nor could I finish without dissolving again.

The five of us crowded the one-room stone hovel in Lizards
Alley where Neri and I had lived since the Shadow Lord had
thrown me out and exiled our parents and our eight living siblings. Neri had been born in this house and never lived anywhere else.

When we'd arrived, I touched every one of our meager pos-
sessions, the walls, the window, our clothes chest, the shelf

where I kept extra parchment and ink, the table and stools we had bought on our first day as a family of two. The door Neri had built us—the first useful thing he had ever created on his own. All the way from Bawds Field I had feasted on recognition and memory—even the most painful ones—as if I were starving and could never get enough.

Neri leaned forward, as if worried I might not hear him. "When Fesci told me you'd not brought her my message, and the shop was locked up, and you weren't here though I knew you had writing work to do, something seemed off. Germond said he thought he'd seen you, only it wasn't you, just someone scared. I found Placidio and we fetched Dumond and Vashti," said Neri.

"That was well done," I said. "I could have been anywhere. Another hour like that . . ."

That Vashti, Dumond's exceptional wife, had joined the search for me was a blessing. Not solely because I would have tried to kill any man who tried to touch me—lucky for Dumond I had only ripped his sleeve and grazed his arm—but also because once the others had got me walking, she'd kept telling them not to fret when I burst into tears at the sight of Germond the ironmonger's signpost shaped like a hammer or the row of message boxes in front of my little scriptorium on the Ring Road. "Think about it," was all she'd had to say. "This is Romy."

I wasn't sure I felt entirely like Romy as yet. Sometimes I turned too fast or blinked untimely and for that one instant I was back in that dark void where a few sketchy circumstances—a nonexistent panderer and her house, a whore's particular skills, and an encounter with a self-important lackwit—were the summation of my life, the entirety of my soul.

"Should never have happened." Placidio stood leaning on

the door, arms folded across his chest. "There's enough things go on that can't be prepared for. But this . . . There's always scoundrels drift over from the prison when they hear there's something on at Bawds Field."

"I should have been more aware of my surroundings," I said.

"Pssh." Placidio waved me off. "You went to where I said, aye? Because you expected my conditions were understood and my orders followed."

"Yes," I said. To blunt my answer would have accomplished nothing.

Neri's coloring deepened three shades. "I just didn't—"

Placidio didn't budge. "When I say *stay in one particular place, don't show yourself, remain there till all's done and clear,* I trust you to assume I have reason for it. I trust you to do as I've said unless an earthquake opens the dirt beneath your feet."

Neri's cheeks burned. "But you didn't say there'd be scoundrels, and I wasn't expecting Romy to come, and I thought I should get the best view I could—"

"But even when your whim took you to a different spot, you didn't stay there till it all was ended."

Placidio didn't have to raise his voice to make his point. If Neri had been where he was supposed to be, he would have been with me when Cinnetti came down the prison path. If he'd stayed in his chosen view point until the duel was over, he would have seen me running—because I'd made sure Druda would head straight for him.

"We four—and those we bring into our lives—exist with ever-present danger." Placidio gave no quarter. "As the Chimera, we've willingly accepted even more. But the price is trust . . ."

". . . and constant mindfulness," I added. "I put us all in a bad spot because I wanted to prove a point about responsibility, but lack of attention got me in too deep." I stood and shoved my stool aside. "Thanks to you all, it's over. Madness averted. And now I'm hungry. Do we have anything in the house to eat?"

Vashti insisted on making tea—her solution for all upheavals—and though our neglected larder provided nothing more than the remains of our morning's bread, some cheese, and a bowl of plums and apricots, we made do. Placidio and Dumond sat on the floor, Neri on his pallet.

"Any notice of our prisoner's arrival?" asked Dumond, offering a welcome change of subject. "By my tally it's six more days until Cantagna has to turn him over."

The prisoner in question, a citizen of Mercediare, had been arrested thirteen days previous in our city's northernmost territory, accused of selling stolen papers. By treaty, Cantagna had twenty days to turn foreign criminals over to their independency's nearest representative—in this case, the local Mercediaran ambassador—for transport back to their own city. It was usually a straightforward transaction, even dealing with Mercediare, our city's greatest rival. For either party to violate the treaty could reap heavy fines or restrictions on commerce, shipping, or banking.

"No word," I said. "I've heard heavy rains and mud slides have blocked the Argento Road, causing terrible travel problems. Neri's been scouting prison yards—the Pillars, the Asylum Ring gaol, even the Prisoners Walk behind the Palazzo Segnori—listening for rumors."

I looked to my brother for confirmation. He shrugged agreement, showing no sign of his usual excitement at a mention of our Chimera ventures. He hated when Placidio found fault with him.

"Would've been nice if the Shadow Lord could have told them where to stash the fellow, so we wouldn't have to watch every cell in the city." Placidio downed another apricot smashed atop a wedge of cheese.

"He can display no interest whatsoever in the prisoner," I said. "He dares not do anything that might make the Mercediarans suspect the prisoner's true identity, elsewise they'll hound the Sestorale into turning the fellow over immediately."

Sandro had seen evidence that identified the prisoner as an elusive thief, spy, and broker of secrets known as *Cinque*. He very much wanted the man questioned before anyone else got wind of the connection, because among Cinque's known assets was a document he called the Assassins List—a sworn pact between certain powerful people, some of them Cantagnese, to *assassinate Mercediare's Protector when the time was right*. Rather than tip off the Mercediarans, he had asked the Chimera to discover the location of the Assassins List and ensure it never reached Protector Vizio's hands.

No one who valued human decency would defend the thuggish tyrant who called herself the Protector of Mercediare, but such an open-ended threat of assassination sitting in that woman's hand would certainly precipitate a campaign of murder, kidnap, and rapine against the signers. Her vendetta would cost our city valuable citizens and valuable allies, spilling over into every aspect of the city's life.

"Why would anyone sign such a paper?" asked Vashti. "Promising to kill someone in the future? If you think a person wicked enough to be dead, you should be bold and do it!"

Placidio grinned and raised his mug of tea to Vashti. "Now we know why Dumond is such a dull, solid citizen. Remind me, all of you, to hide all my wickedness when we're together like this. Wouldn't want this woman to get any notions."

Laughter burst out all around. Even from Vashti, who ducked her head, and Dumond, who nodded broadly. Even I, who yet felt lunacy much too close, joined in.

Vashti's ferocity was truly no surprise. Anyone who saw her with her four daughters could not but envision the Lioness of Paolin—her homeland's goddess of the Hearth, always depicted as rampant, guarding her cubs.

When we had sobered again, I gave her the only answer I could think of. "From what *il Padroné* told me, the signers weren't agreeing to assassinate Vizio, only to contribute money to hire someone *else* to do so when her primacy in Mercedi-are became untenable. Just in case she started choking off trade routes or raising tariffs on shipping or some such."

"Such subtlety won't make a difference to her," said Placidio. "If she gets hold of that list, the consequences will be the same as if each signer had a dagger at her neck."

The city bells rang the Hour of Contemplation—three hours before midnight. Dumond and Vashti left to fetch their daughters from a friend. Neri returned to the Duck's Bone to work off some of the hours he had missed.

Placidio didn't move, except to fill his cup from our little ale cask at his back. "Are you going to be all right, lady scribe?"

It would have been easy to make a glib answer and send him on his way. But, in truth, I didn't want to be alone.

"Don't know. I've a flask of Porchellini brandy I could open.

Client gave it to me for pointing out he'd entered the wrong name in a contract."

Placidio waved me off. "I'd say . . . don't drown what happened today before you know how it's maintaining. Drink can ease a great deal. But some things . . . it'll leave you defenseless. Makes the aftermath far worse."

"Worse? I don't think it could be."

"I'll vouch." He raised his hand as if swearing. "And I'll stay. You don't have to talk unless you want. I could nap. Or I'll play cards. For beans . . . dry, of course. Pebbles? Lint?"

A year ago I'd tried using wine to deaden grief. It had near ruined me. Now I thought of it, I didn't want anything dulled or erased just now. It was sleep frightened me. How could I let go? What if waking life never came back and I was left the shivering, weepy wreck I'd been a few hours before?

Perhaps the discipline that brought me back last year could work again. "Tomorrow. Maybe a lesson from my swordmaster? I've been lax of late. Next time, I want to fight off the demons with a blade."

"Woolhouse at midday."

"I'll be there. So you can feel free to—"

"I'm still staying." From a pocket in the scuffed canvas armaments bag on the floor beside him, he pulled out a palm-sized wooden box and tossed it up onto the little table in front of me. It was made of olive wood, beautifully carved with sea creatures.

"What's this?"

He hefted himself off the floor and onto one of my stools. His big hands slid the lid smoothly off the box. "Cards. We're playing high stakes primera. You provide the beans."

• • •

I slept until the sun was high enough to penetrate Lizard's Alley and our tightly closed shutters. Save for the first dreadful, horrifying gasp when the world was yet a blur and I was back huddled in a corner of the ruin Beggars Ring folk called Fortunata's Doom, all was well. My hands quivered a little as I scraped together the scattered piles of dried beans and shoved them back into their jar. I owed more than beans to Placidio's account.

He had stayed with me, playing primera, coché, triplets—every card game known in the Costa Drago—keeping me lost in tricks and trumps and wagers until I could no longer hold my head up or make out the painted faces on the paper rectangles. Even when I stumbled to my pallet, shaking for terror of sleep, he promised he would neither leave nor close his eyes until Neri came home.

That had happened at some time, as Neri's bed was jumbled in a different disorder than the previous night. But Neri himself was not there. Maybe Fesci had more work for him.

The city bells rang the hour before midday. That hurried my morning ablutions and gave me little time to dwell on whether I would need to work or play myself into oblivion every day from now on. I hoped a dose of my swordmaster's discipline would reduce my need of his cards or his shoulder.

I checked the message box to see if we had word of the prisoner from the Shadow Lord. We didn't. And I stopped for a moment to speak with the ironmonger whose house and yard sat across the Ring Road from Lizard's Alley. But by the time the bells pealed the midday anthem, I was outside the city walls, hiking briskly along the bank of the River Venia—Cantagna's lifeblood.

Past the old city docks and the untidy remnants of the fire that had destroyed them and an entire warehouse district two decades since stood one blockish stone building. The wool guild warehouse, abandoned since the plague years by everyone but birds and transient beggars, had held little but rotting timbers, vermin bones, and a reputation for hauntings when we chose it for Neri's lessons with Placidio. Now thick leather bolsters for punching and stabbing hung from the rafters, hay bundles served for archery practice, and the floor of pounded earth was clear of rubble, ready for combat practice of all kinds.

No one would mistake the taskmaster that awaited me for the companion who had shown me such generosity the previous night. He started me off running—all the way to the scarp called the Boar's Teeth—and climbed the steep rocks right behind me, a silent dare to slack or dally. Pausing at the top only long enough to swallow a sip of his *restorative tea*—a vile concoction of ginger, salt, and lemon—we picked our way down again and raced back to the woolhouse. Only then, when I was drenched with the sweat of midday summer, did he toss me a leather jaque, a pair of leather gloves, and a short sword, pull out his own wickedly sharp main gauche, and set to.

It was well done. For two hours—very near eternity, it seemed—I'd no choice but to bring every muscle, nerve, thought, and imagining to the problem of keeping my feet moving and my skin intact. He never spoke a word beyond *attend, you're dead,* or *again*.

It was exactly what I needed.

Afterward, we sat drinking for a while, Placidio his ginger

tea, I from a cask of clean water I had installed in self-defense. When I could muster spit enough to speak, I said, "Tomorrow? Same time?"

He reclined against one of our hay bundles, dragged his hat across his face, and grunted in a vaguely affirmative tone.

"I'd say earlier when it's cooler, but I might sleep late like today. This will help get me to tomorrow."

"Good," he said. "Harder tomorrow."

A hot, heavy gust off the river set the bolsters swaying. "Did you work with Neri this morning? He was out early. Did he say anything when he came home?"

"No and no. Best if he sweats a bit. Don't make it easy on him. I won't."

Placidio was right, of course. The hard experiences Neri and I had gone through had been necessary. I'd just hoped we were done with the contentious part. Maybe family was like training; you were never finished.

Placidio's breathing settled deep and regular.

I roused my creaky limbs and moved off to the hanging bolster farthest from him and went through the punching and kicking exercises he'd taught us. My conscience—voiced in Placidio's flat baritone—forced me through the entirety of them three times. And then through the slow, stretching, thoughtful sword moves, using repetition and concentration to embed them in my muscles in the same way as walking, running, sitting, and standing. One additional run-through—fast—and I was done for. My body felt like a glob of hot wax.

I cleaned the salt and sweat from the blade, wrapped it carefully, and returned it to Placidio's armaments bag. My jaque and gloves went into the small chest I'd bought to hold some of the costume pieces Vashti had made for my last impersonation. I'd found the chest in a cloth merchant's stall in the Market Ring. The bombastic merchant and his eye-fluttering daughter with a singular devotion to Lady Fortune had given me the idea for the practice impersonation I'd been working on with Placidio and Neri.

Spirits, was that only yesterday? I closed up the little chest, shoved it behind the hay bundles, and tapped Placidio's shoulder. I had no illusion that he was sleeping as soundly as it appeared.

"Move your sorry bones and come with me, swordmaster. Germond the ironmonger wants me to meet him at the Duck's Bone this evening to draft a new will; I think Basilio's wooing has made a soppy idiot of him. But it's not time yet, and I'm dreadfully thirsty for something with a decent taste to it. So I'll stand you a mug from Fesci's secret tap."

"Got something on this evening."

"Mayhap we'll get word of our prisoner's arrival tonight. Time's getting short."

Five days more until Cantagna would turn over the prisoner to the Mercediaran ambassador. The Sestorale always waited the full span of time the treaty allowed for relinquishing custody of the prisoner, like children proving to street bullies that they weren't going to be pushed around. Once we found out where the prisoner was being held, it should be simple to get him to tell us what we wanted to know. Such a man would know how Mercediaran interrogators would relish getting their hands on an infamous spy working against the Protector. Only one aspect of the transaction bothered me . . .

Placidio had begun snoring at such a volume he drowned

out the sound of evening birds along the river. I jabbed the toe of my boot in his ribs. "Have you ever been in prison?"

"A time or three. Never long enough for the rot to set in. And I'm still alive. Not looking to do it again."

He did not elaborate. Any reference to his history fell behind his well-protected boundaries.

"I've been thinking . . . this Cinque . . . we can't set him free, no matter what we promise."

Sandro had left the matter of the prisoner's fate up to us. Destroying the Assassins List without evidence of Cantagna's interference would neutralize the danger that concerned him so fiercely.

Placidio shoved his hat aside just enough to peer at me. "Aye, that seems clear enough. Beyond the fact that the fellow's a mercenary spy—thus not so trusty—if he were to vanish from a prison cell in Cantagna, it would raise all sorts of uncomfortable questions."

"Such as who had arranged it," I said.

"And the logical answer would be the Shadow Lord. There are certain difficulties with being as notorious as Alessandro di Gallanos is. And as ruthless . . ."

". . . as he certainly is." My partners did not yet comprehend that I truly understood the darker aspects of the man who had been my entire world for nine years. "But to abandon anyone to such a fate . . ."

An ugly fate it would be. Mercediaran prisons were the stuff of nightmares. If the Mercediaran ambassador had any notion the prisoner was more than a common thief, it would be worse. Mercediarans were sophisticated in the nasty arts of retrieving information from prisoners.

"Seems that leaves only one clear alternative."

"We cannot just kill him," I snapped. "No matter if you're comfortable meting out death."

"I am never comfortable with that." No teasing this time.

"The Chimera is *not* a cadre of assassins."

"And I'm saying you'd best be thinking about that." He pulled his hat back over his face, folded his arms over his chest, and drew a deep settling breath.

My insult had been unfair. Placidio took his profession seriously, just as he did his role of swordmaster. He forever prodded me to consider the possibilities and consequences of every action, pushing me to be more observant, to think deeper, and to constantly improve my skills to cope with a dangerous world. I welcomed the teaching, but it could be most disquieting.

"Why are you lolloping here?" I said. "I thought you had something on for this evening."

"Never said that something wasn't a nap."

"At some time, I want—I *need* to work on the relinquishing. I can't ever risk what happened yesterday happening again. Will you play Merchant Baldassar for me?"

"I will. Not tonight, though. I've a rough match coming on. N'more than that till we're dead or done with this prisoner venture."

"Good. Don't take too bad a beating." I headed for the door, calling back over my shoulder, "Remember, fluttery young Monette needs her papa sober."

"Yeah, yeah. Pesky females, the both of you."

I laughed as his mumbled jibe followed me into the riverside wasteland that separated the abandoned woolhouse from the city. But as I picked a path through ruins and river wrack, the exchange with Placidio nagged at me. Yes, he had a point, but we were sorcerers. We should have better ways than murder to solve inconvenient problems.

3

The fishermen's path climbed the slope from the river-bank to a narrow slot gate in Cantagna's southwest wall. The warden waved me through without a glance. No one cared who passed into the Beggars Ring, the poorest, most crowded, and most dangerous of Cantagna's five concentric districts, on a steamy afternoon. Those who'd not spent their childhood years exploring its crumbling tenements and the ramshackle dwellings that sprang up overnight like mushrooms from the muck could wander for days before finding a way out of it. At night the guards were a bit more nosy.

Once back to the Ring Road, I stopped at a narrow house front adorned with a double row of small locking boxes under the window and a carved plaque beside the door. The plaque read:

L'SCRITTÓRE

COPYING, LETTERS,

CONFIDENTIAL MESSAGE EXCHANGE

After my dismissal from *il Padroné*'s household, taking up my exiled father's profession as a law scribe had seemed a reasonable way to keep Neri and me from starvation. When I'd grown the business enough to move it out of our house to a little room that opened onto the Ring Road, Neri and I installed the row of locking boxes. Customers could rent one for a small fee. The Chimera's box was still empty.

Cursing my squirming conscience, I unlocked the shop, stuffed my journal and a sheet of parchment into my writing case, and headed for the Duck's Bone alehouse. Most of my clients were lawyers and notaries. But a growing number were Beggars Ring folk who needed someone to draft a letter or a will or a business agreement. They often felt more at ease meeting at the Duck's Bone. It was my preference as well. To work in their familiar place instead of my own granted me a certain anonymity.

Until yesterday, this ordinary life had seemed but an impersonation. Surely my *home* was the house where I'd lived with Sandro. The city of Cantagna was the city he had shown me in the walks we'd taken, in the stories he'd told. My friends were his friends. The art, the conversations, the books, and studies, and confidences I'd shared with him were my true life. Except for my brother and partners of the Chimera and those exceptionally vivid moments of magic and adventure the four of us had shared, the world of the Beggars Ring and Cantagna's lower city was a world of strangers. A place I would never belong. Yet losing all this, even for a few hours, being so lost, made me more appreciative of my circumstances.

"Lady scribe," said Neri's employer as I entered the smoky alehouse.

"Fortune's benefice, Fesci." The fierce, granite-boned taverner would threaten a fist in your face if you called her *Mistress* Fesci.

"Surprised to see you in," she said.

She thunked a crock of pickled fish in the middle of her longest table, already crowded with chattering customers. Brisk and efficient, she carried an overloaded tray of empty mugs and bowls back to her counter, angled across one corner of the overheated room. After shoving the tray into the arms of a girl with a straw-colored topknot, she planted her hands on the counter.

"Neri said you were ailing again like yesterday, so he had to forfeit his hours today."

"Forfeit? Oh—" I stuttered. "Yes, I've been—"

"No need to give him excuses. The lad's got ten girlies and a few of the boys making to lure him down under the bridge. Didn't take a philosophist to skin he was inventing his story. Do it too many times, though, and I'll find someone else to toss my rowdies."

"Too many times and I'll stop feeding him," I said, angry at Neri for more evidence of irresponsibility and at myself for attempting an excuse. Fesci could ferret out a lie better than any magistrate born. "He oughtn't take advantage of your patience."

And I'd thought the horror at Bawds Field had touched him.

"Have you come for more than that scallywag?"

"I'm to meet the ironmonger for business later," I said. "But a mug of your best would do me well for now."

"Someone was in earlier, asking for 'the lady who wrote letters.' Thought she might be another doe pining for the young buck, but she claimed it were the scribe she had an urgent message for. She called herself Tarenah di . . . Gilfi? . . . something like that. Said she'd look for you elsewhere."

"Tarenah?" Astonished, I raised a finger to stay Fesci's hand on the tap. "I should find her. Hold the ale till I come back. I'll leave my things."

I abandoned my writing case on a corner table where I often sat, and left by the door into the horse yard behind the tavern. *Tarenah di Guelfi.* Only a few knew that name—one of my impersonation pseudonyms.

My partners knew, of course.

The Shadow Lord suspected, though he was far too careful to use it.

His wife Gilliette, a spiteful girl of fifteen, had heard the name. And she was of an age with those who so admired Neri's winsome ways. But she'd no reason to suspect Tarenah was me, or that I might be found at the Duck's Bone alehouse.

After a careful scan of the street to find no one obviously loitering, I slipped into the afternoon business of the River Quarter and strolled toward Lizard's Alley.

"Hsst . . ."

The source of the noise was a sheltered doorway. I passed it by. Didn't even look.

Another hiss, and then, "Back here."

Most definitely this girl was an amateur. I walked a little faster and rounded the corner into Lizard's Alley. When someone dashed around the corner in my wake, I grabbed the small cloaked body, spun her around, and shoved her face gently, but firmly, to the brick wall. "A spy should not be so free with names."

"Oof." The rapid outbreath was followed by a familiar giggle.

I yanked down the person's hood and a pair of intensely dark eyes peered at me excitedly over the slender shoulder.

They belonged to a young girl with blade-sharp cheekbones and lips the hue of pomegranates that could reduce Neri to a gibbering idiot in a matter of three heartbeats.

"Cittina," I said, keeping my voice soft and tight as I stepped back, *"what* are you doing here? Does your mam or da know? Do you understand that the name you tossed off must never, *ever* be connected to Neri or your parents?"

Dumond and Vashti's eldest daughter was a clever girl fully aware of the dangers her father's magical gift brought to her family, but often silly, nonetheless.

She twirled around and pressed her back to the wall. "I brought a message from Neri. He swore me not to be seen and not to say your name aloud. But I figured he meant your ordinary name, or how else was I to get your attention? So sorry if I chose wrong."

"Neri's at your house? He was supposed to work this afternoon."

"Nearly on his knees, he was, when he begged me to bring the message." Cittina breathed a little sigh of satisfaction. "Told me that you'd walk right by the Duck's Bone sometime in the afternoon. And here you are. He's *such* a clever one, in't he?"

"Clever is not what I'd name him just now. What's the message?"

"He says he and papa have important work doing. Says you and the swordmaster must meet them in the Piazza Livello at the Hour of the Spirits, and you're to use the 'path of the dead,' which sounds rather dreadful, but that's what he said, and he told me you'd understand?" Curiosity stretched her eyebrows almost to her sleek black hair.

"Not a dreadful path. Just a route to a gate." A *secret* gate that the Shadow Lord had shown me to pass between the Merchants Ring and the Heights. It sat at the end of the Street of the Coffinmakers—thus, *the path of the dead.* "It's the *time* is dreadful. You're sure of it. The middle of the night? Whatever for?"

"He says to wear your sneaking clothes," she whispered. "He's found your prisoner."

. . .

Though I hammered on Placidio's unpainted door at a volume that could revive the slaughtered beasts in the butcher shop below, he didn't answer. No real surprise. Between the sultry weather, the ever-present stench, and the noisy street outside, I doubted even Neri could sleep in Placidio's cramped quarters in the afternoon. But I'd hoped to give Placidio the word about the prisoner and our meeting time in the Piazza Livello. He'd not said whether his "rough match" was this evening or next morning.

If not napping, his primary preparation for any match, Placidio would be eating, the second most important preparation. I poked my head into three of his favored establishments without success before heading back to the Duck's Bone to await Germond, the lovestruck ironmonger.

My blood raced as I walked. *Sneaking clothes. The Hour of the Spirits.* The third hour after midnight. Neri and Dumond must believe we could get to the prisoner tonight. As every time the Chimera prepared for action, part of me wanted to get to it immediately, and part of me wanted to wait more, to plan more, to ensure we hadn't overlooked any details. If I'd thought I'd need to do an impersonation, I might have kept walking right out of the city.

It surprised me that the news came from Neri and Dumond rather than the Shadow Lord. Did Sandro not know the prisoner had been delivered? That seemed unlikely; he ran the most extensive ring of spies in the Costa Drago. If he'd changed his mind about the mission, he would certainly have let me know.

That Cinque was imprisoned in the Heights surprised me too. That meant he was jailed in the Sestorale Prison, the holding cells for newly arrested felons awaiting their hearing before a magistrate. That was good news in a fashion, as it suggested the arresting authorities still didn't know the prisoner was a hardened spy like Cinque. Even so, it seemed lax for a criminal awaiting a politically important transfer. It also made things riskier for the Chimera. Neri and Dumond and perhaps Placidio would be using magic in the most public, most secure, and most important building in Cantagna. Magic sniffers were frequently abroad in the Heights.

As ever at the thought of sniffers, my fingers rubbed the small bronze luck charm in my pocket. Dumond had made it. Supposedly the engraving—a triangular form of three intersecting arcs, one concave, one convex, one sinuous, bracketing a tightly coiled spiral—masked the shimmer of magic in a sorcerer's blood from those able to detect it.

The crowd had gotten rowdier at the Duck's Bone. I shut off thoughts of the Chimera, and returned to being *lady scribe*. Everyone in the neighborhood seemed to have taken up Placidio's mode of addressing me. I supposed it avoided the difficulties of choosing between *damizella* and *Romy*. *Damizella* had an overtone of carnal innocence inappropriate for a woman rumored to have been a whore for someone very important. *Romy* likely struck them as too familiar for an odd stranger with habits far too refined for the Beggars Ring. *Was she truly the girl who had vanished when she was ten, only to turn up again fourteen years later, just as her father's hand was lopped for thieving?*

Fesci had a cup of ale in my hand before I could reclaim my belongings.

"All's well?" she said as she wiped her hands on her apron.

"It was indeed one of Neri's admirers," I said, which was absolutely true. "She hoped I might provide a key to his heart."

Fesci burst into laughter appropriately robust for her out-sized frame. "Thought so. I doubt his heart is the part rules him nowadays."

"Indeed not," I said. "I do appreciate your giving him more work hours. Between you and the swordmaster, he's generally too tired for outings *under the bridge.*"

• • •

It was later than I planned when I left the Duck's Bone. The ironmonger, a shy giant of a man, had insisted on buying my supper. Basilio, a fellow whose infectious good humor made him seem almost as large as Germond, had shown up to join us with a glow of good cheer. No coincidence, as Germond had just expressed his wish that Basilio inherit his house and business if aught should happen to him. It seemed only right that I stay to wish them well.

The city bells rang half-even, three hours before midnight, when I raced up the stair to Placidio's room the second time. He'd not shown up at the Duck's Bone, which was his unvarying habit after a match—easy or rough as it might be. Which meant the duel had not been at sunset.

Still no answer. So I used the lingering afterglow to charge through the streets and out the River Gate to the woolhouse. Perhaps he'd actually chosen to sleep in the quiet of our practice arena or use the cooler hours of the evening to loosen up for a difficult match at dawn.

Sunrise and sunset were considered the most fortuitous times for such fraught events as duels. Legend said that the boundaries between the human world and the Night Eternal were thinnest at those times, and that petitions might actually reach the ears of the Unseeable Gods, rousing them to action. Supposedly our creator gods had retired to the Night Eternal millennia ago, driven to exhaustion after imprisoning the monster Dragonis under the earth.

Believing myself god-cursed, I'd had little use for divinities in my childhood. Only in working with Placidio, Dumond, and Neri—and at last the fullness of my own magic—had I come to believe that those who used magic were *not* intrinsically corrupt and destined for madness. None of us rejoiced that fiery ash spewed from Aesol Mount had buried the city of Fugano three decades ago, nor did we feel compelled to dig into any volcano or dive into ocean depths to set some monster free so he could ravage the world. As far as I knew, it was humans—primarily the Philosophic Confraternity—who had blamed every disaster on sorcery and decided that those tainted with magic needed to die.

Yet magic itself, the destiny that entwined some of us humans while ignoring others, had infused myth with some kind of substance in my mind. The Chimera's first mission had involved a small bronze statue of great antiquity, greatly desired by a devout and scholarly grand duc. The statue seemed quite ordinary—a depiction of the god Atladu, Dragonis, and a third figure that had been broken off and lost over the centuries. Unlike every other image of that millennia-long relationship, the god and the monster had not been engaged in combat, but in a race or a hunt or some other side-by-side endeavor with their lost companion.

More astounding was what happened when, at Dumond's urging, I had reached for magic while touching the statue. I had been taken—transported, it seemed—to another place, a palazzo of sculpted grandeur, arches, pillars, domes, and mosaics. Deserted, filled with sadness, the place had promised knowledge to any who sought it, even as molten fire and cracking stone threatened its destruction. Had Dumond not experienced a similar vision, I'd have believed I was under the mind-shredding influence of mysenthe.

We had never come up with an explanation. Nor had we been enlightened as to the grand duc's understanding of the statue. Someday I *would* understand its place in the world.

The walk to the woolhouse was fruitless. Placidio wasn't there either. Hot, tired, and frustrated, I set my writing case by the door and fetched myself water from my cask.

Sitting in the doorway of the woolhouse, hoping some heavy breeze off the river might cool me down, I sipped the lukewarm water as night swallowed the last vestiges of sunlight. Perhaps Placidio had found a companion for the night. Neri seemed to think his swordmaster had a longtime partner or two who shared a bed with him on occasion. But that might just have been that Neri's mind could not conceive of a healthy man foregoing such pleasures. For myself, I could not imagine Placidio sharing such intimacy. Not from lack of desire or inability, but because of his fierce protection of his privacy. Thinking on his generosity of the previous night, I could only grieve for such a choice—both for him and for whomever might be able to capture his heart.

I hefted my writing case and headed homeward. Only to turn back immediately, dig out flint and steel, and light the woolhouse lantern.

The Month of Fogs was aptly named; a turgid cloud of yellow gray had settled over the surging river, the fog's whorls, ripples, and swells miming the green-black water below. Even with the lantern, it was near impossible to find my way. The lamps of the distant docks and bridges were but pale smears. The torchlight atop the city walls glowed dull; the city's rattle of evening business, audible on a clear evening, was silenced. The farther I walked, the worse things got.

I knew the route across the wasteland as well as anyone could. But the familiar broken walls and chimneys along the riverbank path had become apparitions, looming unexpectedly out of the fog as if the thousands of plague victims who had died in the woolhouse had descended all at once and rearranged them. When a trip over a broken foundation stone placed me much closer to the water than I intended, I halted, wondering if it was riskier to go back and spend an uncomfortable night at the woolhouse or forge ahead before the murk grew deeper yet.

"*Skatá.*" The breathless epithet was almost lost in the quiet slopping of the Venia. Had the sound of agonized retching not followed so quickly, I'd have thought it the plop of a fish or shifting flotsam caught in the snags. Had I not paused my steps, I'd never have heard him.

A drunkard, most likely. The count of such lackwits outnumbered the stars. It would serve him right to wallow in the mud.

Yet the ensuing silence pricked my conscience. Dissipation could sneak up on a person, as I well knew. Even a drunkard didn't deserve to drown.

"Who's there?" I said. "Do you need help?"

Frogs croaked. A night bird screeched from the wooded hill on the opposite bank. Water gurgled around the remains of the old docks. Then came a deep slosh and the unmistakable groan of painful effort. *Theía Mitéra, dose mou dynami—*

The whispered petition broke off in another bout of heaving.

Any scalawag thinking to lure a passerby into his clutches might feign sickness and call on our Unseeable Goddess mother to grant him strength, but what common soul would do so in Annisi, a language not spoken since humankind learned to craft swords with iron instead of bronze? Even then it was spoken only in the realm of Typhon—thirty or forty southern islands absorbed centuries ago by Mercediare.

Another—weaker—splash, then silence.

"Who are you?" I called.

Not a shift or a whisper hinted anyone near. But he hadn't gone anywhere. I would have heard him slosh and creep away.

I knew better than to go looking for a stranger in the fog. Beyond the threats of common rogues, *il Padroné*'s enemies were countless. If one of them had traced his vanished mistress . . .

Drawing my dagger, I edged closer to the river. I was not defenseless. I almost hoped it was Lawyer Cinnetti.

The language belied that fantasy—and drew me onward. A pious man or scholarly one might know a bit of Annisi. So did a wealthy collector's whore, one who had learned enough of it to read the inscriptions on her owner's tablets and statuary.

Sandro had ever delighted in my enthusiastic embrace of his passion for art and history.

Then, too, a man might know a few words of Annisi if he was born on one of Mercediare's two hundred tributary islands. Once I considered that, I couldn't shake the notion that this might even be our Mercediaran prisoner escaped from his captors. If he lay insensible in the shallows, the current could swallow him at any moment. Whatever the truth, I couldn't abandon him.

Every few steps through the fog I paused to test the ground ahead for sinkholes or steep banks and to locate the sound of the eddies around the ruined docks. That's where I'd heard him choking. Unfortunately the closer I got to the river, the thicker the fog. The lantern light reflected from the murk, revealing naught farther away than my own feet.

Neri had heard tales of sorcerers who could use their raw magic to create a light as well as fuel their own particular talent. We had tried it several times. He'd had no success. One time I believed a glow emanated briefly from my hand. Gone as quickly as it had come, it had left me feeling chilled and sick, which I learned were symptoms of weak or ill-formed enchantment. So maybe it was possible.

Using magic was always a risk, even outside the city walls. But tonight my choice was either risky magic or a risky search or abandoning the desperate stranger to the river. Perhaps Lady Virtue would look kindly on the favor. And attempting a light did not require me to leave my soul behind.

Closing my eyes, I reached deep into the well of power inside me. Familiar now, the heat flooding veins, muscle, and bone, speeding my heart's beat, quickening my breath, sharpening my perceptions so that I could see, hear, smell, taste, and feel with heightened acuity.

Certain, a body lay somewhere down and to my right. Solid. Astonishingly cold. Heart beating so slowly it was scarce detectable. Fog and rippling current masked his exact position.

Infusing my desire with magic and need, I focused my will on my hand . . . on seeing . . . on light to penetrate the fog.

Spirits! A soft ivory beam shot from my hand. It revealed no colors, but rather left everything in its narrow range stripped of all but black and gray: the urgent river, the weedy, rutted earth, scattered rocks and shards of brick. The rotting understructure of a broken dock. And a slender man sprawled in the muddy backwater amid the forest of old pilings. The river tugged at his floating legs, drawing him slowly, inexorably, into its grasp.

4

I abandoned my case and the flickering lantern on a flat rock. "Hold on!" I said, not imagining the man was in any state to hear as I slid down the steep embankment, scrambled over logs and uprooted saplings, and slogged through slime and mud. Wavelets sloshed his face. He did not stir, even as the hungry current dragged him another handspan farther into the flood.

Planting my feet, I grabbed him under the arms and hauled him onto the muddy bank. Another heave. He was damnably heavy for a man very near my own size. A groan slipped through his teeth when his foot caught on a snag, but the pain didn't wake him enough that he could aid me. A few more heaves got him to the drier ground atop the embankment.

My magical light died.

Already breathless from the effort, now fighting the wave of cold and nausea that always followed imperfect magic, I bent over, hands on knees, swallowing hard. My skull bones ground against each other. *Breathe. Hold. Blow out slowly. Breathe . . .*

I knelt beside the sodden figure, and rolled him carefully to his back. He lay as cold and still as a man twelve hours dead, but my ear on his chest confirmed my earlier perceptions. His heart was beating, but at the pace of a funeral processional. My damp cheek detected a thready breath at his mouth, though the rise and fall of his chest coincided more with the pace of the seasons than with healthy respiration.

Grabbing the abandoned lantern, I took a better look.

An unraveling braid of pale hair marked him a foreigner, but beyond that, had he been my own brother I could not have guessed his age or what he actually looked like. His eyes were swollen shut, his lips split, his face and hands mottled with cuts and bruises. His nose was surely broken.

The light revealed no significant issue of blood elsewhere, though I couldn't judge his state of wounding without better light and far less mud on him. Yet from the condition of his face I couldn't discount something dire. Someone—or more than one—had been at him with fists and boots, taking him to the point of death and then dumping him into the river to drown. That he had not done so said something about his endurance.

"Hey, fellow! Wake up!" I shook his shoulder, gently at first and then more vigorously. "I really don't want to leave you this way. Wild dogs roam this riverbank, and they'll delight in ripping out your throat. Wander about on your own and the fog will have you right back in the river."

He stirred, then sank back into his stupor.

Strange for our tepid weather, he wore as many layers as a winter-born babe: tunic, shirt, doublet, netherstocks, trousers, over-jacket, wool cloak, and a second mantle atop all. All were visible, because all were torn and slashed to shreds. He'd no belt, weapons, purse, or waist pockets. His attackers must have taken his valuables, even his earrings. Ragged wounds on his lobes testified to a brutal snatch. In the southlands men wore earrings just as women did.

"Come on. I can't carry you, and there's no one else about."

I shook him again, tugged at his hair, wriggled his legs. Each time he moved a little more, but to no lasting effect. Hating to do it, I slapped his mauled cheek.

He stifled a gasp and rolled to one side, drawing up his knees.

"Sorry, sorry," I said. "But you've got to get up. I can't carry you, but I'll help you into the city. Maybe you've kin in Cantagna?"

His whole body twitched.

Theíko Patéra, voíthisé . . . The quiet plea for help, threaded with pain, had no more substance than a wisp of the fog.

I patted his cold hand. "No divinities have been seen in Cantagna for millennia, I'm afraid—Fathers or Mothers either one. Tonight you'll have to take help from a scribe."

Shoving my arm under the man's shoulders, I raised him up to sitting. His head drooped, chin resting on his chest. An attempt to breathe through his nose set him choking.

"Stand up," I said, shaking him when he'd got his breath again. "*Síko páno.*"

Had I pronounced the words correctly? How would I even know?

"I know it's hard. But after a bit of a hike, we'll find you a bed. Get something hot inside you. Never felt a man so cold who wasn't dead."

Whispers of bone-deep terror ghosted past my ear. *Not dead. Blind.*

Was it the ongoing residue of feeble sorcery that made my bones quiver, too?

"Maybe not blind," I said, relieved that he comprehended at least some of my words. "Whoever had at you, they did a right thorough job."

Draping one wet, cold arm over my shoulders, I hauled him up. He got one foot under himself, but the other refused to bear any weight. Thankful for Placidio's nagging insistence on developing my arm strength, I kept the fellow from collapsing while switching myself to his weaker side. The awkward move felt like trying to dance a galliard with a giant fish.

Balancing him upright, I grabbed the writing case and hung it on my shoulder. The lantern would have to remain behind. Now to move.

I shuffled forward. One of his feet moved, the other dragged, eliciting a faint moan.

"Well done." I expelled the words with a grunt.

He said nothing during that agonizing journey. Breathing through his mouth was difficult, through his swollen nose impossible. I spoke only what breathless encouragement seemed necessary. All my focus was on keeping him moving toward the faint red smear that marked the River Gate.

Surely two hours had passed by the time the red smear and a blaze of firelight from the gatehouse near blinded me to the hulking shape bawling a challenge. "Hold up. Who's come?"

I looked entirely disreputable, damp hair straggling, garments sodden and covered in mud. My back and shoulders screamed so loud, I could scarce think. What to answer . . .

"This fellow was— He's—"

I floundered for words that ought to come smoothly. I

needed to be someone else, but without using magic. Swaying on my feet, I dug deep into exhausted confusion. *Think, Romy.*

"What's your business out riverside on a night like this?" The spearpoint that pricked my breast spoke a warden with too little to do.

Mystiko. Secret. *Maybe something risqué for bored gate guards.*

"Aright. Aright," I blurted, shaking my limp hair over my face. "Found this sweetum at the Rusty Knob. We was just takin' our first roll, out where 'is mate wouldn't see. Guess he had a swig too much to rise his mettle for the plunge. Me, too, maybe, so I needs must reposit him where I found him or his mate'll 'ave his nuts, which'd be a waste beyond thinkin', I can tell you, pretty as they are."

Fortunately neither of us had weapons in hand to damp the wardens' hilarity. They shoved us through the gate with their boots, laughing louder when I stumbled and crashed atop my injured companion in a puddle of muck.

"Somewhere under that mud might be a fine figure of a woman," one snorted to his fellow, "but you'd have to haul the body through the cistern at the Pipes even to find which parts it has."

By the time I dragged my companion to his feet and coaxed, berated, and begged him as far as the tarry blackness of Lizard's Alley, the watch was calling the hour before midnight—and the man was so limp my jellied muscles could scarce hold on to him. My constant shivering didn't help. His chilled body had surely leached every bit of warmth from the world.

I kicked open the door and hauled him through the dark into the curtained alcove that held my bed and Neri's. Supporting him against the wall, I yanked back the blanket, then let him sag into a sodden heap on my rag-and-straw-filled pallet.

I wanted to collapse as well, but he'd be dead soon if I didn't get him warm. If I let go of thought for even a moment, I'd not be awake to prevent it. Damned if I'd let him die after all this trouble.

In the dim recesses of my wit I questioned why I'd brought him here. Yes, I had good reason to bypass nosy gate wardens, but I'd passed at least three taverns on the Ring Road and never considered dumping him on their doorsteps. It wasn't like me to be protective of strangers.

I grabbed a shawl from the hook beside my bed and wrapped it around my damp shoulders. Then I fetched the tinderbox and forced my trembling hands to strike sparks in a little wad of cattail fluff and shaved bark. After many more attempts than I liked, tiny flames licked the kindling in our brazier. Once there was a steady vigor to it, I piled in a few chunks of coal from the hod. A tin pot of water sat atop the clay surface.

Visions of the ever-ready fires in *il Padroné*'s house and his instantly available carafes of rare, expensive coffee mocked me as I worked. I erased them with memories of the squalid, bitter days when my parents and most of my twelve younger siblings crowded this same room, forever stinking of mold and piss.

By the light of a small lamp lit from the growing fire, I fetched blankets, rags, and Neri's spare shirt from our chest.

"Got to get you out of these wet scraps else I'll never get you warm," I said, teeth chattering as I unfastened the laces, buttons, and pins that held together the ruins of his sodden garments. "I've seen more men naked than you'd like to think on, including my brother who'll likely combust if he spies a stranger in my bed. So you've nothing I've not seen before."

Only he had.

From neck to ankle, wrist to wrist, his pale flesh was marked with wolf-gray ink in a variety of lines and curves, purposeful designs large and small, all of them pleasing to the eye. Here, a pair of interlinked circles. There, a straight line with thorn-like protrusions along its length. Here, a starburst. Eerily familiar designs, though I had never seen them on living skin, only on painted figures decorating a painted urn—one of *il Padroné*'s most prized antiquities. He believed the urn fired in the Typhonese city of Umbra Lunae a thousand years ago.

Gingerly, I pushed the man's long wet braid aside and blotted his back, arms, legs, and buttocks with the towel. The markings were fixed in his skin—as were plentiful cuts, bruises, and oozing stripes from repeated beatings with belts or chains.

I rolled him over. More ink markings. More mottled bruising, more broken and abraded skin.

My breath stopped. A palm-sized pattern over his heart comprised a triangular form of three intersecting arcs—one concave, one convex, one sinuous—bracketing a tightly coiled spiral. Intimately familiar.

I yanked Dumond's bronze luck charm from my pocket. The engraving on the charm was exactly the same design, even to the placement of the three arcs—the concave on the left, the convex on the right, the sinuous curve across the bottom. The charm supposedly masked magic in the blood. Was this man a sorcerer?

Unfortunately, Dumond lived halfway round the city. I couldn't easily roust him to ask why the symbol on his luck charms might be inked on the skin of a half-dead man who spoke Annisi.

After confirming that my guest yet breathed, I nourished my little blaze with fuel and begged the water pot to heat before I shivered my bones to dust. Failing anything hot to drink as yet, I filled a cup with Placidio's salt, lemon, and ginger tea. Neri believed in its efficacy, and kept a ready supply in a stone flask.

Though the injured man showed no other signs of waking, he swallowed the nasty liquid voraciously. Then I finished drying him off, eliciting quiet groans when I pressed gently on his discolored belly and his horribly swollen left ankle.

My brother's old russet shirt swallowed the man's upper body, but scarce covered enough length to keep him modest. Struggling with his dead weight, I'd not noted how thin he was, his height all angles and bones.

"Your bones must be lead, whatever-your-name-is," I said as I propped his head on a rolled blanket, drew a sheet over him, and laid a wet compress over his eyes and nose. "But by the Holy Sisters, that's all I can do for you until the pot boils."

I slid to the floor, my back to the wall beside the low bed.

Not lead. Not dead. Need fed. Name is Teo.

The whispers came as much from inside my head as above or beside me . . . and I'd have sworn they were wrapped in whimsy and tied up with a fervent blessing.

"Rest, fish man," I said, laughing. "Soon as the water heats, I'll feed you."

I patted his blanketed arm, then drew my dagger and laid it close to hand. Though I willed myself to stay awake, my thoughts soon dissolved into realms unknown, mostly centered around why in the name of the Unseeable I had brought a stranger into my house . . .

The stink of scorching metal stung my nose. My eyes blinked . . . sticky with sleep. "Ah, confound it!"

The overheated tin pot was long dry and the ashes were pulsing with the death throes of my fire. At least the room was warm. Plenty warm for me, though my guest . . . Teo?

I knelt up and laid my ear on his chest. Heart still beating. Breath still pumping, but with no more vigor than before. His forehead and cheeks had warmed a little, but his arms and legs were still cold as dead fish.

"Sorry. I'll try again."

Something nagged at me as I replenished the fire and used some splintered sticks to get it blazing again. *Need fed* . . . Spirits, the poor fellow was starving!

He welcomed another sip of the ginger tea, but surely he needed something more substantial.

Cooking was not an element of my education either at the Moon House or in *il Padroné*'s household. Neri would eat anything he didn't have to make, but our brazier wasn't very efficient and coal was more expensive than food we could fetch from the Beggars Ring market. Edible was the best that could be said of that, but anything was better than my fitful attempts. My prowess was limited to boiling—eggs, dry noodles, or gruel.

As I waited for the steam to rise, I drew a stool to the side of the bed and leaned my back against the wall, still tired and muddle-headed. Certain, I could sleep through until tomorrow's afternoon. Warm and drowsy, I started talking to keep myself awake.

"What am I going to do with you, Segno Not-Lead-Not-Dead-Now-Soon-to-Be-Fed? You pose mysteries too interesting to let go. Why do you cry out in a lost language? What are these marks, especially this one over your heart? I think you must have secrets with so much hidden under your dozen layers of garments."

My eyes itched from the smoke. I squeezed them closed. *Golden stars sparked through wavering glass. A watchful peace . . . drifting . . . healing. Silver lights darted past. Fronds of deep green teased the skin. A tracery of white far below prompted a wave of pleasure . . . and sorrow. Home . . .*

I jerked and jumped up, knocking over the stool with a clatter. The water on the brazier bubbled and steamed in its pot.

"Not all boiled away," I said, relieved when I inspected the pot. "I'd have felt a right idiot if I'd done it again."

Stirring in some oats I'd crushed to powder, I let them stew a bit, then added a bit of salt and a dollop of sagging butter from the dish on a shelf. I returned to Teo's bedside with a bowl holding a few spoonfuls.

Though his puffy, blackened eyes did not open, the taste of gruel on his tongue prompted more reaction than even the ginger tea. Not only did he not choke, which I had feared, but he licked his lips and panted a shallow breath as he swallowed. I paused between the minuscule bites to ensure he'd got them down, prattling to fill the interval as if he might bite me did I not distract him.

"You are experiencing a rare privilege, segno. My longtime master was the last person to be fed from my exquisitely trained hand. There are numerous ways a courtesan can present food and drink to the master or mistress, all of them beautiful and graceful—though perhaps it would not be seemly to mention them to a man I don't know, an injured man whose . . . ah . . . level of worldliness I cannot judge."

I touched the spoon to his lips. The bite of gruel vanished with the same small, desperate breath.

"Are you a worldly man, Segno Teo?"

His lips opened for the gruel. Nothing more.

"Perhaps. Perhaps not. Indeed, I am a woman of ill repute. Be warned, however, I no longer practice that profession and would wreak severe injury on anyone who assumed I desired to take it up again." Unless he snuck up on me and trapped me beside a stand of firethorn . . .

I shuddered and fixed my attention on my guest. Such a strange state he was in, more animal than man. Perhaps more like a worm in its cocoon . . . focused inward, transforming itself, doing what its nature prescribed. I could not fear him, any more than I feared that worm.

Which was entirely stupid, said my sensible self for the thousandth time.

Keep talking. "For two of nine years my master was like a god to me, expanding my world to include the wonders of art and history, teaching me the power of law, allowing me to experience true beauty. For the last seven years—a surprise to both of us—he was both friend and lover. Though who can say what love or friendship is when one is bound unconsenting to the other—even when the chains are silk."

Strange the words that popped to mind. I'd never spoken so frankly even to Neri.

Teo took another bite, though his vigor was flagging. His eyes yet remained closed, signs of sentience elusive. It seemed rude just to poke food down him in silence, so I kept nattering on.

"My master was dreadfully ill that last time I fed him, done in by a poorly roasted fowl at a good friend's table. Actually, he *thought* the man was a good friend until months later, when the fellow tried to betray him over a small bronze statue of the god Atladu."

My hand paused. What had Teo said, down at the river? *Theíko Patéra.* Divine Father. Atladu?

The Unseeable Atladu, god of Sea and Sky, had raised Leviathan who finally defeated the monster Dragonis. The god was always depicted with a barbed spear and earrings . . .

I almost dropped the spoon. Where had my mind been? Whether carved, cast in bronze like the grand duc's ancient statue, or sketched with a charred stick on a cave wall, Atladu's earrings were always shaped like the coil of a wave. The god always carried a barbed spear, his hand marked with sigils of power: sometimes the three linked coils called a triskelion, sometimes a starburst symbol of the sun, and sometimes a sinuous curve to represent the power of the sea. A sinuous curve like that on Teo's chest and Dumond's luck charm.

Symbols were often used within artworks to communicate stability or political power, optimism, fear of death, nobility of spirit, identity, or a simple connection to myth. Sandro believed that a city filled with glorious art would inspire Cantagna's people to greatness in all areas. At the simplest triggering, his passion would overflow. I had gulped and swallowed every detail of his teaching about symbols, techniques, styles, and history, not just because it gave him such joy to have an eager listener, but because those concepts had filled a void in me. Art imposed an order and beauty upon a universe my childhood had interpreted as random cruelty.

Teo's lips twitched soundlessly. I fed him another bite.

Certainly Teo was no muscled divinity. Nor did I have reason to believe his missing earrings had been like to those on the bronze that my partners and I had so recently returned to the grand duc of Riccia. But the barbed line and the starburst inked on Teo's flesh, and the curves and spirals that appeared both on Teo's body and Dumond's charms surely spoke to that same lore.

"Are you some kind of priest, Teo? Are these marks on your skin your way of imposing order on the world?"

I had never met a priest of any deity. Of those few people of the Costa Drago who held the belief that Atladu and Mother Gione, Chloni the sexless Creator of Stars, and the rest of the Unseeable Gods might someday return from the Night Eternal, most had given it up after the ravages of the plague. Yet from time to time visitors to Sandro's house had reported a cult of believers on the rise here or there. Only the Philosophic Confraternity considered them any threat, insisting that those who dismissed reason and logic in favor of vanished gods were the most susceptible to the lures of Dragonis's wiles. Philosophists had encased the Creation stories in stone and proclaimed the end of divinity. They kept watch on ruined temples and holy sites for signs of belief reborn, then brought in sniffers to scour for magic, just as they did for augurs and diviners and other servants of Lady Fortune.

Teo swallowed half the pot of gruel before soundlessly rolling onto his side and curling himself into a knot. He would likely have eaten more if I'd forced it, but experience warned not to overstuff a sick or starving man.

Before I could think what to do next, the bells in the tower of the Palazzo Segnori rang the slow tolling of the hour. One. Two. No mistaking the dark outside my shuttered window for afternoon. And Neri's bed was still empty . . .

Spirits! Neri! I was supposed to meet him at the secret gate in the Via Mortua at the Hour of the Spirits—third hour past midnight. One hour from now.

I removed the pot from the brazier and threw another blanket over my sleeping visitor. With such injuries, I'd no worries that he might prowl my house and find the little bag of silver I kept hidden under a foundation stone. It was much more concerning that I might get back and find him dead.

"Sorry again," I said. "I have to go out. Sleep well, and don't die on me."

I washed the mud from my face and hands and quickly changed my muddy skirt for the black trousers and tunic I'd used for my work with Placidio. Lamp in one hand, dagger in the other, I headed through the dark, deserted streets. First I'd roust Placidio. He was surely abed by now if he had a dawn match. Then we'd head for the gate to the Asylum Ring and the long steep Via Salita that would take us up to the heart of Cantagna. Though ever mindful of my surroundings, I contemplated all the delightful ways I might throttle my brother for his wretched timing.

5

/

I was not a superstitious person. No subtle fears of ghosts or spirits prompted me to festoon my door and window with prickly juniper. I felt no compulsion to bury a dead cat under an oak at midsummer to keep away the plague. But in truth, strolling down the Via Mortua—the Street of the Coffinmakers—in the quietest, darkest hours of the night gave me the flutters.

The narrow dirt lane lined with tidy shopfronts smelled of sawdust and grinding stones, not mortal decay. Indeed the shop owners, cognizant of public feeling, sent sweepers out first and last hour of every business day to ensure their street did not offend eyes or nostrils. But every soft breeze that brushed those shopfronts whispered of grieving. Every scuttle of mouse or cat hinted at souls fading into the Night Eternal. And the pitchy darkness beyond the last shop devoured my feeble lamplight with disturbing greed.

It didn't help at all that I'd to make the journey alone. Placidio was still nowhere to be found. If he'd had an unusually late evening match, he would be sleeping it off. If it was scheduled for dawn, he'd surely be abed so as to be at his best. But his rumpled sheets were long cold.

Even if Neri's suspicions of intimate companions were true, the disciplined Placidio would never compromise a morning match—a rough match—by late-night dalliance. Nor would so private a man impose the burdensome aftermath of his chosen profession, whether wounds or despair or the risk that came with using his magic, on someone he cared for. I didn't like it.

The debris-strewn end of the coffinmakers' lane butted against the high wall that separated the Merchants Ring from the Heights. I pulled away the rotting slab of wood that leaned against the wall to expose a black-painted door of ironbound planks with no visible locks, hinges, or handle. Beyond it lay one of the Shadow Lord's secret paths.

Sandro liked to explore the city without fanfare, avoiding the crowds at gates and public markets and the clot of bodyguards they mandated. Thus he made use of several discreet byways that had been abandoned as Cantagna's population grew. I had considered it a lark to accompany him on his anonymous strolls about the city, when I could pretend we were an ordinary couple who delighted in each other's company.

Fortunately, Sandro had shown me which planks and iron strips hid locks or latches, and how to use a hidden rope to pull the rotted plank back up to mask the door once I was beyond it. Twenty steps through what had once been a drainage tunnel under the city's original defense wall brought me to a locked iron grate with a short alley on the other side. I released the latch, covered the lantern, and closed the grate quietly behind me.

Two dark shapes waited at the end of the alley, outlined by the wavering light of Piazza Livello's torches.

"Who goes?" My brother's voice was unmistakable.

"The woman you summoned to go hunting. Would have been nice to come yourself and make a plan." No matter how often we'd talked of our meeting with Cinque, I felt unprepared.

"Just you?" My brother was uninterested in my annoyance. "You were supposed to—"

"Couldn't find him. He had a match either last night or this morning. Perhaps with more notice, people could arrange their schedules to answer your whims."

I chose not to mention the complication of abandoning mysterious drowned strangers in our house. *Lady Fortune, please whisper in this Teo's ear and tell him not to die in my bed!*

"I'm happy the prisoner's here at last," I said, "but we didn't expect him to be in the *Palazzo* cells. We need a more specific plan. We've five days left, including today. What's so urgent we need to do this tonight?"

I joined Neri and short, solid Dumond who stood in the deepest shadows, his attention on the broad span of the deserted piazza. Dumond's satchel of paints and brushes hung from a strap over his shoulder.

"This is a fortunate situation for us," said Dumond, "and we don't know how long it's going to last."

"The prisoner's not in a cell," Neri burst in with a quiet excitement.

"Escaped?"

"No. He's inside there." Neri jerked his head in the direction of the Palazzo Segnori. "This tenday, while hanging around the Prisoners Walk listening for rumors, I joined up with a regular group of fellows do the same, heckling and spitting, throwing rotted figs at the prisoners."

"But you could easily have been—"

"Just listen. Turns out one of the night wardens has a rat dog he brings in every shift. Nifty little bugger comes to the fence to lick your hand. The hecklers say that dog demolishes rats better'n any cat ever lived. Wouldn't mind having a little dog like that for myself. Clear out the vermin in Lizard's Alley. It came that I could follow this little fella anywhere he went. Now I've got a regular map in my head of the cells underneath the Palazzo."

"You used *magic* to follow a *dog* into the Palazzo Segnori dungeon?"

No need to see his face to feel his smirk. If my brother could fix on a detailed image of something he desired, his magic allowed him to walk directly to it. He might tread streets or passages, stairs, open doors or windows—those were easiest—but no lock, barrier, or wall could prevent him getting where he was going. He said it was as if he dissolved and reformed again on the other side.

Biting off a rising fury, I damned the necessity for us to stay quiet. I wanted to yell a reminder of his recent irresponsibility, of the trouble his rashness could bring. I could still feel Cinnetti's fleshy mouth on my neck . . .

"First off, I got myself into the guardroom outside the dungeons."

Even worse.

"What if this dog had been in a warden's lap?" I snapped

quietly. "Or if one of the nullifiers who patrols the palazzo had brought his sniffer anywhere close?"

Neri leaned his back on the alley wall, as if my anger had pressed him to it. He knew exactly what I was saying.

"No matter what happened at Bawds Field—and I'm sorry it was awful—I've been working at my skill just as you've been." His voice remained stalwart. "As long as I hold my mind to what I'm after, I can pause along the way and figure out what's going on in front of me. One time following that dog, I started through the last wall, caught the nasty smell of the lime pits— where they throw them as die in the cells. I turned right back. And if somebody's there in the place I end up, I can duck back out quick enough they never quite see me. None'll believe a prisoner that says a stranger just walked into his locked cell while the rat dog was chasin' vermin."

"But, spirits, Neri, down there alone . . ."

My joints near melted at the thought of Neri caught where it was impossible for him to be. A year previous, Neri had committed a crime only magic could have enabled; it was why Sandro could not afford to have me near him any more. Only a halfmonth had passed since Sandro had lifted his parole in thanks for our help with the grand duc's statue. There would be no reprieve for either my brother or me if Neri was arrested for anything, much less an obvious use of magic.

"Pssh," he scoffed. "'Twas a deal more useful than danger- ous. I hung around out of sight and did some listening. Found out what we need to know."

I wasn't ready to let him off. "We wouldn't have known what happened to you until they came to arrest me. Unless *you* knew what he was up to, Dumond?"

Dumond held his hands up in surrender. "He only brought me yesterday. Risky, no doubt. But you'd best listen to what he learned."

The urgency in the unflappable Dumond's demeanor set my skin prickling. "So tell me."

Even in the dark I could see Neri's satisfaction as he pointed in the direction of the Palazzo. "See that window on the northeast corner, second level—the one with the bit of light. Bars on it, if you look close. As of today the spy is not down in the dungeons at all, but right there in a snugged-up-tight little chamber. Guess they didn't want him to get bit by a rat or pick up a disease before the ambassador guts him."

"Up there? But why?" I was mystified. Of course they'd keep him unharmed. Cantagna mustn't be responsible. "The Mercediarans expect their prisoner is secured. Certain, the Shadow Lord hasn't sanctioned a loose confinement, nor would he allow the Sestorale to do so. He told me that when he proposed this venture."

"Here's what I know." Neri dropped his voice even lower. "Yestermorn I heard the warders in the guardroom talking about how a prisoner escort party—condottieri—had showed up just before daylight. Usually, if mercenaries bring in a prisoner, they pay off the wardens, stick the prisoner in a cell, and be done. But the prison governor Taglino had left word that he was to be notified when the new prisoner arrived and *before* he was put in the cells. So, a messenger was sent off to fetch him. The wardens were afraid they were going to miss out on their cut of the fees, like maybe the prison governor was going to set the man free."

"Surely he didn't do that," I said.

"Nah. I scuttled round to the governor's office and hid while he was fetched, so I could hear what was said. After handing over a purse, Governor Taglino told the condottieri captain that they didn't dare put the prisoner in the cells, as they'd got word of assassins being after him and Gardia wardens bribed to allow it. So he hired the condottieri to guard the prisoner for another five days."

It made no sense. "Gardia wardens believed themselves cut out of their usual pay. But Taglino tells the condottieri that those same Gardia wardens have been bribed to let in assassins. What is Taglino playing at?"

"That's the question, eh? I tucked myself into a hole where I could watch them bring the prisoner in. He's not a man you'd think a dangerous spy. Smallish fellow. A dandy. Wore a baldric set with enough diamonds and rubies to buy the independency of Argento entire!"

"A diamond-and-ruby baldric . . ." I'd heard of something like that, but couldn't remember where. From Sandro? Salon gossip? Myth?

"And there's more." Neri presented each detail with the pride of a cat presenting another dead mouse. "They escorted him inside that very secure little room, jewels and all, and told him to lock it from the inside."

Stranger and stranger. "Lock himself in . . . With his jewels?"

"Aye. To be sure, they did lock it from the outside as well, and set a guard on him just like Taglino told them."

"Did you hear any mention of notifying *il Padroné* of this arrangement?"

"None."

"I checked the message box again on my way up here," I said, staring up at the barred window and its faint light. "Sandro's still not sent us word of the prisoner's arrival. So I'm thinking he doesn't know as yet."

Was Taglino purposely keeping the Shadow Lord in the dark? Certain, Taglino was no friend of House Gallanos. His position as Governor of the prison and Commander of the Gardia was humiliating for the grandson of a landed baron. Sandro's grandfather had persuaded the Sestorale to do away with hereditary titles . . .

Dumond moved in close. "As we'd not heard different from you, we thought the same. And we figured as soon as *il Padroné* got wind of the matter, he might insist on putting the spy somewhere more secure, so we'd best do what we want tonight. This would be a deal easier than breaching a cell down in those dungeons."

"True." Even so, getting into the Palazzo Segnori was only the beginning. "But we have to get out again—and without Placidio."

"Neri watched my back, while I fixed us access to a back stair," said Dumond. "The stair will take us up to the second level, two empty rooms over from the prisoner. None's using that stair or those rooms this time of night. Give me a quarter hour with my paints to make a second door, and you can walk right into the man's cell and talk to him."

Neri was near bursting his skin. "The right thing happens in that room and we're done with this job."

The prisoner was here. Available. Under very strange circumstances . . .

"We can't afford to leave a trace," I said. "A whisper. A scuff mark. The Mercediarans could assume interference."

"That's always been a risk, no matter what the plan," said Dumond.

Neri was bouncing on his toes. "The guards won't see us. And the prisoner won't remember we were there. Your magic will fix that, right?"

My stomach squirmed. "Right."

From the age of three until these last few months, I had believed my only *gift* was the ability to corrupt a mind. If a person shared an experience or a story with me, I could deliberately replace it with a falsehood. All I had to do was touch the person's flesh while I willfully told a new version, and the lie replaced the truth. Forever. Just as I had done with Lawyer Cinnetti a year ago.

But I didn't know how to seal off every thread of those stolen truths—the feelings, motives, or beliefs that shaped them, or any other associated details—so my victim could be left broken or confused by a memory that made no sense. Like my father who could never recall the hero tales he'd loved to tell me when I was small. Like my onetime maidservant who would forever be confused when considering the events on the day of my dismissal. Such confusion and unresolved conflict—empty spaces where there should be a piece of life—could drive a person mad. After my experience at Bawds Field, I knew exactly how that felt.

It was Neri, Dumond, and Placidio had taught me the true wonder of magic and encouraged me to reach deeper for the truth and wholeness of my gift. Not only had I embraced it, the strange experience with the grand duc's statue had left me eager to discover more. But I had vowed to use that loathsome offshoot of my talent only for direst necessity. Bawds Field had strengthened that resolve.

And yet . . . The Shadow Lord knew this venture was a

risk. He was hamstrung and had asked me to try, trusting my judgment. He would assess no blame if we failed, though if we were *caught* in the doing, he would deny any knowledge of our actions and do nothing to mitigate our punishment. I had to weigh that risk against the considerable benefit of striking early before the situation changed.

The goal was worthy. The opportunity too good to be missed. "All right. We go."

• • •

Torches flickered at each corner of the Palazzo Segnori's roof and above each graceful arch of its harmonious loggia fronting Piazza Livello. Oil lamps burned in the stained glass windows of its famed tower, as if providing an incandescent stair should the Unseeable Gods decide to return from the Night Eternal. The result was an impressive view of the Palazzo itself and a well-lit venue for those taking a stroll on a pleasant evening. The light also allowed sneakthieves like the three of us to see the Gardia warders at their posts—four of them—and to note the absence of any nullifiers or their leashed magic sniffers. For the moment.

The concentration of light on the Palazzo's facade meant that the cobbled lanes threaded between it and the huge Gallanos Bank building on its right and the Philosophic Academie on its left were abandoned to shadows that seemed darker than they might otherwise. Long-needle pines had been planted down the middle of the side lanes to discourage cart traffic squeezing between Cantagna's greatest edifices.

As a result, the stretch of windowless wall nearest the rear of the Palazzo was as dark as a nullifier's heart and as deserted as an alehouse when its barrels were dry. Some time earlier in the day, Dumond had found a secluded venue behind a trio of long-needled pines to paint the image of a splintery, half-height wooden door just above the Palazzo's ancient foundation stones. Any daytime passerby who glimpsed it through the branches would think it a sewer access or some equally uninviting portal. Anyone curious enough to touch it would realize it was not wood at all, but merely solid masonry beneath a layer of paint.

As for me, I viewed it by the light of blue-white flames flickering above Dumond's spread palms. Magic.

"*Cédéré*," whispered the smith as he laid his hands on the door.

The flames were snuffed instantly, but with the snap of a latch and the drag of old wood on masonry, the metalsmith opened the door to a rectangle of paler darkness. Unlike Neri's magical pathways that allowed him—and only him—to bypass any obstacle to reach an object he desired, Dumond's painted doorways simply opened a hole in a wall that anyone could walk through to the other side.

My brother and I pulled on the black masks Dumond had supplied us. Then Neri, sword in hand, ducked and scrambled through the opening.

"All clear," he whispered.

I followed on hands and knees. The dark passage on the other side of the wall smelled of old stone and dusty corners. To my right, stone steps led upward toward a pale illumination. To my left, a tight corner led deeper into the dark—a ground level passage through the Palazzo.

As I followed Neri up the age-scooped steps, Dumond

dragged his door closed behind. He used no magic to seal it yet; it was our way out.

The dim light revealed a landing above. Neri reached it first and vanished around a corner. Dumond and I held below the landing until my brother reappeared to wave us onward. We slipped past the dark passage leading into the first level, and followed him up to the second landing, where a small oil lamp provided the dim illumination.

With the surety of any good scout, Neri motioned us to stay quiet and follow. The short sword in his right hand had been joined by a main gauche in his left. Small weapons, as Placidio advised. A youth wearing a longsword in the city was always at risk of questioning.

The three of us slipped soundlessly along the passage wall so the lamp from the stair would not expose us. Another lamp gleamed a hundred paces ahead. My stomach lurched as a dark bulk moved in front of the light.

We halted and held our breath.

Mumbled words in a deep voice elicited a quiet laugh. Guards.

The body passed in front of the light again and all fell quiet. As if in intentional unison, we breathed again and moved forward.

A few steps farther on, the wall we traversed ended in a black void. Much to my churning belly's alarm, we crept past the open doorway and ever closer to the guards and their lamp. When I believed I could smell the wine on their breath, a second void gaped in the wall. Neri dodged through this opening. Dumond and I followed, feeling our way cautiously into the pitch dark room next door to the prisoner.

Neri laid a hand on my shoulder. A signal to stay still.

I obeyed, even while marveling that my rash, angry sixteen-year-old brother had acquired such calm assurance. Placidio's good teaching—even if all the lessons weren't yet learned. For the thousandth time I approved the desperate choice I'd made to hire the swordmaster in days we weren't sure we'd be able to eat.

A quiet shuffling occurred at the doorway and then a soft light sprang from Neri's hand. His black cloak and Dumond's were hung across the opening to the passage, preventing the ivory beams from escaping to give away our presence.

"You mastered the hand light," I whispered, gazing in wonder at the glow that had no source but Neri's own magic. Of course he had. That's what he had used to illuminate Bawds Field when they were hunting me.

His eyes sparked as he illuminated a dusty stone wall where Dumond was already wiping down a rectangle to prepare it for paint. This doorway would get us directly into the prisoner's locked room without any guard the wiser.

I took Neri's short sword so he could help Dumond, drew my own dagger, and positioned myself beside the cloak-hung doorway. The chamber was a windowless closet, adorned with cobwebs, a rolled rug that looked as if it might disintegrate if you touched it, and a broken stool. A servant's chamber, perhaps.

Only a few moments and I wanted to scream at Dumond to work faster. The sound of each brush stroke inflamed my nerves. Would the magic not work if he put in fewer details? We'd never talked of that. Surely he'd not insist on perfect shading and color if it wasn't necessary. But logic didn't make the time go faster. This door would be taller than the first, so we didn't have to crawl. Better for a quick retreat.

I pulled down my mask to hang around my neck. The wool itched my face and was near suffocating me in the stuffy chamber.

A distant voice snapped a command and determined footsteps sounded from the direction of the stair. Dumond's brush stilled. Neri's light winked out. I pressed my back to the wall as if it might absorb me. I dared not breathe as we waited to hear the chink of a chain and the shuffling of silk-clad feet that would announce a sniffer.

In moments the footsteps—two men in boots, matching strides—passed by the doorway. No rattling chain accompanied their passing. No wordless howl—the sound of a sniffer who detects his prey. Would they detect the acrid fumes of Dumond's paint?

Still we waited. Interminably, it seemed.

Keys rattled. A door slammed. An easy laugh and the clink of pottery—mugs and pitcher—followed. This was no hunt, but a standard changing of the guard. Nerve scraping, nonetheless. *Spirits . . . if we'd been a quarter hour later . . .*

More tramping boots, less brisk than the previous, passed by and receded toward the stair.

Quiet descended once again. Neri reignited his light, and Dumond resumed his work, dabbing on an extra wash of yellowish brown for the latch. A new strip of black along the lower edge had me curious, until I closed my eyes and opened them again to see the new door as a whole. He'd left a gap at its base, so it wouldn't scrape, and layered a tinge of oil on the hinges and latch.

Before my nerves could settle again, Dumond closed the lids of his paint jars, buckled their holding straps, wiped his brushes, and stowed all in his bag. As he rolled up the spattered cloth he'd used to catch stray dabs of paint, he glanced at me. His hand waved at his door and his eyes widened.

I knew what he was asking.

I nodded that I was ready, though assent was a certain lie. Not at all ready. How would I even begin to explain my presence? If the prisoner was sleeping, I'd have to wake him, muzzling him before he shouted. Placidio was supposed to be here for this part.

Dumond shouldered his bag, stood before his artwork, and spread his arms. Blue-white flame appeared above each of his cupped hands. *Sisters! How does he do that?*

Neri pointed to his mask and then to me. He took back his sword.

I pulled up my mask and stepped up close. Neri's ivory light winked out.

Dumond laid his flaming hands on the door. *"Cédéré."*

No squeak of hinges or splintering wood intruded on the quiet, as the door opened to a dimly lit chamber. Dumond stepped aside. He'd stay behind to keep watch.

Neri took Placidio's role, entering the opening first. But he moved aside as I followed him.

After brief impression of a comfortably furnished room—chairs, bed, washing cabinet, writing desk, a gleaming brass lamp mounted high on the wall above the bed—my eye focused on a dapper gentleman in his shirt sleeves. Wide awake, he was seated in a cushioned chair, his stockinged feet propped on a footstool. Gold hooped earrings and eyes of brilliant ebony gleamed amid tight curled black hair and beard. Diamonds and rubies sparkled in the lamplight from a wide strip of brocade that lay on the bed alongside a velvet cloak and doublet.

"Gracious," he said softly. "Who in the names of the Nameless are you two? And where did you come from so late of a night . . . or early of a morning? If you think to assassinate me, it might be a bit more difficult than you think."

He twirled a silver poignard.

For the first moment of my astonishment, I could only gape and flounder. Then sense returned, and I dropped my hood and yanked off my mask.

"Rossi!" I said with a grin. "Now you're a *pirate*?"

6

Few pleasures in the world can match knocking a supremely confident jouster off his high horse. Though our only field of honor had been the chambers of the wealthy and our only weapons words, playing cards, and bits of information, Fernand di Rossi and I had spent many an hour in determined, delightful combat.

"What do you—?" He sat up sharply. His ebony eyes blinked. But his scrutiny quickly softened into a wondering amusement.

"I am visited by an apparition, it seems, the ghost of a dead woman and her, mmm"—he gave Neri a sharp appraisal—"protective demon from the Night Eternal? Yet you both appear quite substantial."

"I have, indeed, departed the life where you knew me," I said.

"So facile with words, my friend. Yet even if you are unattached to that life and certain terrifying men who came with it, I'm guessing that I am still not permitted to carry you away on my noble steed to hunt Frost Wraiths in the Mountains of the Moon or to forge masks of gold in the dragon lairs of the Land of Smoke and Silk."

How could I have forgotten that the tales of a diamond-and-ruby baldric were attached to this man, the most fantastical storyteller I had ever encountered? No one of *il Padroné*'s acquaintance ever inquired about the origins of a Moon House courtesan; we were born on the day our masters or mistresses claimed us and would never be so crass as to speak of our private lives. But every host or hostess in the Costa Drago begged Rossi to grant their guests the story of his origins.

Never boring, the tale differed hugely from one evening to the next. One night he claimed to be the natural son of a Lhampuri mangalla, run away before he could be executed when he came of age. Another day he was a beggar's child, adopted by a traveling philosophist. I'd heard variant versions of his being raised by wolves beyond the mountains to the north, a fifteenth cousin to the grand duc of Riccia-by-the-sea, or stolen from his crèche by the dancing fae and spirited away to the isle of Eide.

The mundane truth had always been apparent. Rossi was the most common family name in the Costa Drago, the majority of its bearers sturdy, freckled farmers, laborers, or washing women with red hair. With his tight ebon curls and skin the hue of smoked bronze, Fernand would never be mistaken for a Rossi. Forever short of money, he lived and dined comfortably in great houses throughout the Costa Drago by virtue of the delights he brought to any company. His manners were flawless, his dignity unbreachable, his erudition undeniable, and his very expensive garments reeked of impeccable taste, though worn at the seams and sorely out of fashion. He was universally assumed to be the scion of a great house fallen on hard times. Guessing which one provided amusement almost as intriguing as the man himself.

"Even if I were willing to ride along, it does not appear you *can* ride away just now, Fernand, unless your fae kin come to spirit you back to Eide."

He smiled and leaned back in his chair, laid the poignard in his lap, and raised a glass of wine from a chair-side table.

This was no frightened prisoner, no hardened rogue, no simple turncoat. Rossi changed the game entirely. The poignard and the glass of wine belied his status as a prisoner, no matter window bars or guards.

"You assume I *wish* to run away, lovely Cataline. Yet here I sit, comfortably secure. This cup is filled with a decent Cantagnese vintage; my bed is good down and wool; and I am promised a fine omelette for breakfast. While you, my dear, arrive in company with a young ruffian and. . . . tsk, tsk . . . so shabby, so unlike the luminous woman who had every wife in Cantagnese society plotting her ruin. Not dead, it seems, but banished to your origins, perhaps? I've heard rumor of such, though never spoken beyond whispers in certain . . . dangerous company."

A grimace of mock terror widened his eyes, exposing their whites. But even such bald humor could not mask his curiosity.

His hand waved at a nearby chair. "Come sit. Sorry I've no more wine. My kindly caretakers did not leave me the flask."

I declined. Rossi's greatest weakness was his vanity. The few times I had bested him in our contests of wits had distressed him inordinately, but even more he had resented that I was a finger's length taller than he. So I remained standing and stepped even closer, where he'd have to push me aside to rise from his chair. Instinct had made me unmask, promising that our history of friendship would easily convince him to trust me. But I was less certain of that by the moment.

Neri flattened his back to the outer door, his eye on Rossi and me, his ear listening for hints of movement in the passage.

"Have you turned assassin, mistress? Or"—his gaze darted to the baldric and his left hand curled into a fist about his ring—"thief, perhaps? The condottieri captain warned me it was foolish to wear my pretties into this building. But I chose to enjoy the symbolism of it—entering on my own terms and not those of my captors."

In many of his stories, told with the exquisite detail induced by his host's brandy, Fernand featured his inherited family treasures: a gold bracelet fashioned in the shape of a dragon, a gold ring engraved with laurel sprays, and a baldric sewn with diamonds and rubies. He always wore the first two; even now they gleamed at his wrist and finger. But I'd never seen the baldric and assumed it existed in the same mythical realms as his kin, the fae.

Though I knew some essential things about this man, I clearly didn't know everything.

"Consider me a benevolent phantom in search of opportunities," I said. "I've come in response to a rumor about this new-arrived prisoner, though I doubted its truth. He was arrested fifteen . . . now sixteen . . . days ago for selling stolen shipping schedules to an Invidian pirate, and I was most intrigued by his situation. Infinitely more so now."

"Go on. You had my attention at *benevolent*. And *opportunities* are always of interest."

Of course they would be. An eagerness lay beneath his relaxed posturing, just as when someone proposed the rules for a new challenge of wits.

Returning my dagger to its sheath, folding my arms as if ready to scold a naughty child, I wrinkled my brow at him. "Piracy reaps a quick hanging in Cantagna, so it doesn't surprise me that you claimed foreign citizenship right away. That the affiliation was to one of the parties of the Triumvirate Treaty also made sense, as it gave you twenty days to figure out a strategy to prevent your neck being stretched. The astonishment is that, of the choices available, you claimed *Mercediaran* citizenship. Not only do Mercediarans hang pirates, they do so in dreadful fashion, with ropes and knives and fire . . ."

Neither his amusement nor the spark in his black eyes dulled in the least with my lurid references.

". . . which suggests that you are a common tool of Her Most Ferocious Excellency Vizio, the Protector of Mercediare, and believe she will protect you."

"Oh, my dear, you of all people know what I am . . . and am not," he said. In my mind's eye, I saw him make a mark to his favor on a scoring tablet.

"Exactly so. I can no more accept that Fernand di Rossi is a bootlicking servant of Cerelia Balbina di Vizio than that you're a stepson of fairies. Indeed over the years you've expressed your opinion of her often and with far more sincerity than you told the story of your origins." I bent down a little. "Such deep-seated loathing could not have been feigned."

The Protector's ruthless corruption had been the only thing I'd ever seen heat Rossi's blood beyond a simmer. I'd never asked what past events caused him such pain, fearing he might consider it an invitation to pry into my own resentments.

He did not acknowledge my saying. Neither did he deny it. A tick mark in my column perhaps.

The notion that Rossi was more sharp deceiver than impoverished gentleman was disheartening, but far worse was imagining any person I'd ever called friend to be Vizio's lickspittle. Her depredations equaled those of Sandro's depraved uncle Lodovico—and her ambitions were more grandiose.

"Which means that you are something else altogether, and that perhaps the whispers I've heard of the new prisoner's identity are true."

He set his wine aside. Paid closer attention. His hands were nowhere near the poignard. "I am perched on this chair like a bird on a branch, awaiting the winds of spring. Tell me who I am."

I did not need to see the scrap of Cinque's handwriting the Shadow Lord had shown me or match it again to the script on an intercepted message from the prisoner to his pirate customers. Of course Rossi was Cinque. How perfect a disguise. How perfect the opportunities of a shabby aristocrat to listen, to overhear, to snatch important papers or intercept messages while being discounted in the games of power. He could meet contacts at any time in any house with no one to suspect he was present for any reason but a free dinner and an audience for his stories. Even *il Padroné* dismissed Rossi as a charming, slightly desperate man, one of his own circle to be welcomed as he himself would like to be welcomed did Lady Fortune ever turn her back on him. But *il Padroné* had never sparred with him, and it was Rossi's determination to best an opponent who had exposed a dazzling intellect.

"You, segno, are the notorious purveyor of secrets who uses

the nom de plume *Cinque*, a man no more beholden to Protector Vizio than to your hundred other employers. Am I right?"

"A most interesting supposition. Though to be sure, if I were such a cynical merchant, whyever would I admit to it?" His eyes glittered in the lamplight.

"You might not—not to me—but the Protector will command her minions relieve you of all your secrets before you die. I understand she's very good at it."

"Even if she believes me to be the notorious—and likely quite useful—Cinque?"

"Because of it," I said. "Surely Protector Vizio has heard the same rumor that came to my ears—that over a number of years, Cinque has gathered a list of witnessed signatures, notable personages committed to assassinating her very self. Vizio would bleed her own child to possess that list."

Rossi gazed up at me, a sly smile touching lips, eyes, and brow. "I think you attribute more maternal feeling to the Protector than she has ever owned. There are many things that she would bleed her only child to possess. But you can only spend blood once, and that bargain was made many years ago. Maybe her ambassador knows what became of him."

Vizio's *child*? Blood spent years ago? No time to pursue that mystery.

"I'm curious, Fernand. Why would notable personages sign such a pledge? And why would Cinque let such a document lie fallow?"

"Notable personages with large treasuries think nothing of committing a portion of that wealth to furthering their aims— an investment, like buying a new sailing ship or a new horse or a new magistrate. It might pay off. It might not. Spies, I would guess, must bide until they can get maximum value for their information."

A glib answer, quite the same as I'd given Vashti. What value did Rossi expect to gain? Something more than his life?

"You're to be turned over to Vizio's loyal ambassador," I said. "No matter whom you've bribed to bring you wine and omelettes and silver poignards, if Vizio discovers the truth of you, you will exist in torment until she gains possession of that list. Then you will die in torment, because more listeners than I will have heard your true opinions of her, and because you've only offered her the list when you are in her power."

Rossi took my hand in his. "Cataline, you are kind to worry about me—and bold to insert yourself and your young companion between one you believe a *notorious purveyor of secrets* and the Tyrant of Mercediare. But I assure you that I have *many* bargaining chips to play before I die."

I wrenched my hand away. "No matter what you offer, Vizio will never trust you enough to leave you alive. And even if so, none of your other clients, especially those signatory to the Assassins List, would trust you, knowing you were once in her hands and walked away unscathed. To violate those clients' trust to save yourself would ruin Cinque's reputation forever. You've no good way out."

No one would expect a hardened spy to quiver in terror or vomit at the reminder that the consequences of a life of perfidy were imminent—and horrible. But his calm both astonished and fascinated me.

"So your purpose here, damizella, is . . . what?"

"To ensure that the Assassins List never reaches the Protector."

His brow creased. His fingers twitched as if to grab the poignard. But he did not reach for it. "To *kill* me, then, or kill this Cinque, should we prove to be one and the same?"

"If that's the only way." Please, universe, let that not be the only way.

"Ah." Rossi settled deeper in his chair. "*He* desires to own this list. Alessandro. I must say I never thought of the Shadow Lord using his discarded mistress as his hunting hound. That's a bit crass."

The pointed jibe could not wound. Its target had long grown numb.

"My former owner does not know I'm here. My break with him was permanent and irrevocable." No lies there. "I've plans for my own future and will not allow your schemes to stand in my way. But I would much rather destroy the Assassins List than destroy you."

"Destroy it!" His exuberant laughter was unforced. "Certain, I'm guessing, but the kind of information you speak of could bring you a considerable fortune to ensure that future."

"I've no stomach for the kind of life you must have led all these years. Work with me, Rossi. You know enough of Protector Vizio—more than enough. She would launch a vendetta against every family represented on that list. We've seen this before. Her thugs would spread throughout the Costa Drago, and there would be no end to the murder, torture, rapine, hostage-taking. I prefer to live out my days in peace."

"Perhaps you believe one of the names on this list could buy you this peaceful future." He beamed at me as if I was Lady Fortune herself, assuring him of a lifetime of good luck. "Are you offering me rescue in exchange for this inflammatory document?"

The thorny question.

"Tell me where I can find the Assassins List and your freedom can be arranged."

He propped his chin on his hand, and his gold-ringed finger rubbed at his lip. His gaze did not leave my own. Assessing. Considering his next play.

I pushed harder. "You know the danger of ink and paper, Rossi," I said. "Spoken knowledge is ephemeral, because lies can serve as truth, even under mortal duress. But a written page itself does not lie, not with authenticated signatures. You would not have destroyed such a valuable document before you fell into misfortune and got arrested, and the Mercediarans *will* pry its location out of you. I've seen the horrors powerful men can wreak on each other, and though you feel safe here with your little knife, there are locks on the outside of your door, as well as inside. The guards are awake and very well armed. If you've misjudged your position—your bargaining chips—you condemn a great many more than yourself to a terrible fate. I cannot let that happen."

With everything in me, I willed him to believe me.

A soft exhale signaled an ending to his contemplation. "I think you are quite naive, Cataline."

Spirits, what can make him listen? So arrogant. Was he so greedy for payment and reputation that he would gamble with such disastrous stakes?

No. I was spitting into a desert, trying to make it bloom. Rossi relished games of skill, not chance. He truly was not worried, which meant he had a play in mind . . .

"Sssst." Neri twirled a gloved finger at the door. A stirring in the passage outside. It could be nothing, but I'd already drawn this out too long.

Rossi's sideways smile was undiminished. "You should go. I am not afraid, dear lady, and I need no rescuing. Though Egerik is quite formidable, I have gamed with him before. Yet neither do I wish to die this night, especially at the hand of woman I admire. So what if I offer you this? The Assassins List is no-where you would ever think to look for it. I will not turn it over to you—not for money or love. Nor shall I refrain from using it to my own purposes. But I swear upon the hours your generous spirit offered me friendship without judgment, thereby turning the tedious necessities of a lonely life into pleasure, that list will never find its way to Protector Vizio's hand."

He held out his hand. We clasped wrists as was the Cantagnese way to seal a contract. His hand was warm, his pulse steady. He either believed what he said, or he was the finest liar in the universe.

"I would so like to believe you," I said, "but there is the matter of this other use you have for it . . ."

Neri jerked an urgent thumb toward Dumond's door. We'd no time to discover Rossi's plan.

I was no murderer. Nor was I a torturer who could persuade the man to yield what he would not. What made him so confident? Allies or secrets or covert friendships that could force Mercediarans to withhold their worst? Blackmail? Or was it *Egerik*—not *Sinterolla* or *the ambassador* or the more distanced *this man Egerik*—with whom he had gamed before? By the Night Eternal . . . had he given me a clue, encouraging me to pursue the hunt to prove how clever he was? That was just like him . . .

All the more reason Rossi must not remember that Mistress Cataline was here questioning him about the Assassins List and hearing his clever play.

My spirit curdled at the thought of what I had to do. But I forced my speech steady. "May I offer you a farewell blessing before I go, Fernand? Sadly, I do believe this parting will be our last."

"Every man can use a blessing. I'm only surprised to hear the offer from one I believed a pure skeptic in matters of divinity. Have you gained faith in Lady Virtue or her divine ancestors since your path diverged from *il Padroné*?"

"I've gained faith in many things since my downfall," I said with an exaggerated sigh. "Not so much in the Lady, but in friends—honorable men and women, maybe even a few who are not so honorable. I fear for you, old friend. I can withhold my own dagger on your promise, but there are other assassins who don't know you as I do."

"Then a blessing, by all means."

"Close your eyes," I said.

He glanced up with a merry squint, flicking his gaze to the pocket that accessed my pearl-handled dagger. I had scandalized him when I mentioned that the Shadow Lord allowed me to keep a weapon sheathed to my thigh. "This *is* a blessing, you say, and not a blood sacrifice?"

"A plea for Lady Virtue to share her wisdom with you."

With our hands yet linked, I reached into the pool of magic that lay inside me and released its warm, thick otherness into my veins.

"All blessings of the Lady Virtue and her sister on you, Fernand di Rossi or Cinque, whichever . . . whoever . . . you are . . ."

I paused as one does when offering a prayer. But my mind raced, considering Rossi's surprise to see his onetime acquaintance, everything he had heard from me in this hour, his every question and every answer, every reaction. Sadly, I knew too little about the Assassins List—its shape, size, wording, or provenance—to erase *that* from his memory.

Once all was gathered, I devised a new story to overlay the truth, and whispered it on a stream of magic: *Such a vivid dream when I drifted off to sleep. The Tibernian Contessa . . . such a lovely woman . . . we were playing piquet. But the cards had no numbers, and every face on the knights and queens was the same, so how could I make sets or sequences? And she played her tricks so fast I could not see if her cards were distinguishable. I had promised her a tale of Eide if she won, and she had promised me a kiss, and my pride was sorely stung that she defeated me so roundly, one capet after another. But she felt sorry and granted me the kiss anyway when I finished the story of my fairy kin and a blessing thereafter. So it was a fine dream . . . but such a shame I spilled the wine as I woke. My kindly caretakers did not leave me the flask . . .*

I glanced at Neri and nodded him to our entry door. He pressed his hand on the latch.

Smoothing Rossi's brow, I swept my hand over his eyes to keep them closed. To seat the new memory, I spoke the finish of the blessing aloud, as if it were but the lingering of his dream.

". . . and may the divine Lady grant you wisdom throughout a long and healthy life. We Tibernians believe our land is the Twin Sisters' earthly home, leaving us always in their hearing. And this last is because I won our game . . ."

Bent over him, I kissed Rossi's forehead, released his hand, and reached under the side of his chair, upending the chair and the man himself. The poignard in his lap went flying. His nose and his wine cup slammed onto the hard tiles. I dropped the heavy chair on his back.

"Ow!" Rossi yelled. "Contessa?"

Fists thundered on the outer door, and keys rattled in the lock.

Prostrate, hand to his bleeding face, Rossi raised up his head. But all he would see was the shattered cup and spreading pool of blood and wine. I yanked up my mask and darted through Dumond's open door.

As soon as Neri pulled it tight, Dumond slapped his hands on it and snapped, "*Sigillaré.*"

The door vanished—wood, metal, paint, and all—leaving the bare wall as we'd found it.

As Neri unhooked the hanging cloaks, anxious voices clamored in the passage. The door to Rossi's room scraped open. When we peeked into the passage, no one was in sight.

Without a word, we raced toward the stair, down, and out into the dark lane. Another "*sigillaré*" and the door in the foundation vanished as completely as the other.

Like phantoms, we hurried silently about the peripheries of the Piazza Livello. As we halted to unlock the Via Mortua grate, a screeching yowl like that of a great cat split the quiet night, leaving a skim of ice sheathing my skin.

The sniffer's hunting cry spurred us downhill. We made sure to run through a pond—because rumor said traces of magic could not be followed through water—and we snatched berries from junipers and crushed them as we ran to remove the taint of magic from our fingers. Rumors, stories . . . after millennia of extermination, there were no books of lore or academies of sorcery to teach us what we were. How long did traces of magic last? How long did we need to be afraid? Spirits, I needed to interview a cursed sniffer!

Once in the jumbled stews of the Asylum Ring we three went our separate ways. We'd meet at Dumond's in an hour. Then we'd have to decide if our mission had been a success or a failure or perhaps had only just begun. I had an uneasy sense it was the latter.

7

For a good part of an hour I huddled at the deserted ruin of the Leguiza Hospice to ensure I'd not been followed. Only then did I trudge through the last few streets and across the sawdust litter of the cooper's yard just outside Dumond's house. Neri was already waiting.

"A successful exercise of burglary, thanks to you two," I said, when Dumond joined us. "This prisoner is most definitely the spy called Cinque, and he most definitely possesses the Assassins List. But he refused to turn it over. He claims he needs no assistance, and is not at all concerned about torture or execution."

"A stupid man, then," said Dumond, we followed him inside. "Bad luck, that."

"No, not at all stupid. That's the difficulty. I used every argument I could think of, even intimated I was willing to kill him. He wouldn't yield the list, but at the end made me this promise and dropped what I think could be an important clue . . ."

While we consumed the food and drink Vashti had waiting,

I recounted my past dealings with Fernand di Rossi and everything I could recall of the night's interview.

"You see the dilemma. The Assassins List still exists in a place unknown, and he intends to use it—sometime. For who knows what? I do believe he despises Vizio, so I'm tempted to believe him when he promises she won't see it. But in four more days, he'll be in the ambassador's hands. A man he has *gamed* with, as he always gamed with me. No word Rossi spoke was unconsidered, so I believe his use of the ambassador's personal name *Egerik* meant something. I'll wager my house that Ambassador di Sinterolla—this Egerik—is more than a mere functionary in a prisoner transfer."

"But are they opponents or allies in this game?" Dumond blew a tired exhale.

"That is the question."

We were all exhausted. It was foolish to address the conundrum without sleep.

"We should gather this afternoon to decide on our next moves," I said. "For now, we all need a nap, and I've something I need to see to . . ."

That something, of course, was the odd stranger sleeping—I hoped—in my bed. I'd a mind to ask Dumond about the symbol on the luck charm, but thought I'd see if my drowned rat had died or vanished with my pens and pots before telling my partners about him. I felt entirely foolish for dragging the man home. Neri would enjoy pointing out *how* foolish.

Vashti refilled our cups one last time. "The swordmaster will come in the afternoon, yes?"

As well as serving the Chimera as a rescuer of lost souls, as a generous purveyor of food and drink at unlikely hours, and as a seamstress who could transform one into a contessa, a tart, or a shepherdess with a few scraps, ten buttons, and a feather, Vashti provided intelligent advice and a certain detached clarity that kept us focused.

"We've got to find him first," I said. "But he'll be here."

Neri and I made our farewells and headed homeward, a not inconsiderable walk halfway around the Beggars Ring. We'd be lucky to reach our beds before first light.

"You did well tonight," I told Neri as we set a modest pace along the Ring Road. "You've learned a lot in a year."

"Got no choice with you and Placidio always on me. Like badgers, you two."

"We are, no question."

I could have told him how much change I saw and how proud I was, but I heeded Placidio's advice not to let him off his caution too easily. Certain, Neri was still young and frighteningly fearless. But he honored his swordmaster above any other person he knew, his sister included.

"Where could Placidio be?" I said.

"Did you look in at Jaco's Spoon? It's not so close, but he likes their sausage loaf after a hard fight."

"I checked everywhere you've mentioned except for the one you weren't sure of—the Bull something. No one had seen him since I left him at the woolhouse."

"Don't like it," Neri said, his concern feeding my own. "Where was this rough match to be?"

"I don't even ask any more. If he doesn't tell me on his own, asking only annoys him."

"Yeah. I'll find him."

Matches between registered duelists were not intended to be death matches. But the weapons used were neither wood nor blunted steel, and any wound could be deadly. Official referees helped prevent the most severe injuries, but the duelists themselves had to pay the referee's fee, and both participants had to agree to do so. At least half of Placidio's matches had no referee. Every match carried risk, even for a duelist with magic as his ally.

Our anxiety trailed after us like a lonely dog.

Only a few people were about so early in the day. A giant of a man in a leather vest dragging a wood cart. An elderly woman carrying a cage of chickens, destined for the poulterer. Neither gave us a second glance. Two skinny cats darted into a shadowed alley.

"Why'd you pull your mask off when you went into that room?" asked Neri after a while. "I thought you'd gone loony."

"All those years, Rossi and I were neither of us quite respectable. I was a whore; he was poor—very different from all the others who gather around *il Padroné*. We spent a lot of hours on the peripheries of social gatherings. As we both loved contests of wits, we became friends. Tonight I believed Rossi would listen to me. Dreadfully naive, as I look back on it."

"You never suspected he was a spy?"

"Never. Though it makes all kinds of sense. People discounted his intelligence because he was short of money, charming, and told wild stories. But he had traveled everywhere, seen so many things, and once you got beyond his fantastical tales, he was so intelligent and witty. A perfect persona for deception."

"Sort of like what you do with your impersonation magic."

"Better." For an instant, the yawning emptiness of Bawds Field rolled through me, a cold wind whistling through my ears. "Safer." Would I ever be able to use it again?

A few hundred paces ahead of us, two horses whinnied.

Our feet slowed. Horses were a rarity in the Beggars Ring and rarely meant anything good.

A linkboy emerged from a lane of shabby tenements and market stalls, his torch illuminating the horses and the yellow blazon on their caparison. Praetorians—the military auxiliaries of the Philosophic Confraternity.

Shouts and protests accompanied the party that followed the boy into the street. Two men in scarlet-trimmed yellow dragged a wriggling scrap of a yelling woman. A small party of men and women erupted from the lane behind them, shouting and waving their arms. Rocks flew, startling the horses and infuriating the praetorians.

A praetorian drew his sword, whirled around, and ordered the protesters away. His partner soothed their mounts, then fixed a rope from the woman's bound wrists to one of the saddles.

Though tempted to bolt or halt to watch the confrontation play out, Neri and I rounded the next corner as if we saw such things every day while strolling the Ring Road before dawn. Indeed, nothing but the hour was unusual.

"That was Nandi the Palmist," said Neri, in a choked whisper. "A fey girl, always laughing. Likely getting ready for her dawn readings. She thinks Lady Fortune sees better at dawn."

"Certain, they're just going to warn her," I said, as soon

as my heart abandoned my throat and returned to beating. "Preach at her about the evils of augury. Put a scare into her."

That was the usual. Certain, if the woman was being arrested for magic, there would have been a nullifier and his unholy sniffer there as well. No law explicitly proscribed fortunetelling, though the Philosophic Confraternity proposed one to the Sestorale every year, claiming the *spiritual arts* led our citizens into *realms of unreason*. The Philosophists enforced the sorcery laws.

We returned to the Ring Road well past the site of the arrest.

"We can't just leave this mission go, can we?" said Neri. "Since your friend didn't say where was the cursed List."

My mind was in the same place as his. Using our magic was ever a risk.

"No. I think we must try again, even if the damnable thing is somewhere we'd *never think to look*. How can Rossi possibly guarantee it won't get to Protector Vizio if he's to be a prisoner of Mercediare? That says to me that someone else knows what and where Cinque's prize is—which I find difficult to believe. Or that he doesn't expect to be a prisoner very long."

"Does he think the ambassador will set him free?"

"Possibly. Two years . . . now three that would be . . . the ambassador's been posted here, so he could have encountered Rossi. But Rossi was never shy about his opinions of Vizio, and no Mercediaran earns the post of ambassador to Cantagna without being one of Vizio's most trusted, loyal bureaucrats. So why is Rossi not afraid of him?"

"Maybe Cinque has something on the ambassador himself, not just Vizio," said Neri.

"Extortion. Very possible, which says our next step must be to learn more about Ambassador di Sinterolla."

As Neri trudged along in silence, I considered how we might do that. I'd never met the man. Sandro had taken his young wife to formal diplomatic functions, and the Mercediaran ambassador was rarely seen in the more relaxed company where mistresses were welcomed. He was a widower, and gossip named him a straitlaced sort. Of course, the Shadow Lord, desiring to know as much about anyone of influence in Cantagna, always had his spies investigate newcomers posted to Cantagna. And all the information they gathered was kept in a safe place . . .

"Mantegna," I blurted.

"What's that?" Neri's head popped up.

"Cosimo di Mantegna is a lawyer. Prosperous and well-respected. Unknown to most people, he also happens to be the Shadow Lord's consigliere, his advisor in matters of the law. He has access to all information gathered by the Shadow Lord's spies—which should include something about the Mercediaran ambassador."

The streets burst into life with the predawn light as if the sun had entered the tenements and hovels and tapped everyone on the shoulder at the same time. Carts laden with vegetables, coal, and hanging cook pots clogged the Ring Road. Laborers with picks or sledges over their shoulders strode out of the side lanes. Girls carried buckets of water. Boys herded pigs.

As we entered the *Quartiere dell Fiume*—the River Quarter, where Neri and I lived—Neri spoke up abruptly. "I'm off to find Placidio. Doubt I can sleep anyways."

"Someday we're going to learn why your talent lets you walk through walls to find a silver bracelet or a biscuit, but can't take you to your swordmaster or your sister," I murmured. "Does every magical skill have a major flaw like that . . . like my relinquishing problem? Or is it just that we don't know what we're doing?"

"Thought for a while it might be the luck charms, since I can't walk to those neither. But Placidio and I tried it. With or without, if he's hid, I can't walk to him."

"Did Dumond ever tell you how the charms work? Or what the mark engraved on them means?" The bits of bronze supposedly masked the magic we carried from sniffers. But none of us could detect dormant magic in each other with or without the charms.

"Nah." Neri kept his voice quiet as well. "He only said that 'twas not the bronze itself, but the *graving* kept sniffers off us. I didn't know to ask if it were the exact mark—or if any other mark might do as well. At the time I thought it was likely the grooves in the metal held the magic . . . like troughs, you know." He glanced at me from under the locks of dark curling hair the local girls found so fetching. "Stupid, eh?"

"How could you have known different?"

Neri wasn't at all stupid. But he'd lived his first fifteen years in Beggars Ring squalor, ignorant, angry, scared, with a houseful of bawling infants and parents who were terrified of him. The only person in the world who might have understood was his elder sister, the whore who lived in luxury with the most dangerous man in Cantagna. If Sandro had not thrown me out, Neri would have been dead by sixteen.

I laid a hand on his shoulder. "I'll meet you and Placidio at Dumond's at midday. Find him, Neri."

"Be sure of it."

He vanished into the cramped lane that would take him to Placidio's room. Sometimes I envied those who had gods to ask for protection for those they cared for.

• • •

Weary to the bone, I pushed through the traffic to Lizards Alley as if I were tumbling down a well. I didn't even slow to check the message boxes in front of the shop. My clients would have to wait. If Lady Fortune was kind, Teo would be gone, and I could collapse on my pallet. Or at the least he would be snoozing peacefully with a normal heartbeat and I could collapse on Neri's pallet.

I shoved open the door.

He was still there. *Damnation.*

The house was still warm when I shut the door on the noisy morning and dropped to my knees beside the mound of blankets on my pallet. *Don't you dare be dead!*

I touched his covered shoulder. "Teo? Are you alive? Awake? Feeling better?"

He didn't move.

Steeling myself for the worst, I loosened the blankets and rolled him onto his back. Only to fall back to sitting on my heels. Teo's face . . .

The swelling, the bruises, the cuts and abrasions had vanished, revealing a narrow face of fine bones and wide-set eyes. Still sleeping, he breathed slowly through a long, straight, and decidedly unbroken nose. How was that possible? Anyone would think it had been a month since I'd seen him, not a few hours.

I yanked the covering from his leg and stared, wonder-struck. The swelling in his ankle was down, the bruising faded to pale green. Equally astonishing, the ink markings on his legs were no longer gray, but raven black. Brazen, I pulled back the blankets to expose the rest of him.

Like those on his leg, the inked markings, including the one so like that on our luck charms, had turned a vivid black. Faint reminders of the worst cuts and bruises from the beating remained. So I wasn't a lunatic.

I laid my cheek on his breast. After a noticeable interval, his heart thumped. His chest rose ever so slightly. Paused. Fell. Much, much too slow, and his flesh remained terribly cold.

Teo's state had not been some figment of the night and the fog. He'd been horribly beaten, near drowned. Terrified. His face had been so badly swollen he feared blindness. But the man in front of me might have posed for one of the marble statues in the ruined Temple of Atladu in the Market Ring—tall, sexless, serene, sculpted in a time when the popular style rejected natural muscle and bone in favor of the sublime.

Never had I heard or read of such rapid healing. The only thing I'd seen that approached it was certain magic—on a day when Placidio had touched a poisoned wound with fire and power, bringing himself back from the verge of death. Even that marvel could not measure to this.

My fingers gripped Teo's slender wrist and I closed my eyes and plumbed every sensation. No fiery power coursed through me as happened when my brother, Placidio, or Dumond called on their magic.

"Hey," I said, shaking his arm, then his leg. I slapped his cheek. He didn't even twitch. "Xýpna, Teo! Wake up!"

I pulled the blankets back to his chin.

Why in the name of the Unseeable had I brought him here? Of course it was irrational. I'd known it at the time.

"I was simply exhausted," I said aloud, as if Neri, Placidio, and Dumond were standing around me accusing. "And honestly, he was in a dreadful way. I was sure he'd die if I left him and I just couldn't allow that. Which I can't explain either, much less how he's recovered from his injuries so fast or why these marks are darker than they were. I was *not* mistaken about those. I couldn't leave him helpless."

I had thought his marks were simply skin art, similar to drawings on the walls of caves or figures painted on urns. Now I wondered if they masked what he carried in his blood, as the luck charms purportedly did, or were they talismans, carrying power in themselves?

Power. Sorcery. Magic. Teo must be a sorcerer. I knew nothing about the varieties of magic in the world, much less the intrigues related to it. Even so, I couldn't believe him a danger. He had been lonely and afraid and hurt . . . grateful for my help.

Which led me to another mystery. I'd not seen him speak a word, nor make a sign of communication but his hunger when I fed him. So how was it I knew these things about him? That he feared being blind. That he had a whimsical humor. *Not lead. Not dead. Need fed. Name's Teo.*

Surely he would wake soon. Spirits, he could be dancing or running up the scarps of the Boars Teeth by noonday if he continued this rate of healing. The moment he opened those eyes, I would demand answers.

So I sat beside the pallet to wait, dagger in hand. Rossi, the

Assassins list, Teo . . . my thoughts soon dissolved into murky confusion . . .

Sweet fronds of deep green, fruits of red and purple both sweet and tart, succulent leaves, perfect to wrap little crabs and tiny shrimps . . . such beauty here. I glided onward, till they joined me in the garden with the news. Another new crack in the pillar wall; it had been one per year, warm water seeping through a jagged opening in the foundation. Concerning, but a novelty. Then it was one per cycle of the moon. Water still, but bubbling hot, a pleasant warmth unless you poked an appendage inside the fracture. But now the foundation was crazed with them, and the pillar wall suffered. Mosaics that had lasted a hundred generations fading, colors washed out like dead fish on the sand. Two a day the rents appeared; some spat molten red streaks that sizzled and dissolved the flesh of the unwary. Time was running out . . .

The test is upon us . . . we cannot hold much longer as we are . . . your time has come early, along with opportunity . . .

A quiet moan accompanied a rustle of movement. I sat up abruptly, panic like lightning bolts in my limbs. I shook my head to clear away the detritus of sleep. So vivid a dream . . .

I rubbed my eyes. Bright daylight streamed in around the shutters and the door. Teo was turned halfway round, his legs hanging off the low pallet as if he'd tried to get up.

"Let me get you straight," I said, "raise you up a bit. Spirits, you must be thirsty. Were you having terrible dreams like I was?"

I refilled his cup with the salty lemon-ginger tea and propped his back and head high enough for me to put the cup to his lips more easily than the previous night.

Though he never opened his eyes, Teo sipped, swallowed,

and then opened his mouth again, as eager as a child tasting his first watered ale. He continued until the cup was drained. Then his head lolled sidewise.

Was he dreaming, too? Creeping destruction. Urgency. Ruin. Very like the visions wrought when Dumond and I touched the grand duc's statue with magic. Mine had been pillars and graceful stone arches, faded mosaics with fiery cracks in them, niches containing bronze artworks. Dumond had seen a grand city abandoned and overgrown with fungus, and a cave room with carved walls creased with fractures. Chests of books and manuscripts had filled that crumbling room. The differing scenes had engendered similar emotions in Dumond and me— sadness, yearning for hidden knowledge, grief, a certainty of magic. Perhaps the presence of this strange man, the wonder of his healing, had but triggered the recollection as I slept.

I needed to get moving and meet the others at Dumond's. Fortune grant that Neri and Placidio were gorging themselves at Vashti's bountiful table.

Meanwhile the matter of the Assassins List and Rossi came rushing back. Rossi had persuaded me that no argument, bribe, or threat would persuade him to turn over the list. And even if my alteration of his memory had worked perfectly, the injury to his face would have put his guards on alert, making any play in the Palazzo Segnori far more dangerous. A second foray into Rossi's chamber would accomplish nothing. We had to approach the problem less directly.

Pulling parchment, pen, and ink from a shelf, I scratched out a message to Cosimo di Mantegna. Disguised as a request for employment references to benefit my brother, my message asked for what information the Shadow Lord might have on the Mercediaran ambassador.

Once the letter was sealed, I cleaned myself up a bit and fetched a few things hanging beside our door. Tied some knots. Knelt at Teo's bedside.

"I must go out," I said to the sleeping man. "I've customers who need work done today, and it might keep me out late. But no matter what my common sense advises, I'm not going to throw you into the street. I've a notion that could cost your life and you might very well not even understand why. These are entirely unsupported beliefs, and I'm a most practical woman, despite my nonsensical ramblings, so I'm going to do something that is not very kind."

I slipped loops of wire-twisted rope over one wrist and his ankles, including the ankle that had been broken and now was not. Padding his skin with strips of fabric, I tightened the knots. The rope between the loops was threaded through an iron eye-bolt I had pounded into the foundation stones a year previous, on a day it was the only way I could keep Neri from getting us both killed. A second length of rope left a little slack for Teo's other hand. He wasn't going anywhere without my approval. If he was truly a sorcerer, maybe the wire would prevent him using magic to get free. Stories said so. For certain, Neri's attempts had not got *him* loose.

I tapped Teo's hand as if keeping him awake when he was clearly not awake, but it soothed my conscience to explain. "I'm sorry for the binding. I want to trust you, but I'm not sure I trust my own judgment in this case. I don't want you falling in the river again, and if my enemies show up, you will appear to be a wholly innocent victim of my wickedness. If *your* enemies show up . . . well, how would they? We weren't followed from the river. I've left you more of the ginger tea here." I touched his slack-bound hand to a filled flask and set it by the bed. "Have all you want of the nasty stuff. I'll be back before nightfall."

8

Dumond maintained his workshop as well as his little stone house behind the cooper's yard. Closer to the street, between the cooper's yard and a chandler's shop, sat the market stall where he sold bowls, spoons, metal jewelry, and small bronze castings.

When Neri was a small boy, Dumond had caught him stealing a bracelet from his locked stall—a gift, Neri had said, to persuade his lost elder sister to come home. The metalsmith gave him a small bronze charm instead, saying that anyone with special talents like Neri's needed to keep a luck charm with him at all times. Neri had persuaded him to make one for me, too.

At my knock, one of Dumond's black-eyed, black-haired younger daughters opened the family's sturdy front door. As the child darted into the alley, she called over her shoulder that her papa was eating lunch.

The stone walls of the boxlike room bore Vashti's mark—

needlework tapestries of vibrant colors, hanging ribbons of red and green beadwork, and exuberant watercolor paintings of wildflowers and vineyards. But Dumond was alone, still wearing his leather work apron and seated on a floor cushion beside a low table.

He nodded a greeting and took another bite of noodles.

I pulled up a cushion opposite him. "Neri and I believe the Mercediaran ambassador is the key to unraveling Rossi's intentions. So I've sent a query to the Shadow Lord's consigliere. He'll know whatever Sandro's spies know about the man." I laid out our reasoning.

"'Tis a curious business, no doubt." The smith continued eating as if I'd told him I'd seen the sun rise or had breakfast. "But will the lawyer answer? The Shadow Lord told you he'd send word when the prisoner arrived. Did he ever?"

"No." As well as dispatching the message to Mantegna, I had checked message box number six on the way. "Which is strange of itself. Why would Governor Taglino accommodate the prisoner so comfortably and so secretly that Sandro's spies haven't learned of it? Has someone else in the Sestorale ordered it?"

"Simplest explanation—a bribe. Man with a diamond-studded baldric could likely afford it."

"Possibly," I said, a bit deflated. "Maybe Rossi thinks to buy off the ambassador, too. Sandro didn't believe any Mercediaran knew the prisoner was Cinque. Even so, Vizio's loyal servant would never let off a man convicted of consorting with pirates."

"Unless he is not a loyal servant," said Dumond.

Not loyal. History and logic had told me that Vizio's ambassador was a loyalist, but only a fool would anoint a logical assumption as a certainty. Philosophy taught that the strongest theories were built by keeping one's assumptions to the minimum necessary.

"So it makes doubly good sense to learn more of the ambassador. If he is bold enough or fool enough to let Rossi walk free, then we need to be there to catch them at it . . . and make sure Cantagna is not implicated."

Dumond drained the contents of his cup and refilled it from the flowered teapot in the center of the table. "Makes sense to me. Are the others on their way? If we're going to do this, we'd best get to it."

"Neri went off hunting Placidio."

Dumond twisted his mouth in disapproval. "Nasty profession, dueling. Wicked that the man can't protect himself better."

Neri said nullifiers occasionally brought their sniffers round to the dueling grounds "lest sorcerers intervene in arguments where Lady Virtue should be the final arbiter." *Spirits, where were they?*

I picked a cup from the stack beside the flowered teapot and filled it. "Did you sleep this morning?"

"I've work pressing," said Dumond. "A coroner up to the Merchants Ring ordered a batch of natalés to have in stock for customers who can't afford to have them crafted special. My friend Pascal will cast them this evening if I get the molds done. It's good pay for simple work."

"Your natalés are exquisite," I said. "The coroner can see they're a bargain."

Though Dumond used no magic to create his bronzes, celebrity was a risk. From what I'd glimpsed of his talent, he could take a place with the finest sculptors in Cantagna. Instead, he confined his artistic skills to cups and bowls and the little bronze statuettes parents placed on the graves of their dead children to distract demons from their tender souls. Unless, that is, the Chimera needed him to forge a statue of great antiquity to prevent scoundrels from fomenting a civil war, as we had so recently.

"Have you come to any theory about the grand duc's bronze?" I said. "Why our magic made us see visions when we touched a statue of Atladu and Dragonis?" Visions clearly connected to each other in subject and emotion.

"No theories. Too many other things to think on." Dumond never used three words if he could get away with two.

"Since then . . . have you dreamed anything like what you saw in the statue?"

He glanced at me sharply. "Nothing like. I don't recall my dreams. Have you?"

"Once," I said. "This morning, in fact. Something else came up last night . . ."

I told him of rescuing Teo, of the man's strange state, his rapid healing, and the coincidence of the triangular symbol on his breast.

". . . so what can you tell me about the mark?" I shoved my charm across the low table.

He glanced at it over the bowl of fragrant noodles, his spoon paused between bites. His gaze flicked up to meet mine, then returned to his lunch. "It's lucky."

I pressed harder.

"What does the design mean and why would it be inked on a man's chest? How does the charm prevent sniffers from locating a sorcerer? Is it the mark that does it?"

The spoon settled back into the noodles.

"Maybe you're the one should be answering questions." Dumond was as unyielding as his front door. "You left a stranger—someone with power you can't explain—in your own house while we used magic in the Palazzo Segnori. And that was right after Placidio raked Neri over the coals for carelessness. What were you thinking?"

Dumond used the same calm tone as he would if asking his three-year-old twin daughters if they truly wished to paint each other yellow while standing on their mother's prized rug brought all the way from Paolin.

"It would have been murder to leave him," I said. "The current would have swept him away in moments."

"For an intelligent woman who thinks of herself worldly wise enough to spy for the Shadow Lord, that has to be the most nonsensical decision ever made. Strangers die every day."

"You'll be happy to know that he is currently tied up with wire rope, and nothing's within his reach but a blanket and a flask of ginger tea, even though his heart is still limping along like a lame donkey in a horse race. His mystery is too important to let him leave before I can speak to him."

Dumond's glare scoured me. His eyes were not the common mellow gold or black-brown of most Costa Drago citizens, but the gleaming obsidian of the Shadhi.

Dumond's father had been a factor for the largest mysenthe trading house in the Costa Drago. Sent to Paolin as a young man to maintain the trading house interests, Dumond the elder had wed a Shadhi woman. Only a few years later, the woman had died tearing her own flesh with sharpened nails for need of the same pleasure-inducing potion her husband traded in.

I deemed it an eternal irony that Dumond the son had

returned to the Costa Drago to pursue his love of sculpture and bronze-casting, only to meet a young Shadhi woman whose father was also a mysenthe trader. Vashti's father had been slaughtered by his customers because he could not supply them fast enough. The customers planned to sell the girl to a brothel, but Dumond had killed them and married Vashti. There was good reason mysenthe was called *the soul-killer*.

"Did it never cross your mind that the fellow might have been there to ensnare you?" said Dumond. "You frequent that riverbank, you who once lived with a very wealthy Cantagnese banker connected to strange incidents where *magic* might be involved. That might explain the man's quick recovery."

I wasn't having that. "There was no deception in Teo's pain, Dumond. Nor that his sickness made him cry out in *Annisi*, of all possible languages. Certain, if someone had been watching Neri and me cross the wasteland for a year, that would seem a perfect place to lie in wait. But for what? And why with a drowning man, instead of a sniffer? Nullifiers need no warrant to invade my house or question my friends."

He had no answer.

"And even if Teo *was* lying in wait for me—which I will not concede—why would he be wearing that particular symbol? He has dozens of symbols inked on every part of him save his face and hands. Have you ever encountered such skin markings? I've only seen them adorning painted figures on pottery or walls—very old pots and very old walls. If I could understand what this symbol means, I might be able to figure out what the others mean as well."

The smith's jaw held a firm line in his sparse beard. He snapped up another bite.

"Why won't you tell me? How many people carry charms like ours? Do you know other symbols of magical importance?"

It was entirely frustrating to know so little about something so extraordinary as magic.

"Tell her, Basha," said the woman who hurried through the fringed curtain. She carried a fresh pot of tea, an armload of fabric, and the scented grace of summer breezes into the windowless room. "You and Romy-zha are pledged to each other with the most solemn oaths. You trust her with our lives, so I think you worry overmuch about your secrets."

As ever, Vashti's arrival softened Dumond's sober mien. Only she could accomplish that. Though never harsh with their four daughters, he was ever somber around them, as if unable to shake his fear for their future in a world so hard. My experience had not eased his worries.

Vashti kissed his thinning hair. "You would not have left an injured man to drown any more than you abandoned a Shadhi girl to ruin, when you had every reason to believe she was a mysenthe slave who would betray you for three crystals of the soul-killer."

Vashti set the teapot on the table, laid the garments carefully over a carved wood trunk, and lowered herself to a worn cushion like those Dumond and I occupied. As she refilled our cups and poured her own, the scent of jasmine flooded the room. "Pardon, Romy-zha. I was listening in the kitchen as I did the washing. The girls are in the cellar practicing their drawing."

Her shoulder bumped Dumond's. "So tell her."

"Bah." Dumond growled his defeat. "I didn't invent the charms. I cast them, but I made the mold from a charm that was given to me. There is no enchantment on them that I can detect. That's why, just as I've told you, they cannot *attract* a sniffer."

"But I thought—"

"Do they truly hide the magic in the wearer's blood?" He forged on as if now the dam was broken, he couldn't stop. "How could I know? Can *you* detect the magic in Neri's blood if he's not using magic? I cannot. I knew your brother carried the taint because he walked through my wall to steal that bracelet. But the charms do *something.* I've walked right past sniffers, and they've never turned their green heads toward me. I've ever thought . . ."

He rapped a knuckle on the table as if to jar individual words into a pattern with meaning. "Sniffers are just sorcerers like us, with greater or lesser talents. Yes, their focus is honed because they're not allowed to see or hear or think of anything else, but there must be more to it. Something they're taught after they've chosen slavery over death. The Philosophic Confraternity has been exterminating sorcerers for thousands of years, and they're the ones who train sniffers. Stands to reason they'd know more about detecting it than those of us born to magic. So I'm thinking, if you want to know more about that symbol and what the charms do to divert a sniffer's attention, you needs must ask a philosophist. Right before the devil ships you off to the Executioner of the Demon Tainted."

"But you can locate the charms."

"I can locate the charms when they're separate from their owners—as I did with Neri's on the day we met—because I've developed a skill to detect my own crafter's mark. Just here."

He turned my charm to the back and pointed to a tiny circle with a vertical line bisecting it.

"I shape the magic inside myself, like I do the fire above my hands when I work the portal magic," he said. "The person who gave me the luck charm taught me how to make the fire to speed my workings, how to create a crafters' mark so that I would only detect it if the charm was separate from its owner. It is exactly how I told you to create the handlight. Only way I can describe it is to channel the power straight from your soul to the work, instead of through your particular variant of magic. I don't know why some of us can do certain things and some can't, any more than why one of us can do your kind of impersonation and one turn painted portals into doorways."

He scraped the last noodles from his bowl, but the spoon didn't move to his mouth. I waited for the flood to spend itself.

"As to numbers, I've given out seventeen charms over the last twenty years and retrieved two that got separated from the owners. Never told any of the seventeen that I cast the charms, nor that I carried the taint myself. Don't know any of their names, save yours and Neri's. Never wanted to know. I just hoped they were protected when they needed it. That's the sum of what I know of magic or charms or marks. Nothing."

He stuffed the last noodles in his mouth as if I were going to snatch them away.

"No enchantment on the charms. Nothing more." I was confounded. Since the day I'd met Dumond, when I'd watched him paint a door on a solid wall and then stepped through it after him into a place that was not the one which actually existed on the other side of that wall, I had believed he held the answers to every question I had about magic. Yes, he was reticent about that part of himself. We all were—even Neri. How else could one live, knowing that exposing your true self could get you bound in chains and thrown into the sea? But I'd thought that if we worked together long enough, grew comfortable with each other, Dumond would soften his barricades enough to let me learn from him. It was doubly wrenching to learn that the answers weren't even there. Clearly it grieved him, too.

I tried to temper my disappointment. "So who was it gave you the original charm and taught you these things?"

"An old woman in Varela, where Vashti and I met. I was practicing my wall magic in a sea cave, and I made a wrong choice somewhere. I still don't know which one of the thousand caves along the Varelan coast she lived in. She didn't seem all that shocked when I walked in on her breakfast. She gave me this"—he tugged on a braided string around his neck and drew out a charm identical to mine—"and said to wear it always, as it was the surest protection one of the demon-tainted could carry."

"Protection from what?" I said drinking the cooling tea.

"She told me it could *not* prevent a sniffer from detecting magic as I worked it or prevent them following the traces that magic left behind on me or the wall or whatever I touched with it. So I assumed that meant it masked the taint inherent in our blood. I believe it works." Dumond shrugged and shook his head. "Maybe your ink-marked fish knows for sure."

"If he ever wakes up." I drew the charm back across the table and retraced the simple lines. "I think the sinuous line refers in some fashion to the sea. To Atladu, perhaps. Teo called on a *divine father.*"

"Among god-believers, the opened inward curve always represents the embracing earth," said Vashti, her slender finger joining my ink-stained one on the charm, "or, with wider vision, the strength and power of the natural world. The curve that opens outward is sometimes interpreted as air, wind, and things unseen. But in Paolin, where people feel freer to speak of such things, the outward curve from a centered design would be interpreted as magic."

"So three kinds of power—the natural world, the ocean, and magic—set as three equal sides of a triangle. A stable boundary, so I was taught," I said, my finger tapping the charm, "but surrounding, protecting . . . what? The tight-coiled spiral can mean so many things—life and death, journeying, change. It's used everywhere and has been for centuries. Unwind it a little and it is Atladu's uncoiling wave. Unwind a little more and it becomes the Typhon symbol for wind."

"In Paolin the spiral is a snake bearing knowledge," said Vashti, "and as the snake uncoils, we learn. Learn what? That is the story surrounding the symbol's use, its . . ." She wagged a summoning finger at Dumond.

"Context?" he said.

"Yes. Perhaps the context of your visitor—the story of his mark's use—will be more revealing than the context of a bronze charm."

"I've come to think Teo's *context* is very important. While dozing this morning . . ."

I told them of cracked pillar walls and faded mosaics and seeping fire.

"Demons!" Dumond's elbows rested on the table. His clasped hands, scarred from years of dealing with molten metal and edged tools, rested on his mouth. "That is *very* like the visions from the statue. And you believe you may have heard things he wished to tell you, things barely whispered, if even that. Perhaps . . . You were right to keep him."

I drained my cup, as satisfied as if I'd just trounced Placidio in a duel. Certain, it could be mere coincidence that I would dream such a dream this day; little more than a tenday had passed since I'd experienced the vision from the statue. But I didn't believe in coincidence.

Dumond slipped his own charm back in his shirt, emptied his cup with one swallow, and stood. "But then again, maybe you should give this drowning fellow back to the river and let Lady Fortune entice someone else to fish him out—if she cares."

Dumond kissed his wife and left, just as the city bells clanged the first hour past noonday.

"He's in a foul mood today," said Vashti. "The price to share time in Pascal's foundry has gone up again. But he refuses to use the prize money from your last escapade to pay. Says it has to be put away for me and the girls if he's going to be working with the Chimera to prevent wars and vendettas."

"Does he want to stop? We can't doubt what we're doing."

Vashti's laughter could light the moon.

"He believes he should want to stop," she said after a moment, "but I told him I'd take the girls off to Paolin if he did. The Chimera has waked Dumond from long sleep. Using magic for worthy purpose glories his soul, and his soul feeds his art which is his first love—beyond me or the girls."

"I don't believe that."

Her fine brows arched. "You should see the painting he is working—"

The front door burst open.

"Bandages, *vaiya!*" Dumond yelled as he and two cloaked figures crowded through the narrow opening.

"We'll need his bag. I dropped it in his shop." Neri's voice grated from under one hooded cloak. He and Dumond were supporting the third man—bigger and taller than either of them. Placidio. With far too much blood on him.

9

Lay him here," said Vashti, shoving all the worn floor cushions into a heap.

A dreadful groan followed me as I bolted from the house and down the alley to Dumond's workshop. Placidio's armaments bag, splattered with blood, lay in the doorway. I grabbed it and ran.

Dumond already had Placidio's blood-soaked shirt and breeches torn open, exposing a dreadful, bloody gash from breastbone to hip. "Vash!"

"I'll bring the box," she said. "Romy-zha, in our bedchamber press will you find linen sheets. Bring several and whatever blanket looks raggedest."

She hurried toward the kitchen and called down the cellar stair, "Cittina, take the littles to Meki's house for the night."

The girl's shining black hair appeared at the top of the stair. "What's—?"

"No questions just now, sweeting. Out the back way."

"*Aicha, naihi.*" Cittina sighed hugely.

As the children bustled down below, I raced the upward steps three at a time.

Dumond's family slept in one large room the same size as their kitchen and sitting room together. Two corners were walled off by colorful draperies made from scraps, while shelves, stools, and clothes chests were set orderly about the remaining space. In the center of the fourth wall stood a white lacquered cabinet painted with scenes of forest and field, red deer, bears, and a great spotted cat.

I rummaged through the cabinet. Belly wounds meant sepsis; sepsis meant death. Another bellowed curse rattled the walls as I returned downstairs with two many-times-mended folds of linen and a clean blanket that looked like it was old when Dumond was a babe.

"Stop that . . ." Placidio's breathless growl came as Neri cut away the rest of the swordsman's garments.

Every jostle spurred another curse, bubbling in the blood streaming from his nose. "Blighted udiverse . . . Debonshit!"

Dumond blotted and wiped the duelist's face most efficiently, muzzling the noise. I could not but be pleased to hear the inventiveness of the curses that squeezed through the wad of linen. Certain, Placidio would not die without a fight.

Vashti passed Dumond my sheets and blanket, and immediately dragged me back to the kitchen. She told me to fill a bowl from the huge kettle she kept on her brazier and bring it in. She fetched a box from a high shelf and took it and a wad of rags into the other room.

When I brought the bowl, she set to washing the blood from Placidio's belly. The box from the kitchen was open to a little knife that looked extremely sharp, a set of bone needles, and thread suitable for sewing wounds. Dumond and Neri had brought a hard pallet from the cellar and spread the old blanket on it.

"Hold on," said Neri, crouching by Placidio. "We've got to move you one more time."

"Touch be, boar snout—and I'll roast—balls—for breakfast." The swordsman's croaks were punctuated with short explosive exhales. "You, too—you hab-handed son of debon-rutting—"

An agonized gasp swallowed Placidio's stream of invective as Dumond lifted his shoulders and Neri his legs. They shifted the swordsman onto the pallet.

Once he was down, Dumond and Neri retreated, and Vashti returned to her attempts to get a closer look at the wound. *Deep . . . oh spirits, so deep.*

Placidio dropped his head back to the pallet. Took a few shaky, shallow breaths, screwed his face into a grimace, and blew a long slow exhale. "'S not so bad. As it looks."

He could scarce get the words out through his clenched jaw. Sweat dripped from his forehead.

"The wound looks fresh," I said. "When was the duel?"

"Last. Night. Match went bad. Second . . . and friends . . . chased . . . ambush."

"Found him over to the Leguiza Hospice," said Neri, "after looking over half the city for him."

Only a few streets away.

Neri folded his arms. "Started out hunting for where he'd fought, which was *not* an easy place to locate when this hardhead *won't tell none of us his business*. It weren't none of his usual."

Neri's anger at this old grievance was very pointed.

"Had to traipse all the way up to the old barracks yard and ask the Dueling List Recorder, who sent me all the way downriver to the Fens, only to find him and everyone else long gone, but a dead man laying there and blood everywhere. No referee marker neither."

A dead opponent. No referee. *Spirits, Placidio . . .*

"As I couldn't follow *him* with magic, I followed this instead. 'Twas the same as that scabby Buto threw at him. Buto, what started all that when you—you know." He held a scrap of gray cloth, stiff with dried blood. The scrap was a dueling badge embroidered with a lizard atop two crossed pikes, a family blazon everyone in Cantagna knew.

"By the holy, blasted Twins, Placidio, Buto stood for one of the *Pizottis*? And you marked Buto's face, so of course in this duel you had to fight another of them."

"Four. Had to win. To be rid—legal."

"Because they had called a vendetta!"

If any family in the Costa Drago kept the outlawed tradition of the vendetta alive, it was the collection of hotheaded dullwits who occupied a mouldering fortress upriver from Cantagna. Unfortunately Digo and Falla Pizotti had four daughters, five sons, and innumerable nieces, nephews, and cousins, none of them with any ambition beyond winning contests of cards, jousts, dogs, chariots, cocks, dice, or drinking than the rest of their siblings. Inevitably their competitions had brought them into conflict with every family in Cantagna.

No Pizotti would take a defeat, a rebuff, or a slight in stride. Once you let yourself into their world of challenges and retaliations, it was near impossible to get out.

I bit my tongue. No one needed me to explain that the win might cost more than Placidio could pay.

"I followed the badge—found two fellows hamstrung," Neri continued. "Then to the hospice ruin, where there was a third mostly dead fellow alongside this *stronzo*, who was trying to magic his own wound. Told me he didn't need any frigging help, but he was so shaky he was spilling—"

"And. Then. You?" Placidio snapped.

"I bashed him in the nose to make him stop, so's I could get him here. Not sorry."

Neri's defiance slumped quickly into genuine worry. No matter Placidio's growling assertions, only pigheadedness was holding the man together.

"So, perhaps much of the blood is from the nose—and perhaps from these dead and wounded men?" said Vashti, rinsing her rag in the bowl. "But your pain is true."

She glanced across the room at me—and the worry in her face did not mirror her optimistic theory. Dark blood welled unceasingly from the horrid wound.

I wrapped my arms about my own belly, as if that could keep Placidio together.

"Knife nicked a rib," said Placidio, his breathing fast and shallow. "Hurts like devil's own, but it'll heal. For the cut— need fire and cauter salt. Like before." He looked straight at me. "The mission . . . I'll be ready . . ."

The fire quickly faded from his glare and his head lolled. His lips were bloodless. With a nicked rib, he might not even be feeling the belly wound, but that's what would kill him. Vashti's rags and apron were already soaked.

"We must do as he says right now," I said, answering Vashti

and Dumond's questioning looks. "We've seen him use fire and magic to drag himself back from the verge of the Night Eternal. Neri, do you know what cauter salt might be?"

"I've a guess."

"And we'll need a lit taper, Vashti."

"I'll fetch it."

"Stay with us, swordsman," said Dumond, slapping Placidio's cheek. "Damned right you're going to be ready for this mission. Not going to get me to do swordfighting or impersonating."

"Ham. Handed." Placidio could scarce whisper his riposte. "Just sear—the rip—let me rest."

"Good," said Dumond with a jerk of his head. "Vashti's got a powder. Won't mend the rib, but can ease it."

Neri scrambled back to Placidio's side with a brown vial he'd pulled from the armaments bag.

Dumond glanced from Neri to me. "So which of us is going to do this fire thing?"

"Me." Neri blurted his answer before anyone could pre-empt it.

If we'd not been watching his lips we couldn't have heard Placidio's answer. "Not Neri."

"Fine." Neri shoved the brown vial into Dumond's hand, and then bent over and shouted into Placidio's face. "This is what he'd pulled out down at the hospice, but he weren't able even to open it. I could have helped him right there. You know I could."

Placidio had drifted off again, so didn't answer Neri's resentment. But I knew why he didn't want Neri to hold the taper. Placidio believed he was going to die, and didn't want Neri left with the burden of it.

Dumond held up the vial. "So what do I do?"

"Cover the entire wound with whatever's in the vial," I said, "then use the taper to sear the wound end to end." I moved around behind Placidio's head. "The three of us will hold him down."

"*Burn* him?" Dumond's horror reflected my own from our prior experience with this.

"Touch the flame to the wounded flesh, yes. Carefully, of course. You'll know when you've done enough. Evidently his magic protects him while he works the healing. That's why he's got to be awake."

I leaned over and spoke directly into Placidio's ear, in hopes he could hear me. "Signal when you're ready for the fire, swordmaster. You need to use your magic."

Neri held Placidio's ankles. I gripped one wrist. Placidio's pulse raced like squirrels in spring.

Dumond used his one hand to gently spread the long, ugly, and very deep gash open and the other to sprinkle fine white crystals into the surging blood.

Placidio's eyes blinked open, and his face drained of what color had remained. His sinews tightened, his fists curled, and his whole body began to tremble.

Dumond set the vial aside. Vashti passed him the taper and grabbed the swordmaster's other wrist. When the last of the white crystals had dissolved in the ooze of blood, Placidio's colorless lips moved slightly, but no words came through his clenched teeth.

"I think he's ready," I said. "Sear it, one end to the other."

At its first touch to raw flesh and treated blood, the flame blazed white. Fire flowed through my hands as well, Placidio's magic grown into a thunder and lightning that raced through his limbs. Not with the searing pain racking his body, but a living elixer of magic—sharp, clarifying, forcing my every sense alive. I could hear sparrows picking at the waking seeds outside and felt the surging power of the Venia as it wrapped Cantagna in its soulless embrace.

But as Dumond moved the taper slowly along the dreadful wound, the flame darkened. Flickered weakly. A putrid scent impinged upon my senses—a taint that threatened to overwhelm all other sensations. The firestorm in my limbs yet rumbled, but cooler, fading.

"His magic's failing," whispered Neri. "We need to help him."

"I don't know how," I said.

"Draw your power as when you practice the handlight," said Dumond. "Will it to go where he needs it."

Fouled blades caused deadly sepsis in a living body. I'd seen it—the fever, the purulent fluids building. Perhaps if I aimed my magic at that . . .

I drew on the fire waiting inside me, but instead of touching an ancient statue to release its mysteries or imagining a light glowing from my hand, I envisioned Placidio's corrupted flesh and willed my magic to cleanse the vileness.

As if my swordmaster had grasped the lifeline of my power and hauled it to him, my magic surged into the racing current.

The river became a flood tide—multiple, distinct streams, creating a heady mixture greater than any one of them. One current, thin and bright, was hot as molten silver. Whimsy named it Neri's magic. A deep, quiet, steady warmth put me in mind of Dumond. Certain, the mighty flow that surged through hands and heart with the unruly power of a thunderstorm was Placidio's, now heated anew by the rest. But twining with these others and my own was yet another stream—immensely strong, but not at all fiery. Rather, cold and clean like a winter freshet. Perhaps that icy flow was the potency of Placidio's cauter salts, but it felt as live as all the rest.

As the magic reached a crescendo, Placidio could no longer hold back his screams—agony, yes, but edged with triumph. With defiance. With life.

But by the time the taper reached the lower end of the wound, Placidio lay still. All sense of foulness was gone, and the torrent of magic had collapsed into a slow moving rivulet. Letting go of Placidio's wrist, I lost the sense of the remainder.

Dumond doused the taper in the basin of bloody water. The stink of burnt hair and scorched flesh mingled with the iron stench of blood. Neri released a breath so long, one might believe he'd held it since he first heard Placidio was missing. Vashti fetched a clean towel to blot Placidio's sweat-soaked face.

That cool stream of magic that felt so different . . . Was Vashti hiding something from us? Did she know? She'd sworn she had no power for magic, but her hands had touched Placidio's skin like the rest of ours. Or perhaps what I'd felt was no individual thread of power, but only a product of our joining.

Dumond squatted beside me. He inspected the dry wound and the ruined, red-black flesh around it. "Looks fairly awful. Don't know as we've healed anything, but at least he's asleep." He prodded Placidio's shoulder without eliciting so much as a twitch. "For sure, this time."

"This is a new wonder to the world," said Vashti, softly. "I yearn to hear what you sensed of this, Basha. Each of you. Your faces told me this was the work of all."

"I'd like to hear what you experienced, as well, Dumond," I said. "Anything odd? Anything surprising?"

"Whole damnable thing's odd. Felt the magic, sure. By the Creation, that swordsman's got a powerful gift, and he definitely sucked down some of mine. Maybe yours too. Couldn't tell. Couldn't see what he was doing. The flame turned color, which was likely these salts burning away as they do in a kiln."

Perhaps my notion about the mingled streams of magic had been entirely my imagining. What did I know of it? What did anyone know of magic?

Vashti nudged Dumond aside and tied a loose bandage over the charred skin. "For now best keep it dry, so my *naihi* taught me. We'll apply a cooling salve later. It's the rib will pain him more when he wakes. Injured ribs are like dragon's claws; as long as they are inside you, anything you do just makes matters worse."

Dumond sat back and scratched his head. "I suppose we'll see what's what if he wakes."

"*When* he wakes," said Neri. "He said a few hours would see him good."

Amusement crept closer to Dumond's surface than usual. "As you say, boy: *When*. I shall be eternally resentful if he was wrong about that. Only four days until the prisoner's turned over."

While Neri, Vashti, and Dumond cleaned up the bloody mess of rags and torn clothing, sponges and basins, I moved Placidio's bare arms to his sides and pulled the edges of the blanket up to cover them, while leaving the bandaged wound exposed. Though his eyes were closed and his body still, his clenched hands were quivering.

"Are you all right, swordmaster?" I said quietly, tucking the blanket around his chest and shoulders.

"Will be," he whispered, eyes closed. "Just . . . need . . . time."

"You need sleep. Dumond says Vashti has something to ease—"

"No."

No surprise. A man of secrets who didn't allow himself to sleep deeply would never approve such remedies.

Even after such a storm of the unexplainable, life resumed its forward course. Neri settled himself at Placidio's shoulder with the swordmaster's own flask of restorative ginger tea at the ready. His somber gaze didn't waver from Placidio's face.

Dumond returned to work, saying he'd be at his friend's forge in the Asylum Ring until dark. Vashti changed her blood-soaked clothing and loaned me a fresh tunic. Then we bundled the pile of bloody linen to her washhouse behind the kitchen. I offered to do the scrubbing.

By the time I returned to the sitting room, Vashti was tidying Placidio's sheet. The two of us retired to the kitchen to make more tea.

"Our swordsman does not rest easy," she said. "But I see no sign of sepsis. A true wonder, what he did."

"No disputing that."

"Wait!" Neri's cry from the other room spoke panic. "Don't—"

"Fortune's frigging blasted dam! Stick a shiv in me!" The croaking epithets silenced Neri and hurried me to Placidio's bedside. He had attempted to roll to his side. A terrible mistake.

"Someone already punctured you," I said, helping him settle on his back again. "Sleep it off."

He threw an arm over his eyes. "Tie me down so's I don't move."

"Hold up. Before you get back to snoring, I got your frog piss here." Neri waved the flask of the salt-and-ginger tea in front of Placidio's nose. "I've been taught it helps the body recover from just about anything."

Neri dribbled a few spoonfuls of the salty tea down him. As I pulled the blood-stained blanket over his bare legs, Placidio mumbled, "Go run, lad. All the way. Round the Ring. It's today's . . . lesson."

His eyes remained closed; his breathing shallow; his unshaven face a mask of pain.

Fear wreathed Neri. I turned him away from Placidio. "Better you go upstairs and sleep. You've been more than a day without, hunting this fool of a swordmaster. I'll watch him until you're back. You can have the night watch."

Grudging, Neri agreed. But he didn't retire upstairs. He threw several of Vashti's cushions on a bench along the wall, laid down, and was asleep before I could blink. Placidio, on the other hand, did not sleep.

After a while of watching him struggle to hold still, I said, quietly, "How long does it take for a deep wound? For the magic to knit things back together?"

"A few hours to get well on the way." As I suspected, he was nowhere near unconscious. "Feels likes snakes in there. Biting. Chewing."

"Would it help if I talked to you? We've had interesting developments with regard to the prisoner and the Assassins List. And I've a mystery to share."

"Anything." A whisper of desperation wrapped the word.

Vashti motioned that she would be in the kitchen.

Laying a hand on Placidio's rigid arm, I began. "Your student who so diligently dragged you in here so we could save your life has been spending his days chasing a rat dog . . ."

I told him about Neri's sneaking, and our magic, and Rossi-Cinque who was not afraid of being turned over to those who would torture and hang him, yet had promised me that the Assassins List would not reach Vizio's hand. "Dumond and Neri and I agree that we should make another attempt to acquire the list, but, as I've laid out, revisiting the Palazzo Segnori would likely get one or all of us caught for nothing."

"Atladu's balls."

"Unfortunately neither manly Atladu nor any other divinity has provided insights as to our next step, except to learn as much as we can about our current rival for the Assassins List— the Mercediaran ambassador."

"Elements. Of combat," said Placidio through his clenched jaw.

"Elements . . . ?"

Of course! Placidio the swordmaster. He insisted that the best way to survive any contest was to consider three essential elements before engagement—even if there were only moments to choose. Thus, before any practice scenario in our training sessions, Neri or I had to review the elements to prove we'd thought them through completely.

Though his eyes were yet closed, my back straightened and my mind focused on the problem. "The first element is opponent. My assessment of our proper opponent is in progress. Currently it is the prisoner. No one knows anything about Cinque beyond rumor and the sample of his handwriting. As to Rossi—I know as much as anyone, because I paid attention over a span of seven years. He is far more intelligent than anyone gives him credit for. He is clearly skilled at deception, but vain and determined to win. I judge him sincere in his belief that he can survive and also in his promise that Vizio is not to get her hands on the Assassins List. Together those lead me to the conclusion that he expects to bribe, extort, or charm the Mercediaran ambassador. Before I arrived here this afternoon, I dispatched a request for information about Ambassador di Sinterolla to the Shadow Lord's consigliere."

"Terrain?"

"As I outlined, I believe re-entering the Palazzo Segnori would be excessively dangerous and ultimately fruitless. Barring some unpredictable occurrence like fire or earthquake, the next place we can find our opponent will be the Mercediaran embassy four days hence. The Palazzo Ignazio in the Quartiere di Fiori of the Heights serves as both embassy and ambassadorial residence, and what information is known about the building could be obtained in the City Architect's Office, a place with which I am more than passing familiar. Indeed . . . I could do that tomorrow. As to the third element—the weapons . . ."

The corner of Placidio's mouth turned upward ever so slightly. "Us."

"Yes. The Chimera and our magic. Time enough to decide how we use it once we have our opponents and the terrain more clear. I must allow . . . I hope it involves no impersonations. Though today's magic"—I tapped his wrist—"reminded me of its grandeur."

I spooned a bit of the ginger tea into Placidio's mouth. He wet his lips, but little more.

"Now we have a start on our plan of engagement, are you up for another story? A mystery unrelated to spies and assassins?"

"Please."

"Last night, I was walking home from the woolhouse . . ." I told the story of Teo, the mark, the dream and how it felt so similar to the visions Dumond and I had experienced.

"Fortune's. Dam. Woman."

Placidio's exclamation was quiet, but forceful.

The disbelieving echo from behind me was equally fierce, but much louder. "A *stranger* in our house? A sorcerer? Someone who gets into your head with words and dreams? You're always asking me if I'm a lunatic. Time to take a look at yourself!"

Neri looked as if he'd been awake for a while.

"Dumond agrees with you that I was a bit foolish—"

"Of course you were!" said Neri. "Think, Romy. Even drunk or mostly drowned, seems he was well enough to poke his name into your head and make it all the way to Lizard's Alley. You could have left him down to the Duck's Bone or over at the Pipes. Someone would have found him there. We four have important things going on. Risky already. You convinced us. Reminded me of it after Bawds Field. And now you park a stranger in your bed, and no knowing what's wrong with him, if anything?"

I sympathized with Neri. It was tiresome to hear people telling me how stupid I'd been and awful to have the notion they were right.

But I gritted my teeth and remained cool. "Even beyond the notion that I've never left anyone to die if I can help it, even admitting that Teo might have somehow coerced me to take him somewhere safe and hidden, how can I get rid of him now?

Assuming he returns to a condition to go anywhere, think of the answers he might have for us. About magic. About ourselves. About the Antigonean bronze . . ."

At that last I glanced specifically at Placidio, who steadfastly refused to speak of the Grand Duc Eduardo di Corradini who now owned the statue, much less to speculate on why the nobleman was so intent on owning that particular artifact. Placidio's eyes remained closed, but his stillness reflected concentration, not vagueness, especially as I told of the visions and the dream.

"Of course, it is a risk for all of us. But tell me what else I could do or can do but see it through, even in the midst of a Chimera scheme."

Not even Neri had an answer.

It was no use trying to describe the trust I felt for Teo, his palpable distress, and my sense that I could ease it. They would rightly attribute it to the very reason I understood his needs without his moving his lips. But why was I not afraid? Was this what demon possession was really like?

"Burn candles around him as he sleeps," whispered Placidio. "Five at least. Won't harm him. Leave no water inside the ring. Don't ask me why."

Even spoken in a whisper without inflection, I knew this information came from beyond one of Placidio's unbreachable boundaries. Something to do with his youth. With his magic. With the bronze statue. With the mystery of an unnamed young man who had leapt to his death in the sea, and with the devout and honorable Eduardo di Corradini, grand duc of Riccia, collector of antiquities. Someday I would know what else lay beyond those boundaries that might link those stories together.

"I'll try that."

The city bells tolled five hours past noonday. I'd already left Teo bound half a day with naught but the ginger tea—assuming he could help himself to it.

I squeezed gently on Placidio's arm. "I need to get back and see to him. I promise to be careful. And discreet. Nothing will interfere with what we decide to do over the next four days. The prisoner is still the gateway to the Assassins List. We'll see if I hear back from Mantegna, and I'll unearth what I can about Palazzo Ignazio."

Placidio said nothing. His arm was definitely less rigid than when I'd started. Perhaps he had at last fallen asleep. Even better, his breathing was even, and his skin neither clammy nor fevered. Neri moved onto my cushion as soon as I was off it.

"Watch out for him," I said. "And meet me in the Piazza Livello tomorrow at half-morn. I've an idea how we can filch a map of the streets around the Mercediaran embassy from the City Architect's office. Two of us will make it easier."

"You'd trust me stealin'? Can't imagine that, useless as I am."

"I trust you with my life, Neri. So do we all. Placidio well knows who saved his today. And he well knows who it was got him—and you—and all of us involved with the Pizottis, of all the blighted lunatics in this world. None of us are without fault."

I crossed the room and poked my head into the kitchen where Vashti was doing something ravishing with a skillet, garlic, and fish. "I'll see you tomorrow. Neri's staying to help with Placidio. If it's all right I'm taking that slit skirt and the purple hat you made for me. I'm feeling the need for a disguise."

"Virtue's hand, Romy-zha. We'll take good care of both of them. And certain, take the pieces. Have a care in all your works."

After collecting the garments, I closed Dumond's door quietly behind me and strolled down the alley behind the cooper's yard to the mundane harmonies of hammers and saws, bellowing mules and carts. Late afternoon was a busy time for the barrelmaker and his neighbor the chandler. I took my usual circuitous route between the stacks of casks and barrels and the head-high pyramids of planks awaiting conversion to useful occupation.

There was naught to be done about resentful young brothers but trust them to come around. At least Placidio's regimen had settled my mind as to our next activities. For the moment I paid attention to my surroundings, scanning the latticed roof and the intersecting alleys, peering into the dappled light that made mysteries of the corners and niches of the cooper's yard. I would not be complacent even in such commonplace surroundings.

If not for that, I might have mistaken the shapeless pile of blankets in a dim corner near Dumond's workshop for a shapeless pile of blankets, instead of a huddled, blanket-draped person with bare feet. Feet smeared with black mud . . . or . . .

"Fortune's dam! Teo?"

10

I mpossible. "Teo, how in all grace did you find me?"

The blanket—my own blanket—slid from snarls of fair hair to reveal a pair of wide-set eyes filled with genuine astonishment, a slender *unbroken* nose, and a smile that could illuminate a solstice midnight. "*Kyria!* How in all grace did you recognize *me*?"

Impossible not to return that smile. "The feet," I said. "Many Cantagnans lack shoes, but I've seen no other foot inked with the uncoiling spiral—the Typhonian symbol for wind."

He leaned over his knees to peer at his feet. "The mark speaks wind to you?"

"You didn't know?"

"Every symbol has a thousand meanings. I wanted something to make me feel fast when I run. The inkmaster said this would do. Wings would have looked more . . . complicated."

Not the answer I was expecting. Certainly not the answer to

my original question or any of the hundred others pelting me like hailstones.

"I'm sorry for binding you; I meant no harm. How did you get loose?"

"Please don't apologize. I'd no desire to fall in the river again or run afoul of your enemies, though I cannot imagine such a generous person having enemies."

So he'd heard what I'd told him. My cheeks heated when I considered some of the things I'd said when I thought him thoroughly insensible. Was he like Placidio who never slept deep enough to miss a spoken word, or was he something else entire?

"Enemies can appear from anywhere," I said. "The world can be a harsh place."

"Harsh, yes." He unfolded himself and popped to his feet in the corner of the cooper's shed, as if he'd never been broken or drowned or jousting with death. Expression sober, he inclined his back in a graceful bow. "*Kyria* Romy, I am not your enemy. I owe you my life, a debt I shall carry always. My service is yours in whatever way I can give."

"Come, let's walk. I'll take payment in answers."

"As you say!" The cheerful note of his reply seemed at odds with dreams of fracturing cities that leaked boiling water and spat molten fire.

The Assassins List and the dangers it posed had to remain my chief concern, but it was too late to get Teo lost and abandon him. If he was a risk to us, I needed to discover it, and if he carried answers regarding magic, I'd be a fool to throw away this opportunity to learn. So I'd start with simple things, gain his trust, learn what might illuminate his purposes, and only then lead into the dangerous topic of magic.

Teo trailed behind me into the sunlit lane. I was happy to see he'd found Neri's outgrown slops that we were hoping to trade for new ones, so he wasn't entirely naked under the shirt and the blanket wrapped round his shoulders.

"Are you still cold?" I said, as we joined the afternoon bustle of the Ring Road. The air was tepid, the milky sky not quite shed of the previous night's fog.

"In truth, yes. I'm accustomed to warmer climes."

"You've come from the south, then," I said, waving him up to walk beside me. "Mercediare?" I kept my inquiries conversational.

"East and southerly of that. The Isles of Lesh, beyond the Hylides." Spoken without a hint of guilt or anxiety, just before he darted across the road to peer into a wood-slat pen, where a dozen weanling piglets were squealing for their recently departed mam.

Though I'd heard of the Isles of Lesh, I wasn't familiar with them. Thousands of islands bordered the Costa Drago. *Beyond the Hylides* would place them halfway across the *Mare Lacrimé*— the Sea of Tears that separated the Costa Drago from the tribal kingdoms of Empyria. At least a month of sailing island to island would be required even to reach the mainland at Varela or Mercediare.

"You're an adventurer, then, traveling all the way around the tip of the Costa Drago and upriver this far inland."

"No adventurer," he said, spinning full around as he walked to watch two ragged dancers leap and twirl past us. Their orange ribbons fluttered; their garishly painted faces leered; and their flailing rattles, clackers, and bell sticks clashed with the six slow chimes marking the Hour of Gathering. "I've not left the Isles before. I'm a foolish, naive traveler. Please do tell me what are those two doing."

"They're members of the Order of Demon Dancers," I said. "They believe that constant noise and movement prevent demons from infesting a house or a street or a city. These two will dance along this Ring Road until they drop from exhaustion— sometimes eight hours or more. At the very moment they stop, two more believers will take up the dance. And so it goes on."

"*Never* stopping? Are they successful at their chosen task?"

His open wonder and serious question belied suspicions of lies or secrets. Childlike, some would say. But then, those bearing Dragonis's taint could certainly mask their lies. Just half a month past, the man I'd lived with intimately for nine years had looked me in the face and believed I was a demure young scholar of antiquities. Did Teo carry the same magic as my own? It was maddening not to know if that was even possible.

"These two belong to an Order family who've danced the Beggars Ring continuously since I was a child. And I can truthfully say I've never seen a demon in the Ring Road. Unless you are one." Fear of my own gullibility put an edge to my offhand jest.

Teo darted in front of me and halted in the middle of the road, forcing me to stop in turn. "*Kyria, you don't* truly believe that I—? What is your experience of demons that you see such possibility in me?"

He was no longer bantering, either with death or with me. Furrows creased his brow, and trouble deepened his eyes. Such eyes . . . They stole my breath away. I'd never seen any like, so deep with subtly shifting color. In one instant a rich and bottomless green, in the next, bluer than a mountain lake at midsummer, then a cool gray, and then green again, flecked with gold . . . and filled with a soul-deep horror.

Beggars Ring life swirled around us, as if we stood on a rocky islet in the Venia at flood. I'd wanted to approach the deepest questions more gradually, but the fear carved on his narrow face drew them out of me. Perhaps my jest was not so offhand.

I spoke low enough no passerby could possibly hear. "You healed overnight from a beating that would have prostrated another man for a month, assuming he survived it at all. Over that same night your ink markings changed color. Your heart was scarce beating, yet you told me your name. You freed yourself of my wire ropes that I believed would hold a sorcerer, yet you found me halfway round a city of a hundred thousand people. What are you, if not a demon—or one who bears the demon taint of magic?"

A long exhale smoothed the furrows on his forehead and a wan smile eased the fear I'd glimpsed in him and felt in myself.

"Please believe me, *kyria*. I am not one of these magic users who so terrify the world, nor am I of demonkind. I was able to free myself because I've lived my life with boats and ropes and knots, and you, gracious rescuer—judged by the appearance of your knots—have not. My *melani*—the body marks—change color with the body's heat; it is a facet of the ink my people have used since some boat brought the ink to Lesh from—depending on the taleteller—the Isla Nagra that marks the southern boundary of Ocean or the sky-touching mountains of Lhampur, where I will never venture, as I've heard the people live in houses of ice that never melt." His brow crinkled. "As for the rest—"

"Are ye turned to stone there, girlie?" A woman laden with baskets of straw and what smelled like ordure from the piglets' pen jerked her head toward the side of the road. A mule cart with a broken axle blocked half the way, leaving no room for her or the child trailing behind her marshaling five geese with a large stick to pass.

"Fortune's blessing, goodwife, " I said, urging Teo around the corner to a down-sloping portion of the Ring Road. Once clear of the blocked lane, I took up my questioning where we had left off.

"All right, knots and ink. What of your astonishing recovery?"

"That is . . ." His brow wrinkled, puzzled, as if only now realizing that what he had done was odd. "I can't explain that, except that my family—my *aya*, my mother's mother—taught me to turn inward and stay out of the way to let the body repair itself. You could likely do the same thing if she taught you. And you learned my name . . . perhaps because I *was* dying."

His gaze met mine, thoughtful, wondering. "The wall between life and death is so fragile, thinner than a skim of ocean on a stone. Your voice . . . your words . . . found what was left of me. You reminded me of life. I know this all sounds strange, and I wish I could explain it better. I seem to be a bit . . . muzzy . . . today."

He fell silent, shivering a little, and scrubbed at his tangle of dirty hair. No twitch or tic or movement, or lack of one, hinted at dishonesty.

After years of observing the people who surrounded, petitioned, or befriended *il Padroné,* I believed I knew all the forms of deception. I had enjoyed testing myself behind the painted screen where I sat to observe Sandro's visitors. When he would come to me afterward, I would point out the liars: *This one's eyebrow twitched when he spoke of his brother's illness,* or *that one's hands never stilled until she claimed her steward cheated.* His investigations most often proved me right, even when he had not caught it himself. He came to rely upon my judgment.

This Teo . . . Any reasonable person must doubt his saying. Either he was a terrifyingly good liar, or he truly could not explain his own mystery. Certain, he could be working some kind of beguilement, magic very like my own, to make him so convincing. Yet his horror when I had accused him of being a demon had been instinctive and truly wrenching. He hadn't tried to deflect my questions, but to answer.

So many remained. His purposes in Cantagna. The fight that had left him in the river. He'd not yet told me how he'd managed to follow me to Dumond's. It was tempting to refuse to take another step until he told me all. But my stomach's reaction to the fine smells coming from several market stalls just ahead of us suggested I stay with a more oblique approach. There would be time for confrontation.

"Lady Fortune's dam, you must be starving," I said. "I'm not a generous rescuer at all. I throw insulting questions at you, when I left you with naught but salt-and-ginger tea."

At some point I had to turn my mind back to the Assassins List. But for now . . . "We should eat."

Teo spread his arms wide with a dramatically mournful expression. "Shamed am I to tell you that my belly is in such a state of collapse that I could be tempted to devour this deliciously warm blanket and suffer the chill. Yet it appears I've not even a boot left to trade for a meal."

It was all I could do not to pat his head and tell him all was well—even as my best blanket slid from his back into the muck.

His face went scarlet, and he snatched up the blanket and wrapped it around his shoulders again. "Forgive my foolishness."

"Forgive *me*," I said. "I've not even asked if you have friends or family here in Cantagna. I could likely help you find them."

His grimace was an artist's rendering of distressed embarrassment. "I know nothing of this Cantagna where we seem to be, and I know not a single body who lives here. My father sent me to a city named Cuarona."

"South of here. Downriver." I motioned him to continue as I guided him to Neri's favorite noodle maker.

"I was to meet a woman, a former servant of my mother's. She was to help me search for . . . something . . . I've been sent to find. The search . . ."

The long pause seemed a search for words that refused to come. He shook his head as if to clear it. Easy to recognize when his mind settled on something he was sure of.

"I carried gold and precious stones to pay my way, but foolishly did not keep them hidden. Not long after I boarded the river barge at a city—Sollebocca—three of the rowers waylaid me and stuffed me belowdecks. They said they would let me live if I led them to the coffers where the valuables in my purse had come from. They refused to believe that those coffers lay halfway across the Sea of Tears, and that half a year would pass before a boat would return for me. Day after wicked day they tried to convince me to tell them a better story. They moved me to another boat, and another, and I'm not sure if I am on the same river where I began. I tried to turn inward . . . to repair . . . to stay alive . . . but they never left off for long enough, one and then the other and then the other . . ."

He winced at the memory, eyes fixed on his grimy fingers, knotted in front of him as he told the tale. "In the end, they gave up and decided to be rid of me."

"Your injuries were dreadful," I said.

I sensed no untruth, and yet there were many things in the world I didn't know, and far more that I had never experienced. In no event could I imagine such injuries healing overnight even heeding the advice of the divine Mother Gione herself. Placidio was the only person I knew who could manage such a feat . . . and only with fire and pain and magic. Was it possible a person could work magic without knowing it?

Teo's distress was soothed by a cup of noodles in tomato-and-garlic broth. I'd thought no one could vanish Goodwife Nocilla's noodles faster than Neri, but when Teo dipped his bowl in the wash barrel and handed it back to Nocilla, he'd not even lost the thread of his tale.

"I didn't understand those boatmen," he said. "I am no child to misestimate the wickedness of the wide world. But in the Isles of Lesh, those who sail and row are the guardians of the waters, indispensible aides to our livelihood, the bridge be-tween our families and friends. They bind us together, know our names, and would never prey on travelers who stupidly expose the contents of their purses. I carried the means to sus-tain me for half a year, and now I've nothing and not a notion of what to do next. So many are depending on me . . ."

His words trailed away as we walked on toward Lizard's Alley.

"Your family, you mean?" I prompted.

"Everyone in the Isles. Everyone."

"Perhaps if we could get you to Cuarona, to your mother's servant . . ."

"Those boatmen said no one would ever know what had happened to me." His fingers tugged at the open neck of his shirt. "They stole the bit of coral I wore on a thread. It was supposed to lead me to the woman, and now I've no notion how to find her. I've a terrible certainty that I've forgotten something about the meeting with her, something I was to ask that would make my course clear."

"Your 'course'—your search, you mean."

"Yes, that." But he didn't sound entirely certain. "You will ask, search for what . . . but I cannot—"

He broke off, his long fingers rubbing his brow so hard I thought he might bring back the faded bruises. Was his head damaged after all?

"It's no matter for now."

He sank into a restless quietude as we walked.

I was educated enough to know that not every society developed in lockstep with Cantagna. Mechanical clocks would seem like magic to some outside our borders—as they had seemed like magic to us until a century ago, when a Paolin trader brought one to Varela. Each of the nine great cities of the Costa Drago was different from the other, and I could well imagine an island state could be as different from Cantagna as Paolin. Yet, human behavior had its similarities. What family would send a son so ill-prepared into a land he didn't know, to people he'd never met?

We rounded the corner into Lizard's Alley. "You had no companions on your journey?"

He shook his head, a mortal sadness weighing the air around him. "I had to come. There are duties both here and at home that only I can— There are so few of us left."

"*So few,* you say. Did the plague reach the Isles?"

"No. Not disease. Just time. We do not increase as we need."

The sun was sliding westward. While I unlatched my door and set out a flask of wine and two cups on the table, Teo stepped into the alley to shake out my blanket.

He'd left the house tidy. The ropes I'd used to bind him with were coiled neatly and set beside the tea flask. No breaks, no ragged ends, no burn marks testified against his tale of knots. The rags I'd used to dry him and blot his seeping blood were folded and stacked with the remnants of his garments.

"I'll wash this," he said, rolling up the blanket, leaving the great damp muck stain on the outside. "And the bloody towels and garments as well. Though as with everything, I must beg you tell me where and how to accomplish it. We're a long way from the sea, I think."

He was not asking if it was far. His wistful declaration said he knew. His tale of his islands' boatmen had spoken clearly of his home and how he missed it. How different it must be to live with the sea on every side of you, pervading everything you saw, everything you felt, smelled, tasted.

"Aye. It's four long days' walking to the shores at Tramonti," I said, nudging the cup of wine toward him. "We'll take care of the washing later.

"I think you dreamed of the sea in those first hours in my

house." *Drifting . . . healing . . . a watchful peace . . . green fronds teasing the skin. Home.* Certainly not *my* home, not since my parents had brought us to Cantagna where my demon magic could be better hidden than in their village by the sea.

Teo took a swallow and then set the cup down, his mouth working oddly, as if he'd bitten into a bitter nettle. "Have you some of the drink you gave me before? It is more what I'm accustomed to."

"The salt-and-ginger tea instead of wine?" I blurted. "Honestly?"

No one in the world could actually enjoy Placidio's restorative potion. Certain, no citizen of the Costa Drago or its island neighbors would prefer it to our land's lifeblood.

"You must be a lunatic as well as just generally odd."

Teo grimaced charmingly. "I hate to burden you."

"It's no burden. Empty your cup into mine and refill it from the cask just there. We've no shortage."

I pointed to the cask sitting beside our larder chest. Neri, a devoted disciple in all things Placidio, had taught himself to make the wretched brew.

"My brother finds it useful when he's worked hard in the heat." I did too, though I didn't care to admit it.

"Your brother," he said as he filled his cup. He downed the salty draught in one long gulp. "I wasn't sure . . . the clothes . . . not a husband?"

"No husband. Though my brother is eight years the younger, he believes it his job to protect me."

"Then he is likely not too happy about me."

I chose not to inform him that I could take care of myself. "I hope he has no reason to be worried."

"Indeed not," he said, earnest as ever. "I wish I could prove my sincere gratitude."

"It will be enough to see you safely on your way. You'll need work to earn your passage home, I'm thinking. Or at least as far as Cuarona or Sollebocca. Our city employs laborers to dig, haul, or lay pipe or brick for our new coliseum."

"Aye, that makes good sense. Earn my passage. And my livelihood." A sheen of rose brushed his fair complexion. "I need clothes I've not stolen from your brother's things, and food that you or some other kind soul has not paid for. I can do without a roof, and I don't wish to take a bed that belongs to someone else. Yes, I'd very much like to go home, though I need to—" His brow creased with effort.

"Find something, you said."

His hand acknowledged the point, though his attention had wandered elsewhere. "It's so strange," he said after a moment. "You asked how I followed you to the cooper's yard this afternoon. I sit here trying to answer and what my mind tells me is that I was not following *you* at all."

His features that had already taken on as many aspects as the sky in spring shifted yet again, as if his wandering thoughts had led him to a new and devastating understanding. "I've come to the wrong place."

"You said that already." I was wholly confused.

"Not just different than Cuarona, but this thing I've come here to—" Again he shook his head as if to clear it. "When I reached the shore where you found me, I felt as if I'd reached my destination, no matter the boatmen's interference. But certain, as I came back to myself this morning, I knew it was not here either"—he looked around the room as if seeing it for the first time—"and I had to look farther. So I went seeking, but it was not in that place where you found me, even though I had felt such *certainty* take me there."

His gaze met mine. And again I saw the traces of fear dim his brightness. "None of this makes sense, does it? To me it doesn't."

"None at all." But it brought me to think of Placidio's marvelous healing magic that could not repair bones. "You suffered a terrible beating. Perhaps your grandmother's remedy can heal bruises quickly, but takes longer to ease the other damage . . ."

"You think my head is not yet working properly," he said in resignation. "I'll not argue that. The truth is so close, but I cannot reach it."

One more thing. I could delay no longer. "What are these *melani*? I've seen nothing like them save in artworks from other times."

"Memories," he said. "We add them throughout the years to remind ourselves—and others—of joys and sorrows, of stories, of people and beliefs and lessons learned."

His pleasure shone through his skin. You'd think that skin transparent, the way his every emotion was so apparent. Perhaps that was what made it so difficult to disbelieve him.

"Some, like the marks on my feet, are foolishness. I do love swimming fast or running or rowing fast. Dancing, too. Some marks are more meaningful."

He pushed up his sleeve and showed me a simple outline inked over his left wrist.

"A comb," I said, squinting in the flickering torchlight.

"That is for my *aya*, because she was ever the strongest, wisest, noblest member of my family. On the day she died, I had the inkmaster put that here, where my lifeblood pulses, so that she would be with me every moment. She holds us together."

"As a comb holds strands of hair together."

"Yes."

He fell into a deep silence after that. A distance came between us, as if he'd forgotten I was there. Perhaps he was lost in mourning or in prayers to his gods.

"What of the mark over your heart?" I said after a little, when he took another sip of the tea. "The triangle made of three curves—inward, outward, sinuous. I've seen it somewhere before, but never heard a good explanation."

He laid his palm over his heart and smiled through the glisten of tears. "That is the mark of my family."

I didn't push to discover a history behind the symbol or mention I'd seen it on luck charms found in a sea cave. I didn't trust him enough as yet to hint that this one particular symbol carried meaning for me or that magic had anything to do with it.

Implausible as it all seemed, his responses felt genuine. The longing when he spoke of his home and family. The frustration and worry when he spoke of his duty and failure.

Chiming bells announced another hour gone.

"I need to sleep," I said. "I've important business tomorrow morning and will likely be away for most of the day. But I'll see you in the evening."

I emptied my waist pocket on the table. One silver solet and a dozen coppers. I pushed them toward Teo. "These are for you."

His eyes and mouth opened in astonishment.

"I'm not usually such an easy mark, but I seem to believe everything you say no matter how odd. Consider the money a loan until you can get work. You can continue to sleep on my bed. I'll take my brother's while he stays with friends. To-morrow while I'm gone, you can eat whatever we have on the shelf or in that chest, and use my paper and ink to write letters if you need. Tell your correspondents to send replies to Box 1, L'Scrittóre on Beggars Ring Road, Cantagna. Go round the cor-ner to the Duck's Bone tavern, and Fesci the taverner will tell you how to find a post messenger to carry your letter to a barge or to Cuarona if you can recall more of your mother's servant. Fesci's food and ale are cheap, if not the best. She can also tell you where to buy decent clothes. Tell her you're Romy's and Neri's cousin from Varela; we wouldn't want word of a survi-vor from the Isles of Lesh to get about, just in case your attack-ers should hear of it. Beyond those tasks, let your head heal. I'll be wanting more answers when I get home."

I wanted to speak to him of the mark on his chest and more about his dreams and my implausible suspicion that I had shared those dreams and that they bore some connection to the sadness that beset him. But I needed to be clearheaded when morning came.

He shook his head, disbelieving. "So generous . . . first my life and now coin and a bed."

"This is a *loan*, as I said, until you can find your way again. I've been lost before—separated by unimaginable distance from a life I treasured as much as you seem to value your home. But I had my brother beside me to keep my feet pointed forward, and we remained in a city I knew. You have neither."

Teo rose and crossed his arms over his breast. "Before I left the Isles, I sought every kind of information about the Costa

Drago. I was told of magnificent cities and flourishing fields, of mighty rivers and forests thick with life, of artworks that would lift my soul, wealth that would astonish me, sorrows that must grieve the divine Mother herself. But no one ever spoke of such welcoming to a stranger as you have shown me." He bowed from the waist with an easy grace. As he straightened, he flashed a sidewise grin. "Especially such an *odd* stranger!"

Sober truth damped my laughter too soon. "I wish I could say there's no reason to fear. But you must take care. Spies and magic sniffers are everywhere. If you're caught using magic, you're dead. Showing your markings, even speaking too much of the goddess mother or divine father can create suspicions. Do you understand?"

"*Deíxe éleos,*" he said softly, eyes closed. *Have mercy.* "Sorrowfully I understand and will behave as you say. Careful. Sleep easy, *Kyria* Romy, and may your tomorrow business prosper. I shall repay this loan in the moment I am able, as well as provide whatever you might need of me—whatever is in my power to give—from this moment until the end of days."

I extended my hand. As I clasped his wrist firmly, he did the same to mine. Was he merely following my lead, or had someone told him how contracts were sealed in the Costa Drago? Perhaps he was merely a traveler, sent to meet a family friend. But my bones told me that he was something else as well. Priest? Perhaps. Sorcerer? Almost surely. But a danger? I didn't think so. Whatever he was, I didn't believe he understood it right now any more than I did.

Teo was asleep before I could blink. Before doing the same, I hurried out and around the corner to the shop.

Two items sat waiting in message box number six. One was a simple curl of wood. The shaving from a pen and a very sharp penknife was Sandro's agreed upon signal that the prisoner had arrived in Cantagna. Again I wondered why the delay and whether Sandro knew the prisoner was our old acquaintance.

The second missive—a folded half page at most—was sealed with silver-gray wax and bore the imprint of crossed scrolls, the symbol of the law profession. Unable to wait, I broke the seal right there and read:

Segna,

> *Our mutual friend recommended your recent inquiry to me. Fortunately I am in possession of references for the gentleman you mentioned. You may view these references in my chambers on any day between the Hour of Business and my midday walk. I am most often in the courts all afternoon.*

> *I commend your brother for his aspirations after his troubles with the law and you for supporting him. May Lady Fortune and Lady Virtue assist him.*

> *Cosimo di Mantegna,*
> *Lawyer registered to the Cantagnan Magistracy*

"Ha!" Experienced in the Shadow Lord's intrigues, the wily lawyer Mantegna had told me that not only did he have information about the Mercediaran ambassador, he would present it to me himself. His *midday walk* always took him to a particular tea shop in a quiet corner of the Merchants Ring where *il*

Padroné would encounter him by seeming chance if he needed to discuss some matter. Mantegna knew I was familiar with the arrangement.

A fierce heat rose in me—the heat of the chase that had propelled us through our first adventure. Our new game was full on.

11

I circled the Piazza Livello fountain for the fifth time in the damp, heavy sunlight, threading the crowds that surged and waned in the thriving heart of Cantagna. Every citizen had business there sooner or later. To pay fines or taxes. To procure licenses to sell wares in Cantagna's markets or unload barges at her docks. To stand witness or accused in a magistrate's court. To attend a lecture at the Philosophic Academie or seek a loan in the Gallanos Bank, an ornate temple to a god of prosperity, did there exist such a divinity. They came most often to the Palazzo Segnori. Its ordered rows of windows promised security and clarity in all works. Today I would enter by the front door.

I dipped a hand in the fountain and wiped the grit from my neck as I observed three wardens of the Gardia Sestorale standing post in the shade of the Palazzo Segnori loggia. Their gray-blue tabards left them almost invisible. Somewhere patrolling nearby would be the ever-present danger . . .

There. The milling crowd in front of the Philosophic Academie parted like soil to a plowshare. A burly red-haired man with an axe at his belt strutted through the Academie's grand doors and down the wide steps as if he were a senior philosophist instead of a hired axe-man. He was a nullifier, charged with ferreting out magic users and dispatching them to the Executioner of the Demon Tainted—whole or maimed, the Executioner didn't care which. Behind him, attached to his belt by a chain leash, slunk his sniffer, sheathed head to toe in a skin of green silk. Even eyes and ears were covered by the green silk skin, only two holes left for breathing, giving him the appearance of some worm-like creature of ancient times crawled out from the seams in the earth. Sniffers were male sorcerers who had traded certain death for existence as a slave. Gelded, chained, ordinary senses dulled by the skin-tight silk, they were allowed only a single purpose—detecting the use of magic.

I could not withhold a shudder.

As did most people I had ever regarded sniffers as inhuman. Until the night Neri and I had come face-to-face with one at a gate crossing. Under the stretched silk covering his eyes, his eyelids opened, and I'd felt his gaze on us—a free woman and her companion, going about our business on a cold, rainy night. It had occurred to me what a painful sight that must be for one who had no hope of warmth or companionship, no purpose but the death hunt.

If the sniffer recognized the taint of magic inside us, he had made no sign of it. Perhaps Dumond's luck charms had protected us; perhaps he truly couldn't see what we were unless we were using the fire inside us. I liked to imagine it had been . . . a gesture . . . something human. No matter which, I'd never again looked at sniffers the same way.

Fortunately my morning's business required no magic. Still, I fingered the bronze luck charm in my pocket until the unholy pair vanished into a side street.

The City Architect kept records of all building plans, not just those for houses and public halls, but maps of sewers, water pipes, graveyards, wells, anything and everything. While I distracted the clerk on duty, Neri could sneak around behind the clerk and steal the detailed drawings and maps of the Quartiere di Fiori—the very private neighborhood where the ambassador of Mercediare lived and conducted his city's business.

I made another loop of the piazza. An hour past the time we'd set to meet, Neri had not yet come. He would think my plan boring, as this impersonation needed no magic. I could work the scheme alone, yet it would be riskier without a partner. So I delayed a quarter hour and then another and another. Each interval screwed my gut tighter.

Whenever I didn't know where Neri was, I worried. For an exuberant youth gifted with magic, life was a constant risk. I hoped it wasn't resentment kept him away.

Perhaps Placidio had taken a turn for the worse. Guilt nagged, insisting I should have stayed with them instead of trying to untangle the mystery that was Teo. Distraction was a certain danger in schemes like ours.

Another circuit of the massive fountain. The only quiet islands in the rushing current of citizens were artists sitting on the paving stones sketching portraits or doing charcoal renderings of the Palazzo Segnori facade or the gold-tipped bell tower. I paused behind a young woman doing a watercolor study of the fountain itself. Under the hand of towering Atladu, a bronze Leviathan broached chiseled waves, his jaw open, his mighty tail readied to sweep the monster Dragonis from the sky. The mid-morn sunlight transformed the water flowing over Leviathan's back to molten silver yielding the beast a rippling life. The woman's rendering comprised only a few splashes of color, yet she had translated all the energy of the sculptor's art and the water's life to her page.

When asking for our help with this matter, Sandro had told me how easily Vizio's campaign of vengeance could blossom into war. I had envisioned a few besieged households engaged in bloody retribution, perhaps some shortages of food or wine or wool, not a real war that would affect us all. But if Vizio unleashed vendetta, it would not fall only on the signers of the Assassins List, but on their families, their servants, their tenants, on the villages who prospered from their trade or tending. In such a world, what would happen to a young person who could now sit peacefully among these passersby, slaking her thirst for art and beauty by creating wonders such as this drawing?

Cantagna still had too many hungry people and too much corruption, but these islands of hope were rising everywhere. Fragile hopes in a world where peace was so unaccustomed.

The mid-hour bell in the Palazzo Segnori tower chimed twice past half-morn. Only an hour remained until midday when I hoped to meet Lawyer Mantegna in his favorite teashop and discover interesting things about the Mercediaran ambassador. No time remained for dallying.

As I hurried into the deep shadows under the palazzo loggia, I pulled a voluminous gray mantle from a large bag and fastened it around my shoulders. Pausing beside one of the great pillars, I twisted and pinned my hair into a sedate knot at the back of my head. A fat, plushy toque of peacock blue covered it all and drooped an ugly veil across my eyes. I finished by pulling folds of a plum-colored underskirt through slashes in my workaday skirt.

Genevieve di Lac would be an ambitious young matron, wealthy, but not supremely wealthy, of respectable family, but not an old family, one of many such women scrabbling to find a place among Cantagna's elite. Women like Genevieve were cruel to their maids and rude to clerks and seamstresses and courtesans, but often got tangled in their own plumage when in the presence of those they aspired to join.

Even without magic, I had to believe I was Genevieve. Segna di Lac would neither hesitate nor duck her head. At my imperious wave a footman opened the leftmost palazzo doors, and I hurried through the babble of the city's business toward a downward stair. My back prickled. The call could come at any moment. *Mistress Cataline? I thought you were dead!* Or, *Scribe Romy, have you forgotten your position? How gaudy you are!* Or it could be simply the howl of a sniffer.

A cool quiet enveloped me as I descended into the labyrinthine lower halls and the City Architect's domain. With a calming breath, I swept through a marked doorway into a workroom that smelled of old parchment, old wood, old dust, and fresh ink, and announced, "I am Segna di Lac of Strada del Mele and I wish to set the route for my sister's wedding processional."

The startled clerk seated at the drawing desk opened his mouth. "Segna—"

"Leila is dithering about gowns and jewels, leaving the most important plans withering from neglect. The processional must traverse the finest circle route available through the Quartiere di Zefferile of the Merchants Ring, avoiding certain unlucky houses along the way, and ensuring that we arrive at the Ucelli Gardens at the Hour of Gathering, which is the most auspicious time."

"Segna, the Ucelli Gardens are located in the Quar—"

"Do *not* patronize me, young man. I know exactly where the Ucelli Gardens are located and there is no more fortuitous prospect in Cantagna. I wish to see every map of the districts involved, with notations of clean benches available for those who cannot walk too far, and of fountains and arcades lest the day be too warm. And we must pass the Domata Ponds, where we might encounter the great spotted cuckoo to ensure a prosperous first year, and the Pillar of Hymonides, which with the proper invocations to Lady Fortune will naturally ensure Domenico's—"

I pressed a finger to my mouth as if the mention of a groom's potency might sear my tongue.

"Truly, segna, with greatest respect, the Domata Ponds, the Ucelli Gardens, and the Hymonides Pillar are not even in the same—"

"Hop to it, clerk!" I rapped a knuckle on his desk. "The route was recommended to me by several most influential persons. My dear friend, Segna Beatrice di Mesca herself, whose daughter has made a most fortunate marriage, told me that her personal soothsayer insisted a wedding processional must visit three particular sites, and I'm sure those are the correct names. Bring me the maps I've requested, and you'll see."

The clerk hopped to it. The wealthy patroness of the arts

Beatrice di Mesca's name was none to be trifled with. Her daughter's marriage to Tibernia's conte had involved such an outrageously elaborate wedding processional that no one in the city could be ignorant of it.

"Please have a seat, Segna di Lac. I shall return expeditiously."

With a bow, the clerk retired through the archway into the vast warren of the archives to gather maps of at least four different quartieres in order to explain to me how the route I suggested was impossible and nowhere near the Quartiere di Zefferile.

Cantagna was divided into five concentric rings—five districts, each with multiple *quartieres* or neighborhoods. Over the past quarter century our city had been quite forward-thinking in gathering all documents, maps, plans, and histories into a collection for each district. The materials the clerk sought for Genevieve would be catalogued nowhere near the ones the Chimera needed.

Now the more dangerous step. I'd never planned on doing this alone. What if he forgot my instructions and came back? What if my notion of the chamber's layout was wrong? *Spirits . . .*

Counting to three, I circled behind the clerk's tall desk and peeked through the doorway.

No sight of him. Muffled footsteps yielded to the rattle of hinges and creaking wood far to my right. Satisfied, I hurried leftward, pausing only to read the labels on the long rows of document racks and cabinets. Five, six . . . the seventh row should be about right for Quartiere di Fiori of the Heights.

The Heights comprised this most elite innermost district of Cantagna, where the heart of Cantagna's governance was surrounded by sun-blessed, palatial homes of the city's oldest families. The Quartiere di Fiori, named for its lush flower gardens, was the Heights' most remote neighborhood. Vine-draped gates and private guardposts protected the quarter's reclusive residents—mostly hostile diplomats, landless nobility, and a few wealthy eccentrics.

Neither Beggars Ring folk, common artisans, nor duelists below the top ranks were allowed to wander the Quartiere di Fiori's avenues. Even *il Padroné*, only a junior member of the governing Sestorale despite his unquestioned power and influence, was rarely invited there, and never had he taken his mistress. Without maps, the Chimera was blind.

My fingers brushed the carefully inked labels above crowded scroll cases, shelves laden with bound books, and wood boxes of flat maps and drawings.

Wrong aisle. These were Asylum Ring materials, not those for the Heights. I sped farther down the row to a crossing aisle and moved leftward again. Partway down the crossing aisle shelves had been cleared away for a broad table laden with tools, wrapped clay, and the model of the new coliseum rising in the Asylum Ring.

Il Padroné loved taking guests on tours of the City Architect's workshops, especially the sculpted models. He hoped to create an outward magnificence that would inspire Cantagna's inward illumination.

He had taken his mistress there at night *lest she be a distraction* to those diligently developing his visions. His lamp had lent a fantastical quality to the miniature cityscapes. We had pretended to see ourselves and others we knew hurrying through the arcades of his coliseum, strolling beside fountains and ponds, and enjoying performances in a theater that would be carved into the side of a hill where an ancient king's armory had once stood.

I scurried past and entered an aisle labeled Heights, eastern districts. My finger traced the labels for the Quartieres of Songs, of Apricots, of Vines . . .

Had the collections grown so much in a year? Had the Archivist rearranged things? This was supposed to be quick, yet every passing moment seemed interminable . . . until my finger touched *Quartiere di Fiori* and I found everything I wanted. A map of streets dated last year. The always important plots of water resources and sewers. The building plots of fine residences. A moment's hunt located Palazzo Ignazio and three random houses just in case someone noticed the missing maps.

My bag could not hold everything. Yet every moment choosing brought me nearer detection. A little farther up the shelves stood a defensive study of the district and a pamphlet called *The Plague in the Heights.* I added them to the bulky bag.

Time seemed stretched, as if I'd been in the archives for hours. So I tucked the bag under my mantle, raced back to the end of the row, and peeked into the outer aisle.

Night Eternal! The clerk, his skinny arms thrown about a deep basket filled with standing map rolls, was closer to the exit door than I was. Surely he couldn't see over his load or hear my heart thumping.

His abrupt halt signaled otherwise. "Segna?"

Nothing for it. I dashed at full speed in his direction, halting only at the last possible moment before bowling him over.

"There you are, clerk! You've taken so very long and I thought you would have come back to ensure that you had every detail of my plan correct. But I failed to mention that my

sister's wedding processional will involve at least twelve cano-
pied litters so we cannot use avenues that are too steep like that
horrid Street of Threads that approaches the Domata Ponds.
Because you've taken so long, you must work up the plan yourself. I shall return tomorrow to examine your plan, because
I am near fainting for lack of coffee, and I am to meet Segna
di Mesca to pry out more details of who it was provided extra
swans for her daughter's stop at the Ponds."

I patted him on his confused head and swept through the
door ahead of him and out of the office, ensuring my mantle
billowed enough to mask the strange bulge at my back, but not
enough to expose it.

His whine wafted after me. "But, Segna di Lac, the City Architect does not provide—"

My progress on the upward stair muted his voice and left
me alone. I stripped off the gray mantle, wrapped it around the
bag of books and rolls like a sack, tossed in my hat, and tied
the loose ends into a knot. Reaching under my skirt, I yanked
the plum-colored folds back through the slashes, as clever
Vashti had taught me, leaving my skirt plain black again.

As I loosed the knot of my hair and shook it out, clattering footsteps brought a pair of well dressed young gentlemen
down the stair. I threw the knotted gray sack over my shoulder,
stepped aside, and dipped my head as a servant would, making
sure my hair frowsed over my face.

They passed without a look. Once they rounded the corner
at the bottom, I raced upward and out into Piazza Livello. Neri
would get an earful for leaving me to do this on my own.

Busy Cantagnans still churned around the fountain. The

bronze Leviathan still threatened the sky. I slowed my racing heart, breathed deep, and pushed through the throng toward the wide gate. It led me downward toward the Merchants Ring and the tea shop where I would meet Mantegna. Likely the lawyer only, and not his most private client. Likely.

Yet my blood warmed, and my feet moved a little faster at the imagining. I hated that.

. . .

"Damizella Scrittóre?" The puffed-up young man in black stepped in front of me before I could pass the vine-draped lattice that barred direct view of the tea shop's outer tables.

Bathed in the fragrances of brewing lavender, lemon balm, and rose hip tisanes, I peered over his ribboned sleeves into the sun-dappled dimness beyond the lattice. Impossible to see anyone.

"And who are you?" I said, though his emphasis on my lack of any name but a profession hinted at all there was to know about him. A glance confirmed my impression. Oiled curls. Ill-fitting doublet. Stained teeth. He was no one.

And he had no idea who I was—or had been. His puffy lips pursed as his puffy eyes narrowed to slits, assessing my plain garb, my tousled hair, and my breasts.

"Segno?"

"Uh—" He blinked and regained his wits. "I am Tommaso di Minimo, clerk to Segno Cosimo di Mantegna. You are the person I addressed—the scrittóre?"

I maintained a sober dignity. "Indeed I am the law scribe granted a interview by Lawyer Mantegna."

His mouth shriveled as if he'd bitten an unripe pear. "With *apologies*, my employer is unable to see you. He asked me to pass along the document you requested."

Minimo held out a sealed scroll—only a page, perhaps two.

I'd counted on a face-to-face meeting, so I could ask for more information, learn things Mantegna might not have wanted to commit to paper, such as why Sandro only received word of the prisoner transfer two days after it happened. I wanted to pass on the news that the prisoner was Rossi. But in no wise dared I pass such information through this man, even in code.

Harnessing my disappointment, I reached for the document. Minimo's soft fingers tightened as if he wished he could ask for a witness to verify my worthiness to receive something from such an elevated personage as himself.

My finger tapped the scroll. "Tomasso, if you please . . ."

Evidently the shock of hearing his personal name from my lips unhinged him enough to loosen his grip.

I picked up the gray sack I'd set beside the lattice wall. As I slung it over my shoulder and turned to go, a derisive sniff came from Minimo's direction. There was a time when such behavior at my detriment could have cost him his balls from one of Sandro's attendants—not that such had ever happened to my knowledge. Not that it would have been right or just. But it gave me a certain satisfaction to think that the person who would have happily done that for me would never in the world trust young Tomasso. The boy, so foolish as to display his personal feelings about an assigned duty, had risen as far as he would rise. Unfortunately, the damnable clumsy sack of scrolls and books made it quite difficult to retreat with dignity.

Only a few steps down the sloping avenue on, I stopped for

a moment and broke the seal on Mantagna's scroll. The report comprised two closely written pages. I stuffed it in my waist pocket and glanced around.

A very tall man with shoulders wide as the Palazzo Segnori and a shock of white hair that jarred with his pale, unlined complexion loitered just inside an alley between the tea shop and the next house—a spot from which he could observe all comings and goings. His pale eyes met mine, and before I could drop my gaze, he nodded ever so briefly.

Gigo. The Shadow Lord's bodyguard. Gigo, who held his master's complete trust, would know that Mistress Cataline yet lived and would be able to recognize her in any situation—unless she drew on the magic she couldn't get herself out of.

So *il Padroné* was inside the shop. Certainly he could not be seen with any woman who might be unmasked as a spy or a sorceress. I understood that. But every time I thought I was well healed, events would sting the bitter wounding of my exile yet again.

The walk down to the Beggars Ring and around to Dumond's house was long and empty.

12

Where's Neri?" The question burst from me the moment I spotted Dumond in the alley outside his house.

"With you, I thought," said the smith, opening his front door. "That's what he said when he left here at first light. I've been up to the forge, though, so maybe he's come back."

Astonishing how quickly fear could erase fury. "What was he up to so early? We weren't to meet until half-morn."

"No idea."

I entered the house on Dumond's heels, praying to see Neri at Placidio's bedside. But it was Vashti sitting at the table sewing, while a pale, drawn Placidio lay asleep on the pallet.

"How is he?"

"Restless earlier in the night," said Vashti. "Accepted a few drops of my infusion for pain. In the last hour he's not moved."

"Can. If I need to." The words issuing from the motionless body might have been spoken by a tree frog. "Prefer not."

"Neri's missing," I said, setting the bag of maps and books by the door. "Never showed up this morning. He was so angry yesterday . . . and then I was so angry when he didn't come. But now . . ."

"My fault." Placidio muffled a curse as he rolled to one side and attempted—without success—to sit up. "About the healing. Should have thought."

Keeping his breath shallow and regular, he gripped his pillow and buried his face in it.

"I know exactly why you refused him," I said to his back, "and you were right to do it. But I never expected he wouldn't show up this morning."

"I thought he might head home to meet your aquatic friend," said Dumond, shedding his leather apron. "His britches were burnt about that, too."

"Teo was up when I woke, taking his leave," I said. "Neri hadn't been there."

"Boy's not a fool," said Placidio from the depths of the pillow. "He'll be—"

A hammering on the door shot Dumond, Vashti, and me to our feet. Placidio struggled onto his knees, one arm clutched tight about his middle, the alter hand gripping his dagger.

"Sword. Dumond," grunted Placidio. His unsheathed blade lay beside his pallet.

Dumond snatched up the sword, more adroitly than I expected for a man I'd never seen draw a weapon. "Who comes?"

"Let me in! Cursed crazies . . . lunatics!"

Rolling his eyes, Dumond returned the sword to its place, drew his heavy latches, and opened the door. "You didn't lead any lunatics *here*, did you, boy?"

"Wouldn't never."

"Then again," murmured Placidio, his face a knot of pain as he eased back to the pallet. "His wit's not entirely ripe."

Relief allowed me to indulge my annoyance. "Just when I think I can trust him, he demonstrates that again."

Neri burst into the room hissing like a burnt cat, one eye purpled, shirt torn, balled fists bleeding. "Crazies out there this morning. Two of 'em tried a snatch near the Nittis' sausage stall, chased me halfway round the Ring till their partner showed up and they funneled me down Fig Alley, doing their best to make sausage out of me. I got loose and climbed over the wall into the old laundry. Hid under a rusted tub. Stupid place to hide as I couldn't walk . . . You know. To get away. And the *stronzi* wouldn't leave. Kept circling, shouting, hunting, but too stupid to look under the tub. Likely couldn't lift it. Hours I was under that blighted iron cauldron. That's why I didn't come." His rant faded and he looked at me squarely. "Wasn't gonna ditch you, Romy. Wouldn't."

"I didn't want to believe you would."

Neri dropped to the floor, peering at the overlarge knot that was Placidio. "Are you all right, swordmaster?"

"Alive. No estimates beyond." Placidio didn't lift his head. "Who was chasing? Anything to identify them?" Belying his state, the question was as hard and cold as a frostmorn. I'd not want to be any person Neri named once Placidio was on his feet.

"Don't know who. My age. Drunk. Fierce. Kept hollering *cheat* and *coward* at me, along with some other names that don't bear repeating if Dumond's nubbins are anywhere around."

"Could any of them be Pizottis? You know, Buto's lot from the day you didn't stay hid?"

"Could have been. Maybe." Neri's high color faded. But he firmed up his jaw and continued. "But before all that, before they started chasing, I took a peek at our prisoner. He's still there where we left him. Asleep in that bed with swollen nose and a bandage around his head. The baldric's not out in plain sight anymore, and there's lots more guards."

"Again, Neri?" I spluttered. "I know you can get in and out fast, but—"

"Basha!" Vashti called from the kitchen, sparing Neri my tongue lashing. Idiot boy. Though I wasn't sure who exasperated me most—Neri or Placidio, whose drunken insult had drawn the ire of the Pizottis.

Dumond retreated to the kitchen and emerged with a tray holding a basket of bread and four bowls of basil-scented broth. "Vashti says eat, don't talk. She's bringing something plainer for the invalid."

Neri swooped in on the food. Grateful, no doubt. We all obeyed Vashti.

"I thank you both. But not yet," whispered Placidio. "Soon though."

Observing carefully, I judged this comment was more about soothing worries than predicting the future.

"Is it the gut or the rib?" I said quietly, as Dumond joined Neri at the table.

"Both. *Fiery* snakes today. But improving. Truly."

"Your gift is truly glorious, but it would be nice if it worked faster."

"Up tomorrow."

Once we soaked up the broth with the stale bread and cleared away the bowls, I fetched my bag from beside the door.

"While Neri dodged crazies and Placidio snored this morning, I played messenger, thief, and supplicant. First off, we received *il Padroné*'s signal that the prisoner had arrived alive. That's likely why Neri observed more guards."

Neri waved his spoon. "All of them wore Gardia colors."

That made sense. Using Gardia Sestorale regulars rather than a House Gallanos cohort to boost the prisoner's security demonstrated no overt interference in the transfer, as Sandro intended.

I spilled my morning's bounty onto the table. "Thanks to a very confused clerk at the City Architect's office, we should be able to find our way in and out of the Quartiere di Fiori and the Mercediaran embassy if we choose to do so."

"Terrain!" Excitement erased Neri's resentments.

"And"—I tossed Mantegna's little scroll on top of the books and rolled maps—"we received a reply from the Shadow Lord's consigliere. Mayhap we can glean a reason why Rossi thinks to diddle the ambassador."

"Good work," said Dumond.

Neri still refused to sit down for lessons in reading or writing, but Dumond had a skill for goading him into it. As he and Neri unrolled the maps and drawings and began sorting them into some order, matching areas of interest from one to the other, Dumond would point out words and make Neri guess what they meant.

I returned to the floor cushions beside Placidio, where Vashti sat teasing a few spoonfuls of tea into his mouth. Only a few and he shook off more, and buried his face again. Frowning, Vashti set the bowl aside and felt his hands. Apparently the result was better.

"Shall I summarize Mantegna's report for you as I read?" I said to Placidio's hunched back.

"Certain." The words found their way through the pillow. "If I snore, you can kick me. Gently, please."

Vashti and I laughed, and I began reading.

After scanning a few paragraphs, I reduced the lawyer's verbiage to the essentials. "Ambassador Egerik di Sinterolla, a widower with no children, is aged nine-and-forty. He studied rhetoric, philosophy, and art at Mercediare's Philosophic Academie, apparently with the ambition to shake off the nastiness of his birth family, who traded in mysenthe and bawdy houses. He rejected all contact or identification with them, but only after he'd come of age and taken his proportionate share of their fortune."

"Not stupid then," said Placidio.

"Clearly not. Mmm . . . he made his own fortune in a merchant house that specialized in medicinal wines, using his cleverness to expand their wares to new uses *and* to marry the owner's daughter, Oriana. He even took her family name, Sinterolla."

"Well played."

Vashti winked at me, approving Placidio's quick response.

I perused a little more, my interest rising. "Listen to this. *Shortly after his marriage at age thirty, he took on a succession of tasks for the Protectorate and has maintained his usefulness for an unbroken succession of Protectors since that time. His support in the bureaucracy was key to Protector Vizio's ascent to power.*"

Placidio's cinder-gray eyes emerged from the gray, rag-stuffed pillow. "A man of opportunity more than belief. And agile."

"Agile, indeed," I said. "That's nineteen years he's survived. At least eight Protectors in that span . . ."

Mercediare's Protectorate bestowed immense opportunities

for wealth on whatever family, faction, or tyrant was strong enough to win it. Some had lasted only a few days; some a few months. Vizio's ten years was by far the longest since Dedino di Rossignoli, Mercediare's last king, was overthrown a hundred and fifty years since.

"... so Egerik manages both to make himself useful *and* to avoid assassins."

"Loyal to Vizio for now," said Dumond. He and Neri had left off map-shuffling to listen.

I tapped the report. "Others certainly judge him loyal. Members of the Sestorale and city commissioners note Egerik as *mannerly* and *thoroughly faithful to the positions of his employer.*"

"Which leads us back to why Cinque the spy is not afraid of him," said Neri. "Blackmail?"

"I've not seen an answer to that as yet," I said. "This affirms what I heard after Egerik came to Cantagna. He is man of elegance with very expensive tastes and had a wife who was an extraordinary beauty. Only a few people ever met her—this Oriana. Supposedly she was very pleasant, but quite frail and never left the house. She died only a few months after arriving in Cantagna. The ambassador refused all social invitations after her death, pleading mourning. Mantegna says here that *no mistress or other romantic liaison has been identified since, nor is it known whether he prefers women or men in his bed.*"

"Maybe he killed his wife for her father's money," said Neri.

"Possible," I said. "Mercediaran family intrigues are notorious. But they'd been together almost twenty years. And with no liaison since her death ..."

"... perhaps his mourning was sincere." Vashti finished my thought.

My eyes darted further down the page. "Here's a piece that's curious. *His personal attendants and bodyguards are all his countrymen and extremely loyal. He does hire local house servants, but few stay on because he is so exacting in his requirements with regard to household duties, cleanliness, and adherence to an elaborate system of wards, talismans, divinations, and other mystical practices unusual in a man of his education and stature. The ambassador stipulates that anyone in his employ must sever all ties with friends and family.*"

"All ties. Truly?" said Vashti, shocked. "I never heard of this."

"Nor have I. Not in any house, foreign or other," I said.

People did odd things for fear of disease or other sorts of bad luck. But insisting his servants sever *all* ties? And to adhere to *mystical practices* like divination? Very odd.

"He wants perfectly loyal servants," said Dumond. "Sounds like he's hiding something."

"Anything else?" said Placidio.

"A list of affiliations: the Philosophic Confraternity, the Society of Public Men, the Fellowship of Poets, and such like." Similar to those of every person of status in Cantagna. "Something called the Brotherhood of the Exquisite, which I've not heard of."

I glanced up, but saw nothing but shrugs, even from Placidio.

"All that's left is a list of his earlier postings. Before he was sent here, he held ambassadorial rank in Cuarona, but he resigned his post after little more than a year. He called Cuarona a *corrupt and undisciplined society run by rabble.*"

"Now that's odd," said Dumond. "If any independency suffers from *rule by the rabble*, it's Mercediare."

The longing for a return to the days of the Rossignoli kings yet lingered in older Mercediaran Houses. Cantagna was not so different in that regard. *Il Padroné* believed that elevation of mind and just application of law would create prosperity and peace for all citizens of Cantagna, thus bringing glory to the city and House Gallanos. Yet more than half of our governing council, the Sestorale, believed this enlightened vision impinged upon the rightful privileges of their own long-established Houses. That kept our city a gnarled mess of plots and intrigues.

"I know someone who might be able to shed light on Egerik's time in Cuarona," I said. I'd met Cuarona's local wool-guild commissioner on several occasions. She was an intelligent, interesting woman.

I ran my finger down the page. "Here's one earlier posting of interest. Eight years ago, he served as a trade liaison in Argento, but the Argentians sent him home before a year was out. And this: *There were certain whispers at the time of a salacious scandal involving several wealthy Mercediaran exiles, all of whom died within months of Egerik's departure.*"

I could well imagine what kind of scandal. Knowing we would be sold to members of the privileged classes, our Moon House tutors had taught us how to accept the depraved with grace.

"Old scandals, strict secrecy in his household, a dead wife. Neri could be right about the blackmail," said Dumond.

"And a man who seizes opportunity without scruple could very well have mutable loyalty," said Placidio, halfway to sitting. Vashti stuffed two cushions behind him, unable to hide a smile.

"And he's superstitious enough it gets noticed by the Shadow

Lord's spies," I said. "I'd say Egerik is a more interesting person than one would imagine. So I'm thinking . . ."

Neri looked up from another bowl of soup he'd fetched from the kitchen, the glint of the hunt in his black eyes. "We need to get into his house."

Instinct told me there was substance here with Egerik, who spoke loyalty, but had demonstrated a certain suppleness of conscience. And secrets. And oddities that might be exploited to learn more.

"Whatever game Cinque has planned is going to occur three days from now," I said. "We must get some idea what Egerik plans to do when the prisoner is turned over. We know that Rossi isn't afraid of that event. Maybe his certainty has nothing to do with the Assassins List, maybe it does. But the only way for us to know for certain is what Neri said—get into Egerik's house. Spy it out—and its owner as well."

"Egerik isn't going to sit for an interview," said Dumond.

"No." The more I thought of it the clearer it became. "We have to insert ourselves into their gaming, whether they are partners or opponents. So how do we do that? I could apply to be a servant. But that could take longer than we have."

"And you'd be alone," said Placidio. "Better it's two of us inside. Another day or two . . . I'm good for that."

"Mystical practices," said Vashti, brow narrowed in thought. "Whether this ambassador conspires with the prisoner to betray his tyrant Protector or is subject to extortion, this is a fraught time. A man who relies on auguries will seek assurances."

"It might seem a bit coincidental for a fortuneteller to show up at his door," I said.

"Romy," said Neri, tapping his spoon on the empty soup

bowl. "That girl at the market, the cloth merchant's daughter you imitated for your practicing, didn't you say she carried a needle bag?"

"*Ascoltaré* needles, yes," I said. "And every other word she spoke invoked her divine mistress. She believes she is Lady Fortune's chosen voice."

Espe, Lady Fortune, and her sister Aea, Lady Virtue—the twin daughters of Gione and Atladu—were the only divinities left to supervise the human world. Unfortunately, the Twins could not intervene directly in worldly affairs. Believers said Lady Virtue would whisper wisdom in the ears of the righteous. Her sister, Lady Fortune, gave us guidance through augury and divination, whether palmistry, cards, crystals, omens, portents . . . or the Needles of the Nine Mysteries.

"Baldassar and Monette shall come to life again," said Placidio. "The ambassador dresses well, you said. Expensive tastes. Very particular. So a cloth merchant tantalizes him with . . . what? Lhampuri brocades? Paolin silks?"

"Cloth-of-gold," said Dumond. "Any man on the rise in public office would jump for cloth of gold at a good price. Happens I've got a sample. False, not real, though there's still enough gold filament in it to show. A weaver wanted me to draw brass wire for her to substitute for the gold threads in her cloth. Showed me how the fakery was done. Before I could tell her I didn't want to get crossways with the Weavers Guild, she got herself caught— by the Weavers Guild."

"Monette could distract the ambassador from his business," I said, "first with herself . . . and then with her soothsaying. If she could intrigue him, we might learn a lot. And her papa could observe the goings on—mayhap the preparations for a prisoner exchange. If naught else, we could find something for Neri to fix on so he could sneak in and hunt for Rossi once he's in the house."

"Certain, I could do that." Neri looked ready to go right then.

"You can forge me a set of the needles, Dumond?"

"Aye. I can cast them so you can detect which is which, and weighted, so you can make them fall as you will."

"And I can show you how to manipulate them," said Vashti. "My auntie taught me finger tricks for merchant faires. Good for catching a few coins a day. But I do not know the arts of soothsaying."

"Maybe I'll have the real Monette cast her needles for me," I said.

In the space of an hour we had a plan. Dumond and I had drawn diagrams of nine slim, wrist-to-fingertip lengths of bronze, embossed with the traditional symbols of the Nine Mysteries of Lady Fortune: Mysticism, Presence, Power, Substance, Relationship, Reason, Judgment, Jeopardy, and Order. Practitioners of the Nine Mysteries cast the needles onto a flat surface, then used the needles' positioning, their relationships with respect to each other, and the symbolic meanings of each needle to interpret Lady Fortune's message.

While Dumond retreated to his workshop to prepare models and molds, Neri hurried off to make his apologies to Fesci yet again and work his shift at the Duck's Bone. He promised to return later so he and Dumond could become familiar with the maps. A finger pointed at the now perhaps-really-sleeping Placidio spoke my brother's true intent. Vashti winked and nodded.

I worked with Vashti a while, deciding what Damizella

Monette and her father should wear if the ambassador agreed to see them. She would need time to find what pieces she could in rag shops and markets and to sew the rest. Then I took Mantegna's letter and set out for home.

Once there I would dispatch an application for Baldassar di Fabroni, Cloth Merchant, and his daughter Monette to present their exceptional wares to the noble Egerik di Sinterolla, Ambassador of Mercediare, along with some forged letters of recommendation. I'd consider how best to approach my acquaintance from Cuarona to learn if she knew anything about Egerik's brief sojourn in her city. Then I would give thought to what kind of divination might entice a Mercediaran bureaucrat to reveal his secrets to a devotee of Lady Fortune.

Our mission was to locate the Assassins List and destroy it. But first we had to insert the Chimera between the two men Fortune would bring together three days from this.

13

The moonless night was pitch black on my hurried walk around the city, and the Month of Fogs again held true to its name. Wisps and tails of mist drifted through the quiet streets alongside me, so I felt like a phantasm spying on the dreams of ordinary folk.

The hour didn't seem a fortuitous beginning. My eyes burned from the smoke of outlaw fires sparked by desperate souls in alleys and lanes where they cooked scraps gleaned from offal pits. My boots were already a muck-sodden mess from the impossible-to-avoid sewage of the Ring Road. And it was much too early to barge into a family house, where a man who ought to be dead recovered from a grievous wound.

But I couldn't wait any longer. I marched across the cooper's yard in a fizz of agitation.

A yawning Vashti opened the door to my knock. "Blessed morn, Romy-zha. Never thought to see you so early."

"Blessed morn, Vashti. How is Placidio?"

"A better night," she said. "But who knows?"

I followed her inside. Neri and Dumond sat at the low table eating buns filled with cheese. Neri was the only one who looked at all awake. Placidio didn't look as if he'd moved since the previous afternoon.

"I've brought news," I said, slapping the gilt-trimmed fold of parchment onto the table. It bore the dolphin-and-hammer crest of Mercediare.

Dumond picked it up and read aloud.

Segno Fabroni,

> *The Honorable Ambassador Egerik di Sinterolla, Anointed Agent of Her Eminence Cerelia Balbina Andreana di Vizio, Protector of Mercediare and the Two Hundred Islands, Savior of the Southern Coast, Commandante of the Bannered Legion, will be pleased to receive a call from Merchant Baldassar di Fabroni of the Cloth Guild and his daughter Damizella Monette at the Hour of Business on Sixth Day at the Ambassadorial Palazzo. Bring samples of materials suitable for men of rank, especially those which could be made available to His Excellency's tailor within the day.*

> *Mella di Bonsi,*
> *Housekeeper to His Excellency, the Ambassador*

A fierce heat rose in me as it had when I first opened the letter. The Hour of Business on Sixth Day. Dawn—

"Tomorrow!" said Neri.

"And it appears he wants a new garment for the next day," I said. "The day of the prisoner exchange. What does that mean?"

"It means this will be a very busy day," said Vashti. "I've a good start on costumes. For Monette's papa, I found this fine jacket and fashionably wide trousses at a dye shop in the Asylum Ring. I'll show you."

From a bag on the stair, Vashti pulled out voluminous garments of such a garish shade of yellow as to rival a field of wild mustard.

"That is grotesque." I would still see the horrid satin with my eyes closed.

"Nicely made and very expensive," said Vashti. "But, alas, the dyer used much too bright a yellow for their owner—the governor of the Pantagi Asylum—who then abandoned the garments without ever wearing them. Because, you see, the dyer's grandmam had died in misery in Pantagi Asylum and to ruffle the nasty governor made the dyer very happy. I do fear our Placidio might fall on his sword when he sees them, though." The mischief in Vashti's face was beyond price.

Next, she showed me folds of deep, vibrant red. "The last of my ruby silk will allow Damizella Monette to draw the ambassador's interest even before she demonstrates her skills with soothsaying. Bodice and underskirt are done. Get them on so I can work on the sleeves and gown, and perfect the fit . . ."

As Placidio slept, Vashti stood me on her low table, fitting and stitching a respectable garment for a cloth merchant's daughter. She was an artist at cutting apart old clothes she'd found in scrap shops, dyeing, embroidering and combining them with a few lengths of more expensive fabrics into garments that looked to have cost a hundred times my year's income as a scribe.

Meanwhile, Neri, Dumond, and I talked quietly about possible ways forward without Placidio. Dumond expressed the enthusiasm of a tree stump at the prospect of playing Baldassar.

Neri was dogged in his belief. "He'll be ready."

Vashti gave me a hand down from the table, and then clipped some stitches to release me from the stiff red bodice and trumpet sleeves. "These will be ready for you by morning."

Next, she took Dumond in hand. "Upstairs with you, Basha, and into Placidio's costume. I must understand how much altering would be necessary if you needed to wear it after all."

I retired behind the kitchen curtain to exchange the flowing red gown and underskirts for my plain blue kirtle and black sleeves.

"By the Great Anvil! This will not do!" Dumond soon followed his horrified protest from the stair.

I bit my lip before saying anything or, more unforgivably, bursting into laughter. Placidio would have enjoyed the sight immensely.

The grinning Neri voiced the only words that could apply. "'Tis a giant duckling! Aye, Romy had best go alone lest the ambassador throw you on a spit and roast you!"

Though overlong, the garish doublet might do, as Dumond's shoulders were those of a man who'd worked a forge to support his family as well as his art. But the voluminous satin trousses would never work for short-legged Dumond. The fashionable stiff codpiece reached halfway to his knees.

Vashti pressed her slim hand to her mouth before speaking. "Indeed if you are pressed into service, husband, we shall have to find something else."

Dumond vanished so quickly up the stairs, she had to call after him, "Careful as you take them off, Basha!"

She laid my costume aside. "Now I'm off to take morning blessings to my girls, and make sure Meki will keep them another night. I'll be back, and we shall put a finish on these costumes."

"You need to see what we've found, Romy." Neri shoved his emptied bowl aside and sprang from his cushion.

Atop an extra table made of planks supported by two of their neighbor the cooper's casks, the building plan of Palazzo Ignazio lay open. Lead weights held down its corners. The plan was little more than a smudged sketch of the main house and outbuildings—kitchen, stables, steward's house, gardens, and walls—with lines and notations of distances and water conduits.

I couldn't understand Neri's excitement. "I suppose there's no sign of a dungeon where Egerik might stash a prisoner."

"None. But Dumond read that book you brought about city defenses."

Neri unrolled one of the city maps on top of the drawing. One finger firmly on the Palazzo Ignazio plan, he pointed to a detail on the second map. "Right here is the ambassador's house and his kitchen house, and it looked to me like there's this same pairing on this other map, which Dumond says is a drawing of old defense works."

"Tunnels," said Dumond, who was tying on his leather apron. "This city's built on an anthill. They were used to store food and armaments back when Cantagna was just an outpost protecting the highroad off to Riccia. Ordinary folk hid in them, too. Did you ever hear mention of them when you lived up there with the rich and powerful?"

"No. *Il Padroné* showed me his own secret ways, but never mentioned tunnels."

The smith leaned over the old pages, squinting, and traced a blunt finger down the faint line. "Neri spotted it right off. This passage goes between Egerik's main house and his kitchen house. It looks to us like another goes straight downhill underneath the Merchants Ring wall and comes out square into the Ucelli Gardens. They could be used for hiding things or people or weapons. Or working magics we want to be out of sight."

"Have to figure out how to get in or out of 'em," said Neri.

"Escape routes," I said. "The Quartiere di Fiori has its own gates—and guards that we might need to avoid."

My stomach was full of toads. Some combination of my brother's talent and Dumond's could get us through almost any barrier. But they needed specific destinations for their magic, and the diagram made it clear that guessing would not be fruitful. The Mercediaran Embassy and Ambassadorial Residence was a sprawl.

Now we were actually going to act on my guesses about Egerik's belief in augury, the flimsier those guesses seemed. What could Damizella Monette *foresee* that would make him reveal what he knew of the Assassins List or his plans for the prisoner to be delivered to him the following day? How could I ensure we could get inside the embassy when Rossi was actually present?

"I'll need all my wits to play this right," I said, trying to implant the positions of halls and courtyards in my head.

Neri looked up from the map. "When you worked the memory magic on Rossi, I guess you couldn't take away his memory of *you*."

"Impossible. We've probably met fifty times or more. The best I could do was replace the story of that one meeting with one that had nothing to do with me or you or the Assassins List—and then set him up to think the experience was a dream. I hope it worked." But I knew what Neri was really asking.

"So yes, I must use my magic; the moment Rossi walks into the palazzo, he could recognize me. But once I become Monette, *her* ideas will drive her reactions, and those ideas—the instincts I create in her—could be entirely wrong."

The *Ascoltaré* rite would be familiar to any man of Egerik's inclinations. But Monette had to entice him into the rite without seeming to do so. Then I had to make sure the augury she cast would lead to Rossi and the Assassins List. If he didn't take the bait, she would need to do something different.

"You'll figure it out. Placidio says the first impersonation worked perfectly, and you didn't even know what you were doing."

"My brother, the optimist," I said.

But it was true. A month previous, when I had appeared before the Public Arts Commission, I'd not even realized that magic had made my impersonation into a true mask. What had made it work? Tarenah's story had been solid. I had made her a self-effacing daughter of a fisherman, and the articulate, devoted sister of an antiquities scholar. I'd given her desires, curiosities, and knowledge that enabled her to do what we needed.

Certain, the key had been the interior voice that influenced Tarenah's actions. Her respect and love for her brother had been her guide. It could just as easily have been the voice of her mother, a mentor, her conscience, or a deity. So, for Monette it could be the voice of Lady Fortune herself. Even more so than the real cloth merchant's daughter, Monette must be a true believer, waiting to hear the voice of her goddess. Maybe then she would interpret Romy's wishes and Romy's interpretations of events—even Romy's fingers manipulating the needles—as divine Espe's influence.

"Inventing new human beings is complicated," I said.

"Does your anxiety have more to do with what happened at Bawds Field or with *this* situation?" Dumond glanced in Placidio's direction, making clear what *situation* he was talking about.

For an instant, the room blurred and shuddering emptiness gaped in front of me . . .

I shook it off. "If Placidio is well enough to go," I said, "I trust he'll be able to do what's needed for me. Push me when I need it. Keep me from heading off in the wrong direction. Certain, you could do the same. Mostly my jibbers are simple uncertainty about what we'll face. But . . . yes. Recalling what happened that day, I wish I had more time to prepare. To build a way back to myself."

Dumond laid his hands firmly on my shoulders and focused on me with those Shadhi eyes, until I was near lost in their gleaming black. "Be sure of this, Romy-zha," he said. "We will always bring you back. Always."

Just then I understood why his daughters were such happy children, even when shuffled off to friends in the middle of the night or when their parents spoke in hushed tones about things they could not know. I believed him.

A weight akin to the Boars Teeth rocks rolled off my back. I nodded, not trusting myself to speak my thanks.

Neri shrugged and went back to perusing the maps. "Anyways, if you didn't use your magic, you'd be wasting the best trick you've got."

"Which reminds me," said Dumond, who vanished immediately out of the front door.

Before I could guess what he meant, he returned with a small roll of leather that he passed to me. "For the Chimera," he said. "A new trick."

I unrolled it to find nine beautifully wrought, wrist-to-fingertip length bronze needles. The points on either end were exquisitely sharp, the embossed symbols so perfectly defined that I could identify each one with my eyes closed.

"Dumond, these are beautiful," I said. "Yesterday afternoon, I spent several hours with the cloth merchant's daughter. When I professed my devotion to Lady Fortune with a donation of silver to her purse, she taught me the lore of the *Ascoltaré* and even allowed me to practice casting her needles. Hers were not half so easy to distinguish."

Eyes closed, I ran a fingertip over each needle and tested its balance.

"Each one slightly different, you see," said Dumond. "Practice to learn how they fall, and you can lay them exactly as you please."

"I'll have to do nothing else until we arrive at Palazzo Ignazio."

I placed one needle between each pair of fingers and the ninth between my thumbs, held for a moment, then spread my fingers all at one. The needles fell in a tangle, ready for interpretation. Surely a month would not be enough to master them. I had a day.

"We've got to figure out what to do with these tunnels," said

Neri. "We could make things appear and disappear. We could take this ambassador on a walk to someplace he don't expect."

Dumond rejoined him at the map table. "You and I will go scouting, lad. If the tunnels are clear, they could be useful for many things. Not one of the other maps shows them. I'll vow they've been forgot."

"Collapsed they are, sure as rabbits rut." The voice from across the room startled us. "And I approve your choice to become your true diviner self, Damizella Monette, daughter mine."

As one we spun to see Placidio sitting up, propped precariously on one quivering arm.

"What do you mean, collapsed?" blurted Neri.

"If they're the same tunnels as those down to the old barracks in the Asylum Ring, they're not going to take you anywhere you want to be. Back when I was training Gardia recruits, fellows would duck in those caves to cool off, hoping no one would notice they'd miss a round or two. Couldn't go ten paces in without finding a rockfall. Half of my boys came out spooked from the dark, the damp, and the wind howling through. And could someone please come catch me before this arm collapses and sends me bawling into the Great Abyss."

Placidio's *voice* was strong if naught else.

"Told you he'd wake," murmured Neri to Dumond, after they'd got Placidio not only supported, but out to the alley to relieve himself. The swordmaster now sat on a bench, a blanket across his lap, his naked back propped on Dumond's wall, and his head back and eyes closed as he contemplated the rigors of that journey.

"Leviathan is with us!" said Vashti, returning from her errand with a whoosh of damp air.

We all stared at her mystified.

"A fighter, yes?" she said, pointing at Placidio. "Dormant, waiting for the world's need. Is that not your Costa Drago legend of the great beast?"

"Indeed so," I said. "The beast Leviathan swept Dragonis from the sky so that Atladu and Gione could prison the monster under the earth and sea. I just never thought of Leviathan as a *human* beast."

"I've seen him shown that way," said Placidio, his head still back, eyes still closed. "He's always naked. Like Atladu. As am I under this sheet. You have been generous beyond measure, good Vashti—and I do thank you immensely—but I am a modest man and would appreciate breeks at the least. I understand there are delightful ones awaiting the input of my warlike ass."

No, Placidio did not sleep sound. He was always listening . . . like Teo.

As Neri and Dumond approved Placidio's attempts at good cheer, and Vashti flew up the stairs to fetch garments that might fit Placidio, my thoughts shifted back to Teo, who had waked in my bed surrounded by candles while I was getting ready to leave the previous morning. He'd been startled at first, and then he seemed to close himself off. No more whimsy. No curiosity. No emotion at all.

I'd said something about a friend recommending a ring of candles for those with terrifying dreams or injuries to the head. He didn't argue it, but didn't accept it either. When I offered him cheese or eggs for breakfast, he bowed politely and said it was far past time to take his leave. To find work, he said. So he could repay me.

"Are the candles bothersome?" I had asked. "I didn't mean to offend."

His smile was genuine, but distant. "How could I take offense for a well-meant gesture from a woman who has gifted me so much?"

Which was no answer at all. I could not but feel that I had hurt him deeply, and I was too shamed to ask why. But if ever I saw him again, I would ask. The moment he'd left, taking his mysteries with him, the world seemed . . . less. Thinner. Paler. Transient. It was impossible to explain, even to myself, how the man affected me.

I shook my head and tied up my hair. Today our minds must be on Chimera business.

Vashti offered Placidio some of Dumond's slops and hose. Neri volunteered to fetch some of Placidio's own garments from his rooms in the River Quarter.

"Before we install your backside anywhere, swordmaster," I said, "or proceed with this plan, you must prove you can stand and move without falling."

Dumond loaned Placidio a hornbeam cane wrought with a brass horse's head as its handgrip. The metalsmith was supposed to shorten the cane for a diminutive buyer, but had not as yet. It worked perfectly.

Wearing only his blanket-cape, Placidio walked around the room without grunts or groans or fainting. Carefully though. His left arm protected his injured ribs. After the demonstration, he unbandaged the burnt red slash across his torso. Though ugly, the wound showed no signs of sepsis, swelling, or seepage. He left off the bandage.

The bells rang a single strike—the first hour past the Hour of Business.

"This time tomorrow we need to be sitting in the ambassador's residence, showing him our wares. We know you're strong and determined," I said. "And clearly your healing is well on its way. Now tell us honestly if you will be able to keep your mind focused, recall what we've planned, and do this thing. We're your partners and value your desire to take part in something you do so well, but we also share your risk. You can't decide alone."

It was a measure of the seriousness of his injury that instead of blustering, bullying, or teasing us for holding back in the face of risk, Placidio considered deeply.

"I can play the part," he said at last. "My head is clear, though, kind Vashti, please give me no more of your tipsy tincture. If it were today, I'd doubt I'd have the stamina to walk up the damnable hill. But if I'm as much improved tomorrow as I am from yesterday, all should be well."

My spirits plummeted. If Placidio couldn't walk up to the Heights, we were left with Dumond, wholly unpracticed in impersonation. Or me alone.

"Before deciding," said Vashti. "I've a friend owes me a favor. He has a *kieyu* to lend, and two loyal workers who, for no more than ten coppers each, will carry it. Basha, *kieyu*"—she wagged a finger at Dumond—"chair. To carry."

"A sedan chair!" I guessed.

"That is it. The workers speak only the Invidian tongue, so would not be discomforted by your talking. Would that be acceptable?"

"More than acceptable," said Placidio. "Papa Baldassar might display a touch of gout—and if he is deemed nonthreatening by these Mercediarans and spies, all the better." He glanced at me. "And they will be *wrong.*"

"I'll see to it," said Vashti. "And now we must finish the costumes. Damizella Monette can practice her needle casting, while I ensure Papa Baldassar's warlike ass is resplendent."

None could hold back laughter at genteel Vashti's bawdy humor. But while she gathered her sewing case and costume materials, Placidio sobered quickly.

"We've one thing not yet decided," he said. "What if our gambit fails? What if this Egerik ends up with this cursed list, whether by purchase or partnership or torture, or Rossi walks away with his secret intact, through extortion or murder or whatever. Romy and I addressed this issue once, but did not solve it, and now the Chimera's leader has bespoke the spy and found him no nameless rogue, but a onetime friend. It's time to talk. Do we allow either man to control a document with consequences we cannot see clearly?"

Silence ruled for a few moments.

Dumond broke it. "Killing one or the other will violate the treaty interference clause. But I can't see trusting Cinque's word to keep it from Vizio. For myself, I think Treaty fines and hard times are always preferable to Mercediaran fire cannons. And, if we're choosing, 'twould be better to kill the spy before he gives over the list than the foreign ambassador after."

"It might come down to killing both," said Placidio.

"I'll kill him," said Neri. "Whichever one or both. Give me a place to find them, and I'll walk in and do it."

"No." The answer burst from me like a bolt from a crossbow. "You are not an assassin, Neri, and the Chimera is not an assassins' cover. We'll find another way. Trickery, blackmail, diversion . . . those are our weapons. We are sorcerers, not murderers. Not demons."

"Sometimes there be no choice," said Placidio, blunt as a horse's hind end. "Sometimes you have to let people reap the harvest they've sown."

What he said made terrible sense, but I was far from ready to concede the point. "We've too little time to argue."

"There'll be *no* time later. Think on it."

14

The fires of Palazzo Ignazio burned perfectly in the center of each hearthpiece, stoked to emit heat that was perfectly comfortable for those sitting just in front of it, yet expending no wasteful fuel on anyone occupying the vast portion of the room that remained behind them. It was an oddity in a house filled with them.

Dumond and Neri had faded quickly into the side streets of the neighborhood as soon as the Palazzo Ignazio gates came into view, the dolphin-and-hammer ensign of the Independency of Mercediare whipping in the gusty wind. They planned to explore the routes and passages they'd learned from the maps, and hoped to locate the tunnels from the old fortification drawings.

Antone and Vargo, Vashti's Invidian friends, carried Placidio and our sample case in the *kieyu*—the upholstered chair supported on twin poles. I trudged alongside, as we were admitted through the Palazzo Ignazio gates, where we faced the widest, deepest household sleugh I had ever seen—the first oddity of the morning.

It must have taken buckets of oil and water to fill the deep, iron-lined trench as custom dictated. We had to cross it on an iron footbridge. Egerik must worry about a veritable host of demons wanting to cross his threshold. It nicely affirmed our choice to prey upon the ambassador's superstitious bent.

A guard in gleaming armor had escorted us to a stone welcome hearth approximately the size of a temple, with a tiny fire precisely in its center. Placidio and I were seated on stone benches set close, with our backs to the rest of the massive stone entry hall that had likely not been truly warm since the fires of Dragonis scorched the earth.

After a slightly longer than comfortable wait, a slim, handsome woman in flowing white had introduced herself as the housekeeper, Mistress Mella. Polite but brisk, she escorted us to the "invited guest reception chamber."

Vargo remained in the entry hall with the *kieyu*, while Antone followed us with the sample case to our second tidy fire. Tall, straight-backed armchairs drawn up close to the dark walnut hearth were intricately carved into shapes of beasts. The design of the chair arms was very like iron teeth and just as comfortable. No one would be tempted to linger. Nothing encouraged me to admire or even notice the rest of the room. Odd.

Our present waiting location in Ambassador Egerik's outer chamber was a green velvet couch set only a few paces from a marble hearthpiece twice my height, containing, yes, a third small, neat blaze exactly in its center. Such tedious waiting time was not the usual in Cantagna, where business was conducted with brisk efficiency. Perhaps the languid airs of southerly Mercediare made such the custom.

The peculiar arrangements of seating and fire in the three chambers could simply signify a miserly conservation of fuel. But why occupy such an extravagant residence if the cost of wood or coal was a concern? If Ambassador Egerik wished visitors to admire the magnificence of Mercediaran culture, then why did he not care whether his guests viewed the entirety of his chambers?

No other visitors were in evidence. Perhaps ours was the merchants' entry, and diplomatic or personal guests waited elsewhere. Certain, the house upheld Egerik's reputation for cleanliness and particularity, from perfectly polished floors to perfectly groomed servants. Not a dust mote dared show itself on either one.

Placidio, resplendent in the canary satin trousses stuffed as wide as his shoulders, stiff matching doublet, billowing ribboned sleeves, and high, ruffled neckpiece, sat very still on the green couch, keeping his breathing shallow. No matter Antone and Vargo's smooth gait, the crack in Placidio's ribs had forced us to stop three times on the long climb to the Heights to let him vomit up whatever ginger tea remained in his belly. Vashti's rouge ensured he displayed the florid complexion expected of a prosperous merchant, but the colorless knuckles gripping his cane's brass horse head gave a truer estimate of his state. He swore it was only the rib, that the gut wound was well healed and painless. I was pleased he was upright.

The housekeeper had vanished beyond the twin doors of cast bronze at the far end of the chamber to announce us. Antone stood patiently behind the couch with our sample chest.

I, incapable of staring at a fire for another moment, strolled around the room seeking to settle nerves already overstretched.

With Dumond's clever forging and my determined practice over the past day and night, the Needles of the Nine Mysteries should fall exactly as I wished. But interpretation of the ritual cast was fluid, and any hint of the ambassador's true nature, desires, and interests that I could channel into Monette would make her divinations more useful.

Our hope to get the Assassins List was to interfere in the dealings between Rossi and Egerik. So I would use the divination to sow a wariness of dealings with the prisoner and suspicions of the prisoner's loyalties—whatever Egerik supposed those might be—using only oblique references to the document itself. The best result would put us in the house when Rossi was delivered. After Placidio's sobering reminder of failure, I was determined to make our plan work without assassinations.

"This house is something different from the Palazzo Segnori, eh, daughter mine?" Placidio's booming baritone reflected no weakness. "Peaceful."

I cringed at his bellicose intrusion on the quiet. The shaven-headed footmen who stood at every door wore crimson slippers that made no sound on the marble floor. The brisk housekeeper wore slippers as well, and spoke in softly measured tones swallowed by the high ceilings.

"Indeed so, Papa. This room is so different from the usual," I said. "Interesting."

Certain, it was a very odd chamber for someone so particular about his surroundings. The mosaic floors were uninspired, abstract patterns of wheels within wheels set in gray, dull blue, and white. The wall on the left as one entered from the reception chamber was striped with five floor-to-ceiling windows of clear, paned glass, too narrow for a view of the gardens beyond or to admit much light at this dim predawn hour. The plain wall opposite the windows was hung with long, narrow silk tapestries. Rather than an exuberance of scene, each huge hanging contained but a single image. A peacock. A leaping fish. A gnarled tree. Each of them lovely, expensive no doubt, but cold. They told no story.

I relished the artworks *il Padroné* sponsored for the public buildings of Cantagna, as well as his own residences. Paintings, frescoes, panels carved from wood or stone or cast in bronze were filled with exuberant, lifelike portrayals, whether the subject was a mythic encounter or a celebration of a grape harvest. Sandro believed that every ceiling, wall, and dome should infuse the people's souls with beauty and give them pride in their city. What was the purpose of *this* odd arrangement?

"The tapestries are especially beautiful," I said. "Is Mercediaran art all so serene and elevating?" Boring, truly.

Just then, the city bells rang the Hour of Business—the hour of our appointment. At that very same moment the sun peeped over the eastern horizon and shot its beams through the narrow windows. The mosaic chips in the floor took on new life, the light giving depth to the blue circles, slightly less to the white and gray, so that their image became swirling waves like the sea that surrounded Mercediare. Not serene at all; I could almost hear them crashing. In a blast of rose and gold, the dawn light bathed each of the tapestries with the perfect angled beams to bring out the subtle colorations in the designs, as if a thousand threads of a thousand other colors had been worked between the ones the eye saw, only visible when the light was angled perfectly.

"By the Holy Sisters," I said, overwhelmed with astonishment. "Papa, look! This whole chamber is the artwork!"

The room was alive, ablaze, an exquisite harmony of color and light. But only for these few moments. Even as I blinked, the sun shifted; life and color began to fade.

This was ephemeral artistry, more so than jewel-colored frescoes that dampness set peeling in less than a decade, more even than a sculpture built of sand. How many times a year—once, twice—would the particular combination of time, season, and weather display the floor and tapestries in their fullest glory?

Was that the ambassador's design? Perhaps he had other chambers decorated entirely for other instants of time. Or did he have different teases for different visitors? The hour chosen for our appointment and the slow processional from the gates to this spot could not have been coincidence. Yet a visitor who remained on the couch could miss the entire display. A visitor who arrived for an appointment late . . . or early . . . or who failed to apply at all would never be able to appreciate the owner-creator's cleverness. Did Egerik care if that was so?

A door closed softly behind me, back the way we'd come in. No one had joined us from the reception room. Yet high on the wall above that door—at the level a second floor of rooms might exist behind the wall—was an intricate brass latticework. I would swear I glimpsed the outline of a door behind it.

A squint! I knew as well as I knew my own name that someone had been watching and listening from behind that lattice, as I had once sat behind a painted screen listening to the Shadow Lord interview his petitioners. So the ambassador *was* interested in how his visitors reacted.

Everything I'd learned showed Egerik di Sinterolla to be an ambitious man. It seemed he was also one who reaped satisfaction from his own superiority. However trivial the game, he wanted to see the outcome of his play.

Mantegna's report had portrayed a man ready to accommodate any tyrant so long as he retained his position and his private pleasures. One who valued static perfection and loyalty. A man looking over his shoulder rather than in front of him. But this room evidenced a person who shaped his own world. Perhaps one who played other people, not one who allowed himself to be played.

I swept across the fading tiles, reclaimed my seat on the couch, and made sure to speak clearly. "I've never seen anything like this room, Papa. Such magnificence! So exceptional! This ambassador must be a *very* intelligent man. So clever and sophisticated."

"When this noble ambassador sees our wares and notifies his countrymen of our extraordinary selection, we shall travel to his glorious homeland and see its wonders for ourselves," boomed Placidio. "I've heard that Mercediaran art is surpassed only by the region's true landscape of fields, sea, and sunlight"— he leaned close as if sharing a confidence—"and that those are only surpassed by the splendors of Mercediaran women!"

"Papa! Decorum, segnoré."

We played the parts, but Placidio's cinder eyes circled the room, and a slight nod told me he understood exactly what I was saying.

Unexpectedly, masked by the draping of his cape, my partner took my hand. Cool fire consumed my skin as his huge paw massaged an ointment into my fingers. "A last-minute gift from Paolin," he murmured. "As discussed."

Vashti had told us of an ointment that made pinpricks bleed more than expected, but she was afraid she'd forgotten how to make it. I squeezed his hand in acknowledgment of the surprise.

Mistress Mella emerged from the inner chamber and extended her open hand to the twin bronze doors in invitation, her expression unrevealing. "Merchant di Fabroni, damizella, His Excellency will see you now. Your servant may enter for long enough to deposit your chest on the carpet beside the display table."

"Good, good," said Placidio. "Such a quiet house and comfortable accommodations could send a man dozing, even when he has stimulating business at hand!"

Indeed. The silent slippers and the seats facing the hearthfire could keep guests unwary of what surrounded them. Or imply that the magnificence a sideways glimpse revealed was not truly intended for their eyes.

For the first time I was pleased that the circumstance of Rossi forced me to use my magic. Such a man as I imagined would have no interest in a merchant's flirtatious daughter with a playful avocation of augury. Monette had to be absolutely convincing. A true believer in Lady Fortune, not a dabbler like the girl who inspired her. And not a flirt, but a desirable woman susceptible to his mastery.

I slipped my hand under Placidio's arm, hoping to provide a bit of extra support. No need for us to reveal more than necessary of our weaknesses. He rose slowly, smoothly, avoiding groans or grumbles.

"Cei will make you welcome," said Mistress Mella. "I shall escort your servant to an appropriate waiting chamber."

"You are most gracious, Mistress," I said, motioning Antone to follow us.

"Papa, are you ready for our most *serious* business?" I squeezed his arm in two sharp bursts—a signal I'd used before to tell him I was going to draw on my magic. "We shall have no foolery in a *great man*'s house."

Placidio glanced down, thoughtful and perceptive. Then he smiled broadly. "I do relish meeting new customers, my lovely Monette. I am always ready for serious business."

"Then onward."

As we followed Mistress Mella across the vast chamber to the great bronze doors, I allowed Placidio to guide me. Closing my eyes, I reached deep for the power I'd kept walled away for over half my life. Thanks to Neri, Placidio, and Dumond, I envisioned my magic as a cask of strong liquor to be relished, rather than a nest of cold vipers to be avoided. I had learned to seize the power that waited, rather than hesitate; to wield it purposefully rather than tease and dash away. I must not allow the terror of Bawds Field to rob me of that grace.

Warmth flowed around and through me, honing my senses, heating bone and blood, mind and wit, and I set my mind to the masquerade. I had to become Monette, but I could not let Romy get buried too deep. I must infuse Monette with all of Romy's questions, and the words I chose to invoke my magic must shape a woman capable of exposing the purposes of the man who had brought us to *this* room at *this* hour.

Thus I began my change: *I am Monette di Fabroni, a woman who intends to burst out of her father's sordid shadow to become the most respected woman in the Costa Drago. Sweet Espe, Lady Fortune, daughter of the Unseeable divinities, whispers in my ear . . .*

A sturdy arm supported me. My father's arm.

. . . laying the needles I cast in patterns that speak of things to come. I know it. I believe it. The Lady's breath is warm upon my cheek and the certainty of truth lives in me as she speaks through sharpened bronze.

But I am still learning how to read those patterns, and until I've honed my interpretations, I need coin to live and to surround myself with accoutrements that befit the Lady's favored handmaiden. The Lady has graced me with a natural comeliness. Ravishing, *so many serious men have told me.* Luminous, *I've heard from women whose pleasures lie in that way. But a diviner—even a beautiful one—who dresses in rags and roosts in the Asylum Ring with bricklayers and pimps will appear a charlatan, no matter that she speaks the Lady's truth. So I use my beauty as I use all my skills . . . in service to my Lady.*

For today, Papa's profession is more exciting and profitable than earning my coin as a chambermaid or scullion. Our new customer is something different from usual. A man who can change lives. A wealthy man with secrets and particularities that I must learn. He could be my path to Lady Espe's service.

Lady Espe promises to forgive my minor transgressions if I remain open to her guidance and prepared to denounce my father as a pithless cheat when the time is right to give her my all.

And so we play our game again . . .

15

Greetings of the dawn hour." Another shaven-headed young man held open one of the bronze doors to Ambassador Egerik's inner chamber. Cei, Mistress Mella had called him.

"And to you as well, segno," said Papa.

Of course, no *gentleman* would be holding the door with his head bowed, not in such a house as this one. The woman hadn't even dignified him with a title such as *aide* or *understeward*. Papa made it a practice to "bounce the honor" as he called it, offering everyone at least a step more rank than they owned. Part of my job as Papa's partner was to take accurate note of such matters for future use. To prevent him acting too much the fool, more like.

Without dignifying the servant with a glance, I followed Papa into the spacious room. Quite elegant it was! Uncluttered, with fine coffered ceilings, and a floor of light wood, polished like a mirror glass. Wide windows looked out on greening hills and vineyards. At one end a single modest doorway stood open to an indeterminate passage. At the other end stood twin painted doors of soaring height. Surely those must lead into another grand chamber.

No ambassador was present as yet; nonetheless, the room revealed much. So much clear glass would have cost a bucket of gold. Certain, Papa had noticed *that*; he could smell a clot of gold dust the size of an olive pit halfway across the Costa Drago. Once our hired porter deposited our sample case, the cold fish of a housekeeper showed him out. The young man closed the doors behind her and turned to us with a slight bow.

"Honorable Merchant, Damizella Monette, welcome. Ambassador Egerik has commanded me to make you comfortable until he is available to speak with you."

When the young man straightened from his bow, my heart near seized. Were the naked god Atladu himself standing in the middle of that room, it was this Cei would hold all attention.

Cei was simply the most beautiful man who had ever come into my view. A plain sleeveless tunic and flowing trousers of soft ivory linen set off skin that glowed like burnished copper. My insistent eye traveled the strong curves of his shoulders and arms for their full extent, before moving on to the fine bones of his face, hands, feet, and shaven head—bones that would seem too prominent did the sweet skin that covered them not fit so seductively. His lips were neither miserly nor slack; his firm, shapely chin had not a bristle to be seen, yet he was undoubtedly man, not boy. Long lashes fringed eyes that remained humbly lowered. I liked that.

"We thank your master for his hospitality," said Papa. "A chair would do me well. The damp has set me a proper torment of aches and pains these few days."

"Certainly, Segno di Fabroni. But before all, if you please . . ."

With charming humility, Cei motioned us toward a waist-high table of red lacquer inlaid with ebony that stood just inside the entry door. A bowl of water sat in its exact center and a stack of white linen squares on the shelf beneath.

"It is our house custom for all to cleanse their hands when entering one of His Excellency's private chambers." Cei's voice was neither gravel nor tin, but the rich in-between that could loosen a woman's knees with even such mundane verbiage.

"Hmmph. An unusual custom." Papa leaned heavily on his cane, pivoted smartly, and returned to the lacquer table. "But I wish more of my customers would take it up. My heart breaks to see fine fabrics mauled by greasy paws. *Not* that I would expect His Elegancy to have such."

Papa passed me his horse-head cane to hold, while he inspected his knuckles and dunked them in the water, disturbing the floating curls of lemon peel.

"Pass me a towel, Monette. Best you do the bending and not me."

I reached for the towel, only then noticing the little bronze statue sitting beside the towels. It was a natalé, like those people put in the graves of dead children to keep demons from eating their souls. What did a natalé signify in a reception chamber? When I passed Papa the towel, he winked approvingly. Which made no sense.

Cei watched closely as I dipped my own unstained fingers in the bowl and blotted them carefully on a linen square—so as not to wipe off the oil that kept them soft. I wished I'd taken the time to henna my fingernails. Alas that it was his master's attention I needed to entice.

This Egerik collects beautiful things. Like a parent's slap on the cheek, this odd phrase rose up unbidden. And just like a slap, it forced me to look at Cei with new eyes. *Unblemished* was the word that came to mind. *Perfect.*

Disquiet whispered through my blood. No accounting for it.

"Merchant Fabroni, will this be satisfactory for your wares?" Cei gestured to a long, polished table where our samples could be spread for clear inspections. That was not how Papa liked to do things. I mustn't allow myself to be distracted. For now, the game was his.

"Let me be seated first," said Papa. "My daughter can judge how best to show our wares."

"Sit as you please in any of these." The three chairs Cei indicated were padded with slim cushions of gold-broidered black like those in the waiting room. His gesture pointedly excluded a high-backed armchair of gleaming ebony which had no cushions at all.

Interesting this Egerik. Particular about all things, as we had heard.

"Here, Papa," I said, pointing to a wide chair that would support him best in his state of aches and pains. Unfortunate that his gout had picked this day to flare.

Once Papa was seated and his foot propped on a low stool, giving him clear relief, I asked Cei if he would move the sample case closer. "We prefer neutral light, neither too much nor too little. You understand, I think, how important light is to an artistic display."

Dared I imagine the young man's rich coloring deepened ever so slightly? Down to his bare toes. Lovely toes! He alone of all the servants we'd seen wore no shoes.

Monette! Attention to business! I swallowed an ill-timed tease.

Divine Espe held a firm grip on my conscience. I always heeded her words.

Cei bowed in agreement and gestured with an open hand.

I thanked him and showed him to put the case beside Papa's chair.

Once the case was in place, Cei offered wine or tea and sweet cakes.

We refused as always. It's difficult to speak clearly or handle samples to best advantage with hands juggling cups, or lips and fingers sticky with honey.

"I shall notify the ambassador that you're settled," said Cei, retreating through an inner door that was but one of many pale, cherrywood panels of a not-windowed wall. Cleverly done.

"What do you think, Monette?" my father whispered once the panel was vanished into the wall again. Perhaps he thought someone was eavesdropping.

"I think the ambassador is a man of exceptional taste," I said at normal volume. Best not seem to be conspiring, and I wasn't at all sure that whispering would preclude our being overheard. I took my place at Papa's shoulder.

"This house is a marvel of beauty and order. Pleasant and bright, not grim." Though why I should expect it to be grim, I didn't know. "Such well-disciplined servants and clad with such simple elegance! I can only imagine this man Cei wearing *our* ivory silk, with just enough of Dama Aliota's embroidery to enhance his perfection."

Papa heeded my cue, leaning back in his chair. "Never seen the like. Perhaps you should take a walk around this lovely room and see where a customer might gain advantage from our wares, other than dressing handsome young men."

Papa's gout always left him grumbling, as did my interest in handsome young men. He had no idea of my true aspirations. Lady Espe alone would shape my choice of husband.

Dutifully, I circled the room. Though a pleasant chamber, as I'd noted, signs of the master's appreciation of the mystical world were everywhere. Ghiris—the spiky knots of pomegranate twigs—were woven into the draperies above every window and door to filter out bad luck. The hand washing—not merely a house custom, I guessed, as lemon peel was said to cleanse away the oily spoor of demons. More natalés had been tucked in unlikely places—under tables, in corners, beside or behind other statuary. Chains of dried sea lavender twined the candelabra on the table, and wreaths of it circled the base of every lamp. The warmth of lamp and flame released the scent that barred the malevolent dead from plaguing us who yet lived.

What does he fear? My fingers brushed the needle bag at my belt.

A small shelf set in front of the wide windows held an array of glass candle lamps, a handbell, and a rectangular box of jewel-colored enamelware. Something treasured, most assuredly, yet here on display for visitors to see. My curiosity leapt ahead of my sense and I tipped up the lid of the lovely box. It held a simple gold ring, set with rubies, a lock of hair the color of sunlight, and a few dried rose petals as a bride might find on her marriage bed. I closed it quickly, shamed at my boldness, though wondering why something so private would be on display here.

Why, indeed? A treasured memory? A reminder? The Lady ever prodded me to question.

A brass latticework of the kind used to vent smoke centered a wood frame mounted on the wall of cherrywood panels.

"Be observant, daughter," called Papa. "Would a fabric screen serve better than the brass?"

That would depend on whether there was anything behind the latticework, of course. I peered between the interlaced withes. There were varying thicknesses to the darkness, but the lattice was too fine to give any sensible shape to them or detect any movement.

"Perhaps a draping of silk to soften the edges," I said and moved on to the next wall.

The painted doors were flanked by two statuary niches lined in gold mosaic. One niche held a life-sized figure of Gratiana, the mythic queen of Mercediare, holding Dragonis's tail. She had cut it off to prevent it obliterating the two hundred islands its flailing had broken from the mainland. A wide marble plinth centered in the second niche stood vacant.

"If His Excellency grants us a second visit," I said, "we must pester Labrier until he yields us some lengths of lampas—a shame it is so rare. Our merchandise must be worthy of such an elevated person."

No, the plinth wasn't vacant. A servant must have left behind the red rose—a bud just on the verge of opening. Beside the rose lay a small knife with a bone hilt and thin blade, slightly curved at the tip. The knife must be as sharp as it looked, or perhaps the great thorn on the rose stem was, as a single drop of fresh blood stood on the polished white marble.

Why did two items and a drop of blood, carelessly left, so disturb me?

Because this man does nothing *carelessly.* Certain, that was clear.

I was not squeamish. The rose and knife were laid out quite artfully on the white marble. The man had a taste for perfection. I approved.

"His Excellency Egerik di Sinterolla, Ambassador to the Independency of Cantagna by appointment of Her Eminence Cerelia Balbina Andreana di Vizio, Protector of Mercediare and the Two Hundred Islands."

Cei's announcement hurried me to Papa's side just as he lumbered to his feet and the ambassador stepped through the open panel.

Dipping my knee gracefully, I allowed my crimp-curled hair to fall over one shoulder, as it displayed both hair and ruby silk bodice to best advantage. As a man of such position would expect, I lowered my eyes . . . but not before I assessed our mark.

Trim in the body; slightly more than modest height. Clean copper-brown hair swept back from a wide, intelligent forehead; a thin nose; a finely drawn mouth advantaged by the brief shadow of beard surrounding it. Attractive for his middling age, if not handsome. I had expected a wizened, miserly sort.

His appearance is as carefully considered as his chairs or his man Cei.

"Excellency." Papa bowed deeply, gripping his cane. My hand crept under his elbow. The pain in his foot must be excruciating.

"Greetings of the morning, Excellency," I said, laying two fingers of my left hand on the silver lacewing pendant at my breast.

"Please sit." The ambassador's voice was pleasant enough, crisp and light.

Papa returned quickly to his chair. I stood at his shoulder.

Egerik swung himself into the uncushioned chair. I admired his brisk ease.

At that very moment, he looked straight back at me. His eyes were not sunk under the narrow shelf of dark brows, but open and clear, his gaze forthright. He did not disguise his assessment of me. I took the slight lift of one eyebrow as approval.

His attention reverted to Papa. "Your fabrics come highly recommended, Merchant Fabroni."

We always saw to that. I had a decent hand with pen and ink, and enjoyed composing recommendation letters on varied types of parchments. Papa collected seals. Some from junk bins at a market. Some from unhappy or annoying customers. He relished devising signatures appropriate to the names.

"We take pride in the value we provide," Papa pronounced most sincerely. "I have cultivated suppliers from as far away as barbarian Eide, where the chill and the wet produce stout sheep with exceptional wool. Our wool guild is just now beginning to accept—"

"Forgive me. My time to indulge my interest in fabrics is limited." The ambassador offered both the apology and the statement of priority without sentiment. Also without the contempt I expected from such an elevated man to the likes of Papa and me.

"Silk of pale hues interests me," he continued. "As does lampas wrought in the blue of midnight, threaded with true silver. I hear that is difficult to procure, but I would like to see samples as soon as possible."

A quiver of amusement at the corner of that fine mouth

accompanied a quick glance in my direction. He'd been eavesdropping on us! Why would he admit that? Did he think we were too dull to notice?

"For Cantagnan winter I prefer a figured velvet of black and gray," he continued, "and solid black to match. The climate of Mercediare does not favor velvet, but I very much appreciate the luxuriant feel of it, the sheen, the depth of color. *Nothing* in canary, if you please."

There was the contempt. Papa's nostrils flared enough to demonstrate he felt the sting of it, though his attitude of careful attention did not diminish. I had warned him that the yellow on a man of his imposing bearing was excessive, but he insisted a merchant of his stature should demonstrate the height of fashion. He never listened to me.

Egerik's soft doublet of fine blue wool striped with brick-red braid was perfectly fitted. His shirt's black collar rode high on the back of his neck with a scarf of matching red tucked into the front. His black sleeves were not puffed and slashed but comfortably loose, fitted at the wrist with the same red braid. Handsome. Every material the best. No, we would never see a rag-stuffed codpiece on Ambassador Egerik, or a hat with a brim the width of my forearm and a crimson-dyed plume that drooped over half his face as Papa's did.

"Is anyone else to join us, Excellency? Your wife? Guests?"

I held my breath. Papa knew very well that Ambassador Egerik's wife was dead.

"No." The word could have sliced rare beef.

"All right, then. Monette, show his Excellency what we have. We've the silks and the figured velvet, though I believe we've only shades of blue and rose in our case."

I dipped my knee to Papa, something I rarely did, but it seemed proper to remain dutiful in the face of the ambassador's disdain. Kneeling beside the case, I pulled out our hemmed lengths of white, ivory, cream, and pale rose silk, unrolled them, and laid them over my arm. Imagining them draped over *Cei's* skin surely heightened the color in my cheeks.

As I set other rolled samples aside to unbury the velvets, I glanced at Cei. He stood beside the panel door, directly behind Papa and me. Hands clasped behind his back, he was perfectly still, perfectly beautiful, and his focus remained on the floor in front of him. Interesting that Egerik hadn't acknowledged his presence once. Not even a glance. That puzzled me. If one enjoyed beautiful things, why not look at them?

I crossed the few steps between Papa and the ambassador, and offered the gentleman the pile. "The items you mentioned, as well as an example of the finest embroidery in Cantagna."

It would be paining Papa terribly that he couldn't stand at my side, his imposing height diminishing the man in the chair, even as he bathed him in flattery.

Egerik did not look at Papa. "Bring that footstool over here, damizella, and be seated there as you display your samples for me," he said. "One at a time, if you please."

"Of course, Excellency."

I laid the samples in Papa's lap, gave him our anything-for-the-rich-customer eyeroll, and then carefully shifted his painful foot from the little stool to the floor. Perhaps this was Egerik's revenge for the mention of his dead wife.

"So you serve Lady Fortune," said Egerik, as I drew the stool to his chair. "Several of the recommendation letters mentioned your talent of divination. I find that most interesting."

"Indeed, Excellency. I am humbled to be favored by the Lady. My father has indulged my studies even as I share his honorable trade."

Not entirely honorable. I had mentioned my vocation in the letters apurpose. Along with a mention of our exceptional price for cloth of gold.

It was rumored that the ambassador craved cloth of gold, that rarest of fabrics. All the more reason for me to gain his trust and distract him from the quality of our sample. For us to buy even a sample length of authentic cloth of gold would leave us in penury. But the profit to be made from a decent order of our less-than-perfect fabric could set us for a year or more, making it worth the trouble to move on and restart our business in Varela or Riccia, well away from the customer's wrath. Were the profit sizeable enough, I could call an end to this deceitful business and follow Lady Fortune's call.

I positioned the footstool as the ambassador wished, well aware that this would put me in a subservient posture. Papa was aware of it, too, and displayed a ferocious scowl when I retrieved the samples from his lap and blocked the ambassador's view. I returned the scowl and squeezed Papa's knee in reassurance before taking my seat at Egerik's feet. No need for pique to interrupt a presentation that could change our future.

Draping my skirts to display the red-and-black pattern and my hanging sleeves to best advantage, I beamed at the man as if it pleased me to look *up* at him. If he didn't make a substantial order, I would be vexed that I had so abased myself. But then, Egerik was an attractive man . . . and obviously very rich.

"We supply only authentic Paolin silk, bought from private traders." Allowing my sleeve to slip back to my elbow, I offered the sample of the ivory, letting it drape across my wrist and hand. It was the best and largest sample we had.

He didn't take it, but held a fold with two fingers and drew them lightly along its length, not stopping when his fingers left the silk and continued up my bare forearm. "Exquisite."

Gracious Lady, his fingers were warm, and very sure of themselves! Powerful men thought they could do anything. Yet I refused to take it amiss. If he appreciated me, well and good. My task of distraction would be all the easier.

He removed his fingers as I laid Dama Aliota's sample atop the length of silk.

"Imagine this lovely silk trimmed with fine embroidery."

"I am imagining many things," he said. The charming creases that fanned from the outer corners of his light blue eyes deepened. Not quite a smile, perhaps, but pleasant. And interested.

"The silk is also available in pure white." I held out the sample, but he waved one of those excellent fingers for the next.

"And cream." Again the same, though I held the sample a little longer, knowing how well it harmonized with my own deep coloring. Those fingers . . . It had crossed my mind from time to time that an alliance with a wealthy patron with a devotion to Lady Fortune could be exactly the path laid out for me.

We moved on to the velvets, which Egerik deemed inferior to those of another merchant, likely Ganiu Stellani, the obnoxious sow. The ambassador very much liked the sample of the blue dye that would be found on the Kairys-made lampas, however, and agreed to see the samples whenever we acquired them. A small victory which prodded Papa out of his moping silence.

"Is there anything else that interests you, Your Grand Excellency?"

I pretended my father had not let his disapproval of the forward ambassador show beneath his business manners.

Egerik sat back and picked a silk thread from his knee. His gaze remained fixed on me. "Cloth of gold interests me."

Hooked! An ambitious man could allow no other answer. No fabric so evidenced true power as cloth of gold. Only a few in all of the Costa Drago could afford it.

"Cloth of gold interests every man and woman in the world," said Papa, his mercenary spark reignited, "till the price be told. If you're thinking of a suit like mine own, 'twill cost at least the price of your grand house here and weigh near the same on your shoulders as you wear it. Yet, as it happens, I have sources in Lhampur. They cannot reduce the weight, but can offer a bid for your needs well below the price of goods from Kairys or Riccia."

"I am considering a shoulder-to-hip sash—a ceremonial baldric—as a gift for my noble Protector Vizio, who celebrates her tenth year in her office two months from now."

"A most generous and proper gift, Excellency, for the extraordinary lady of Mercediare! Monette, fetch our sample to show the ambassador."

"Yes, Papa."

Sniffing the prospect of a sale, Papa leaned forward in his chair and continued without taking a breath. "You understand the sample is necessarily small, segnoré. Few cloth merchants are able to provide cloth of gold to customers of taste and means, simply because the sample itself is so costly. But House Fabroni has shouldered that burden."

"The expense lies primarily in the material," I said. "Every tiny square of the fabric costs the same as an equal sized square of gold foil. Yet the making adds half again to the final valuing. It requires a weaver of exceptional skill and is so tedious that weaver might produce only a knuckle's length of cloth in a day."

"I specified in my message that I wished goods to be delivered to my tailor within the day. So that's not possible?"

"Ordinarily no," said Papa. "But for a modest length as that you've indicated, there is a slim possibility that some might be available. A change in requirements of size or delivery day. A canceled order. As soon as we leave here, I will dispatch messengers to my warehouse."

While Papa gave Egerik estimates of cost and time to delivery, assuring him that a reasonable length could certainly be dispatched to Mercediare within a month, I fetched a flat, rectangular box of thick-walled bronze from the sample case. My heart thrummed, knowing that this would be our riskiest play. We could not allow Egerik to look too closely at our sample. Were a man of his stature—even a foreigner—to unmask our deception, he could have our license revoked, our stock and samples seized, and the two of us in the stocks for a month.

Seated on the footstool, I arranged my skirts yet again, this time ensuring the red silk bag marked with the Lady's symbols hanging from my belt was positioned correctly.

"Your gift will last your honored mistress until her fiftieth year in office!" Papa flapped his fingers together, impatient as I unlocked the bronze casket and unfolded the soft linen wrappings to reveal the triangle of heavy fabric, each side two small fingers long.

"Ah, here we have it." Papa clapped his hands as if my mother had just delivered him a son. "Still beautiful. Hold it to the light, Monette. See its shimmer, Excellency, a luster like no other. This simple weave is the purest, loveliest form of the rarest fabric in all the world. You will see that our gold wire is wound over a core filament of silk, the strongest of all threads. No common linen or wool. Show him, girl."

Most of the sample's raveled edge was bound with heavy stitching. With sharp, pointed tweezers from the bronze case, I prized apart the brushy threads of the short length left unbound. Unwinding one fine gold wire exposed the silken core. I made sure the wire was one of true gold and not the brass ones used to cheapen the sample's making.

I raised the sample into the light where Egerik could see it, my tweezers gripping the core thread and the unspiraled gold. Giving him only the moment, I enfolded the sample in my fingers.

"Such a marvelous hand to the cloth," I said, kneeling up to show him—as well as granting him an excellent view of my well-filled red bodice and Lady Fortune's lacewing pendant settled nicely in the cleft of it. Distraction.

"Pliable, thanks to the silk core," said Papa from behind me.

"And such a pleasing weight," I said. "Feel it, Excellency. Not unbearably weighty. Reassuring. Valuable. Perfect. When the sash lies across your mistress's breast"—I drew the side of my hand lightly across my own—"she will feel the weight of your regard. And your worth."

I laid the sample in the ambassador's outstretched hand, captured his gaze with mine, and smiled. His appreciative gaze did not leave my face as he hefted the scrap of cloth. His blue eyes were truly quite nice, especially when he responded with a genuine smile of his own. Why had I ever imagined him merely an ordinary man, trying to make himself beautiful by collecting beautiful things?

Reluctantly, it seemed, he turned his attention to the sample. Regretful, I made as if to stow my tweezers in a waist pocket. In truth I stabbed the tweezers' sharp tips forcefully into the red silk bag . . .

"Sweet Lady!" I gasped and drew back my hand with nine exquisitely sharp needles embedded deep in my flesh. The pain was fierce and hot.

"Damizella!"

Papa bellowed, "Monette, sweetling! What have you done?"

I couldn't answer. One by one, I yanked the needles out and dropped them to the floor, feeling the mark of its Mystery embossed on each—Mysticism, Presence, Power, Substance . . . By the time I reached the last, welling blood covered my hand and dripped on my gown, pain threatening my composure.

I clutched my arm to my chest. What had happened? I was only supposed to rip the bag and spill the needles, not impale myself.

Then Papa was there, whipping out his white kerchief and deftly wrapping it around my hand. "Are you going to be all right, daughter mine?"

He drew me to my feet and into his embrace. I buried my forehead in his chest. "The sample," I whispered, a sob escaping me. I dared not forget.

Papa said, "Fortune's dam . . ."

Egerik yet held the triangular scrap, but his attention was fixed on his polished floor, where the Needles of the Nine Mysteries lay tangled, blood spattered all around. More blood than a few needle sticks should cause. And indeed the sight struck me with awe.

"Spirits, Papa, look!" I pushed my father off me. "'Tis the Lady's sign . . ."

I had set out to use the Lady's favored telltales as a show, to distract a customer from our faulty sample. But some force within me—surely divine Espe herself—had dispersed the nine needles in piles laced with blood and pain. It was a sign no one who listened for Lady Fortune's whispers could ignore.

"Your Excellency," I said, hoarse with awe, "someone in your house—"

Egerik's sure fingers touched the pendant at my breast, drawing my gaze to his pale eyes. They bored into my own with relentless insistence until it seemed as if his determined fingers had touched my very soul.

His brows lifted; his lips parted; and he drew in a quick breath.

"You *believe* she speaks to you," he said. "Lady Fortune, the divine Espe, to a common merchant's shill? Can you read the *Ascoltaré*, girl?"

I nodded, unable to speak, overwhelmed at his willingness . . . his *need* to believe. This was what I was made for.

Tears of joy and awe stung my eyes as Egerik took my uninjured hand and helped me to the pale wood floor. We knelt on either side of the tangled, blood-spattered needles.

"Tell me what this means, damizella. A casting laced in blood has significance, I know."

I had not yet learned how to interpret every possible positioning of the Nine, but students of Lady Fortune learned one principle first. "Excellency, an unintended cast, confirmed with blood, means death arrives in your house after the sun's next rising."

16

B egin now," commanded Egerik. "Your interpretation."

"Monette, what are you thinking?" snapped Papa. "His Excellency has no time for your foolishness. We have business."

"You will stay silent or leave the room, merchant." No mistaking the command in the ambassador's quiet word. "And you, damizella, will clarify this warning your needles speak. You'll need candles and . . . ?"

"Yes, candles. Nine. Of beeswax, set in a ring around us."

I clutched my bleeding hand—my right hand—to my breast. Could the urgency of Lady Fortune's work be any clearer? The right hand belonged to Lady Virtue. The left—my uninjured hand—belonged to my mistress, Lady Fortune.

"And a towel of clean white linen."

The ring of candlelight would separate the Lady's influence from common concerns. The linen would hold the needles as I removed them from their positions.

Egerik stared at the bloody needles as if they might stand up on their tips and speak.

Papa hobbled back and forth, seething. But he knew any hope of profit now rested with me. Who could have imagined the Lady would use our scheme to deliver a true warning to our mark? Certainly not Papa, who believed in neither luck nor virtue.

The soft sound of a closing door brought Cei with an armful of candles, holders, and a rolled towel of white linen. With fluid motions, he set the candles in elegant brass holders—each an image of a different screaming mouth—and gestured for me to approve the positioning as he placed each in the circle.

When the last candle was set, Cei folded wooden shutters over every window and brought me a burning taper. Then he withdrew. Egerik had neither spoken nor even looked at him.

I turned my attention to the needles. *Please, divine Lady, let me not falter.*

Lighting the nine candles one by one, I contemplated each of the nine Mysteries—Jeopardy, Judgment, Mysticism, Order, Presence, Reason, Relationship, Power, and Substance—and their eighteen manifestations. Each Mystery had a primary manifestation and an obverse, represented by opposing tips of its needle.

When the candles were lit, I returned to my place on the floor. A halo of light surrounded Egerik and me, the needles, and the blood. Papa remained a shadowy bulk behind the fire. Perhaps he would believe me after this.

I carefully examined the lay.

The sharp tip at each end of the thin bronze needles signified the equal importance of the primary and the obverse. A single embossed ring marked the first third of the length from the primary tip and a double ring the second, so there was no mistaking which end was which. The symbol of each Mystery was embossed exactly in the center of its needle: the arrow for Presence, the crescent for Reason, the starburst for Order, and so on.

The needles had dropped from my hand into three distinct piles of two, two, and five. Easier to interpret than all nine in one tangle. The candlelight set the bronze aglow, the symbols and the rings easy to recognize. Though I had never performed a reading for a stranger, I felt ready.

I breathed deep and began. "Divine Espe, Lady Fortune, whispers in my ear, petitioner. By her hand alone has this casting been laid before us. Humble in the face of her will, serene in the surety of my calling, and steeped in her lore do I venture interpretation."

As I spoke the ritual words, bathed in awe of the Lady's gift, her serenity and confidence steadied my soul. I knew these needles. My hand could read them.

"Will you hear Lady Espe's words from my mouth?"

"Oh yes, I will hear." Egerik devoured the words as if they were bits of tender meat.

"I see three separate positionings," I said. "Isolate, thus not dependent one upon the other, yet unquestionably linked by blood."

The first was a simple crossing of two needles.

"The Mystery of Substance lies atop Presence, primary upon primary."

The forefinger of my left hand confirmed my observation by touching the symbol on the uppermost and then the lower of the two needles without disturbing their position.

"The primary manifestation of Substance is *flesh*; the primary of Presence is *arrival*. Thus, a visitor of flesh will arrive here at the sun's next rising. Tomorrow."

The clarity of my understanding astonished me. The air quivered around us; Egerik's agitation, not mine. My Mistress was with me, guiding my hand and my voice, infusing me with calm. I continued without hesitation.

"The nature of this casting, offered by the Lady without our intent and bathed in blood—blood which marks every one of these needles—tells me this visitor shall be either the victim or the agent of a mortal doom."

Egerik stared at the needles I indicated, a dip of his head signaling acceptance. "You've no idea which he will be—victim or agent?"

The Lady's power surged in me. "Certain, we who read the Lady's intents are taught to consider the simplest interpretation first, until more of the context can be clarified. She has warned of death arriving at your house. Thus I would say that, the visitor *brings* the danger. And because the needle of Substance is not touched at exactly at its tip but nearer its center, the danger is not of flesh alone, like a disease, nor is it a danger of spirit alone, like murderous intent. Without more information, I can say no more of it."

"Go on to the others then." His eagerness fired my soul.

Another two needles lay apart from the rest, not crossed, but almost parallel, their primary tips pointed in the same direction. "These two represent the Mysteries of Mysticism and Power," I said. "They are aligned primary to primary, obverse to obverse. This positioning says each Mystery both affects and is affected by the other.

"*Enlightenment*—attention to the extraordinary aspects of the world, the unexplainable—aligns with *strength*, while Mysticism's obverse of *mundanity*—the preoccupation with the everyday— aligns with *weakness*. One could say strength is fed by enlightenment which in its turn builds strength."

"And mundane concerns feed weakness," he said, "which deepens preoccupation with the mundane."

"Certain, Excellency."

It was a profound alignment, entirely contrary to the truth of life in the Costa Drago where those with political power discouraged any investigation of mysticism.

I glanced at the ambassador. The creases at the corners of his eyes had deepened and furrows of deep thinking lined his brow.

"Again, I cannot interpret these further without moving on," I said. "Unless you tell me where these sayings draw your thoughts."

He jerked his head. "More."

The other five needles were jumbled in a precarious tangle. I examined it from every angle.

"Atop all we find the Mystery of Jeopardy, with its obverse tip pointed skyward—highest of all the nine—"

"—and the obverse of Jeopardy's mystery is *danger*," whispered Egerik, the furrows on his brow deepening. "So danger towers over all."

Though it was not proper for a petitioner to offer interpretation, I'd not the heart to reprimand him with so serious a matter at hand.

"Indeed so," I said. "Jeopardy's obverse tip rests *atop* the primary of the steeply tilted needle representing Relationship.

That positioning implies that the source of the danger is a Relationship, rather than the Relationship resulting from the Jeopardy."

"From an enemy."

"Nay, Excellency, for as you can see, Jeopardy's needle rests on the *single-ringed* end of the Relationship needle—its primary."

His glance popped up to mine. "So a *friend* is the source of my danger?"

"The steepness of Relationship's tilt suggests the relationship is much more than friendship. Your danger could arise from oath, pledged service, conspiracy, sworn fealty, or other relationship of a deep and significant kind."

"And is it one dangerous person or more?"

I considered the stack yet again and invoked the Lady's aid. "Nothing here speaks of numbers. And to say *dangerous person* is inaccurate. All we see here is that the *relationship* generates the danger."

Egerik chewed his lip.

I was curious, but then it was not my role to apply the casting to my petitioner's life. Only to illuminate the Lady's handiwork in the needles.

"So my arriving visitor brings mortal danger with him. The danger arises from one or more relationships of sworn oaths or fealty or pledged service. That relationship might or might not be with the arriving guest."

"Indeed, Excellency, that is how I interpret the Lady's warning."

"Go on. What else?"

Carefully, I removed the top two needles, confirming the

symbols I'd seen on them and their placement with respect to the three below. When I laid them aside on the white towel, blood drips spread eagerly into the fine linen.

I plunged ahead. "These two needles are the underpinning of the danger. The primary of Reason, which reaches high enough to touch the indicator of danger, is *knowledge*. The same segment of Reason touches the obverse of Judgment, which is *unresolved error* or *unpunished crime*, as opposed to *justice*. This positioning implies a most serious crime, like murder or theft. Its connection with *knowledge* implies secrets—terrible secrets. Those are the bones of this augury, Excellency."

"So unpunished crime or unresolved error inflames this towering danger. Betrayal, perhaps. Treason, perhaps. And if I adhere to mundane concerns, I am weakened, but if I travel the path of faith . . . as I do now, for example . . . I gather strength." His first assertion puzzled him, but he spoke the second with confidence.

"Logical conclusions, Excellency. And too—" I peered closely at the remaining needles. "There is one more thing."

I had thought the last needle, Order, unconnected to the divination. Though it lay beneath the large pile, it did not touch any of the other needles. But in truth its obverse came within a fingernail's width of a needle in the first pairing. Heart and mind quivered, alive with the Lady's spirit, filling me with assurance that this was a matter of great significance.

"Here is a fundamental strangeness," I said, pointing to the needle of Order. "*Chaos* is the obverse of the mystery of Order. Look at how *chaos* is all but touching the lower end of the Substance needle, which speaks of *spirit*."

I struggled to make my interpretation into a cohesive story.

"It appears that your arriving visitor will bring death to some in this house. The source of this arriving danger is your relationship with person or persons bound by solemn oaths or the like—coupled with secret knowledge of crimes like betrayal or treason. But the foundation of all these events seems to be yet a third entity, a chaotic spirit. An angry spirit, unable to leave this world."

I sat back on my heels and reviewed the positions of all the needles and everything I had said. Finding no fault in my reasoning, I glanced up, only to see Egerik's face turned to stone and his pale eyes peeling back my skin.

All serenity and confidence dropped away. How absurd for this man to put faith in a merchant's daughter who dreamed of speaking with Lady Fortune's voice.

"Of c-course, there are many ways to interpret these things," I stammered. "I could draw a diagram that you could take to someone more—"

"I want you," he said, in a cold assurance of a man who assumed his desires would never go unfilled. "Tomorrow afternoon. You will cast again, this time apurpose. Then we shall see how the future is arranged. Is it true that if objects or persons in the augury are present or near to hand, it changes the energies of a second cast?"

I struggled to reconcile his wishes and his question with the augury, and the outcome terrified me. To be so close to unnamed dangers . . . death in some unguessable guise.

"Yes, yes, certain, it would affect the cast if any of them were nearby: the arriving person, whose physical presence poses the danger, or anyone bound by oath or fealty which is the source of that danger, or the chaotic spirit. You think one or more of them could be present tomorrow?"

"Certainly the agent, and those bound by oaths. The malignant spirit . . . I hope not. A second cast should tell me more, I think. Of course you *could* be just a silly girl spouting nonsense."

"Calumny, Segnoré Ambassador! My daughter is beloved of Lady Fortune."

Papa stood outside the ring of candlelight, an indignant giant in the gloom, gray-faced and leaning hard on his cane. I'd forgotten him completely.

"My daughter and I have other appointments, and I would not have her in the path of dangerous visitors, living or—"

"Your arrangements are nothing to me," said Egerik, rising to face him. Though his stature in no way approached the figure of my father, Egerik was clearly master here. "Your daughter will be present in this house by the second hour past midday, even if I have to send my household guards to fetch her. She will stay as long as I have use for her. Naturally, I'll pay you well for her services. No need to bring your shoddy cloth of gold, or yourself for that matter."

I wanted Papa to say no. This man who collected beautiful things frightened me. Or was it the Lady's breath on my cheek frightened me more? Conspiracy, death, malignant spirits. The seeing . . . the words . . . had been so clear, as if graven in my soul. My hands had dropped the needles as if Espe's own had guided them. I stared down at my right hand, bundled in bloody linen. Only now had I regained any awareness of the throbbing punctures.

Papa sniffed and wriggled his moustache. "Well, certainly, Excellency. We shall be here by the hour you say. Understand, segnoré: Monette is my only daughter, gifted with talents and beauty as all men dream of. I cannot and will not leave her alone with strangers, no matter how elevated their position. We shall negotiate the price of her services upon our arrival tomorrow."

No matter his pompous words, my stomach churned at Papa's easy agreement—and at the eager glow on his cheeks.

"Damizella." Egerik nodded stiffly. "Merchant Fabroni. Do not be late."

With no more than this curt acknowledgment, the ambassador left the room through the door in the wall panel.

"Your needles, Monette." Papa's reminder caught me before I could get to my feet. My unbandaged hand gathered them onto the square of white linen. Shaking and awkward, I bundled them with the towel. Blood yet stained the pale wood. More blood than needle sticks should produce. The Lady's work.

"May I assist you to the door?" Cei had appeared at our side.

"I can walk," said Papa. "But we need our sample case brought."

"A servant will fetch it." Cei held open the bronze door while Papa walked slowly across the room.

Mella was waiting beyond the door. "This way."

I set out before the words were out of her mouth.

"Slow down, Monette," said Papa. "My gout."

I tried but my feet would not slow. I needed to be out of there. I was suffocating.

The journey through the house seemed endless. I had to stop at every turning to let Papa and Mistress Mella catch up, so that by the time we reached our porters, Papa near collapsed into the sedan chair and I was about to burst. We had to wait even more until a servant brought our case and the written invitation that would get us through the Quartiere di Fiori gates the next day.

I fidgeted as the case was settled on Papa's lap and the porters lifted his chair. I needed to talk to Papa about the morning—and the visit to come. My hands shook with a mix of terror and excitement. Surely the Lady had shown the ambassador some plausible truth through my hands. My dreams of service and glory were awakening, but at the pleasure of such a man . . .

When the Quartiere di Fiori gates were just in sight at the end of the lane, two rough-looking men burst out of an alley and headed straight for us. Papa's eyes were squeezed shut.

"Papa! Attention! Ruffians!"

Papa glanced up, his face creased in pain. "Fortune's dam. I was hoping you two were close. Get this cursed box off me."

His hands were crushed underneath, trying to hold up its weight.

I slipped around to the side opposite the approaching men.

"Sorry for the delay. We didn't want to be seen," said the blockish older man in a quiet rumble. "Resident family guards patrol every crack and knothole hereabouts."

He mumbled something to the lead porter, who signaled a halt.

The younger of the two men lifted the sample case from Papa's lap. "You look terrible, swordmaster."

"Papa, who are these men?" They did seem familiar. We'd seen them on the way in.

The graying older man peered across the *kieyu* at me. "Gods' hammer!"

Dark curls framed the slim younger man's astonishment. "Demonscat, I didn't recognize her. Never seen her looking so . . . I mean I knew she was decent looking, but I never believed what I heard about her these years. She was just my— What's happened to her hand? Is that blood?"

"Aye. We'll tell you all."

"Would everyone stop talking about me as if I weren't here!" I snapped.

Papa snorted. "You're not. Exactly. One of you'd best give my *daughter* a hand, if you know what I mean."

I edged closer to the jogging chair and squeezed words through my teeth. "Who are they?"

"Bodyguards," he said. "Let me breathe a bit. Don't know which is going to have the better of me, the rib or a damnable woman who gets into the game so deep she frights the piss out of me."

I couldn't believe he would speak about our *game* in front of these two disreputable-looking bodyguards. They were filthy— all dust and torn clothes, what looked like cobwebs in their hair, and their sewer stink would have rats chasing us any moment.

"Excuse me, damizella," said the older man, coming up beside me. He held out his hand in a friendly way. "Name's Dumond."

My hands unavailable due to the needle bag and needle pricks that stung like knife cuts, I just shrugged. "My name is—"

He touched my wrist gently. "*Romy,* I believe."

As if a whirlwind lifted my hair and skin, Monette returned whence she came. Every sight, sound, and understanding of the morning was now visible through my own eyes. Romy's eyes.

"Gracious Spirits!" The shock near laid me flat.

"There's an alehouse off Swagger Alley in the Asylum Ring," said Placidio. "We can get a pitcher or two and a bite before I eat this damnable hat, and privacy enough to have a word. We've a deal to talk about and one journey of the sun till we have to be back."

17

Nearing midday, the watery sun had transformed the busy streets and alleys of the Asylum Ring into a sultry stew. Though yet shivering from shedding magic and Monette, my chemise was damp under my layered garments. Antone's and Vargo's backs were sodden as they lowered Placidio's chair to the ground in a weedy, rubbled yard between two blocks of tenements.

"Tell Vashti's men to wait here, Dumond." Placidio eased himself out of the *kieyu*. "We'll send them food and drink. The way ahead's too narrow for the chair. And though Pix will see to our privacy, we must see to hers."

His hair hung in wet ringlets as he tossed his plumed hat into the *kieyu* and pointed the brass-headed cane farther down the dirt lane. Neri and I followed him in the direction he specified. Dumond followed after relaying Placidio's order in an approximation of the Invidian dialect.

We soon turned into the mouth of a narrow alley.

"Pix?" Neri asked the question sitting on the tip of my tongue. I was glad, for if I spoke a single word, everything stuffed in my head would come gushing out.

Placidio, walking with better ease than I expected, stepped gingerly across a puddle of sewage. "First person I met when I came to Cantagna. Runs an alehouse called the Limping Bull."

We turned into a narrower alley. The chair would not have fit.

Down and around the corner we entered a squeeze between a stone wall and a shingled wall. A few dozen paces in, Placidio reached under a shingle set between a scraped oak door and one of two shuttered windows and pulled out an iron key. Buried in such a maze, the Limping Bull must not rely on customers just wandering in. Not even a painted name identified the place a public tavern.

Once we stepped inside, I understood. We'd either come in the back way, or a side way, or this wasn't a tavern at all.

"Get the shutters, lad."

Neri obediently unlatched shutters covering the empty windows and threw them open. Dusty light from the alley illuminated a high-ceilinged room that smelled of ale and baking. A single long table surrounded by a dozen stools and two small corner tables with two sides of benches each were the entire furnishing. The walls to right and left were covered floor to ceiling with scrawled names, words, and drawings, most of them less than skilled. I'd no wit to decipher their meaning.

Placidio sagged heavily to a corner bench. "Now put the key back where I got it. And Dumond, if you would, step through that door and have one of the lads tell Pix that . . . uh . . . Groaner needs the back room for an hour. And we'd like refreshments sent to our porters out on Gamble Row."

The age- and grease-darkened door Placidio indicated shared a wall that was half paintless shingles and half grimy brick. The low iron door in the brick and the black soot traces on the beaten earth floor suggested the wall was the former outer wall of the house, the brick column the back of a hearth.

"*Groaner?*" Dumond's skeptical question was not accompanied by a snicker, but it was a near thing.

"Pix insists on these names . . ."

Neri squeezed past me and back into the alley to replace the key. Desperately clinging to every word and image of the morning, I didn't join in the talk. I didn't want to forget anything.

Dumond pulled open the inner door. Lively piping, a rattling of tabors, and an avalanche of laughter and conversation spilled into the room, instantly silent again as he pulled the door closed behind himself.

Placidio sighed. "Sit, lady scribe. We're safe here. Pix helps people in trouble, as I was when I ended up here the first time. One can sleep quite well on one of these benches."

I sat on the other bench at his corner table. Numb. Shivering. Clutching my bundled needles and my punctured hand. Trying to arrange everything I'd learned into a cohesive whole.

The door banged open, bringing Dumond with his hands full of brimming ale mugs. The person who followed him in was a blaze of lightning disguised as a substantial woman of indeterminate age. Her bounty of tight black curls billowed in every direction at once, her dangling earrings jingled, and her ample form shot across the room to Placidio with a grace and quickness that no twig-like dancer making a grand leap could have matched.

"Groaner! Too long it's been." She grabbed his sweat-soaked

hair and jiggled his head affectionately. "You look terrible. Fat brandy for you. And your friend—"

In a whirlwind of plum-colored pantaloons, she spun around to me and laid a gentle finger on the bloody linen. "Ouch. You are Thorn, I think."

"No, my name is—"

But she had already yanked open the door and stuck her head into the noise. When she retracted it again, she slammed the door and spun back to me. "Fat brandy coming for Groaner. Basin, bandages, and salve coming for you, Thorn. A friend so delectable . . . has Groaner had his way with you? Mmm, I think not. *Thorns* puncture his armor, so he doesn't allow it. I'll guess you know that. And who is this?"

Pix looked back and forth between me and Neri, who looked half a month from finding his tongue. "I see a part of who you are at least, Sapling, you and Thorn. And you four together make a heady puzzle—which I care nothing about."

Her closed fingers snapped open beside her ears as if to ward away secrets. "Your friend juggling ale can only be Anvil."

She leaned close to the startled Dumond and sniffed. "The sturdy scent will always give you away, though you and Sapling are wearing a costume of stink that makes me think my establishment should offer baths to all comers. Hmm . . ."

She retreated to the inner door. "One of my boys is taking refreshment to your porters, so enjoy your hour, Groaner, Thorn, Anvil, and Sapling. My back room is a place of respite. Whilst you bide, none shall enter but my boys. Groaner, tell whoever made your fine suit that I want pantaloons of the same glorious color—and do not be a stranger to the Bull. It's been too long. Apologies to the rest of you; you're not welcome there."

She vanished back through the door, just as three young men in belted tunics popped through. One, with a braid of startling white hair, deposited a tray of four filled soup bowls and a pitcher of wine on the long table. The other, with a well-trimmed scuff of black beard, set a green stone basin, a roll of bandage, and a crock filled with a gray substance that smelled of honey and onions on the small table beside me. The third, a slight youth with russet curls and merry eyes, set a large gray mug, steaming with the fragrance of brandy, almonds, . . . and butter? . . . on the table beside Placidio. *Fat* brandy?

"Knock if you need more," said the merry, russet-haired youth. "I'll wait on the other side of the door for your hour." Only in the puff of air as the door closed behind the three did I notice that the merry fellow had only one arm and that all three belted tunics were made entirely of ribbons.

Placidio took a long, grateful swallow of the steaming posset and set it back with a thump that signaled business.

"So," he said, "seems we've hooked our fish. But I've a notion Egerik di Sinterolla is no fat, slow codfish, but a spike-toothed shark grabbed onto our line and dragging us into the deeps. What say, Romy? You saw something going on before we even met him or his man Cei. And, by the by, that Cei gave me the cold shudders just like when I wake with the knowing that a match is going to the rough. What was it you saw?"

"Egerik is the monster who devours the sharks," I said. "He doesn't care who sees it, because he believes he's more intelligent than any of the other fish. . . ."

While Neri relieved me of the bundled needles, and Dumond's sure fingers unwrapped my pricked ones and bathed them with the warm water in Pix's basin, I poured out the story of the morning. Interweaving what we'd learned from Lawyer Mantegna's report, I described Egerik's dawn light artwork, and how it provoked the startling reversal of my estimate of the ambassador. "He is intelligent, arrogant, and supremely confident . . . every bit Rossi's equal. If they are playing each other, I'd not know which to back. If they're together, I've no idea where this goes."

"You wanted him to *collect* you?" Neri blurted, horrified. "And you made yourself look so—glowing, sort of. Before you changed back, you were *not* my sister. I never really believed what Placidio said about your magic. At Bawds Field you looked more like you'd eaten a lot of biscuits and gone rolling in Dumond's paint pots."

"I wasn't happy about jumping in so deep," I said after Dumond and Placidio had finished their chortling. "But it came clear right away that Egerik is only impressed by perfection. Monette had to sincerely believe in her power, in her closeness to Lady Fortune, elsewise he would have seen right through her as easily as he saw through our cloth of gold. I decided that if he deemed her beautiful, maybe even came to believe she could fit into this very particular world he makes for himself, then he was more likely to overlook her shady origins. He caught on to Baldassaar's game early on . . ."

Maybe as early as his jibe about the yellow garments, now I looked back.

"And you were successful with the divination?" Dumond dabbed Pix's onion salve on the nine punctures on my hand, and wrapped the clean linen strip around it.

"She was masterful." Placidio set his empty cup on the well-scrubbed pine. "He could not take his eyes off her or her needles. Every word of the saying *meant* something to him, too, though the creeping spider wouldn't yield a spit about why. The casting, the blood . . . don't know how you did it, smith, but you'd set the needles exactly right. You had me believing the Lady's own hand set them to poke her."

Dumond signaled Neri to cut the bandage and tucked the freed end into the wrapping. "A sponge in the bottom of the bag held them steady and spread out while she sliced the bag."

"It was perfect. Monette believed it was the Lady's hand guiding her," I said. "The constant repetitions in practice made it feel natural. Leaving *chaos* beside *spirit* was sheerest luck. I was able to make Monette—myself—take advantage of it, but, divine graces, skulls were not meant to hold two minds at once." Yet Monette's crowding had been far less terrifying than Druda's existence as a splinter floating in a void.

Neri shoved my bowl of soup at me—some delectable mix of beans and garlic, stewed in a little pork fat. The others had already emptied theirs. Astonishing to realize that I was hungry.

"You surprised me when you started talking about the angry spirit," said Placidio. "I don't recall us even thinking about that."

"It was the natalés started it," I said once I'd downed a few spoonfuls. "It's one thing to hang ghiris in the windows, dig the biggest threshold sleugh I've ever seen, and require guests to wash with lemon peel. Cleanliness is one of his priorities, obviously, but he had sea lavender wreathed around every lamp and candle in his chamber—"

"Protection against the angry dead!" Neri, the superstitious, pounced.

"And demons," I added. "Placidio pointed out a natalé

under the washing table, and then I noticed them everywhere—twenty of them at least in that single room, though I've heard nothing about a child's tender soul involved in all of this. Perhaps he just sees them as additional protection for his own soul."

Neri again. "Maybe he and those nobs in Argento killed somebody. You said he was the only one left alive, so maybe he had the others assassinated so they wouldn't tell what wicked things they did there!"

"Mantegna said that the men implicated in the scandal all died *after* Egerik left Argento," I said. "But Egerik bit on the chaotic spirit part of the divination so hard, I thought he was going to bite *me*! He's the one called it *malignant*. So there's something there. Maybe we'll find out more soon; I sent a message to the woman I know at Cuarona's wool commission here in the city. If she'll see me, I'll ask her about diplomatic scandals in her city in the year Egerik left his post."

Dumond sat astride his stool as if intending to ride it to war. "Sounds certain he's feared of the dead."

Neri opened his mouth, but Dumond laid a hand on his shoulder. "We'll get our turn. Let her get out what she saw, while it's fresh."

I appreciated that, even as I gulped half a mug of Pix's ale.

"What did you see through the brass screen?" asked Placidio. "I thought I caught a glimmer behind it."

"It's definitely a squint. Someone could sit back there to watch and listen. It must be open to some other place, as I felt a wafting air. For years I would sit behind a screen and listen to *il Padroné*'s petitioners . . ."

A wave of hurt drowned the moment. When I glanced up,

all three had their eyes fixed on me, waiting for more as if I were finally going to rip open the past. I rarely spoke of those days, and wasn't about to start now.

"That's all I noticed."

Neri was still fidgeting, but Dumond's grip checked him again. "Any clue as to whether Cinque is Egerik's friend or foe?"

I shook my head. "I can't even guess as yet. But the arriving visitor, the dangers from those he's linked to by fealty or oath-swearing or conspiracy—and he said himself that it was more than one person—and the knowledge of crimes or dangerous secrets . . . all touched him, just as Placidio said. The malignant spirit most of all. Rossi may be in for a harsher welcome than he expects."

"This Rossi doesn't care if his Assassins List causes a war," said Dumond, with a kind of horrible indifference. "If your words throw the two of them off kilter then it's good."

"So what's next?" said Placidio. "We've only an hour in this room. Egerik wants Monette back two hours past noon tomorrow, ready to cast again."

"I believe I've planted the uncertainties we wanted in Egerik's head," I said. "That the prisoner is part of a something bigger—some kind of conspiracy that threatens his life. Maybe it's Vizio that worries him, maybe it's Rossi, maybe it's both."

"And he wants you back," said Dumond. "Just what we wanted."

"Indeed. The problem with auguring generalities is that we can glean only generalities in turn. But if he believes an angry dead person behind it all, that could help us, too. What I need now is more information. I've practiced needle casting until my fingers are raw . . . and pricked now, too. I'm confident I can get

Monette to create whatever casting layout I want. But I need some new meat to shape my interpretation."

"Figure out whose ghost scares him, and we can use the tunnels to put a fright into him," said Neri.

"We mustn't forget we're after the Assassins List," said Placidio, "not solving the riddle of Egerik and the spy, nor creating false divinations to fool him. Our mission is to ensure that the list Cinque's got stashed away never gets back to Vizio. Straight and simple."

"That's right," I said. "It's not so important even to know whether Egerik and Rossi are allies or enemies; it could be either. We're trying to disrupt their plans—get them to make a mistake or reveal themselves. That's why I spoke to him of oath swearing and secrets and how it could be one or more people who are the danger to him. If we're there, and we know to watch, we can play them to our best advantage to learn about the list and get to it. So as for what else we do next, I think . . . uneasy as Egerik is . . . some malevolent spirit activity might shake him even more."

"So something shows up where it oughtn't?" said Neri, glancing at Dumond. "With all those natalés . . . a string ball, maybe?"

Placidio looked as confused as I was.

Dumond, though, seemed to grasp the meaning. "I could probably come up with a straw doll. Got a leather ball, a thorn rattle, and knucklebones. Sit behind that screen they were talking of, and toss the knucklebones and that'll shake him."

"Children's playthings!" I said. "A fine idea. Start with one and we'll observe his reaction. I could bring one in my waist pocket."

"Needs to be there before you go," said Neri. "You describe a place, I'll take one in. Move it. Put a second, if there's time. And yes, yes, I'll be careful. So where?"

The answer seemed obvious. "Beside the cloisonné box where he keeps the lock of hair and the ruby ring. Even if those are not his wife's, they're a remembrance of someone. So, a quick in and out?"

He grinned. "Certain. If I can see the thing I want well enough, I don't have to parade through the halls like you did. The harder I work at it, the more direct I can go. When I stole those rubies last year, I walked from the street straight into the illuminator's chamber."

He didn't need me to remind him that the *harder he worked at it*, the quicker he would deplete his talents—or that rash decisions could have life-changing effects. *Those rubies* had cost our father his hand.

"All right then." Using a charred stick that had clearly been used for such before, I sketched the plan of Egerik's reception chamber in one of the few bare spots on Pix's wall. I described it in exacting detail as I drew. And then I sketched the shelf under the windows and the glass candle lamps, the brass hand-bell, and the cloisonné box. Neri recited it all back to me.

"Egerik doesn't want Baldassar there," said Placidio when we rejoined him and Dumond. "Wants to buy him off. Buy *her*, maybe—have his own diviner right alongside his own whatever this Cei is. I'm not sleeping at Dumond's tonight, so I'll need you, lad, to fetch my sleeve knife and my boot knife before we meet tomorrow."

"I will," said Neri, "and your sword, too, and have it ready to bring to you. I could stay on to help, as well, if the dire comes.

But certain, we need a signal, so I'll know which to do. Maybe an explosion like last time?"

Only Neri's ferocious exuberance could have sparked smiles in the face of such a mission.

"Going to set you to work on signals," said Placidio with a quick laugh. "Explosions may be a bit too noticeable. I'll think on it this afternoon."

"Moving on to another subject before Neri gets overheated," said Dumond. "The lad and I had a fruitful exploration. There's no unguarded crevice within three streets on any side of Palazzo Ignazio, so if you're being chased out of the house—or need to extract a prisoner—there's no safe route for you to get free. We came near getting caught more times than I've got daughters."

"But there's tunnels," said Neri.

"Aye, and we found that tunnel that goes right between the kitchen house and main house like on the map. Got into it from a cave Neri knew off in the rough. Seems to be well shored up, but we don't know what's beyond the kitchen house, nor whether it goes all the way to the palazzo cellars. Looks like a dead end, but we didn't push our luck. It's pitch down there and the map shows a maze of tunnels we could get lost in. We'll need better light than we can make from magic, seeing as how we don't want to get ourselves too used up to do the more important things. I'm off to fetch my paints and a lantern. We're going back this afternoon to fix a safe way out for you two and the prisoner if need be."

"Well done," I said. "Do the tunnels go beyond the Palazzo Ignazio grounds?"

"The map says we should be able to get all the way to the Merchant Ring. We found where we think it must have come out at one time—a part of the Merchant Ring wall that's collapsed and been repaired over time. The wall foundation might block that end and be too thick for my simple door magic to penetrate. But I've another method might work."

The metalsmith drained his mug of ale as if girding his loins for battle. "Between now and time for you to go in, certain, I can fix us a trapdoor where you can find it in the ambassador's kitchen yard for getting down to the tunnel, and another in a good place to exit. It will just take us some time to figure out where. But we did find something more . . ."

Dumond gestured for Neri to take another turn.

"Bodies!" said Neri. "Corpses . . . hundreds . . . thousands of them down there."

"Plague bones," said Dumond. "None that's new."

"Maybe that's why Egerik's got the willies." Neri's color was high. "Maybe he has relatives down there. Or he could have hid one *under* them."

A tap on the inner door and the cheerful, russet-haired youth poked his head in. "The glass has turned, noble Groaner. You know the rules."

"Indeed so. Express my thanks to Pix yet again."

"Fortune's benefice upon you all."

"Virtue's hand, Guide." Placidio reached for his cane.

"So we have our tasks," I said. "I hunt more information on what Egerik and Rossi are up to—or ways I can shape a divination to find out. Neri spooks Egerik with playthings. Dumond fixes our way out and maybe finds out if there's some route between the house and the tunnels, just in case we can't get out to the garden. And Placidio rests his injuries so Papa Baldassar won't melt into a puddle because his belly aches."

"It's just the cursed rib," said Placidio, "unless someone sets a lead-weight chest on my gut. Do you all know the olive grove next to the Quartiere di Lustra boundary?"

"It's where we met before we did our thieving at Palazzo Fermi." No surprise Neri would remember. That had been the night he first used his magic in a purpose beyond his own desires, a deed of daring and courage.

"That's it. Be there in the morning an hour before midday. Neri can bring my weapons, and we can all report on our tasks."

All agreed.

Placidio pushed himself to standing. "The grove's not so far from Palazzo Ignazio and Egerik," he said, "yet it'll not reveal our destination should any of us pick up a follower. I had a sense on our way over here . . ."

The swordmaster scratched his head, exhaled long and slow, and glanced round at the three of us. "Likely it's naught but Lady Fortune's stepchild breathing cold down my neck. Were it not for all of you—I never knew the gift could be offered, as you did. It's something to add if we were ever to create our own book of lore."

Neri and Dumond's faces reflected my own somber understanding. Placidio had just admitted that his wound had been as dangerous as we'd feared. Lady Fortune's stepchild was Death.

"We're glad you're still with us," I said.

Placidio and Dumond walked out to the alley still confirming details of Egerik's kitchen yard. Neri hung back as I wiped my needles and returned them to the new bag Dumond had ready for them.

"I don't like the sound of this Egerik," he said, "or you going back there with Placidio not at his best."

"I don't like it either," I said. "But even hampered as he is, Placidio has his magic. He'll sense a move coming, and he understands how to fight when he's hurt."

"He should never agree to a duel without referees. He can afford the fees."

But it wasn't the cost. We both knew why Placidio agreed to go without referees if the other party was willing. He wanted to be free to use his magic to control the outcome of the duel. The more familiar with Placidio's fighting, the more likely an observant referee would become suspicious of his uncanny ability.

I flashed a smile at Neri as I tied the needle bag to my belt. "Just think, we might save a thousand lives tomorrow. Then we can go back to scribing and tossing drunkards at the Duck's Bone. But I wonder . . ."

Both Egerik and Rossi were so smug. So confident.

"There is something more to all this. It's been weighing on me since I came back to myself. I just . . . I have this sense that Egerik is more than a simple conduit of dangerous information, more than a bribe or an extortion attempt waiting to happen so Cinque the spy can go free. I wish I knew what he was."

I had shoved the feeling aside because the four of us had so much we had to get straight. The fires, the momentary art. Cei. The vacant plinth, adorned with a rose, a knife, and a drop of blood. None of these were accidental. And then there were the reports of *salacious activities* in Argento. Some connection was lurking in the back of my mind, but I couldn't put a name to it.

"I know someone who might be able to explain whatever

this is that makes Egerik cocky beyond his wealth and position. I hope to find out what that is."

"I'll be in that tunnel," said Neri. "Won't rest till you're out. And I'll come looking if you don't. Just wish we had some kind of magic to signal when you need help."

"A magical messenger bird," I said, as he pulled the Limping Bull's back door shut. "That would be fine. When we finish this, we'll work on it. For now, just be there. I'm counting on it."

As Pix's lock clicked behind us Neri raced after Dumond, who awaited him at the corner of the alley. Placidio had made it about half that far. I joined him, and we watched Neri disappear around the corner.

"I want to trust him," I said.

"He's a good lad."

"Thanks to you."

"You gave him a purpose, plus a bit of adventure, which is a fine thing. Did the same for all of us."

I didn't know what to say to that, so I moved on to the mundane. "You're going to rest until we meet tomorrow, right?"

"I told Dumond to send the *kieyu* and the bearers home. Thought to go round the corner to the Limping Bull proper. Now don't get your back up . . . I'm not going drinking."

Clearly his eyesight was not impaired.

"Pix has some beds that are better than the back room benches. Thought to sleep a bit. The gut is merely tender, believe it or no. The magic works. Can't put salts and fire to bone, though, even with the magic, so I've no remedy for the rib but time and sleep. I can do what needs done."

"I need to introduce you to Teo. I'll swear his broken nose and ankle healed overnight. And no, I've not told him about us—

or about you. No names. Nothing of any of our magic. I truly believe he's no threat. But he's gone now, and I don't think he's coming back. He took offense at the candles around his bed. Wouldn't say why."

Placidio's head did not turn, or did he speak, but he could have. I could read my swordmaster at least as well as he could me. Someday, I would have it out of him.

We walked slowly toward the alley corner. "Pix is interesting."

"Mmm."

That humming grunt signaled another barrier. I didn't interrupt his weighty silence.

"About the fish man," he said at last. "If he returns and you feel . . . discomforted . . . in any way, bring him to me at the Bull."

This was deeper than just a man asserting his protective notions about females. I preferred handling problems of my own making myself, but in this case there was legitimate reason to question my own judgment. And a size issue. Even wounded as he was, Placidio could likely tie Teo into a knot.

"I will."

"And lest the event, I'll show you the way to the Bull's *front* door."

We turned into the corner of the tidy alley. Placidio was indeed moving more easily.

"Why does Cei gave you the shudders?" I said. "Monette thought him *very* attractive. Did you notice that Egerik never spoke to him? Never even looked at him."

Perfect. Unblemished. Had those been Monette's observations or my own, so strong as to break through the magic? Certain, I shared the unsettled feeling that came after, thinking of Egerik the collector.

Placidio paused, leaning on the horse-head cane, a thoughtful frown shadowing his face. "Don't know exactly what got under my skin. The way he never looked at *us*, maybe. The way he moved so quiet—more than the others. No shoes. Groomed to his eyelashes. Have you ever seen a wolf who's been tamed to the leash?"

I shook my head.

"They're not. Tamed, I mean. They're always wild no matter how well they heel. Look in their eyes and you'll know."

"I can see that. Yes." Maybe that was what bothered me as well. Several things bothered.

"Back in Egerik's chamber," I said, "did you see the items left on the plinth in that gold-lined alcove?"

"Rib didn't approve turning round all that much."

I picked at Pix's bandage on my hand. "It was an odd arrangement. The more I've thought about it, the more I believe I've seen something like before. Something that gives me the willies, as Neri would put it. A single budding rose, a small, very sharp, narrow-bladed knife with a curved tip, and a drop of blood. Does that mean anything to you?"

We rounded the corner, stepping carefully between a fetid puddle and a bold rat chewing on something unidentifiable.

"Nay. But from everything else I saw in that house, I'd guess it means something very particular to the ambassador. Maybe that lawyer could make some more inquiries for us."

"Mantegna must remain a last resort. But I've an idea of someone else to ask. Not sure I can get to him . . . or if he's still where I think he is . . . or if he'll even see me. But whatever's nagging isn't going to let me loose until I get an answer. So rest well, swordmaster, and I'll see you tomorrow morning."

The Palazzo Segnori bells began their noontide clangor.

I left him frowning, and had gone only a few steps when he called after me. "But where are you going? Someone ought to know."

I returned and folded my arms in front of me, considering. "I'll tell you, if you'll tell me why you are allowed to patronize the Limping Bull and the rest of us are not."

He donned his I-really-don't-like-your-prying expression. "All you want's the reason?"

"Yes. And then I'll tell you where I'm going to find out about the rose and the knife."

He wrestled with it. "All right. Only duelists are allowed inside. Working ones like me. Or retired. Crippled. Traveling. No students. None that's unregistered. Every city has a place. We like it kept private."

"That makes good sense." There were a number of people a duelist wouldn't want intruding on an hour of relaxation. Angry clients out to avenge a loss. Upstarts who hadn't yet made the Dueling List thinking to make a name for themselves. Vengeful families.

"To find it just go farther down the lane to the next alley past this one—that's Swagger Alley. No signboard, but the Bull's got a blue door. I'll tell Pix to fetch me if you show up. Now you."

"I'm going back to the Moon House."

18

The ancient sweet chestnut tree shading the stone bench where I waited was so large the four partners of the Chimera together could not have wrapped our linked arms around its bole. Rich green moss blanketed its gnarled roots and had crept into the deep folds of its bark.

The chestnut grew in a green swale at the western edge of the Merchants Ring—a bit of countryside in the city. It overlooked a string of tranquil ponds where water birds posed and floated. On the hillside across the swale, just past a stone fence, sat a small but elegant house of pale ocher stone.

Few who sought tranquility at the Domata Ponds or marched their wedding processional along the gravel paths to ensure their future prosperity likely knew what went on in that serene setting. Inside those vine-draped walls, young unblemished girls and boys, taken from the streets or bought from desperate families, were stripped of their names, groomed, and educated in seemly and unseemly ways to become treasured companions for the wealthy. Tutors used willow switches, confinement, isolation, deprivation, and pain of any kind that would not mar the body to teach them everything from how to clean their teeth and sweeten their breath to writing in each of the classic forms of poetry.

Once I left that house at fifteen, it had taken me only a few months of Sandro's gentle tutelage to gain a true joy in learning. What a waste that so much of worth had been forced down my throat with pain.

The Moon House. Never had I thought to return there.

The harsh clanging of a handbell signaled midday. For the next two hours, everyone would be occupied in the refectory, younger students serving a meal to the older, older students serving the tutors, so all could learn how to present or eat delicacies they hadn't even known existed. Proctors would observe, ready with their willow switches.

One of the senior tutors had always elected to take his midday meal in his own chambers. He disliked the hammering instruction, and the inevitable shouting, tears, and whippings that destroyed what he believed should be a peaceful time. His objection always seemed a bit ridiculous, since he was the House Disciplinarian, the one who administered true beatings for egregious offenses like hitting a tutor or scarring another student. The Disciplinarian also served as the instructor in some of the more distasteful of the unseemly arts. Moon House courtesans were precious and valued, but they were also expected to fulfill their owners' every desire with grace and obedience.

Wrapping my red-and-black gown in Vashti's sober black cape, I left my bench and hurried up the gravel path to a place where a marshy gully had undermined the stone wall before I'd been brought here. I wasn't sure whether the Moon House Grand Mistress and her staff had simply neglected to repair the wall, or had decided that the public punishments of students who used it to run away were more useful than preventing the violation.

With a silent apology to Vashti, I hiked up the muddy hem of my gown and traversed the marsh from stone to stone, then followed a path through the animal yards and kitchen garden to the musty stone stair that led to the main house basement. Four times in my five years at the Moon House, I had used this path to sneak a visit to my family. Twice I'd been successful in escaping detection. Twice not.

This time I scurried up the students' stair to the top floor, hoping to elude unwanted gossip, rather than punishment. I ghosted past the deserted chambers of those tutors and proctors occupied in the refectory, to the corner of the house overlooking the Domata Ponds. A brass plate bearing the single ominous label DISCIPLINARIAN centered the otherwise unadorned door.

Rather than inviting a refusal, I opened the door softly and walked inside. A spider-limbed man in soft gray hose and charcoal-hued doublet sat in a comfortable chair beside the open window. He looked up from his reading. The neatly trimmed hair and beard that framed his narrow face were grayer than I recalled, but the keen eyes glared quite as ferociously as they always had.

"You may turn around and leave as quietly and quickly as you entered, young woman." The crisp articulation of his thoughts had not changed either.

"Proctor Nuccio." I lowered the hood of the cheap cape and

unfastened its clasp. I deemed Vashti's red-and-black gown would give me a better hearing, muddy hem and all. "Excuse my intrusion. I am a former—"

"Cataline! So you're not—"

"Dead? No. But consider me a phantasm who will vanish without trace before the interval is over. Forgive my intrusion on your hour of peace."

Proctor Nuccio, a decent sort of man considering his profession, had wept when he told me that Lodovico di Gallanos, an infamous degenerate, had bought me. Though required to give me special tutelage of several unpleasant sorts at Lodovico's request, he had been, as ever, considerate and impersonal. He believed it depraved to take advantage of his position.

On that terrible day, he had consoled me that I was intended as a gift for Lodovico's nephew, Alessandro, assuming the young man survived the multitudinous plots against his life, and assuming Lodovico actually released me to the nephew once he had his hands on me. That hour and the two days following had been the worst of my life, and yet, like Mother Gione's agonies as she gave birth to the world, they were the doorway to the best.

"My curiosity is unbounded," he said. "Be seated, if you will."

I perched on the stool that was the only other seating accommodation in his chamber.

In the days of my schooling, visits here had never encouraged me to take note of Nuccio's chamber. It was as spare as the man himself. Bare wood floors, polished to a high sheen. A book chest, its simple domed lid strapped with leather and elegantly wrought bronze buckles. A small writing table.

A single artwork hung on his cream-colored walls—the

painting of a beautiful, richly dressed young Lhampuri woman
and an equally beautiful man who was kissing her breast as he
disrobed her. A second beautiful young man in the bloody rags
and chains of a slave yearned in the shadows. The work was
glorious in its line and color—and in its heart-wrenching emotion.

"A phantasm, you say?"

"Mistress Cataline is indeed dead, by declaration of her
master," I said. "I now bear a different name and am employed
elsewhere. My new mistress"—I liked thinking of the Chimera
that way—"takes great interest in matters of importance to our
city."

His expressive brows lifted. "I'm fascinated. Go on."

"At her direction, I have introduced myself to a man of very
particular tastes, which I am trying to understand without asking him directly. I'm not certain these tastes fall into categories
in which you enlightened me as a student, but I decided that as
one who studies personal behaviors, you might be able to provide the answers I need."

"You are a *spy*?"

"Would that distress you, Proctor?" Even as my stomach
clenched, I maintained the steady deportment this school taught
so well. Every man and woman of means in Cantagna employed
spies.

His lips pursed as they do when disguising a smile. "You
were a bright student, talented in many ways that would lend
themselves to such a profession, as well as the profession we
prepared you for. I'm simply consumed with curiosity as to the
path that took you from Alessandro di Gallanos's bed to such
work."

"*That* is a most private matter, Proctor, and as anything which touches the Shadow Lord of Cantagna, I would advise you forget your curiosity as quickly as I've raised it. I've been told that he . . . reacts badly . . . if my name is spoken in his presence."

Dare I imagine I saw the cool gentleman swallow his gorge?

"Absolutely," he said. "Already forgotten. Be certain of that. So, to your question?"

"I have visited the home of the wealthy gentleman I mentioned. His house is quite fine, immaculate and tasteful, crafted to please in every detail—to please himself, I concluded, even more than his guests. His servants are every one of them dignified, respectful, and exceptionally handsome, both male and female. In a place usually reserved for statuary, entirely unconnected to our business, I noticed an unusual decorative arrangement. It nags at me, for reasons I cannot fathom. I don't believe it was put there for my benefit. If I'd not taken an opportunity to explore the room before the gentleman entered, I'd never have noticed it, which lends it an extra aura of mystery."

Nuccio laid his book aside, propped his elbows on the arms of his chair, and rested his chin on a steeple of his slim fingers. "Most intriguing."

"The display consisted of a single, stemmed rose—fresh, not dried or wilted—and a narrow-bladed knife with a curved tip. Beside these two was a single drop of fresh blood. My initial reaction was that this was some careless clutter left from an accident. Yet the gentleman was not careless in any fashion. Thus, the more I considered it . . ."

I let the pause hang in the air, thinking Nuccio might take up my sentence. The mention of the rose had already changed his expression. He knew exactly of what I spoke. Yet he remained motionless, save that the tips of his steepled fingers moved to his lips. Was he deciding what to tell me?

His hands settled to his lap. "Why is this odd matter important enough to bring you *here*? Few who leave the Moon House can be persuaded to return for any reason."

Had it been any other of my tutors or proctors, I would have made up a story. But so many years of detecting falsehoods had made the Moon House disciplinarian expert at it.

"I'm not permitted to tell you, Proctor, but I would ask you to believe me that the safety of hundreds of people, entire families—could turn on the character of this man. I need to understand him."

"Hundreds. Truly?" No horror laced his words. Only his usual cool remoteness.

"I speak of grave consequences, Proctor. If what you tell me"—and more and more I believed he could tell me something—"might lead to understanding, I ask you to speak it. Elsewise keep your information as you will. I dared reveal myself to you because I believed you had some sense of honor about you. You did not revel in cruelty as some of your confederates do, so I thought perhaps the prospect of innocent deaths might induce you to answer."

He chuckled, a bit grotesque coming from a man who had beaten me to agony twice without breaking my skin.

"Oh, Cataline—or whatever you call yourself now—I'm astonished you didn't find yourself a place among our independency's finest diplomats. What a life you must have had these years to instill such skills atop those we built inside you."

I reined in my impatience. "Excuse me if I am not grateful for my schooling, Proctor. Can you—will you—answer my question or no?"

My spirit flinched as he rose and crossed the room to a tall, shallow wooden cabinet standing flat against the wall. Behind its single door were hung his canes and other implements of discipline. The right half of the cabinet was a stack of shallow drawers. He picked something out of the topmost drawer and brought it to me—a heavy ring he dropped in my hand.

He returned to his chair as I turned the heavy ring to view its face. A starkly simple design. Three words—*ad sublimi quaerere*—surrounding a rose, a knife with a curved tip, and a single tiny ruby.

"To seek the exquisite," I said, and inhaled sharply as I recalled Mantegna's report of Egerik's fraternal associations.

A glance up and Nuccio affirmed my translation. "This is a token of a society known as the Brotherhood of the Exquisite."

"And this ring is yours?"

"Yes."

Spirits, did he *know* Egerik? My confidence that I'd found a clever remedy for our ignorance . . . my certainty that a visit to this benighted place held no dangers . . . my naive view of this man . . . all came collapsing about my head as if the monster Dragonis had chosen this day to rage against his imprisonment under the earth. I had endangered us all.

"Many Cantagnans take pleasure in a search for the sublime," said Nuccio, "in art, in food, drink, music. In every human endeavor. Certain, your former master does so."

"But he's not—" I snapped my mouth closed. I would not speak of Sandro.

The corners of Nuccio's thin mouth twitched. "Be easy. Though I am sworn by the most serious consequences not to speak of other members of the Brotherhood, I allow myself the freedom to say who is not. *Il Padroné* is not and has never been. Though, in truth, few members present anything to the group to which a woman of the world like you would object."

I wasn't sure I liked Nuccio calling me a woman of the world—his world.

"*Il Padroné's* uncle was a member, but was expelled, as his search for the sublime took some very dark turns. Exquisite pain and exquisite suffering can certainly bring enlightenment just as can the evening light on a perfectly arranged garden, or the taste of a single quail egg poached in espina leaves and dusted with saffron. But Lodovico got very messy. No subtlety. No care. So we dismissed him. Coincidentally, fortunately, he died before he could take the vengeance he threatened."

That was where I had seen the symbol before. In Lodovico's chambers. Lodovico had died of poison in his soup a year after giving me to Sandro. No perpetrator was ever discovered.

I glanced up at Nuccio, whose fingers were again matched tip to tip under his chin. Interested and amused.

If Egerik was a man of Lodovico's ilk . . . and Nuccio, too, was one of them . . .

A frisson of terror spidered through my limbs. Did the Brotherhood dabble in *exquisite* assassination? Did they eliminate those who compromised their brothers in the fraternity? Or foolish people who were too curious about their activities?

"I should go," I said, rising from the stool and fumbling with my cloak. "I've no wish to compromise your associates. Perhaps this person is but an aspirant to your society."

I dropped the ring in his hand.

"Perhaps so," he said, turning the ring so the ruby gleamed in the sunlight. "Leave if you wish. But I doubt I know the man you speak of, if that's what concerns you. I was not born a wealthy man and my position here has not made me one. The most exquisite objects and experiences of this world are often quite expensive. The Brotherhood is not so welcoming of those who lack the wherewithal to share their new experiences of the exquisite with the other members. Thus, I've not been an active participant for a decade."

And Egerik had lived in Cantagna only three years.

"Besides, your description fits at least half the members I know—which is a very small part of the Brotherhood. Come, ask me your questions. What I hear will not go beyond this room. It is amusing to deal with matters that are not students who fail to keep control of themselves."

I hardened my lips against instinctive bitterness and my quaking spirit against the desire to run. The information was important. If Nuccio was lying and intended to expose me to Egerik, leaving would not stop him. And I'd no other resources.

"All right." I returned to the stool. "Why would this man have displayed the symbol of rose, knife, and blood in his inner chamber?"

"To pique your curiosity, perhaps, if he suspects this intriguing avocation of yours. Usually it serves as a message to others who have occasion to visit the room. A notice to the like-minded. Or a reminder to the subjects of his passion."

"His passion for exquisite things—or persons?"

Nuccio smiled proudly, as if I were reciting my lesson back to him or demonstrating the efficacy of his punishments. "Our passion is to *experience* the exquisite—sublime perfection, especially fragile perfection—in all its forms. A rose at full bloom is already dying. Its perfection occurs in only a very few moments between bud and bloom. For some of us, experiencing sublime perfection is a way to rouse emotions and sensations that are otherwise out of reach."

"So it is not the mere viewing of a beautiful painting or sculpture . . ."

"Sometimes the object itself creates the experience of the sublime—eating the saffroned quail's egg or hearing the lutenist fill the air with a perfect melody or seeing a Moon House courtesan dance. Sometimes performing the melody on the lute for oneself yields the sublime experience, or *preparing* a dish of such perfection does it. And sometimes it is *owning* the painting or owning the quail who produces such fat and perfect eggs . . . or owning the lutenist."

His description brought to mind Egerik's chamber of sunlight and mosaic and silk threads—not simply a moment of perfect art, but of knowing that a guest could be in the room and miss it, and only he, Egerik, would know.

"Sometimes it is even more than owning," I said. "Sometimes the pleasure is in *mastery* of the beautiful thing or person."

"Indeed so. As I taught you here in these chambers."

"Yes," I said, half to myself.

How had I not seen that Cei was an expression of this same mastery? Egerik had collected Cei. Flattered him, perhaps. Lured him. Groomed him. Tamed him like a wolf, as Placidio said. And then . . .

"One who relishes mastery might take delight in reminding his subject of their relative positions," I said.

"Certainly. *Subtlety* is an intrinsic element of experiencing the exquisite, as well. Nuance can often make the difference between the sublime and the merely satisfactory."

Every time Cei passed through Egerik's chamber, he would see the rose and the knife and the blood, a reminder of his master's passion. And when Egerik ignored him, was that yet another reminder? *You are nothing,* it would say. *Even your beauty cannot make me look at you. You still lack perfection.* Had he done that with his beautiful wife, as well? Possessed her. Groomed her. And then ignored her?

"Some of your fellows' searches could lead into very complex games," I guessed. "Sometimes harsh."

"Indeed so. And if a member invites a group of his brothers to witness the fruits of his search for the sublime, they are obliged to agree. Without judgment. Which is why the matter of Lodovico di Gallanos's expulsion is still a tender wound with many in the society. I sorely miss most of the experiences I shared while active in the Brotherhood, but a few took me places that I did not enjoy—despite what you may think of me. Here at the Moon House, I teach survival. I take no pleasure in physical torment or death, no matter how exquisite the design of the experience or how beautiful the subject."

"Death!"

Furrows on Nuccio's brow deepened. "I never saw such, but I've heard stories. The rules don't forbid it, in the way they forbid even the remotest taint of sorcery. Violations of *that* rule will reap a most significant consequence in any reputable chapter of the Order. The other members have reputations, families, public positions that cannot be compromised."

Egerik's overweening confidence, his contempt, his delight

in manipulation of his servants and his guests hinted that he would see no problem with death or torture if it satisfied his passion. Certain, a man who shaped a room in his house for a single moment's pleasure twice a year would not be bothered by the ephemeral nature of the experience. His wife had died within months of his arrival in Cantagna three years since—and she was reputedly a great beauty. Grotesque and horrid as it seemed . . .

"Proctor, you said you were not a member three years ago."

"I was not. And lest you ask, besides being forbidden to reveal other members, we may not reveal any experience we've had as members to outsiders, whether or not that experience is entirely lawful. I'll not break my word on that. Someday Lady Fortune might send her luck my way, and I would prefer to be a former member in good standing." He twirled the gold ring and set it beside his book.

"I ask for no names, no violation of such an oath. But this: if you were to speak to some you know and find out if these acquaintances shared an *exquisite* experience of murder in the summer three years since, could you let me know? Just whether or not it happened. I must understand this man. He's the key. I'll swear that what I've told about my purpose here is true."

"To prevent a siege of murder. Truly?" I had never seen—never imagined—Nuccio indecisive. "I don't know . . ."

I couldn't let this opportunity slip away. I hurried over to his writing desk, unstoppered the ink, and wrote *Box 1 at the L'Scrittóre shop on the Beggars Ring Road.*

"Send the answer—as much as you can give—here."

19

As I hiked the gravel path past the Domata Ponds, I wanted nothing more than to forget everything I'd just learned about the Brotherhood of the Exquisite. I comprehended people who spent their lives pursuing new expressions of beauty in architecture, poetics, or sculpture. Exploring the refinements of law or governance or viticulture also struck me as worthy endeavors. Even my own difficult experience had roots one could understand. Though I could never approve the Moon House goal of enforced submission, seeking new delights in the arts of companionship or lovemaking held intrinsic merit.

But how hollow was a life, how profligate a waste of minds and talents was it, to pursue perfection for its own sake? A quail's egg . . . truly? A single instant's artistic glory in a cold, empty chamber? And to seek out some kind of a *perfect* exhibition of torture or death was too grotesque to contemplate.

Hearing that even this appalling Brotherhood had limits soothed me a little. Surely Nuccio had just told me that the lunatic fraternity was responsible for the death of Lodovico di Gallanos. Knowing what I did of Lodovico's depraved pastimes, I could not call such an execution wanton murder. So what of Egerik? Mantegna's letter said he had left Argento eight years ago because of a salacious scandal, and the other men involved were all of them dead soon after Egerik's departure. Was it possible the local Brotherhood executed them for some horrible offense, missing only Egerik because he'd run away? I should read Mantegna's letter again.

Placidio was correct that our sole objective was to prevent the Assassins List from reaching Protector Vizio, but at the moment it seemed equally important to wipe the smirk from Egerik's face. I doubted it was plague victims buried under his house that stoked his fear of malignant spirits. Perhaps it was a guilty conscience.

I needed to go home, settle my mind, and consider how to incorporate the exquisite into a new divination.

When I reached the Merchants Ring market, I headed downhill, threading the colorful displays of heaped spices, silk scarves, and glass and bronze natalés. Why did Egerik populate his house with grave talismans for children? Now there was fodder for a divination, if only I could guess the answer.

A sudden crush of shoppers flooded the narrow lane from farther down, bumping a comb seller's flimsy table and spilling a fruit vendor's baskets of raspberries. No smoke billowed behind the crowd. No one seemed particularly panicked, only somberly determined to be somewhere farther uphill.

Reluctant to backtrack and take a longer way around, I strolled onward into the Piazza Vasaio. The small courtyard, fragrant with pots of flowers and lemon trees, was surrounded by shops filled with fine pottery, glass, and silverwork. This had been one of my favorite markets in the heady years of my residence in *il Padroné*'s home.

The piazza was almost deserted, a number of shops shuttered. Ordinarily, wealthy shoppers and prosperous traders crowded Vasaio at midday. Curious, I strolled over to an open stall, shaded by an awning. The potter was surveying the piazza as she pumped the heavy treadle and smoothed her spinning clay.

"Where is everyone?" I said, as I examined the pots and cups on the shelves lining her back wall. "The day's fine."

"See for yourself." Her finger, gray with watered clay, pointed around the piazza. "There's one over there by Philomene's. Another straight acrost. More in the Quartiere dell Alba, so I've heard."

I peered through the dappled light. Foxes were ever-present city creatures, known to frighten children, and a mad dog could empty a street. Once a wild boar had charged into the Beggars Ring through an open gate, killed two children, and knocked over a barrel fire that burnt half a quartiere.

The pair that emerged from the shop she indicated explained everything. A muscular woman wearing a bilious-green tabard and carrying an axe led a tall, thin sniffer into the piazza by a chain linked to her belt.

My body quivered with the compulsion to turn tail and run. But I dared not. The potter wasn't at all frightened. One shout, one questioning finger pointed at me . . .

"Two sniffers abroad in this one piazza?" I said, proud my voice did not shake. "More in the neighborhood? Has there been another incident?"

The previous autumn a sorcerer had caused an explosion that had killed fifty-three citizens. He had been captured and sent to the Executioner to be drowned, while the Cantagnese aristocrat who'd hired him had been beheaded in a public execution. The only felon more despised than a sorcerer was the one who suborned a sorcerer to his plots.

The potter splashed water on her spinning clay. "Don't know if they heard of something happened or only found the track. Peccio the glassblower told me they traced a magical stink to *il Padroné*'s own house."

My knees jellied. Sandro's house! No, no, it couldn't be . . . Not even a month had passed since I, disguised by magic, had walked into that house to deliver the strange bronze statue to the grand duc of Riccia.

"By the Mother," I said, "is *il Padroné* harmed?"

Last autumn's explosion had been meant to kill him. And even the Shadow Lord was subject to the First Law. Had someone got wind of the Chimera—his own hireling sorcerers?

"Unharmed, bless 'im," she said, smoothly transforming the lumpish clay on her wheel into a graceful urn, a skill that must once have seemed magical. "I heard he were shuffled off to safety when the nullifiers barged in."

Dumond believed magical residue did not linger past a day, but who really knew? Neri and I had tried to detect traces of magic on each other before, during, and after using magic, with and without Dumond's luck charms nearby. Only with a touch of flesh during the work itself could we sense another's magic. As Dumond surmised, there must be something—some sensation, sound, or odor—that enabled sniffers to do so.

I needed to be away from here. Not three hours had passed

since I'd used my magic in Palazzo Ignazio. And even now, Neri and Dumond were using their extraordinary skills in the center of the city, not all that far away.

"The Twins protect us all, if even *il Padroné* is at risk," I said.

The woman's fingers shaped a pouting lip on her urn. "*I've* naught to fear. Animals they are, these sniffers, like hounds what stay on the scent till they catch the demons. Certain, no spawn of Dragonis can pass my wards."

Ropes of prickly juniper hung around her awning and twined around its posts. But, of course, I was standing under that awning with no ill effects.

"Bad luck when sorcerers are about," I said, drifting toward the front of her stall. "I don't know whether to expect the hellish monster to burst through the ground or the city to be flattened by another explosion."

My eyes raked the quiet piazza for the quickest route to get me away as the potter droned on.

". . . bad omens of late. Three men washed up dead to the docks four nights ago. Two swans found headless at the Ucelli yestermorn. And today morn these monsters slither about chasing demons. Summat terrible's in the wind, no doubt."

"Fortune's continued benefice, Mistress Potter," I said, poised for flight, "and for Cantagna, as well."

She bobbed her head. "Virtue's grace."

Sweat beaded my back as I strolled out of the potter's stall, past the shuttered glassmaker's shop and a cobbler's stall. One of the brick arches that marked the boundaries of Piazza Vasaio lay just ahead. A neat signboard read SCALA CIONDOLANTE. The Dangling Stair, a set of worn and very steep steps, led straight down from Piazza Vasaio to the Market Ring Gate.

The day had gone quiet. Conversations had retreated behind walls. Tradesmen lunched indoors. Children and elders had vanished from stoops and benches as if winter frost had dropped down on us out of season.

As if straight from my own horror, a wordless screech split the quiet from a jumble of houses and shops just beyond the piazza boundaries.

I clutched the luck charm in my waist pocket as I walked briskly through the boundary arch, watching my step on the crumbling stair like the other stragglers. A water carrier. Two prosperous-looking clerks in starched ruffs and tall hats. A woman carrying a bolt of gray wool. Perhaps ten others in sight farther down.

A second howl arrowed from the piazza directly behind me.

"Must have a demon on the run," shouted one of the clerks, a gleeful, ruddy-cheeked young man, holding his hat as he took the steps two at a time on his way up to the piazza.

"Maybe we should wait," said the other clerk, huffing to keep up. "Don't want to get too close." His pleated trousses flapped as he jogged after his friend.

I stayed my course downward, away from the confrontation.

"Come on, ma." A boy with tight-crimped hair tugged at a reluctant young matron halted in the middle of the way. "There could be fireworks! Or monsters. Or the sorcerer could get a foot chopped!"

"'Tis evil," she said. "Demon's work."

"Papa would take me. He says it's good to see the law do its duty."

The mother ascended another step lest the boy tear her sleeve off.

"Don't do it," I said as I trudged around them. "Stay away. It's naught for a child to see."

The woman glanced at me, the beads on her woven cap quivering.

"Out the way! Out the way!" The clerk in the pleated trousses had reversed course and near bowled the mother, the boy, and me over as he stumbled down the steps, retracing his path.

I spun around. A howling sniffer raced down from the piazza, the nullifier on his heels, the chain leash between them rattling on the broken stone. The eager clerk had flattened himself to a house front, leaving no one else between me and the green, silk-sheathed finger pointing my way.

"*Esse ancora, lo spirito maligno!*" yelled a graveled voice—the nullifier, commanding the demon sorcerer to be still.

Paralyzing terror exploded through limbs and veins. My feet would not move.

The screech of a second sniffer came from the crowded streets to my right. Closer than before. Closing in. My lungs refused to pump.

The descending sniffer slowed, its howl reduced to a growling moan, its hands raised with fingers spread as if sensing magic on the sultry air. The creature pointed at a doorway. Axe raised, the nullifier beat on the door, ready to smash it if the householder failed to open it.

I released a breath, as my trapped intellect urged me to action. *It wasn't you. You were just between it and its quarry. Move, now.*

I reversed course to face downhill again. *Go left at the red house. Barbers Row will get you out of sight.*

Barbers Row began as a wide and busy boulevard, but after

four or five shopfronts it disintegrated into a maze of vacant tenements, stables, and storehouses. *Il Padroné* had donated the area to the city for a new theater. Until the theater design was approved by the Sestorale, it was an eerie place, good for losing oneself—or slipping through a broken bit of the wall into the Market Ring.

My first step could have required no more effort were I breast deep in the flooding Venia. The second was little better.

A growing cluster of onlookers—braver or more foolish than most citizens—gathered along the stair to gawk and to heckle whomever the nullifier might roust. The two clerks were among them. My leaden feet took me behind them. The red house and Barbers Row were only a short distance away.

Another step down.

A whoop and screech from my left near shattered my skull. The second sniffer closing in.

A slight figure pelted out of a squeeze halfway between me and the red house. Pausing for one moment, he looked around frantically, then streaked for the yawning mouth of Barbers Row.

The moment was enough to recognize him. Pale hair . . . bare feet . . . my brother's slops. Teo!

Placidio constantly harangued Neri and me to develop solid principles for joining any fight, and to hone our instincts to serve those principles. The practice made us able to react quickly without overthinking, and thus more likely to succeed. It soothed guilt and self-condemnation if we failed. And it forced reexamination of motives if the result was not what we intended.

That was why I threw myself to the ground in front of the dark little squeeze between houses that had spat out Teo.

I scrubbed dirt into my face, tore my underskirt, and started cursing and screaming that the fugitive had knocked me over.

"Summon the law!" I yelled as I sat up, legs akimbo, skirts in a snarl. "Who's to defend a poor girl fetching buns for her mam?"

My cries distracted some in the crowd from the sniffer prowling the houses across the lane. I spread my arms in a plea for help. Two dusty hod carriers and a stout woman in an apron came to fuss over me, the four of us very effectively blocking exit from the squeeze.

Just in time.

Pounding boots, clanking chain, and the waver of wordless bawling halted in a shower of dust and gravel. The chasers had come to a stop right behind me.

My spine crawled with worms. My helpers gaped in horror.

"Get out the way, citizens," snapped a throaty female voice over my head. "Move your feet or I'll chop them."

One of the carriers and the woman melted into the onlookers. The other carrier dropped his empty hod, grabbed my shoulders, and dragged me aside.

The flat of a cold steel axe blade pressed my cheek. The snarling, leather-skinned nullifier bent down and said, "Don't never get in the way of hunters, girlie."

"Nay, yer honor," I croaked. "Never would I. Knocked me over, he did. But nay, I would never interfere with the righteous law."

I dropped my gaze as she yanked the chain leash. The sniffer stumbled past me. Its feet—*his* feet—were huge, their silk coverings frayed. Fresh blood glistened amid the street filth. Human feet.

"Find him again, demon," growled the nullifier, as the crowd made way for them.

"Ayeee!" The sniffer's howl of lust and anger and . . . pain . . . shivered me far worse than the cold steel of the axe. Maybe not so human. Maybe mad.

Such a short time I'd given Teo. Enough to hide, perhaps. To stop whatever magic he was doing. Magic . . .

"Are you well, damizella?" asked the crouching hod carrier, his hot breath on my cheek. What skin showed between his thick beard, moustache, and brows was covered with soot, and his hands had likely not seen soap in ten years. But his terror-bright eyes and quivering hands reminded me that no risky choice endangered oneself alone.

I pressed a clenched fist to my breast. "Thank you, goodman. Your courage shames me. Be on your way with Fortune's benefice."

He nodded and hurried away through the scattering onlookers. I stood, remaining inside the shadowed mouth of the alley, waiting for the street to clear and my heart to slow.

The two sniffers waved hands in the air and pointed in differing directions, growling and moaning while their nullifiers consulted. In moments, the woman and the tall sniffer with bloodied feet rounded the corner into Barbers Row, while the other pair raced down the Dangling Stair.

I leaned my back against the alley's brick, taking stock of what had just happened. Teo . . . chased by sniffers. Teo, a sorcerer. Of course he was. If the sniffers didn't snare him, I would. And then I'd beat the damnable liar until he spat out the truth.

A huge black shape dropped from a low rooftop to land at my feet like an avalanche of night. My stomach lurched in upheaval, as the shapeless blackness unfolded into a black-cloaked man. "Atladu's balls, woman, are you an entire fool?"

"Swordmaster?" I could not have been more shocked had a naked Atladu leaped from the sky. "What are you doing here? You're supposed to be sleeping. Healing."

"Followed you from the Moon House. Wanted to warn you there were sniffers about. Decided that rooftops were safer than the streets, and that mayhap it was better we not walk together, lest one or the other of us be taken. May we now get away from here before you attract any *more* devilish attention?"

Wrapping his arm and voluminous cloak about the both of us, Placidio urged me down the cobbled steep.

• • •

"You're sure that was your fish man they were after?"

"Yes."

Placidio had bought cheese and bread in the Asylum Ring market, and we sat on a stone step to eat it. Unlike the *Scala Ciondolante*, these steps were shallow, wide, and open enough no one could overhear us without being very obvious about it.

Though urgency drove me onward, Placidio needed time to breathe. His drop from the roof had done his cracked rib no good.

"But you said he wasn't—"

"I said I wasn't *sure* he was a sorcerer. He denied it. Was horrified at the notion of it. He had reasonable explanations for almost everything I asked. Best liar I ever encountered."

"Yet you played the fool to delay the chase. At least you had a reason. I thought you were going to lure me into a fight with a sniffer for a stranger. So what do you think to do about him now?"

We had circled wide on our path toward the Beggars Ring, avoiding Barbers Row. But it was clear the hunt had moved swiftly down the Rings as well. Casual inquiries around the Market and Asylum Rings had placed the howling sniffers down in the Beggars Ring at the docks.

"Perhaps he's jumped a barge going downriver." Or killed someone else. The potter's omen of three dead men had taken on an ominous integrity.

I passed the rest of my bread to Placidio, unable to choke down another bite.

"Lady Fortune would never ease our path so conveniently," he said, as my share of the loaf followed his into oblivion. "Do you think he saw it was you held up the sniffer on his tail?"

"I doubt it. He was in a panic, looking for escape. If he survives . . . Well, he'll either let me know what's happened or not."

"And if he's stupid enough to think he's bamboozled you, he's stupid enough to lead the sniffers right back to you. You can't go home."

"Clearly he bamboozled me. I suspected he was a sorcerer and still coddled him like a milk nurse." I kicked at a loose cobble with my heel. "But I'm not going to stay away. I'm not going to give up my life in Cantagna. The house. The shop. L'Scrittóre's clients and Neri's work. Besides, I need to practice with the needles before tomorrow, and then fetch my new costume from Vashti. And I'm hoping for an answer from my acquaintance in the Cuaronan Wool Guild."

"Thinking of raising sheep in your little domicile?"

"She may know why Egerik left his appointment in Cuarona so quickly. I'd dearly love to know if it had anything to do with the Brotherhood of the Exquisite."

I told him what I'd learned from Nuccio.

"What I'd give for a flagon of mead to wash all *that* away!" He swiped at his moustache and grizzled chin. "All right. You head for Lizard's Alley. I'll follow discreetly to make sure no one's sniffing around behind you."

"You ought to be resting that rib."

"The rib will mend."

I was glad of him. I could still feel the cold steel pressure of the nullifier's axe blade on my cheek.

• • •

The overwhelming relief that flooded me as I walked into the Beggars Ring was entirely unjustified. Had my little fiefdom of a stone hovel in a rat-infested alley and a shop far smaller than Sandro's dressing closet become the kind of home poets spoke of? The kind of home that brought tears to Teo's eyes?

More likely the relief had to do with the occasional glimpse of Placidio peering out from behind a chimney or creeping across a cracked slate roof. Now that I knew to watch for him, his aerial travels were not entirely invisible. Especially when his boot slipped and he came near tumbling headlong into the stableyard behind the Duck's Bone—the very mire where I'd first laid eyes on him.

The swordsman splayed himself on the roof in a most un-dignified manner to check his slide. I paused to watch two children herding a flock of geese to their doom at Ogi the poul-terer's stall, lest I need to roust a goose rebellion to divert attention from cascading swordsmen. But Placidio deftly righted himself, popped to his feet, and vanished behind the crum-bling facade of the building that housed my shop.

I was pleased to find a neatly folded paper bearing Cuarona's seal in *L'Scrittóre's* message box. And dreadfully curious when I found a second fold of paper underneath it bearing a plain wax seal and no markings.

Romy!

I scanned carts, foot traffic, and roof tops for Placidio to no result.

"Ssst!" The hiss came from the sliver of dead space—the squeeze—between my shop and the rambling house that occupied the corner of Lizard's Alley.

Stuffing the two messages in my waist pocket, I backed up to the wall next to the dark slot and murmured over my shoulder, "What are you doing in there?"

"Sshh." A hand encircled my arm with a grip very like that of Germond the ironmonger's vise, dragged me around the corner, and shoved me into the squeeze. The crooked walls of the adjacent buildings converged, blocking the slot's far end, and the overlapping roofs hid the sky, leaving the dead space in perpetual night.

This was not Placidio. This person stank of fish.

"Could this be the lying wretch who's eaten my food, occupied my bed, and accepted my coin?" I said. "Did you think of something else you wanted from me? My purse? What's left of my virtue?"

"Yes, 'tis I, but—no, I would never . . . I've come to warn, not harm, you."

"Then let me go before you break my arm."

He snatched his hand away and retreated. But only a few steps, and he remained between me and escape. The glare from the street behind him blazed too bright to make him out. Certain, he was dripping wet. Where he'd pressed close to me, I was, too.

"Were you followed here?"

"No. I'm sure of that. But, Romy, the danger is terrible. Up in the city, I was searching, and soldiers were everywhere followed by—I don't know what they were. Green demons? Monsters? Though of human form, they had no eyes. No mouth. Ne ears. No words. They howled like beasts, terrible cries of anger and suffering."

"Magic sniffers. I warned you about them, and you told me you didn't carry the demon taint. But sniffers don't chase ordinary folk, only sorcerers. So the things you told me about the healing, about your grandmother . . . your marks . . . your healing, were they all lies, too?"

"I swear to you I do not lie," he said fiercely. "I have no *magic*. I'm just—I am not where I belong."

"Sniffers are sorcerers. Enslaved sorcerers. They detect *magic*. Their owners are called nullifiers and they *arrest* sorcerers. Nullifiers carry an axe so they can chop off your foot to prevent your running away. Spirits, I was so stupid to believe you."

"I didn't lie. Not apurpose, at least. Nothing makes sense. I've *duties*. I just cannot explain . . ."

I wasn't going to fall for his distress or his excuses this time. "You're sure the sniffers haven't followed you here to the Beggars Ring?"

"I swear not. When I realized they were after me, high up on the cityhill, I sneaked and hid and ran"—even in silhouette, I could see how his chest pumped as if he were still running—"and when I was sure none could see I took to the river near one of the great bridges. Demons cannot follow through moving water. So I swam upriver and came through that narrow gate we crossed through on the night you rescued me. I'd never have risked coming back here, never have intruded on your peace, were I not afraid for you."

His matter-of-fact mention of demons roused the tingling disquiet of midnight walks through graveyards. I shook it off. He was playing me. "Warn me of what?"

"You were concerned about evils in the city," he continued, "and enemies who might find me at your house. These pursuers . . . their evil was clear. Please believe me. You saved my life, and I feared for your safety. Once I was sure I'd lost the pursuers, I didn't know what else to do."

Neri was right. Dumond was right. I was the world's biggest idiot. Even now I wanted to believe him. But I'd seen the sniffers on his heels and heard them howling.

There was only one thing to do.

"We're going back to the river," I said. "Upstream there's a place we can talk freely—an old stone warehouse standing off by itself. We go now. You first."

20

Before leaving the squeeze, I paused to blink away the glare and watch Teo vanish into the sunlight. Placidio was sitting on the rubble wall that fenced off the ironmonger's yard just across the Ring Road watching two Demon Dancers rattle and spin past, orange ribbons fluttering. He bade a good afternoon to Germond as I joined him.

"Thought I might have to come fetch your corpus in that squeeze," he said.

"It's good I wasn't counting on a rescue."

"If you've not learned enough to handle a stripling like that, then you're not the student I thought you were." He glanced down at me. "The fish man?"

"No stripling I've ever met has a grip like his. I'll have bruises tomorrow." I rubbed my throbbing arm. "But I'm glad you didn't intrude. We're heading for the woolhouse, where he's going to explain a few things. I think you'd best follow him discreetly and see what he's up to along the way. Once we get there, I'll introduce you."

Placidio touched a finger to his brow in mock salute and vanished as quickly as Teo had. I hiked through the winding lanes toward the River Gate, mumbling curses, speeding up, stopping to check my shoe so as to catch a glimpse behind or to the sides. I was not followed.

Not another person was in sight along the riverside wasteland. Rumors of unquiet spirits from the plague years, when thousands had died along this section of the Venia, kept fishermen down past the docks or farther upriver on the side streams. Water birds, caring nothing for hauntings, screeked and dove for the neglected fish.

When I ducked behind a broken brick oven and checked behind me, my secret wish that the intriguing complication that was Teo might vanish was dashed yet again. His soggy tan tunic, brown slops, and pale hair made him almost invisible amid the sunlight, rocks, and ruins. Placidio emerged from the River Gate well behind him and ambled over to sit on the riverbank. Unthreatening.

I waited at the door to the woolhouse.

"What is this place?" Teo examined the high beamed roof pocked with holes that allowed stray beams of sunlight to streak the dusty air. The hanging bolsters. The bundled straw.

"My friends and I come here to be private. None can approach without being seen or heard from a good way off."

"So you know yonder fellow who followed me out of the gate?"

"I do." That man was now blocking the path behind him.

"Is he here to kill me?"

Teo might have been transparent, or a rough cut of marble under an artist's chisel. Every line of his thin, sodden form was taut, poised to fight. But it was neither apprehension nor bravado written on his spirit. Only resignation, a touch of sorrow, and absolute confidence.

"No," I said, before Placidio could answer. "You can trust him as you do me. But we need to understand. Now, show us your magic."

"Friend Romy, I told you—"

"Show us your *searching*, then. Whatever you call it. But sniffers follow people wielding magic, not people seeking a new hammer or a lost child. What are you searching for?"

"I so very much wish I could tell you. The world appears to me like a glaring lens, a pool of sunlight where everything is so clear, so loud, so hard-edged—the barge, the river, you, this city. But outside the perimeter of that lens all is mud and murk, darkness and danger—and all these things I can't remember. One shining thread leads through that murk into the glare. I am near blinded, so I cannot see what draws me, though everything in me says I must continue. I use no magic—not that I know. I don't know how to do that or what it would feel like if I did."

I wondered again if the beating had taken a toll on his head. Certain, it hadn't harmed his strength; his grasp could have paralyzed Placidio. Perhaps he actually *could* have swum against the Venia's strong current all the way from one of Cantagna's bridges.

"Show us what you were doing when the sniffers discovered you."

"I simply . . . turned inward," he said. "Composed myself.

Put aside worries and noise and distractions. When I'm settled, I open my eyes and the thread gleams, even in this glaring lens of the world."

"Show us."

As his eyes closed, his whole being changed. His brow smoothed. His cheekbones softened. His back curved ever so slightly. The long sinews in his arms released, until those limbs hung loose at his side. Then he spread them slightly away from his body, hands open and relaxed.

A few moments of stillness and his eyes flicked open. He began to walk in a slow circle about the empty woolhouse examining the packed dirt and straw, the walls, our practice fixtures. Placidio and I might have been the river breezes wafting through the doors.

I sensed nothing untoward, but then I never sensed anything from Placidio or Neri when they worked their magic. Beckoning Placidio to join me, I signaled what I wanted to do.

He nodded. The next time Teo paused to contemplate something, we each took a wrist.

Spirits! A bright, narrow torrent of searing cold rushed through my veins. Magic, certainly, though nothing like the fire of my own or the others of the Chimera. But intimately recognizable. Keen as a honed blade. Clean. Cold.

I dropped Teo's arm.

Placidio had already done the same. "It was his," he murmured. "The boost of magic during the healing rite; the one that felt like melt from a glacier."

Not Vashti, but Teo. He'd never explained how he followed me to the cooper's yard.

"How did you do it?" I snapped. "How did you interfere

when we were helping my friend heal? You were just outside the door, and somehow— Why didn't you see fit to mention that you'd joined in a magical working that day?"

Teo was not listening to me. He spun in place, arms wide, gaping about the woolhouse as if with new eyes.

"Extraordinary! This is just as when you found me on the riverbank. On that night, I was certain I'd arrived at the place I needed to be. Only I wasn't. Nor am I now. But it *was* here—this mystery I seek—though it is no longer. How is this possible?"

I threw up my hands. We were talking of two different mysteries. "We held your wrists just now and felt your power. Why do you tell me you're not a sorcerer?"

He paused his spinning, the flush of exhilaration fading in bewilderment. He peered at his outstretched arms, as if they were a stranger's appendages.

"Because I'm not! Or . . . I've never thought of myself as a *sorcerer* . . . something evil. I try never to do any evil thing, although sometimes—"

Shadows darkened his pale face. His crossed arms pressed to his chest. "Certain, I am not perfect. I get tired. Selfish. Afraid. Angry. Life is hard, and we sometimes do things we ought not. But this thread—the path to this thing I need to find—draws me forward, demanding I follow it. A piece of that thread lies in this very place. It also led me to the barrelmaker's yard where you found me. It led me up into this city today. I wandered the street for hours, but what I seek was not there, either, and I fear it is lost because somehow I am broken."

I knew what evil he had done that sullied his delicate conscience. The Piazza Vasaio potter had told me. Fearing for Sandro . . . and myself . . . I had heard, but not listened to the woman's tale of bad omens. Sniffers, two headless swans, three men dead . . .

"Three men were found dead at the docks on the night I dragged this fellow out of the river," I said for Placidio's benefit. "You killed them, didn't you, Teo? The three bargemen who kept you captive."

He clutched himself tighter and squeezed his eyes tight, and murmured, *"Theíko Patéra, synchorste tin apotychía mou. Synchorste. Synchorste."*

"Forgive your *failure*? Were you supposed to kill *more* people? Or were you after their cargo—salt? pearls? coins? Is that why they beat you and you killed them?"

His whole body shook. With effort, I thought, as if he were trying to lift a mountain. "The story I told you was truth. By the divine father, I swear it. To slay . . . needlessly . . . what greater failure? What greater weakness? I am not meant for killing."

"What are you meant for? Thievery? Spying?"

"By the gods I serve, my brave and patient rescuer, I cannot say."

"Cannot or *will* not? What are you searching for? How will you know when you find it?"

Wincing, he opened his arms wide—helpless. "I very much wish I could tell you these things. They must be important to drive me so. To make me kill from weakness and fear of death. Because I *must* stay alive. Someday I will face a reckoning for those deaths. For the rest . . . I swear I do not know."

I should kill him. He was surely the most convincing storyteller ever born—the most dangerous of all opponents. Thousands of lives could hang in the balance if I judged wrongly, beginning with my brother's, and Dumond's and his family's, and that of the man standing just a few steps away, silent and ready. I had all but admitted to this stranger that I and my friends were sorcerers. But no logic or reasoning could deny that Teo was one of us, whether he admitted it or not. The power coursing through his body, though different, was as recognizable as my own. How could he not know what he was? Why wasn't he afraid of his condition—lost in a place so unfamiliar, committed to a purpose he didn't understand, missing pieces of his life?

"Do people in the Isles of Lesh work magic? Is it permitted?"

Tugging on his wet snarl of hair, he pondered the question much longer than it should have taken. "We are . . . as we are."

"That's not much of an answer," I said, surprised when Placidio did not erupt in scorn. He did not tolerate excuses. But since detecting Teo's magic, he'd kept silent, his cinder eyes narrowed. Thoughtful.

Screwing his own visage into a charming confusion, Teo sat heavily on a straw bundle. "I agree. Again, I beg pardon. Somehow my home—a home that I love and long for—resides mostly in the murk. I recognize that some things I do, like recovering from injury, might seem extraordinary to the two of you, in the way your life without the sea feels so strange to me. But naught that I remember, naught of my own deeds or those of my family, speaks of *sorcery*—those stories of terrible works intended to pervert the gods' making of the world."

He spoke of myth, not common magic. It was our vocabulary that differed.

Nothing for it; I wasn't going to learn anything unless I hinted at the truth. "Each of those places where you followed this *thread* were places where magic had been worked."

Here. Dumond's house. Sandro's house. Mine, too. Had

he also wandered into the Heights where a fiend-for-hire had worked a magical explosion to kill Sandro? Had he found the little street in the Market Ring where I had stolen the memory of my name from Lawyer Cinnetti? Or into the Palazzo Segnori where I'd used magic to corrupt Fernand di Rossi's memory? Perhaps this searching business was his own particular talent, as impersonation was mine and anticipation Placidio's. Perhaps it had come upon him late in life, as abruptly as it had manifested in me at two and Neri at three. Yet even that wouldn't explain what we'd felt at Placidio's healing.

"When you were in the cooper's yard, a great magic was being worked nearby. We felt your power in the middle of that working—exactly what you demonstrated just now—as if you were lending it to the work being done. It was very strong and like nothing I'd ever felt."

I glanced at Placidio for a confirmation . . . or dissent, but his face and posture revealed nothing of his thoughts. Exasperating man. Both of them.

Teo peered out from under his tangled hair. "You felt no evil that day?"

"No. Far from evil."

Grimacing, he scrubbed at his head. "Was it worthy work? A good purpose?"

"Very worthy. Healing a dying man. How did you do that without touching his flesh? How could you not know you were doing it? You were surprised when I found you there. Surely you experienced something different than this 'pulling thread' you speak of. What did you feel? What did you do?"

"I followed the thread to that place just as I told you. While I was seeking, there came an explosion in my spirit, like a glorious sea storm with thunder and lighting and waves as high as the cliffs of Lesh, and warm as the sands of Lesh itself. I opened myself to the storm, thinking I might have found the object of my search. Such beauty it was. Such power! But at the center of the storm lurked a devouring malevolence. I tried to understand it, afraid it might swallow me, terrified that I'd gone mad as you seemed to think—which is why I didn't mention it to you at the time—and knowing I must hold against it with all my strength. After a while, it came to me that the malevolence was not a . . . mindful . . . evil, which made no sense at all. Even so, I dared not yield. After a while, the storm abated, the malevolence seemingly vanquished. I was so drained . . . and so confused . . . that I pulled the blanket over my head and tried to sleep."

"And that's where I found you." He had simply reacted according to his nature—whatever that nature was. He had no wondrous secrets of magic to offer.

I assumed the *malevolence* Teo fought had been the sepsis lurking in Placidio's gut and not our magic. And yet . . .

"What would you call a mindful evil?"

"The three who beat me in hopes of treasure until I could no longer sustain my life." His clenched fist tapped his chest, where his shirt hid a triangle of variant curves enclosing a tightly coiled spiral. "I should have held longer."

He had resisted until he was driven to extremity. So he killed them. And now felt shame at his weakness. Divine spirits, who was he?

Teo cocked his head, wry apology written on him. "I would have offered help freely in your worthy work if I'd known it could be done. I'm glad it was not just a figment of my broken head."

I laughed in spite of myself. "What are we to do with you?"

Again I glanced at Placidio for help. He met my gaze briefly, but just shook his head and strolled over to the open doorway.

"My friend and I have important things to be about today," I said. "And my brother . . . once he's heard this, he'll be convinced I'm a lunatic. He'll want to bash you on the head and throw you back into the river—and I'm not at all sure he'd not be right. What I would really like to do is sit here all afternoon and see what else you can do that you don't understand."

"My talents seem sparse." He wrapped his arms round his bony knees, lost in Neri's slops. "Surely you've thought of that, friend Romy. I recall so little of my purpose. I don't seem to be very good at anything. My father sent me away, thinking this acquaintance in Cuarona could make use of me. But instead of trusting *me* to explain his purpose, he wrote her a letter many seasons ago telling her that someday I would come. Before I left, he gave me a bit of coral to wear that she might recognize me. Perhaps my head is not so much broken, as never very solid in the first place."

It was a wistful assessment. I wanted to pat him on the head and make him feel better. But he was not a child of three. Besides it was entirely ridiculous.

"*Sparse* talents? You helped rescue a good man from certain death when his own strength and that of his friends were failing. You can heal yourself overnight from injuries that would keep an ordinary man on his back for a month. For certain, you swim very well, except when you've been beaten to a solid bruise." I pointed through the door toward the river. "Or was that a lie, too?"

"The beating was true. My soul was but a cooling ember at the end . . ."

"I didn't question the beating. To overcome three captors when you lay at brink of death shows a modicum of skills, whether you are *meant* to have such skills or not. But did you truly swim from one of the city bridges up here to the River Gate not an hour ago?"

"Aye. I am a strong swimmer. The river is friendly, though I miss the salt and the waves, the pulse of living water, not just a mindless running downhill. Perhaps mindless is better for me just now. The sea is . . ."

His voice trailed off as before when we spoke of the sea. His luminous eyes clouded.

"And I'll swear you don't sleep," I snapped, battling sentiment. "You heard everything I said while you were *turned inward* to heal yourself. Your dreams spilled into mine. You spoke to me when you were sleeping, without moving your lips. Can you do that, too? Speak in my head?"

"Pshh. Who could do such things?"

"Someone whose *search* for some inexplicable something can be detected by a sniffer. Which means the searching *is* magic. But he doesn't know what he is or can do . . . and here he is with me, who understands exactly what that is like, because for years I thought I was broken, and now—"

"You're not? That is most encouraging." A bright grin blossomed and faded. "My head bones bulge and crack with all this thinking."

"You told me your name that night and that you weren't dead. You spoke in Annisi. Do you know very much of it?"

"Annisi?" He frowned.

"The language of Typhon. No one's spoken Annisi for centuries, but the first word I heard from you was *skatá*. Crude words don't surprise me, but the language did. Then you called on the goddess mother and divine father, *Theía Mitéra* and *Theíko Patéra*, whom we name Gione and Atladu. I happen to know a bit of Annisi, because—What's wrong?"

Teo roamed the floor again, head bent and brow creased with effort. "I must have heard the words somewhere. My family speaks as you do here—the merchant tongue of the Costa Drago—though with differences in pronouncing. But . . . the Mother of Earth and the Father of Ocean . . . yes, we honor them . . . heed them . . . always."

"Stop," I said. "Look at me and tell me your name. Tell me the truth with no hiding."

I grabbed his wrist as I'd done earlier.

Troubled, he fixed his gaze to mine and offered his other wrist to Placidio. Placidio, so unusually quiet, accepted it.

"My name is Teo. I have come from the Isles of Lesh and I wish no one harm. There are many things I don't remember, and I must believe, as you've said, that my head is damaged."

No magic surged through him to cover lies or place another story in my head, as I had done with Rossi and my chambermaid and my father. He believed what he said. Had someone done to him what I had done to those three and others in my life? Or was he lost in a broken impersonation that he could not relinquish on his own?

"So, this one last test," I said. "Close your eyes, turn inward, and tell us something interesting—without speaking it aloud."

"Without speaking?" His iridescent eyes cooled to gray. "That's impossible."

"Try it." I tightened my grip on his wrist.

Mouth drawn into a knot, finger-deep wrinkles on his brow, Teo shot me one hard, skeptical look, then closed his eyes.

You are a woman of extraordinary generosity and courage, Romy of Cantagna, and wise and clever and most extravagantly lovely.

I dropped his wrist.

But truly your head must be as broken as mine.

Teo's words struck my mind as solidly as arrows slamming a target even after I stopped touching his flesh. His lips had not moved. Not a ripple of magic surged through him. Not magic as I knew it. Not even *his* magic as I had felt it.

I sank to the straw—my joints refusing to hold me up any longer. "Not broken," I said, scarce able to muster a whisper. "Certainly not wise or clever."

"You heard what I said!"

I nodded. How was it possible he could do such a thing? How was it possible he didn't know?

The other two were silent, and I glanced up to see Teo staring at Placidio's back.

"I didn't hear anything," said Placidio. "But you did, Romy?"

"Clear as sunrise." I wrapped my arms about myself, as if to assure myself of their continuing attachment to my commands. When one's mind is no longer one's own, but trespassed by another, no matter how ... friendly? innocent? good humored? sincere? ... as Teo seemed to be, one could take nothing for granted.

Placidio spun around, brisk and sure. "Can you speak back to him?"

"How could I?" I said. "No magic flowed through him when he spoke."

Teo's gaze shifted to Placidio.

"Perhaps it was just too subtle to detect," said Placidio. "Try it. Close your eyes, reach for your magic and concentrate—as we tried when practicing the hand light, as I do when drawing power for healing—and then say something to him without speaking. Does she have your permission to try, Teo?" He bowed ever so slightly in Teo's direction.

My jaw dropped at the gesture of respect.

"Certainly," said Teo, not seeming to notice Placidio's offering. "I would tell you how to do it, if I knew. By the Mother's heart, I don't understand. It is a marvel, truly."

I did as Placidio suggested. Several times. Each time, Teo shook his head, grimacing in apology.

"Perhaps it is only a skill of those born in Lesh who've had their skull cracked."

"Perhaps so," said Placidio. "For now, I need to be off. For what it's worth, I believe your story, Teo, and wish you well in your endeavors. I'm glad Romy was able to help you and wise enough to do so. Romy, I'll see you at the olive grove tomorrow at the time we set."

In a whirl of cloak and dust, the swordsman left. His pronouncement left me flummoxed. What had convinced him?

I closed my eyes and laid my forehead on my knees hoping to break the fascination of this impossible mystery.

Bare feet scuffing the straw-layered dirt brought Teo's cool bulk to my side. He stank of river wrack and the sweat of fear.

"Your friend is a good man. His acceptance means a great deal to me . . . and to you, I gather."

"Yes. Winning his trust is not easy. Truly I wasn't expecting it in your case, especially with this new strangeness. I accused you of putting things in my head, but I didn't truly believe it."

"It makes me wonder what else—good, ill, strange, ordinary—lies waiting outside the bright lens of my seeing. But maybe I don't want to know."

"Mmm." Overwhelmed, amazed, terrified at the possibilities of his talents, I could not muster words enough to make sense of a man who had no concept of his gift, because in his mind, *sorcery* meant something evil, whereas what he did was . . . ordinary. Invading a mind, it seemed, required less effort than healing broken bones overnight.

"I found employment," he said quietly, yanking me back to the mundane. "Down at the docks. In the morning before all this happened. There's a fish-packer named Frenetti, who buys hogsheads of . . . *serdellas*? Little fish. Silver."

"Pilchards." Silly word, when my head was stuffed with so much of magic and not-magic.

"Aye! Pilchards brought overland from the sea in casks of brine. He dries them, packs them in jars of oil, salt, and spice. I told him of the spices my aya used for serdellas, and he liked that, and also that I knew how to work with them, which he says not many in Cantagna do. He says that when a new lot comes in, he could use me to help. And in between, he needs a good hand for mending nets, scraping keels, just about anything needed for his fishing boats or the boats that carry his packed fish to markets up and down the river. I know fish and boats. He says I can sleep in his fish house, and he doesn't mind I lack boots. So, this . . ."

I lifted my eyelids enough to see his outstretched hand. Long, clean fingers holding one silver solet and five coppers. He laid them on the hard-packed dirt at my feet.

"I used the other seven coppers to eat and to buy this shirt. And I shall repay them and return your brother's breeks as soon as possible."

I squeezed my eyes shut. How could he think of coins and breeks and fish, when we had just proved he could speak in my mind? And what of his dreams? Behind my eyelids I saw the broken walls that seeped fire and cracked foundations that seeped water to fade the ancient mosaics. And I heard the voice of warning. *We cannot hold . . . your time has come early.* Was that some kind of truth, as well?

His movement stirred the air stirred beside me. Standing. "My pledge remains, my generous friend. Whatever I can do for you until the end of days."

My clotted mind took a few moments to comprehend his meaning. I jumped up. "No wait, Teo, don't leave—"

He was already gone.

I hurried to the open doorway. Teo moved rapidly toward the distant city, hopping from rock to snag, broken wall to weedy clump as if he weighed nothing. Were the dangers and possibilities of our appointment with Egerik not weighing on me more than ever, I would have chased after him to ask why he dreamed about cracked walls and leaking fire.

21

I was halfway back to the River Gate when the city bells intoned the Hour of Respite. The day that had started so dreadfully early still had hours to run. As I weighed the conflicting benefits of practicing my needle casting against making an early bedtime, when I remembered the messages I'd picked up before Teo's appearance. My hand flew to my waist pocket where I'd stuffed the elaborate parchment of the Cuaronan Wool Guild and the unmarked fold of plainer stock.

I chose the mysterious one first. It had no signature. But clearly it had come from Nuccio.

> *A reliable source from the Brotherhood confides that there have been no exquisite murders presented in the local chapter in the past three years. One presentation centered on a disobedient servant's punishment. One on a member's suicide. One on a game of draughts that culminated in a member's death.*

So Egerik had not murdered his wife for the Brotherhood's edification. What was wrong with me that I could feel crest-fallen at such news? I did wonder if the disobedient servant could have been one of Egerik's. Or if the ambassador might have persuaded some brother of the fraternity to his suicide or into a mortal game of draughts. But I doubted Nuccio could or would enlighten me further.

Hoping for better news from my Cuaronan friend, I snapped the seal on the Wool Guild message. The page bore a few lines of elegant handwriting.

Dama Ginzetti,

> *It is with great sadness that I heard of Mistress Cata-line's passing. When I attended Segnoré di Gallanos's first salon of last summer, I noted her absence, as I was looking for her particularly after such enjoyment at the winter quarter salon. An acquaintance quickly hushed my queries and told me the dread news. I was devastated, even when my friend whispered of rumors that the death was perhaps not exactly a passage from this earthly plane.*

> *I cannot imagine what token of friendship she has left me, but I would be pleased to receive you in my chamber—#5—at the Wool Guildhall on any afternoon during the Hour of Respite. You are kind to see to Cata-line's wishes.*

> *Best Regards,*
> *Lenore di Tessio, Commissioner,*
> *Wool Guild of the Independency of Cuarona*

The Hour of Respite. Right now.

• • •

Like doting aunties, the sober, blockish halls of the *Syndicati Maggiore*—Cantagna's seven oldest guilds—overlooked the teeming heart of the Merchants Ring marketplace. They provided solid assurance that the merchandise displayed under the colorful canopies or on carts, tables, or spread rugs was the finest to be had in all the Costa Drago.

My cheeks pulsed with the heat of my hurry as I ducked into an arcaded walkway between the Hall of Physicians and Pharmacists and the Guildhall of the Wool Trade. Foreign wool guilds rented chambers in the guildhall for their local representatives, so they could have easy access to their Cantagnan counterparts during their incessant negotiations. Lenore, as the sister of a wealthy Cuaronese merchant, made her home in a much finer house, but spent her days in the small sitting room she was allotted for her business.

I paused to run my fingers through my hair and to blot the sweat of my walk with a kerchief.

No one had followed me from the Beggars Ring. I had stopped by the shop on the way just long enough to grab a clean mantle and a new pen I had splurged on a few days previous.

Beyond a side door in the guildhall lay a stone-floored entry chamber devoid of people, furnishing, or any decoration beyond the unartful paintings that covered its walls. The mural's subjects ran to fat, thick-coated sheep, multitudinous bags of sheared wool, and elaborate looms the size of houses, all marked with the crest of the Cantagnan wool guild. The diminutive figures of scrawny sheep and dour shepherds relegated to the background lacked the favored markings. No one would mistake the message that to dally with foreigners on wool business was a losing gamble.

A quick exploration of three branching passages took me to room number five. The cypress and crescent moon ensign of Cuarona hung above the open doorway.

Inside, a woman with great shining loops of hair piled atop her head sat busy at a writing desk. There was no mistaking her. Though of middling years, her cheeks were smooth as an infant's and bore the same charming blush. Unfortunately, those cheeks and her glorious, rich folds of copper hair were the only physical attributes to offset flat gray eyes, equine teeth and jaw, and bones better suited to an ox than a woman.

Lenore di Tessio bore her awkward physiognomy with dignity and a sharp wit that she confessed gave her far better advantage in the wool trade than would more refined features. I had thoroughly enjoyed our few meetings.

Her head turned at my tap on her door. "Commissioner di Tessio, may I have a word?"

"Enter." She wiped her pen, laid it aside, and turned her chair where her weak eyes could see me better.

She snapped to her feet. "Oh my! Mistress Cat—"

"Shhh!" I pressed my finger to my lips. "Please excuse my subterfuge. I am not dead and not hiding, but I've been given no leave to enlighten the world as to my state of breathing."

"Oh, my dear, I—I—" She could not seem to come up with any more words. Her body tried to increase the distance between us without actually retreating. An observer might assume I carried the plague, which, indeed, had much in common with banishment from the Shadow Lord's favor.

"Gracious Dama di Tessio—Lenore—I swear to you there is no danger in speaking with me, nor the least compromise of your position. I'd never wish to cause you embarrassment."

I held my ground in the doorway so as not to threaten, and only when she had lowered herself cautiously to her chair did I step inside.

"As you can see, I am much diminished in situation. But I've managed to make a new life for myself. Quiet and out of the way. And *seemly*, which I always told you would be my only aim did the worst come to pass. As it did. Obviously."

"Good. I'm glad of that. That is ... glad you've made a seemly life. And that you're alive."

She was more flustered than standoffish, which gave me encouragement. I'd no intent to approach the truth as closely as I had with Nuccio. I didn't know her well, and she had many other interests to compete for her loyalty. But she had relished sharing gossip with an intelligent woman outside her professional circles.

"I brought a small remembrance in return for your kindness," I said. "Though we met only a few times, you spoke to me as a person whose company you enjoyed, and not as the Shadow Lord's bound mistress. That meant more than you will ever know. Dare I say that most women who accepted me in their society did so entirely in hopes of my master's favor?"

I set a plain wooden pen case on a table beside the door.

"No need for thanks." Her posture eased, though she certainly did not rush across the room to embrace me. We'd not been that kind of friends. "To talk of something other than wool contracts was a pleasure."

Indeed her gossip had proved to be a delightful source of

sharp observations on Cantagnese society. Not wishing to give her a wrong estimate of the length of my visit, I perched on the arm of the petitioners' bench just inside her door.

"I've come to ask a simple favor. A friend of mine, a notary, has been offered a position as a local agent for the Mercediaran ambassador here in the city. The pay is better than my friend's other contracts, yet I've had a mind to warn him off. Somewhere in my . . . elevated years . . . I heard rumor of a scandal involving Ambassador Egerik when he was posted to Cuarona. I told my friend I knew an insightful person who might shed light on that history—without mentioning any name, of course."

"Egerik di Sinterolla?" Her awkward features took on a lively flush. "Oh, my! Yes, there was quite a story."

"Would you tell me? It would be a kindness."

She needed no more encouragement. Perhaps she'd not found another safe outlet for her gossip since my downfall.

"I only met the man once. It was at one of my first official functions after taking a position with the Wool Guild—a reception for representatives of our guild's best customers. I thought Segnoré di Sinterolla a cold man, pinching his nose at all of us as if we were sheep farmers, not landholders. He scarce had a word for anyone but his wife. But she—Oriana—was charming. Warm, friendly, good humored, truly lovely inside and out, and gloriously with child. Their first and only child, a boy, had died in a terrible accident when he was but three years old. Fell out a window! Oriana clearly adored Egerik. That gave him a bit of grace in my opinion, as did his clear devotion to her. I would say they were one of those matches Lady Virtue uses to show us true worth."

My horrid, lingering hope that Egerik's wife was the malignant spirit he feared crumbled. Though the dead son . . . "So what was the scandal?"

"It was not so much a scandal," said Lenore, "as dreadful tragedy. Only a few days after we met, Oriana was attacked and robbed as she shopped in the spice market. She suffered terrible injuries, and though she survived, her unborn child did not."

"How awful!" I said. Meaning it. No wonder Egerik had named Cuarona *an undisciplined society ruled by rabble*. His wife assaulted. A child dead before taking a first breath. Were the natalés we'd seen some lingering protection for his children's tender spirits? Though why he would install them in his chambers instead of the children's resting places remained a mystery.

"But that's not the whole of it," said Lenore, her smooth cheeks flushed deeper than their natural rose. She had never been one to leave her stories incomplete. "The thief was apprehended and thrown into gaol to await trial and execution. But after only the one night, he was found dead in his cell, beaten and slashed, and— Well, the details of his demise are too dreadful to speak. Wild dogs could have done no worse. The hint of scandal came when a *gendarme* reported that one of the ambassador's servants had been seen outside the gaol that night. A youth—scarce more than a boy. Stories grew that he was the lady's secret lover taking his vengeance."

"Whyever would people think a *boy* her lover?" I asked.

"For the same reason he was recognized; he was most extraordinarily beautiful! For a year every woman in Cuarona—and quite a few of the men—had made fools of themselves over the youth. Wrote him sonnets, drew him, painted him, sighed and moaned and composed dreary love songs. The ambassador never allowed him into company. I assumed the fellow was a dullard or had a voice like a donkey's bray, else why would Egerik hide him away? And having witnessed how Egerik doted on Oriana, and she on him, I never imagined any doings outside their sheets. But all that was before the murder."

Her words stung my hearing like a hot knife. *A servant youth. Extraordinarily beautiful.*

"Whatever the truth," she continued, "the ambassador refused to let the magistrate question the youth, and they had no witnesses or evidence to suggest he had truly done the deed. No one ever saw the handsome fellow again."

Cei.

"Poor Oriana never fully recovered. Oh, she was still lovely, but grieving and sickly. It was not long until Egerik whisked her and, presumably, their murderous servant back to Mercediare. Though Egerik could hardly disapprove the prisoner's demise, I never believed the other rumor that rose among the men of the city—that he had goaded the boy to do it. Though cold and condescending, the ambassador was ever a gentleman."

Certain, I could believe Egerik ordered Cei to do the murder. Was that why Egerik kept him in the house, but could not look at him? If it had been a clean execution, I would understand that; sometimes summary justice was the only recourse. Yet to retain the perpetrator of such savagery so near his wife while she yet lived, a reminder of her pain and their sad loss, seemed cruel. What was exquisite about *that*?

"As for your friend's query . . ."

As my mind raced to make sense of the story, Lenore continued her musings, absentmindedly tapping her pen knife on her journal.

". . . though I attribute no fault or scandal to the ambassador, I don't know that I would recommend anyone to work for him. He is most strict with his household, excessively concerned with cleanliness and petty details. And without Oriana to open his heart, it could be a very chilly situation."

"A certain consideration," I mumbled.

"Is there anything else?" Her glance flicked to me and then to the open doorway in growing unease. "My secretary will be returning shortly."

Collecting myself, I rose from the bench. "I appreciate your frankness, Lenore, and will pass on your recommendation to my notary friend—without referencing your name or the awful details, of course."

We exchanged a few farewell pleasantries. Lenore did not rise to see me out, and though we mouthed politenesses about meeting again for coffee or supper, I knew we never would. Lenore was devoted to her work, and she was clever enough to realize that companioning the Shadow Lord's supposed-to-be-dead mistress could hardly enhance her city's interests.

My feet flew over the cobbles as I descended to the northern arcs of the Beggars Ring. I hoped to find my partners at Dumond's house, as I wanted to tell them what I'd learned. Egerik may not have murdered his wife, but Cei . . . the savage murder . . . there was something there.

22

A noisy processional, celebrating someone's birthday or coming of age, clogged the eastern quarters of the Heights on the morning of our second venture to Ambassador Egerik's palazzo. Troupe after troupe of musicians, acrobats, and dancing children twirling ribbons crowded passersby to each side. Finely dressed celebrants riding expensively caparisoned horses were in no hurry at all to let ordinary citizens pass.

The festive group funneled into the grand boulevard of the Quartiere di Lustra, the residence of some of the oldest and wealthiest families in Cantagna. So much expensive glass had been installed on the great houses of the neighborhood, the glitter in the afternoon light had given the quarter its name—the Shimmering Quarter.

As the city bells rang ten strikes, I turned onto a steep lane that angled away from the processional route. At the far end of that lane stood the gated and guarded entry to the Quartiere di

Fiori where Palazzo Ignazio awaited us. Rather than proceeding directly to the gate, I took a dirt path that plunged into a bit of ancient orchard that had survived as the city grew.

Not a breath of air stirred in the olive grove. Early summer poppies made a red splash amid the gray-green trees, though the blooms hung their heads as if napping in midsummer heat.

No one was there. Spirits! This was the twentieth day, the day Cantagna must turn the prisoner over to the Mercediaran ambassador. We had a great deal to talk about.

Only Vashti had been at home the previous evening. She had helped me with a fresh costume for this morning and with my practice casting the needles. But I'd not been able to tell even her of Lenore's news, as her daughters were at home doing lessons and eating supper.

"Anyone here?" I called softly.

"Mind your back, student."

I spun toward the spitting whisper.

Placidio loomed behind me, sheathing his dagger. Had he been an assassin, I'd be on my way to the Night Eternal.

He yanked me into the shadow of a gnarled trunk as broad as my armspan and pressed the brass horse head to his mouth in warning. After a careful interval, he sneaked a glance back the way I'd come. "Anyone follow you?"

I didn't like admitting I wasn't certain. Thus, I fell back on the world's most ancient strategy for diverting uncomfortable questions.

"Did anyone follow *you*?" My words were as quiet and snappish as his. "Where did you run off to last night?"

"I had things needed doing."

I folded my arms across my chest and gave a clear signal that I was waiting for more.

The rattle and flutter of a woodpecker diverted his attention. He cocked his head, listening carefully until the sounds of the grove settled back to the quiet buzz of insects.

"'Tis none of your business."

He gaze darted from me to the lane and back again. I didn't blink.

"All right. Jumping around rooftops set the rib fussing. Pix has remedies for customers who have to fight again sooner than they'd like. I slept the night through."

"Eventually you have to pay the price for such *remedies*," I whispered. I knew the kind he spoke of. "But something's got you jumpy . . . "

Most of the time, Placidio's big body, exceptional fighting skills, and magic-assisted prescience made a reassuring bulwark against lurking dangers. His twitchy distraction was unsettling.

His shoulders sloughed off concern, even as another furtive glance darted toward the lane.

"What's going on?"

"Pssh." He screwed up his mouth in resignation. "Damnable Pizottis around every corner. Caught up with me in the streets after I'd left the Bull."

"Spirits, they've called vendetta!"

"Only till I get the matter straight with the referees. The duel was registered. The fool who ended up dead was the named partisan—thanks to Lady Fortune for that. The others Neri found were none of them dead right away and can be shown to have attacked me inside the city—which should rightly get them hanged."

"Bawds Field wasn't registered."

"Buto's uglier, but still alive, so Bawds Field doesn't matter. But that lot's like a swarm of blood-sucking mosquitoes. Can't round a corner without finding some lurking. Fortunate there's not a wit amongst them. But either I retire from Chimera schemes or we needs must keep an extra sharp watch for a while."

A public rebuttal to the charge of the Pizotti vendetta would focus unwelcome attention on Placidio. But it would also force magistrates to uphold the law banning the ancient custom. Until then, there were enough members of the Pizotti family—and enough fat purses thrown around for bribes—to discourage anyone who dared call them to account. Most definitely a complication the Chimera didn't need.

"We'll help watch. I've learned more about Egerik's wife—"

"Sssh." Placidio shoved me against the tree, and plastered himself against another.

Tucked away behind the broad trunk, I held my breath.

Turf-muffled footsteps sped toward us through the grove. I readied my dagger. The steps drew closer. Halted. A short, repetitive whistle—a mediocre imitation of a warbler's chirrup—intruded on the insect hum.

Placidio's rendition of the birdcall was astonishingly accurate.

"Mother of Mountains," he grumbled, as he stepped out from behind the tree. "Thought I taught you two something about *stealth*."

"Thought I might be too late." Neri, breathless, swiped a sleeve across his forehead, smearing the black smudges already there. "There's things to tell, things you need to see. We found—"

Placidio's wagging finger stopped him. "You brought my weapons?"

"Did." Neri unhitched a slim canvas-wrapped bundle from his back and dropped it at Placidio's feet. "As you said."

Placidio made brisk work of unrolling the canvas and installing a Varelan stiletto in his old boots and another slender blade up his right sleeve.

"Where's Dumond?" I asked.

"Still working on a portal inside the Via Mortua tunnel," said Neri. "It's the only way he could find to get us out of the tunnels and into the streets. The Ring Wall above the collapsed end of the tunnel is too exposed for him to paint. But did you know that if he paints one side of a door on one wall, and the other side of the same door in a wholly different place, he can take you somewhere that's *not* the other side of the wall you started through? Takes a lot more work and a lot more magic to make them connect, but gods *balls*, 'tis a certain wonder!"

Neri's enthusiasm had Placidio halfway to smiling, even while his gaze darted in search of stray Pizottis.

"I'd always wondered how Dumond made that family bolt hole in his cellar," I said. Of course, Neri vanishing through a wall and Placidio countering a move when his opponent's was scarce begun were certain wonders, too. It was Teo's magic threatened to eclipse all we knew.

Rising from his crouch, Placidio glared at the horse-head cane, then waved his hand at the rumpled canvas. "I suppose gouty Baldassar must have his walking stick with him. You'll have to keep the rest for now."

Neri rewrapped the remaining weapons, a main gauche and Placidio's *spada de lato*—his one-hand-two-hand, slash-or-thrust, ready-for-any-kind-of-fight weapon. As my brother tied the bundle to the straps on his back, he inspected Placidio head to toe. "Are you well, swordmaster? Easy in the gut? Clear in the head?"

"I'll be glad when folk have better things to talk of than my head and my bowels. Such as, where do we get out if we need to make a hasty exit from Egerik's domicile? Did you leave any gifts for our ambassador friend? And are there any clues about this Rossi—the prisoner or guest or spy or whatever he is—and whether he's on the premises yet? And for the lady scribe, what is your news and what in the Mother's name is your plan?"

"Neri's answers first," I said. "You found the reception room?"

"Aye. Your description took me right there. Left a little straw doll on the shelf under the window, as you told me. As no one was there, I did a lookabout, too."

Foolish to think he wouldn't do more than the task we'd agreed on.

"It's only good strategy," he snapped, before I could protest. "You've got to scout the way, right? Got to examine the terrain, see what's there, what's in the way. *That's* what I was taught."

He eyed Placidio. "I figured that if there's a space behind that brass grate you told of, then there must be a way to get in there. You'd said some of the panels on the wall opened like doors, so I tried some. Being careful for sure. Ready to bolt."

Behind his indignation rose a glow like the morning sun.

"You found it!" I said.

"Two panels rightward of the grate. A latch hidden in the left-side molding opens it into a stair closet. A few steps would take you up to a plain wood platform behind that grate. A bit of a scrunch, but someone could sit right there and watch what's going on, just as you said. The stair goes down to the cellars. Which means it connects to the tunnels eventually. One way out of the house. The stair also leads upward to a cross passage. Narrow. Dusty."

"A second level inside the walls!" I said. "A silver solet says it leads to the squint in the odd waiting chamber."

"Didn't have time to explore it. People were coming in and out of the room, servants bringing in chairs, setting 'em outside a circle of candlesticks."

"For Monette's divination," I said. "How many chairs?"

Neri sat back on his heels. "Four when I left."

Who would Egerik invite to hear Monette's augury? Rossi, perhaps. Egerik had suggested he would have Monette cast in the presence of the *arriving guest* and the oathsworn friends he thought might be responsible for the danger I foretold. But who?

"What of Rossi?" said Placidio.

"No signs of a prisoner transfer anywhere I looked."

"A decent scout," said Placidio. "But don't get cocky, lad. You charged into here about as quiet as a contessa bit by a swarm of wasps. Was there a dark corner in that stair closet where you could hide a weapon?"

"Aye. Certain."

"Having the main gauche close to hand could be useful for either Romy or me. If it was found, they'd hardly imagine it was Merchant Fabroni or his daughter stuck it there. Mayhap they'll think it left by an unquiet spirit."

Neri appeared to grow half a head taller. Placidio's trust was better than gold. "I could do that, if the business in that room slows down. Maybe leave another plaything about at the same time."

"Then do it. Careful, as before." Placidio's warning finger was far more effective than any words. "Do we have a clean way out to the street?"

"I'll show you," Neri cleared a spot of dirt with his boot and knelt, sketching lines in the dry earth.

"Here's the main house—and the window in the reception room where Romy sent me. Dumond had me flash a glass from the window so's we'd have it exact."

He tapped on his drawing.

"Here's the back steps come down from the main house. Servants are on those steps and in and out that door all the time. Across the yard here is the kitchen house. Thirty paces left of that is a wellhouse, and right behind the wellhouse"—he poked a finger in the dirt—"most convenient, is a tangle of old trellises and dead vines, like somebody tried to grow grapes there years ago. The smith painted a trapdoor on a square of wood we found and we planted it square in that dead vineyard, just here under the trellises."

Another tap showed us the spot.

"He painted a matching trapdoor in the tunnels, so he livened it with his magic and we tested it. You'd think it had been there since the tunnel was built. Yank on the ring outside or give a shove from the inside, and it will get you in or out of tunnels that will take you all the way to the Ring Wall and the front side of the door he's finishing in the Via Mortua passage. We'll have the way marked."

"Marks we can take up as we retreat?" said Placidio.

Neri grinned. "Certain."

Back on his feet, Neri brushed his drawing away with his boot. "I'd tell you the rest, but you have to come with me now. I know time's short, so's I'm not going to babble about things Dumond says you need to see for yourself. You'll not believe what we found in the tunnels. Once you're through the Quartiere gates, head straight through to the Cat's Eyes at the cliff top. I'll meet you there."

Leaving no opportunity for discussion, he sprinted away. Just as well. We had no letter of introduction to get Neri through the Quartiere di Fiori gate, so he had to get to our meeting place by another route.

Placidio and I made sure the lane was clear of Pizottis and got ourselves admitted to the Quartiere di Fiori. As we hurried through the tree-shaded lanes of the Flower Quarter on our way to meet Neri, I told him the story my brother's excitements had precluded. My father would have named it *The Wool Commissioner and the Murder in Cuarona*.

Placidio listened carefully. "So you first thought Egerik had murdered his wife in one of these *exquisite* pageants, but now you say he actually fancied her and dispatched that half-naked servant to murder the one who attacked her. Certain, I don't see how it could be both."

"I can't say for certain that he loved her," I said. "But Lenore is a good observer, and Nuccio's message tells us that Egerik didn't kill her for the Brotherhood, at least. No servant of Egerik's would slaughter Oriana's attacker on his own. So maybe Egerik set him to it because the attacker dared touch his prized possession or harmed the perfection of her beauty. But together the two stories reinforce what we saw in the house. Lenore said the attacker's body was ravaged like a wild animal had done it; you said Cei reminded you of a wolf tamed to the leash."

"He does that."

"After I left Lenore, I was trying to understand why Egerik kept Cei around after the murder, even while his wife was living. And I told myself that Egerik is clever and determined and does nothing without a reason. If he set someone to take his vengeance, then it was done exactly as he wished. Savagely."

Saying the words aloud helped me make sense of it all. "Five years ago, Cei would have been younger than Neri. How long had Egerik been grooming him to do such things? Has he killed others who crossed Egerik? You see where all this goes?"

"Aye." Placidio paused and tapped the walking stick on the rocky ground. "Egerik has a trained assassin in his collection. Pretty. Barefoot. Most people wouldn't suspect him."

"An *exquisite* assassin."

The cypresses and poplars thinned as we neared the rocky eastern boundary of the Heights. There, the ring wall was actually under our feet—a broad expanse of naked stone, riddled with cracks and littered with rocks and rubble, the top of a stomach-churning cliff. A glance down from the edge—only children or the nerveless ever tried that—revealed the sheer rock face that provided a much stouter defense from an eastern assault than anything humans could build. One might have thought Mother Gione herself had taken her longsword and cleaved the rounded edge from the hilltop to expose the solid underpinnings of Cantagna.

"So is fish man off searching for his mother's servant?" Placidio said, as we paused behind a straggling clump of junipers and scanned the expanse of rock for Pizottis.

"He told me he got work packing pilchards for Frenetti, and is to sleep in the fish house. Then he left as abruptly as you did. I had to turn my mind to Chimera business. If we don't get our hands on the Assassins List today, I'm afraid we never will."

I wanted to talk more about Teo. To ask Placidio why he had changed his mind about him so abruptly. Why he'd shown him *respect*. But across the rocky flat a wiry figure sat waiting atop a half of a lightning-split boulder near the cliff edge. It was time to work.

23

Travelers crossing the rolling fields and vineyards to the east had named Neri's perch and its twin the Cat's Eyes. In the early morning, sunbeams reflected from polished swirls of color in the oddly shaped pair of rocks, giving rise to the story of a great cat that lounged atop Cantagna's heart gazing out on the fruits of her prosperity.

My brother scrambled down and beckoned us follow him into a crack in the cliff. Millennia of rain, wind, and earthquakes had widened the crack into a rugged defile. I held my breath and stepped carefully down the narrow, gravelly, and much-too-steep-for-comfort path. Placidio followed close behind. I wished him steady feet; if he slipped, he'd send me shooting out over the edge and tumbling all the way down to the city's East Gate.

"Sorry the ground's a bit shifty," said Neri. "I explored this years ago. Thought myself an adventurer when I found three caves. Two were no more than scrapes in the wall; but one went deeper than I could go without a light. When Dumond and I were hunting an entrance to the tunnels, I remembered what you said, swordmaster, about the caves down to the Asylum Ring, and I wondered if this one might be connected. The map seemed to agree."

Pebbles squirted out from under our shoes, skittering and pelting down and down and down until I couldn't hear them anymore. Fortunately it was only a short distance until Neri vanished into a hole in the left wall. I stepped in after him, never so grateful to be surrounded by rock and dirt on every side and Placidio behind.

Neri quickly disappeared farther into the dark. My eyes blinked rapidly, dazzled from the brilliant morning.

"Left this here before I came to fetch you." Neri returned into view with a lantern. "Come."

The cave led downward through a tunnel of rock. Neri's light seemed much too pale, but once we had turned a corner where the outside glare couldn't reach us, my eyes attuned to the lamplight. The way was wide enough we could walk two abreast.

The rock soon yielded to a mix of rock and dirt. Sturdy beams had been placed long ago in places where rock had crumbled or dirt slumped.

Neri halted where the tunnel branched at a particularly large heap of stone slabs, dirt, rock, and splintered wood. One route continued past the debris pile in roughly the same direction. The other headed over the pile and into another tunnel.

Neri pointed straight past the mound. "This route we're on takes us straight to Dumond's trapdoor from Egerik's kitchen yard. But that entry we just came in won't do you for *escaping*, as it would send you right back past the palazzo to the guards at the Quartiere gate. So you'd need to turn into this side tunnel. Follow our marks and eventually you'll get to Dumond's new door that will take you out of the Heights and into the Street of the Coffinmakers."

"We'd climb over this heap?" Placidio pointed his walking stick at the mound. "Assuming we've found our way this far."

"Aye. It's not so rough. We've a lantern hung beneath the trapdoor and torches set along the way, ready to fire as you need. Believe me, you don't want to stumble wrong in these tunnels."

Neri held the lantern up high enough to show us an unburnt torch sitting in a bracket.

"Stacks of these torches were already here," said Neri. "Old as the moon, but sitting in nice puddles of pitch. Dumond was able to unstick them. He's getting good with fire and heat."

"Left from the plague burials," I said. Neri's lantern had revealed a massive lintel stone above our heads. It was carved with the ancient words seen at the entry to every graveyard: *Riposa nella Notte Eterna.* Rest in the Night Eternal.

More telling, the carvers had left off the traditional ending of the graveyard greeting: *fino al ritorno degli Dei Invisibili.* Until the Unseeable Gods return. Over half of Cantagna's population had died during the three waves of plague. No one believed the gods would ever come back.

"There's corpses in every direction," said Neri. "For now we'll go straight toward the palazzo."

I covered mouth and nose with my mantle as we squeezed past the mound and entered the first burial chamber. The walls were lined floor to ceiling with niches, each holding a desiccated corpse or two or five, wrapped in crumbling canvas. The dry cave air so far above the river, and the distance of a hundred fifty years, made it possible to pass through without vomiting. The odor was mostly dust and mould. Some places you could see a name scratched in the wood—*Rigo, Gulio, Maréa, three children* . . .

Many of the shelves had collapsed. Burial parties had scraped out side rooms in the packed earth walls. Weak, exhausted, numb as the years of horror passed, they had dumped cartloads of victims there without wrapping or identification.

Through chamber after grim chamber, we splayed our fingers in a sign of Mother Gione's peace, as the weight of mortal sadness settled on our shoulders.

"Not much farther," said Neri softly.

The walls of packed earth pressed closer. Placidio's hat brushed the ceiling. The dark devoured our lantern light. Mercifully, the burial parties had not pushed into such close quarters.

"Here." Neri pointed out the location of Dumond's trapdoor, marked with carefully placed scratches on a well-shored section of tunnel roof. "After you've gone in, Dumond will fire it with his magic. Get out to the garden, yank the ring to open it, and you can drop right down here."

Past the trap, the tunnel ended abruptly in a solid slab.

Nonetheless, Neri beckoned us onward. A very narrow vertical crack seamed the end wall.

"*Through* this?" Placidio was skeptical.

"Worth the trouble," Neri whispered. "You need to see."

To get through the crack, Placidio had to remove his wide-brimmed hat and the fashionable padding Vashti had installed in his yellow doublet and trousses. I had to wrap mantle, gown, and underskirts around me so tightly, I felt like a sausage.

Even before Neri brought the lantern through, I knew we were in a huge space. But the light revealed its immensity. The stone roof was supported by sturdy pillars and beams. Free of the miasma of death, it had been swept, mostly de-spidered, and filled . . .

Neri held up the lamp.

"By the Mother!"

Sacks of oats, flour, barley filled one corner. Stacked casks of ale, wine, and mead lined the walls. Everywhere stood wax-sealed jars bearing the marketplace symbols for dried fish, dried meat, and dried fruit, dry noodles and beans. More sealed jars held nuts and seeds and ever-precious olive oil. A hoard of salt would be the envy of any village in the Costa Drago. These were stores enough for a siege.

"We thought this a bit more than expected for one man and his household," Neri whispered. "And then there's this . . ."

His knife blade made quick work of the lock on a gate of rust-free iron bars, and he waved us through. The walls were festooned with weapons. Pikes, halberds, staves and spears, shields and bucklers. Dozens and dozens of them. Some new, some well used, but clean of rust. Long racks held more of them. Sampling the contents of the long wood chests stacked three high revealed bows and thousands of arrows.

"Atladu's balls, does he have an army hid down here, too?" said Placidio, peering into the corners the lamplight couldn't reach.

"If so, we didn't find it," said Neri. I recognized the very particular grin he was trying to hide—the pleasurable satisfaction of truly astounding a taskmaster.

But this was no game.

Placidio inspected the wall of polearms, examining joints and blades. "Not exceptional work, but, damnation, between this room and the stores, they've spent a grand duc's ransom. There's no city regulations forbid a man, even a Mercediaran, from stocking his cellars. But the Shadow Lord might want to send scouts out to places like the Boars Teeth or the Spikes, where troublemakers could hide thinking to use all this. 'Twould be a clever maneuver for Vizio to send a lightly armed band as her vanguard."

"He scouts those places regularly," I said. "And he has spies—" I stopped. There were things I should not speak, even to those closest to me.

Sandro had two people deeply entrenched in Protector Vizio's house who kept him apprised of every development. And it was only nineteen days ago that he had proposed this scheme to prevent the Assassins List from breaking the ever fragile peace between Cantagna and Mercediare.

"He would know if Vizio was on the move." Unless, of course, those brave spies had been caught and silenced.

Placidio ran a finger along a poleax blade. Rubbed it with another finger and sniffed at it. "These have been sharpened and oiled quite recently, lady scribe. Something's in the wind."

"This changes everything," I said, shaken to the marrow. "This is much bigger than *offer the Assassins List to Vizio to win my freedom* or *blackmail the ambassador to let me go free.*"

"Aye. We're well beyond that." Placidio's sobriety reflected my own. "For a diplomat fairly new to Cantagna to accumulate such a hoard without the Shadow Lord learning of it, he would need expert help. Who better than Cinque the Spy? And Egerik is wily enough that he would never leave himself exposed to anyone he didn't trust. To my mind we've just answered our original question: Cinque is not afraid of the ambassador because they are partners. Makes me wonder if Cinque got himself caught apurpose to bring them together. Today."

"Two days ago I'd have called that madness," I said. "Now I wonder if the Assassins List plays a role in their conspiracy at all or if we'll have to kidnap Rossi to find it."

Placidio opened a deep chest to reveal helms, habergeons, and other simple armor. "Rossi promised you that Vizio would not see the List. Do you truly believe that?"

That took some thinking, riffling through our meetings over the years, and every word of our interview in the Palazzo Segnori.

"I do," I said at last. "Rossi never cheats. He plays to win and would consider it demeaning. This game happens to be much bigger than I knew at the time, but he meant it."

"Which suggests that he and Egerik are not working *for* Vizio, but aiming *at* her."

Puzzle pieces shifted into place.

"Supporting rebels," I said. "We're awfully far away, but then, barges head south from here every day. Safer to accumulate arms up here. The Shadow Lord is not going to be at all happy to discover this city will appear to be supplying rebels as well as assassins. Rebellions fail and Vizio would see everyone in Cantagna as her enemy. And certain"—how had I overlooked the obvious?—"they could use the Assassins List, not for vengeance or a bargaining chip, but for exactly its purpose. Call in the pledges and hire an assassin to remove Vizio."

"Aye, they'll send Vizio a cloth-of-gold sash to celebrate her decade in power in the hands of a well-paid assassin, backed up by a well-armed, well-fed cadre of rebels."

"An *exquisite* assassin," I said, near breathless with the audacity of such a plot. "Perfectly groomed for this task."

"That plays. Whatever the variant details, I'll wager my fine hat that the Assassins List will be inside Palazzo Ignazio today."

"Indeed. Rossi would never let such a valuable instrument out of his control before ready to use it. If we can get a notion of where it is, a location we can describe to Neri, we can have it. I have to become Monette, so you're the one will have to watch, listen, and feed the information to Neri."

Placidio bowed. "Baldassar is a man of opportunity."

"I'll be waiting," said Neri. "But we need to move on. Can't hear the bells down here."

"Yes, of course." I released a long breath. Failure had just taken on a much more terrible face. "Are there any more terrifying mysteries you want us to see, little brother?"

"Just another burial chamber up closer to the house," Neri said. "Recent. Not old. We think it likely his wife's. The place is fancied up, the walls painted like the Palazzo Segnori—"

"Artwork, you mean," I said. "Murals."

"Aye, and a marble coffin with a lady's figure carved on it and gold-work posts at the four corners."

"I want to see it before we go. I need something to drive a wedge between Rossi and Egerik."

"Boy was right. We'd best hurry," said Placidio. "Be late and all will be for naught."

Oriana di Sinterolla's resting place was just off a side passage beyond the storage cavern. No expense had been spared in its elaboration. The four gold pillars at the corners of the tomb, shaped like bundled spikes of sweet asphodel, matched the finest work of Ranila di Baggio, *il Padroné*'s choice to cast his beloved grandfather's memorial statue.

The luminous murals were surely the work of young Tiso di Andillo. His cresting waves and leaping dolphins were so lifelike I could taste the salt flavor of the sea. Muscular celebrants wearing sandals and gold bangles while feasting on heaped platters of grapes, apricots, and oranges were classic images of Mercediaran culture.

I committed every detail of the capacious chamber to memory. The silk hangings of sunset orange-red. Gilt-trimmed urns filled with dried flowers. Perfume flasks and cloisonné jars, ivory combs and bronze hand mirrors laid out on a lacquered dressing table. A couch laid with pillows and silk sheets, as if the lady might step out of her white coffin and take a nap.

A sad life, ended too early. I wished her peace.

Life-sized bronze images of Gione the Mother and Manadi the Huntress occupied two corners. In the third corner, a curved niche lined with gold mosaic surrounded a plinth that lacked a statue . . .

Goddess mother! On the marble surface lay a fresh rose. A thin-bladed knife. And indeed a drop of blood. Quite fresh.

"We need to leave." I pointed at the blood droplet. "Someone was here not so long ago."

The sight brought back all my misgivings about exquisite murders.

A backward glance as we hurried away revealed wreaths of sea lavender encircling the bases of the four gold pillars. A row of finger-high brass natalés stood guard around the base of the marble catafalque. The mystery of their meaning teased at me as I followed my companions back through the storage rooms and the passage beyond.

We sped through the burial chambers as if the dead were pushing us from behind, and reached the tunnel entry and the perilous path upward to the land of the living in an astonishingly quick time. Neri hung back as Placidio and I brushed ourselves off.

"I'm off to meet Dumond," he said, his black curls dusty, his skin ablaze with adventure. "We're to test the last doorway. Soon as we've got the whole route clear, swordmaster, I'll get your main gauche back to the stair. What should I do with your sword?"

Leaving his sword behind damped Placidio's spirits far worse than the pain of a nicked rib.

"No assurance we'll leave by this tunnel route, else I'd stow it in the dead lady's bedchamber," he said at last. "But with boot and sleeve knives, the dagger at my belt, which may or may not be left me, and the main gauche hid in a place I know, I've already more weapons than hands. If I need better"—he bent his head toward Neri and flashed a grin—"I'll just have to borrow one from its owner. Forcibly."

"I'll keep this one with me, then."

"So these storage caverns and Oriana's tomb must connect to the palazzo," I said.

"They do. There's a tangle of passages beyond the tomb chamber. Spooked us, but we found the way all the way to the stair from the closet."

"Glad to know you can be spooked by something," said Placidio.

Neri, reflecting his swordmaster's flash of humor, picked something off my shoulder and tossed away an unsettlingly large spider. "Don't let the creeper collect you, sister witch."

I caught Neri's arm before he could dart away and pulled him close. "I've good reason to believe one of Egerik's servants is a savage murderer, *little brother.* And with what we've just seen, don't underestimate *anyone* in that house. Tell me you hear what I'm saying."

The retort burning Neri's tongue died as my grip hardened and he met my gaze with sobriety. "I hear. *You* remember it, too."

"I will. And Monette will." Trying to smile, I shoved him away. He disappeared into the tunnel.

• • •

As I climbed out of the rift, the city bells chimed the first hour past midday. One hour we had to decide our next move. I was glad of the time. So much to consider.

Placidio was already halfway up the path, and quickly vanished over the rim of the rift. I followed. Once off the steeps, I breathed deep of the clean air, grateful for sunlight, solid ground, and a quickening breeze.

For a moment I thought Placidio had gone off without me. But he stood in the shadow of the Cat's Eyes—out of easy view of lurking Pizottis. But for this moment I didn't think his mind was on drunken swordsmen and vendettas, spies or treasonous ambassadors. Hands propped on the walking stick, he gazed out easterly. The day was so clear, you could almost glimpse the sparkle of the *Mare di Ossa*—the Sea of Bones—or the range of high peaks that curved protectively about Riccia-by-the-sea.

Shadows drifted across his demeanor like wisps of cloud across the sun. Grief, I believed, perhaps prompted by my farewell with Neri. I'd seen it in our brief encounter with the grand duc of Riccia-by-the-sea. There was history between Placidio and the grand duc. Maybe magic. Maybe family. Maybe Riccia itself or something else entirely. All remained fixedly beyond his boundaries.

But today, we needed to move forward, and I wasn't sure exactly of our destination.

"Do you suppose Egerik fancies himself Vizio's replacement?" I said, propping my backside on the massive boulder.

"I'd not think his strict cleanliness rules would hold up well in Mercediare or any independency—except perhaps tidy little Cuarona. More likely he's got some tyrant-in-waiting who will owe him immense favors."

"Truly, Monette could use a few more weapons to sling between these two," I said. "Malignant spirits frightened Egerik more than anything. It would have been convenient if he had murdered his wife."

"You're a cruel woman, lady scribe."

"Then tell me why were Brotherhood of the Exquisite symbols on the plinth at Oriana's tomb." I said. "The rose, knife, and blood are meant to be a sort of clever cipher that only the initiated understand. But if her death wasn't a Brotherhood event, why put them there? Who are they *reminding*?"

"Maybe it serves a different purpose there," said Placidio. "Many families believe in burying their family members with

all the appurtenances of that person's life. Those were surely
Oriana's face paints, her couch, her pillows."

"The art reflected her Mercediaran birth," I said, "and I'll
wager her favorite color was that orange-red of the hangings
and her favorite flower asphodel as in the gold pillars. But
why the symbol of the Brotherhood? For Egerik?"

Placidio harrumphed. "Did you ever consider that maybe
the woman herself was a *member*? No matter name or history,
there's not a fraternity or brotherly order in Cantagna doesn't
have women admitted nowadays. She'd lived with Egerik for a
long time, so likely knew about it. Maybe she shared his obses-
sion with these exquisite pleasures."

"Truly?" Never invited to—or interested in—these fraterni-
ties and brotherhoods, I'd not imagined women members. But
if so . . .

Placidio slapped his forehead. "Mother Gione's ever-
nurturing tits, you heard report of a *member's—*"

"—exquisite suicide." The conclusion struck us at the same
moment. "Certain, that was it! Reports said she was ill. Her
children long dead. No others conceived in the years between.
Some women take that very hard."

"Men, too. Especially those concerned with great families . . . heritage . . . titles."

Born to a family whose multitude of children was the root
of starvation, and having lived with Sandro whose aspirations
to children rested in someone else, I found it difficult to sort out
how childlessness, no matter how tragic, could have driven a
well loved woman to take her own life. "Do you think Egerik
drove her to it?"

Placidio raised his opened palms as if to distance himself

from the knotty question. "Self murder is comprehensible. The mystery is what might drive anyone to embrace this confraternity of perfected triviality."

I could not disagree. A hot breeze snatched at my mantle and tugged my hair from its braid.

"Cei naked," Placidio blurted.

"What?"

"Mayhap seeing Cei standing naked on that plinth was the lady's idea of exquisite perfection. Recruited her to the Brotherhood."

"I certainly won't argue with that particular perfection," I said, "though suspecting the beautiful man capable of savage murder tarnishes the imagining a bit."

Private as he was, I sometimes felt as if Placidio knew me better than anyone in the world. Better than my brother who had never tasted the wider world. Better even than Sandro, from whom I'd hidden a childhood that had forever shaped me and the taint on my soul that would necessarily drive us apart. For certain, Placidio was the only one of the three I could not shock.

I left my rocky support and tugged Placidio's hat around to the rakish angle that shadowed his dueling scar. "So, swordmaster, we know the terrain and our opponents. Our weapons are in place. All we have left to do is fight."

Placidio gave a pleased chuckle, startling a goodly number of pigeons. "A sufficient recitation, student. We need to move. Don't like to stand in one place too long."

He scanned the few passersby carefully before we stepped out from the shelter of the split boulder.

"I'm guessing you saw the natalés and the sea lavender around that tomb," he said.

"I did. Perhaps Oriana is the one who put the natalés about the house, believing her unborn child's soul was still inside her. Some believe that when a child is stillborn."

"So her tomb became the child's too. Yet it still needed warding for whenever the soul took flight? Even though the younger had been three years dead by the time she died? And presumably the child's soul would have flitted away with hers, yet Egerik still maintains warding inside his house? Does any of that make sense?"

I had to agree it seemed strange, but who was I to say?

"The sea lavender could be to ward off the spirit of the man Cei murdered," I said. "Though if that was so, you'd think Egerik would rid himself of Cei, hoping to appease the dead man."

To twist such morbid oddities and theories into some logical pattern, while walking in the peaceful sunlight with warblers and buntings waking from afternoon doldrums in the oak branches overhead, struck me as ridiculous. A laugh bubbled up in me. When I finally let it escape it met a matching chuckle from Placidio.

"Two old skeptics, we are," he said, as we turned onto the boulevard, "trying to make sense of goblin stories and human strangeness. 'Tis not polite to laugh at others' serious business, lady scribe, especially when they're dead."

"Certain, their story is sad. The strange part is trying to explain the spiritual motives of a political functionary. Truly, I would like to know what malignant spirit Egerik fears."

We walked on in quiet companionship. I appreciated what Placidio was doing—inducing a sense of calm before a difficult task. Unfortunately the effort was spoiled from time to time when he would shove me behind a tree or a boxwood hedge without warning. After a moment, he'd say "all's well," and we'd be on our way again. The Pizottis. I'd never seen him so skittish.

The gates of Palazzo Ignazio came into view. As on the previous morning, the dolphin-and-hammer ensign flapped slowly in the heavy breeze. Only . . .

My feet halted, my every assumption, every certainty, every conclusion suddenly in flux. "Placidio, you told me that you could recall everything I read you from Mantegna's report exactly. Yes?"

"Aye. I was very well focused. Elsewise my slashed gut was going to have me clawing my naked skin off."

"Tell me what it said about the *salacious scandal* in Argento."

"There were certain whispers at the time of a salacious scandal involving several wealthy Mercediaran exiles, all of whom died within months of Egerik's departure."

Exiles. One word that could change everything yet again.

"Now look at the pennon atop the gatehouse." The pennon that, like that one flying the previous day, displayed Mercediare's blazon on a field of fiery red orange. Only today the dolphin and hammer were topped by a crown.

"Demonfire!" Placidio's astonished exhalation could have extinguished Chloni's lantern in the moment the sexless god created the stars.

"Most people who leave Mercediare alive are happy to do so and grateful to be accepted elsewhere," I said. "I can think of only one group of Mercediarans who would ever style themselves as *exiles*."

"House Rossignoli. . . ."

No earthquake precipitated by Dragonis's mighty tail could equal the concussion that name set off in my head. Rossi might be the most common surname in the Costa Drago, but Rossignoli was exquisitely rare. Dedino di Rossignoli, the last king of Mercediare, had been dead for over a hundred years.

"Fernand di Rossi lived for some years in Argento," I said, biting my lip, frantic to rebuild our understanding before the next bell rang. "When I first met him eight years ago—my second year in House Gallanos—he had just arrived from Argento. He and Egerik were in Argento at the same time."

Fernand di Rossi, who wore a gold bracelet, a gold ring, and a diamond-and-ruby baldric inherited from his nameless family. What a fine way to eliminate family members one might view as rivals—to have a newfound ally implicate them in sordid activities that could draw the Brotherhood of the Exquisite to eliminate them.

"In every local dialect of the Costa Drago, *cinque* means five," said Placidio. "The last Rossignoli king with the name of Fernand was the fourth of that name, also known as *Fernand Empire Builder*."

Was it possible that Fernand di Rossi was Pretender to the long vacant throne of Mercediare? Even if he'd claimed Rossignoli blood as one of his origin stories, who would have believed it? Rumors of Rossignoli heirs had popped up now and again like ghost hauntings, but were as easily dismissed. Mercediarans were thorough in their purges. And even believing, who would fear Rossi? A silly man, charming, as significant as a household spider.

Yet this particular spider's web reached into every wealthy house throughout the Costa Drago, and his superior intelligence—even the Shadow Lord sorely underestimated it—made than web far stronger than any could imagine. He was armed with a list of rich, influential people sworn to rid the world of Protector Vizio and what other information he—as Cinque—might have gathered through the years. History named the Rossignoli kings both ruthless and wily. Had he installed a cache of arms and stores underneath all nine independencies? Such violence would inflame the Costa Drago to ruination for generations.

And on this particular day, Egerik was flying the royal ensign of Mercediare—enjoying a moment of superiority, imagining all of us common intellects would never notice his audacity.

"We're not speaking of rampant vendettas anymore," said Placidio. "Or supporting a rebellious faction with arms and food. We're speaking of a full-blown revolution."

I glanced up at the heavy banner, filling and whipping in the heavy breeze. "Somehow," I said, "in some way, it is going to begin in Cantagna. Tonight."

As the tower bells struck the second hour of afternoon, the heart of Cantagna's working day, Placidio and I stared at each other, even as the matter of spies, ambassadors, a groomed assassin, a cellar full of armaments, and a compromising list of notable citizens reshaped itself around us yet again. And only moments did we have to judge what we were left with.

24

No possible story could serve as an excuse for us arriving late to Palazzo Ignazio. If we wished to continue this venture, we had to stroll across Egerik's flagstone forecourt and outsized sleugh before the bells' intonation faded, slipping back into our roles as devout servant of divine Espe and jackleg cloth merchant—two fools who had no idea what use their conspiratorial host thought to make of them.

Our earlier conclusions of partnership between Egerik and Rossi were guesses, and now the stakes were much, much higher. Switching Protectors was an internal matter for Mercediare, its consequences rippling through trade and shipping, skirmishes and vendettas. Bad enough. But a revolution to install a hereditary lord—a king—would fracture every independency.

Like Cantagna, every city had those families who longed for a return to the age of kings, and those like House Gallanos who envisioned something new. Two independencies were already ruled by hereditary nobles. Would the upright grand duc of Riccia ride to the aid of a legitimate Rossignoli heir? His legions were the largest in the Costa Drago. What of the conte of Tibernia? If those two powerful lords joined Rossi's cause, his lack of an army of his own could be moot.

I tried to hold on to reason. "Egerik has spent years positioning himself as a trustworthy pillar of the Protectorate. It's hard to imagine him sacrificing his own ambition to a royal Pretender who's spent his life in drawing rooms and lacks his own army to wield those hidden weapons. What does Egerik get out of a revolution? Even a spy's cache of secrets cannot pay for an army, and an impoverished sovereign's gratitude buys no cloth-of-gold. So I need whatever help you can give to confirm or refute our hypotheses. The longer I can go without invoking my magic, the more I can learn to influence Monette when it's time, but Rossi . . ." Rossi could ruin our play with one glance.

We strolled across the courtyard. "I *must* know if Rossi is already in the house," I murmured, "and I must know if they are together in this, and whether this new suspicion is grounded."

Placidio leaned heavily on the walking stick, lest anyone wonder at our pace. "Aye to all that," he said and tugged his wide-brimmed hat lower to shade his face.

Though I doubted Rossi or Egerik either one would be observing our arrival, I raised the hood on my mantle as well. "Once I'm Monette, if ever we've time alone, you've got to pull me out, so we can share what we've learned."

"I'll do that." He gripped my arm with a most unfatherly tightness. "Before all, you needs must think hard on the answer to our endgame question . . . about Egerik and Rossi surviving this mission—this *night*. I've a notion we'll not have luxury to regroup and ponder. Look at the number of footmen, guards, carriages, horses about this court. Looks as if your audience will be sizeable."

He was right. Staggered by the possibilities of royal revolution, I'd not even noticed. The peripheries of the circular court-yard were bustling—servants in varied liveries wiping down carriages, groomsmen tethering horses, linkboys laughing, dicing, or drinking until their services were needed for departing guests. I expected a few conspirators, not guests . . .

A meticulously liveried guard wearing the dolphin-and-hammer crest of Mercediare approached us from the entry.

I glanced up at Placidio, somber, his cheeks flushed, eyes fierce as flaring embers under his thick brows. He was right about the endgame. Assassinating Egerik and Rossi could implicate Cantagna in treaty violations, shaking the Shadow Lord's power, if not erasing it. Yet that could not overbalance preventing a generation of war. Either consequence would leave *il Padroné*'s vision of enlightenment in ruins.

Yet something more was brewing here. Why the guests? Why the divination? Egerik's desire gave us a unique opportunity to discover his game and thwart it. Maybe without resorting to murder.

"The Chimera is not comprised of assassins," I said. "We work for Cantagna's safety. Not Mercediare's, not Cuarona's, not any other city's. Our task is to neutralize the danger of the Assassins List and that we will do."

We could slow our steps no longer. The Mercediaran guardsman arrived to escort us to the sleugh crossing. On the far side of the iron footbridge, Mistress Mella waited in pale perfection, as if she had been carefully put away in a trunk when we left the previous day and just brought out again. Not a hair had slipped from her modest cap. Not a wrinkle or smudge marred her crisp white linen gown. "Merchant Fabroni, Damizella Monette, welcome return to Palazzo Ignazio."

The only slip in the housekeeper's deportment was the flare of her nostrils as she took stock of our wilted appearance. My shoes and hem were caked with mud, grit, and a kind of ash that did not bear thinking about. Placidio's ruffled neckpiece had sagged into something that looked like a noose, and his yellow silks were frayed and streaked with dirt. Both of us were beaded with sweat from our foray into the burial chambers.

"My master asks that I provide his hospitality before he meets with you himself," said Mistress Mella.

I dipped my knee in humble courtesy, but immediately regretted it. *Spirits!* I must keep my wits about me. Monette had left here believing that Lady Fortune had truly spoken through her. That her destiny was coming to fruition as the voice of the divine. She would not be humble before a serving woman. Not anymore.

Placidio rapped his walking stick solidly on the floor three times, arresting Mella's attention. "I must speak to His Great Excellency about his intentions with regard to my daughter. She has been most agitated about his insistence on a particular divination after a long morning's business. He must understand that she is delicate, and that the Lady Espe speaks at her own time, not at her servants' command."

"I will report your request, merchant. But I've been instructed to inform you that you will be compensated appropriately for the girl's service. This is an opportunity that will come to such folk as yourselves few times in this world—to have your talents so perfectly rewarded."

"Hmph."

Placidio's skepticism reflected mine exactly. Even as myself, Mella's responses insulted me. How stupid and insignificant this woman believed us.

I appreciated Placidio's attempt to introduce a delay. A few hours to explore our new theories would be most welcome. But he knew as well as I that the world would not wait.

Mella led us briskly through the waiting rooms we'd traversed so slowly on our first visit, and up a modest, open stair to a less ostentatious hall than we had seen so far. Wood plank floors. Wall panels covered not with murals, but figured fabric. Clerestory windows provided a diffuse light. And four rooms—two on either side—opened from the hall. Between the two solid doors on each wall, a wood bench and a side table holding a pewter candelabra provided the hall's accommodation. No squints. So safe for now.

"Be seated, merchant. I've dispatched a servant to bring ale for you."

"Wine is my preference," said Placidio with dignity. "And my daughter keeps to cider when she is communing with divinities."

He waved his stick at the doorways. "Is one of these where we will meet with the ambassador?"

"You may inform Emilio of your preference for wine when he arrives. And no. These are householder accommodations."

She laid her pale hand on my shoulder and urged me insistently toward one of the doors. "Come, damizella, I'm sure you would appreciate a chance to freshen yourself. His Excellency has guests for the evening."

"Papa, would you keep my mantle? I could certainly use a moment to brush off the day."

Unsure of what *freshening* myself meant in Mella's eyes, I dropped the thing on the bench beside Placidio. An inside pocket of my mantle held my small dagger and my needle bag. I didn't want Mella to notice the dagger, and I dared not lose the *ascoltaré* needles Dumond had modified. More than ever today, either Romy or Romy's voice in Monette's head must tell my hands how to direct their fall. I must *not* go too deep.

Placidio affirmed my deposit with a jerk of his head, and sat, back straight, hands propped on the brass head of his stick.

"We're to meet guests?" he said. "Who would that be? Some of them may already be my customers; all will have heard of our most excellent collection. We did not bring our sample case, but perhaps you could send a servant . . ."

"That will not be necessary," said Mella, not deigning so much as a glance as she held open a door and herded me through. She closed the door firmly behind us, breaching protocol again with a hiss of disgust. Placidio would enjoy knowing he'd driven her to it.

The chamber surprised me. I'd thought Egerik's householders would sleep in hermit cells. Rose-colored fabric covered the walls, and a brightly woven blanket dressed the modest sling bed. A long dressing table was set with a brush, hand mirror, and a selection of small jars and vials at one end. At the other end sat a wide clay bowl painted with roses. Everything clean. Everything harmonious. The whole struck me as a modest echo

of the exquisite burial chamber not so far away. I wanted to be
sick.

"First a wash," said Mella. She filled the bowl with water
from a painted pitcher. "The day is warm. Sit here, so I can do
it. We must have you ready when the bell rings."

"But, mistress, I've no need—"

"Do not argue." She scooped dried rose petals from a dish
and tossed them into the steaming bowl, and then pressed me
down to the stool beside the dressing table.

"Of course this seems strange to a person like you. But His
Excellency has great admiration for your beliefs, great respect
for your closeness to the Lady." Her flat insistence made clear
these were sentiments Mella did not share. "He understands
you would not wish to insult your divine Mistress with filth or
shabby attire. He raises you up in honor to her."

"All kindness, but truly . . . I . . ."

How would Monette answer? I'd never understood how entirely my impersonations grew from the magic. While I stammered, Mella's brutal efficiency had me washed, stripped, and
sheathed in clean linen. My hair was unbraided and brushed
until it spread about my shoulders in a black cloud. My dirty
garments were left in a heap, and she had me step into a soft
flowing undergown of deep blue. The high neck and front panel
of the bodice were overstitched with a spiderweb of silver, the
slim sleeves banded at the wrists with more of it. She attached
a mantle of gauzy indigo at my shoulders with silver clasps in
the shape of lacewings—like the lacewing pendant that she returned to hang at my breast, the sign of Lady Fortune. I'd worn
no garments so lovely since the harsh midnight I was banished
from *il Padroné*'s house.

"I must say, damizella," said Mella as she clipped a simple twist of silver to hold my cloud of hair from one side of my face. "You wear this very naturally, as if you've had other occasions to don such finery."

"Only for customers. To show our fabrics."

A good thing Mella had met me before I became Monette on our first visit, catching only a glimpse of Monette on our way out. Who could have known I would endure such intimacy?

She tossed my cheap earrings onto the heap of soiled clothes, replacing them with knuckle-length drops of tiny sapphires. Egerik wanted me to make an impression on his guests.

Who would Egerik invite here tonight? The carriages and linkboys belied a gathering of mercenary captains ready to provide a legion should Egerik give the word. The guests could simply be members of the Brotherhood come to watch him torture a prisoner fool enough not to fear him. But I didn't think so. I'd seen the crown on the banner.

"Mistress, I must know what quality of guests will see me this evening. Who—and how many. My Lady's truth is often of quite personal nature. Too many observers can confuse my hearing, obscuring the clarity needed for accurate interpretation. And I see no need for such apparel, beautiful though it be and so generously meant. The Lady demands a certain modesty from her communicants."

Mella bathed my hands again, taking her time, paying careful attention to my nails and the red needle pricks from the day before. "You will see whomever the ambassador chooses and wear the garments he sees fit. Those are the conditions of his favor. You will come to understand the rewards of such a life."

"Such a life?" Monette's naivete must be clear. "Mistress, surely I cannot *stay* here. My father has forbidden—"

"Surely your father has wit enough to defer to the ambassador's desires. Our master is a most determined man. If he wants you, he will have you."

So Egerik did mean to collect Monette. I must make sure she had good reasons to accept it, while keeping her wits about her.

Mella pushed my feet into soft blue slippers—the kind she and the rest of the staff wore that kept their steps so quiet. "Now a little darkening about your eyes, a little rouge to highlight the cheekbones."

"Your master's favor honors me and my Lady. Certain, I must trust her bidding."

Moon House instruction rose up from the wastelands where I had buried it. Of course Egerik wanted submission.

For yet one more of ten thousand times, I thanked whatever power in the universe, course of luck, or fortune's benefice had sent me to Sandro. Against every custom of our world, he had allowed me choice in everything from what to wear to the hour in which he came to my bed for the first time. He had nourished my mind and spirit so generously that I'd been able to see multitudes of choices I never imagined. Never had I wanted to walk away, nor broached the subject. But what would he have answered if I had asked him to set me free? Even now as I looked back, recalling how much I adored him, knowing how sincerely he cared for me, I could not guess that answer. I had been his bound servant under the law, but to my good fortune he had seen me as a thinking person. Life as Egerik's collected diviner, I guessed, would be very, very different.

More than two hours had passed by the time Mistress Mella judged me fit.

"You clean up decently. Our master may wish you veiled, but we will let him judge."

"Indeed, a veil might ease my worries, Mistress." Entirely truth. But I could not delay my impersonation magic indefinitely. Egerik's belief in Monette's true gift was essential.

She draped a filmy length of indigo gauze over her arm, smiled, and opened the door. The smile did not extend to her pale eyes.

I followed her out. "Papa, have they told you—?"

Placidio had slumped to one side on the bench, one arm dangling limply to the floor. Asleep? Or . . .

Please all divinities, not this. A wine cup lay on the floor, its dregs staining Baldassar's puffed yellow trousses and soaked into the planking. An empty pitcher sat on the side table. A half-empty ale flagon and tumbled mug sat in a puddle at his feet.

"Papa! Wake up!" I shook his shoulder. It jostled a mighty snort out of him, but his eyes did not open. *Don't you dare be drunk, you damnable sot! I need your eyes and ears. I need you to wake me if I go too deep . . .*

No, no. He'd never go back on his word. The armaments in the tunnels had shaken him. But Placidio di Vasil was another man who did nothing by accident. This was playacting, surely, or . . . By the Night Eternal, had they put something into his wine?

A bell chimed faintly from a distance.

"Come, damizella," said Mistress Mella. "The ambassador wishes you brought to him. Now." Her lip curled, showing not the least surprise or concern at finding Merchant Fabroni insensible. They wanted him out of the way.

"My divining needles are inside my mantle," I said, fighting off panic. Without Placidio I'd have no one to direct Monette's attention to items of importance, no one to fight my captors if the plan fell apart. Without Placidio . . .

The terror of Bawds Field rolled through me yet again, a cold wind whistling through my ears, the memory of a yawning emptiness where Romy's soul should be.

Desperate, I shook his shoulder. Then dropped to my knees. His stertorous breaths smelled only faintly of wine. He was certainly not drunk. I well knew how much it took to drive him to oblivion.

"Papa, I have to go with Mistress Mella. But my mantle's underneath you, and I need to get my needles."

Placidio lay awkwardly on his left arm. I had to shift it out of the way to get to my mantle and the red silk needle bag. It weighed like a dead man's. As I tugged on him I squeezed hard, twice in rapid succession, our signal that I was ready to invoke my magic. Though I laid my fingers in his flaccid hand where Mella could not see, he did not squeeze back.

My heart stuttered. This was no playacting.

A prick of blood on his finger made me cautious as I rummaged underneath him for the red silk bag of needles. It was not tucked away where I'd left it, and indeed four needles had slid out of the bag's mouth.

If anyone else discovered such a circumstance, that might appear natural. But as I practiced the casting, it was Placidio himself who had suggested that I knot the drawstring, so that none would fall out and be lost. And he did nothing without purpose.

Careful to hold the bag tight enough the protruding needles could not move, I rose and frowned at Placidio. "I must apologize for Papa, Mistress Mella. He's been suffering from gout, as you saw yesterday, and it appears he has drowned his pain in drink. To be honest, he is a bit unnerved by my intimacy with Lady Fortune. But if he could be made more comfortable, close by until I'm free to see to him, it would put my mind at ease."

"We'll find a place he can sleep off his wine before sending him home. Men oft give in to pain rather than standing firm through it."

Not Placidio, though. He could endure more than Mella could imagine.

"Now you *must* come, damizella. Emilio will be at the bottom of the stair. We'll dispatch him to take care of Merchant Fabroni." She swept across the room.

I dared not fuss over him more. He'd not thank me for upending this venture for sentiment. Surely he would have suspected a taint in the wine. His profession had taught him of all the ways people could seek advantage over their opponents. So if he'd risked it, there was reason.

Thus, I hesitated just long enough to verify the telltales that ensured these were indeed the needles Dumond had made for me, and to identify the embossed symbol and raised rings of each protruding needle that would tell me which end was sticking out. *Sacred spirits . . .*

Somehow, over the hours it had taken to dress me, Placidio had contrived to learn the answers we needed most. The four exposed needle points were the primary ends of Presence and Relationship, and the obverse of Jeopardy and Order. *Arrival. Friend. Danger. Chaos.*

I did not need Lady Fortune's voice to interpret, but only Placidio's and mine as we had articulated the most important answers we needed. And here they were. Rossi was here. Rossi and Egerik were aligned in purpose. And their partnership was as dangerous as we feared. Chaos.

As Mella turned back to see if I was coming, I bent over and kissed Placidio's forehead—my sincere thanks and an apology for misjudging his state and for abandoning him here.

I dared not delay my magic. Cold sweat dribbled down my back as necessity drove me to the verge of the precipice and I gazed out on the void.

Whatever Egerik's plan, Monette had to do the disrupting. I had to believe Placidio could fight off what they'd done to him. I had to believe my brother and Dumond would keep themselves safe. Dumond had promised they would not abandon me. I had to trust.

Squeezing my eyes shut, I erased the vision of horror and focused on Monette. Interlacing her story with everything I had learned, everything I needed to remember, and everything I needed her to heed, I reached deep for magic. My body and spirit became Monette di Fabroni, ambitious diviner, while Romy settled into place as Lady Fortune's voice.

25

His Excellency is completing his dressing, Damizella di Fabroni." The manservant Cei, eyes properly lowered, tripped the latch on the paneled door. His hands were slim, smooth, and fine-boned, his nails clean and perfectly trimmed.

Cei had forced himself into my thoughts all day. So deliciously handsome and yet so humble. Yet with Papa's example ever with me, I knew better than to trust such a show; servility could hide innumerable vices. Besides, the Lady's favor, so distinctly clear and so nicely recognized by the ambassador himself, set my place far above a barefoot serving man. My aspirations should be higher.

My hand strayed to the luxurious silk and silver gown and to the sapphire drops dangling from my ears. Mine, if I wanted them. And much more beyond those if I worked matters properly. The imagining left me breathless.

Nonetheless, at some time Cei would lift his eyes, and I

could judge more clearly what kind of man he was. His skin and bones were *so* lovely.

Cei stepped aside to let us pass. As before, his shapely feet were bare.

"Move, girl," snapped Mella under her breath. "Eyes down."

Cold Mella clearly saw herself as the lady mistress of this widower's household. I smiled a little as I lowered my eyes. I would choose my own time to defy her.

The gleaming wood under my blue slippers gave way to a thick carpet; the dimness of the short passageway to pooled lamplight. The faint aroma of warmed lavender and hair oil erased the mundane scent of floor polish.

Mella pinched my arm to halt my steps. Her skirts draped as she bent her knee. "Excellency, you said you wished to see the merchant's girl alone before you display her for your guests."

I stood straight, choosing not to imitate her servantly obeisance.

"Just as I expected." Egerik's sigh of satisfaction could have launched a ship. "The deep sapphire, indigo, and silver show her to excellent advantage."

"Do you wish her veiled?"

"No. She wears her belief as naturally as she wears this costume."

I disliked them speaking of me as if I weren't there. Mella's disdain was insufferable. Yet Lady Fortune herself had chosen the ambassador as the instrument of my elevation. Until I understood her intentions, I should do my best to please him without shame.

Dipping my knee but a finger's breadth, I boldly raised my

eyes. "Your Excellency, such a gracious welcome. Your generosity humbles me and honors my Lady mistress."

The ambassador was resplendent in red-gold brocade with blackwork embroidery at his wrists and a ruff of stiffened lace at his neck. His deep-red trousses cut a generous figure, but unlike my father's canary monstrosities, were tastefully *un*-stuffed. *Oh, Papa.*

"Damizella." Egerik nodded in acceptance of my compliments and, I thought, my boldness. "Housekeeper, you are dismissed. I shall ring when the lady and I are ready to proceed to the reception chamber, so you may ensure our guests' wine cups are full when we enter."

Though her serene expression did not change, Mistress Mella's posture stiffened like drying fruit; she'd been named *housekeeper* when the merchant's daughter was called *lady*. She withdrew with all the grace of a broomstick. My cheeks warmed with pleasure.

Amusement flickered across the ambassador's fine mouth.

As ever when I was about the Lady Espe's business, I heard her whispers in my head, teaching me: *He induced exactly the reaction he wished in* both *of you. Be wary of his wiles.*

Papa feared the ambassador intended to keep me here.

Egerik spread his arms in helpless whimsy. "A moment to finish my evening's adornment, damizella. Then we shall have a brief private talk before we begin our evening's exploration of destiny."

Destiny! Feathers teased my skin.

Silent Cei proffered a short cape bordered with a hint of white ermine. Egerik twitched a finger, and the servant clasped the garment at his master's shoulders, arranging the folds to drape beautifully.

The comfortable, windowless chamber hinted at an extensive wardrobe. Three great closets lined the walls. One stood open, revealing suit after suit of rich fabrics, and trays of collars, jewels, and other ornaments. Papa would sniff at the "lack of *abundant* fashion" in the ambassador's expensive garments. He would also grind his teeth at the evidence of so much coin paid to a cloth merchant other than himself.

Anxiety rippled through me like distant lightning in summer. Though I had spent years craving release from Papa's schemes, his drunken collapse worried me. He had sworn to Egerik that he would be here watching out for me. Certain, I did not *need* him at my side, not with gracious Lady Espe in my heart. But Papa did care for me and did *not* entirely trust Egerik, a sentiment I shared. I must follow my Lady's course this night, but I must make sure to check on Papa when I could.

Cei lifted a plain, gold pectoral chain from an open jewel case and laid it over Egerik's shoulders. Once it was positioned in perfect symmetry, the servant withdrew, leaving us alone.

Egerik twirled a finger. "Turn around, damizella. Let me see all of you."

I spun slowly, just enough to loft the gauzy mantle and silk gown. Fair enough recompense for such luxurious garments as he'd provided.

"Yes. You'll do well. All day I've considered what name will reflect you best. First I thought *Maura*, for you revealed yourself with dark tidings, or perhaps *Sancia*, for you believe so deeply in the holiness of your calling."

"What *name*, sirrah?"

He drew quite close and touched a finger to my lips. "Lesson number one. My servants, no matter how lovely they are or how intimate they might be with the divine Twins, do not speak to me or to my guests without my permission. Ever. Frivolous words interfere with observation and with listening. The tides of the world often move in silence . . . and we who heed them need our quietude."

I quickly averted my eyes so he could not see my dismay. I had assumed that a handmaid of Lady Fortune would not be so bound or restricted as his lesser servants.

As if he'd heard my thoughts, Egerik's fingers raised my chin and held it firm, fixing his gaze to my own.

"Lovely damizella, I believe a most lively and complex spirit exists beneath your sincere devotions and your affectations of simplicity. I saw it when you draped silk across your arm yesterday as you partnered with your oafish father. And"—his finger traced lightly along my jaw and down my silver-worked silk bodice—"when you purposefully drew my attention here." He tapped Lady Fortune's lacewing pendant resting at my breast.

"But when you read your needles, I perceived the certain touch of the divinely exquisite. Between that and your extraordinary beauty, I knew I had to possess that lively spirit. But the name must fit as perfectly as the garments. Thus, for as long as you reside in my house, you will be known as Mistress Viviana of the Nine Mysteries."

Certain, I had invited him to look at me that morning to distract him from our cheating. But a new *name*? Divinely *exquisite*? My bowels squirmed.

My perturbation only encouraged his teasing smile. Shameless, he molded that smile into paternal concern. "Do you wish to refuse my patronage, dear lady? In an instant, my bell can summon Mistress Mella to strip off this finery and send you packing with the oaf."

I'd waited for the Lady's call all my life. Certain, I could not refuse it. Her voice was so clear inside me even now: *You are my voice and my hand, Monette di Fabroni. My devoted servant. Mine alone. Trust me and I shall guide you through this strange man's world. Together we shall not only foretell, but shape his destiny.*

Exalted by such intimacy, I knew what I had to do, even if it meant unwanted concourse with this man. I shook my head to refuse escape and dipped my knee. I would remain obedient, but proud, too, my true submission to the voice inside me.

Egerik held out his open palms. "If you choose to stay, then lay your hands atop mine, and as you look me in the eye, tell me you understand that my rules are your law and that my decisions for your life will stand unchallenged."

I laid my palms on his and faced him squarely. With the Lady's help, I devised words to ensure my position was clear.

"I accept that your rules are the law of your household, Excellency. As the price of the great honor you do me, I humbly accept that your decisions shall bind me in all *mortal* dealings. But with the greatest respect, the honor you offer as payment truly belongs to my divine Mistress, Lady Espe, who has granted me her favor. Thus, *her* will must ever be my truest guide, lest her whispers sour and my talents fail your need."

His hands twitched. But his hard expression did not change, and after a moment, he lifted my hands, kissed them—a very dry kiss, I would call it—and smiled, slightly less smug than he'd been earlier. "A proper ordering. I would never presume to interfere in your relationship with Lady Fortune."

Pleasure swelled my breast. I had defied him ever so slightly and prevailed. My fingers flew to my pendant and felt the rich threads of silk and silver beneath. This was how a humble diviner's own fortune would be made.

"Now, Viviana, you shall accompany me to my reception room. I thought a familiar venue might help put you at ease." He wrapped my fingers about his crook of his arm. "There will be several guests there—and more later. You will pay them no heed. Your eyes will either be lowered or fixed to me alone, and you will speak only when I tell you. You will show me proper deference and follow my guidance in all things. Is that clear?"

"Very clear, Excellency."

As he rang a hanging bell, he glanced at me, a bright eagerness in his complexion. "Another rule. You will address me as Master."

"As you say . . . Master."

"When the proper time arises, I shall present you to the company. You will invoke your mystic arts and cast your needles as the Lady guides you. But you will voice your interpretation only in response to specific questions I ask, no matter what else you might glean from the needles' positioning. If no answer is to be found to my question, then that is what you say. Whatever is left unspoken, you will report later when we are private. Do you understand?"

I hesitated, trying to decide if what he asked would compromise Lady Espe in any way. Such a man might expect spoken interpretations shaped to his own desires.

"I can certainly do as you wish, Master. But I must report only the truth of my interpretation, which, as you heard yesterday, is often a realm of possibility rather than a clear answer. I cannot shape that answer to what I suppose might please you. Is that acceptable?"

"Indeed so. I desire Fortune's true guidance. I am a believer, Viviana, just as you are. You have no value to me if you lie, omit, dissemble, or otherwise shade your words."

No mistaking his sincerity. His broad brow and fine mouth were firm and eager, his clear eyes unblinking and most serious.

I dipped my head in acceptance. "Then I accept your preference. I've not done such a focused casting, but I've heard it deemed a productive method. Will the guests ask questions, too?"

His hungry gaze devoured me as if I were a Kairysian pastry. "If it seems useful, I may allow it. But if so, you will address me alone. No one else. Now. Silence and deference. Eyes down."

Egerik lifted my hand as if I were a proper lady and escorted me through a short passage where handsome Cei waited to open the door.

26

His Excellency Egerik di Sinterolla, Ambassador to the Independency of Cantagna by appointment of Her Eminence Cerelia Balbina Andreana di Vizio, Protector of Mercediare and the Two Hundred Islands."

It seemed a year at least since Papa and I had first heard Cei's introduction, thinking we were to make our fortune selling counterfeit cloth-of-gold. How much had changed in the span of a day!

Heed everything, daughter. Even within his rules, you can observe. The guests. The furnishings. The arrangements. Listen to what's spoken . . . and unspoken.

Truly this must be my destined course, as the Lady's whispers sounded ever so much clearer than before. I whispered a prayer of gratitude as we swept into the chamber swirling with the aromas of perfumes and wine. We paused somewhere near the center of the room. The pale wood under my feet glowed with golden light.

"Greetings of evening, grand segnori," announced Egerik, "may the hospitality of Mercediare and whisperings of the divine make this evening illuminating and profitable for you all."

Grand segnori! Not just any guests, then, but heads of some of the oldest, wealthiest houses in Cantagna. Never had I imagined a foreign ambassador's guests would be so illustrious.

"Who is this toothsome morsel at your side, Egerik?" This rude address was delivered in a nasal whine that set me to instant dislike. "Have you at last stripped off the weeds of mourning?"

Though he smiled easily, Egerik's fingers twitched, pinching my fingers. Papa had made the same mistake of referring lightly to Egerik's dead wife. Our informants had warned us that it had been a great love between them and that her death had been a grievous burden.

"Have a care, Segnoré di Savilli," Egerik said, with a bite behind his smile, "this woman has intimate relations with the divine Lady Espe. Even my inferior Mercediaran education suggests that the title you aspire to cannot divert your destiny from Lady Fortune's influence."

Savilli! A name of infamy. It was *his* father, the old segnoré, who had hired a sorcerer to cause a great explosion, killing half a hundred citizens! He'd been beheaded in the Piazza Cambio. One would think such a man's heir could never show his face in company again. I supposed his riches and lands—the most of any Cantagnan save *il Padroné* himself—could buy an invitation anywhere. And *title*? We had no nobles in Cantagna, though long ago we'd been ruled by a grand duc, such as they had in Riccia.

The desire to look up at the rude man was near unbearable,

but surely Egerik was watching closely here at the beginning to ensure I obeyed his orders. He tugged at my hand and I followed him toward the great windows, the source of the sunbeams that made the silver in my gown shimmer like early starlight. We stopped beside Egerik's elegantly carved chair.

"Take your place, Viviana." He pointed at the footstool where he'd sat me to display our samples.

I lowered myself to the stool as gracefully as I could and arranged my skirts, sleeves, and mantle as he would wish.

No! I was thinking as a servant. I must bend, but assert my own will, too.

He had said to lower my eyes, but also to look only at him—contradictory commands that I could use to advantage. I raised my chin proudly as Egerik pivoted to face the half-circle of seated guests. Though I attached my gaze to his back like a faithful hound, I had an excellent view of the company.

A most elegant company it was, seven in all. Two women were of mature age as one would expect for heads of families. One tall and crowlike, one broad-bosomed and solid as a stone tower, they were dressed in a sober elegance of brocade and lampas of rich deep greens and blood reds, wide skirts finished with intricate embroidery and a hundredweight of jewels. Their brows had been plucked to broaden their foreheads; their hair tucked into jeweled nets.

The women were but sparrows beside the varied peacocks that were the five men. Two were slim and elegant, one hugely fat with piercing eyes, one an ugly brute with multiple scars savaging his face, one a dandy, his cascading curls and beard more elaborate than a festival of mummers. No matter size and shape, they had decorated themselves with broad-shouldered doublets, and a full exhibition of capes, ruffs, ribboned sleeves, embroidered peascods, tight hose, and ballooning trousses. Papa would swoon at the prospects of commerce.

Many of the guests studied me with open curiosity. And admiration.

Each guest had a small table at hand and a filled wine cup. In the center of the group was a circle of nine candlesticks . . . the same we had used in the morning. Waiting for me.

I closed my eyes for a moment and breathed deep. My presence here was not as an ornament, but to reveal the Lady's auguries to these masters of Cantagna.

Egerik opened his hands in welcome. "You were invited to a celebration of Protector Vizio's ascension to power, and my kitcheners are preparing a magnificent feast as my invitation promised. But before we retire to the hall and join a few more guests, we've a bit of business to address."

All the curious stares shifted to Egerik.

"The eight of us have significant interests in common," he said. "Far more than you might imagine, considering my position as an agent of Mercediare, Cantagna's perpetual antagonist."

Egerik bowed to the stone-slab woman. "Segnora di Gavonti, if you would pick up that scroll on the table between you and Segnoré di Malavesi. You will likely recognize it as a document that you signed many years ago, supporting a great endeavor. I presume you did so to benefit your business interests across the Costa Drago. Once you have verified that the signature is yours, please pass it to Segnoré di Malavesi . . . and so on around your circle."

The woman unrolled the parchment and glanced at it. The color escaped her skin as completely as the beads from a broken necklace. "How have *you* come by this?"

She shoved it at the curly-locked younger man on her right.

"I've no idea what—" The young man choked as if he'd swallowed a live duck, so he clearly did have an idea. He came near throwing it at the crowlike woman next in line. More protests followed.

"How could a Mercediaran jackal have this paper?"

"How dare you expose this?"

"This was to be secret."

"Forgery."

Six voices of horror and disbelief. One—the man with the scarred face—tossed the scroll onto the table beside him and folded his arms, proclaiming, "I want to hear what he thinks to do with this."

A few gathered themselves as if to leave. My heart raced at the spectacle.

"Never fear, my friends," said Egerik, retrieving the scroll. "I hold no malice toward you! Indeed, I applaud your wisdom to add your names to this document in past years, pledging your family's support to alleviate the oppression of my countrymen. But the time has come to honor that pledge."

What kind of business agreement frightened those who agreed to it? And why would Cantagnese aristocrats care about the oppression of Mercediarans?

Well, of course they wouldn't. That would be Egerik's point. They had made the agreement for their own reasons, and Egerik claimed sympathy with their choice. What had they agreed to?

My hand flew to my mouth lest the crow of victory tickling my throat escape. Yet I felt only curiosity. Surely it must be Lady Espe's good pleasure.

Trust me, daughter. I shall guide your hands. My name is Fortune and together we shall discover truth.

Urgency and excitement filled me. The voice of the Lady ... illustrious company ... important affairs. My dreams were coming to life! I needed to listen well, to take in everything so Espe could guide me true.

"Quite obviously this is a forgery." A tall man with hair slicked into a roll below his ears shot to his feet, quivering with indignation. He was the rude man with the nasal whine. "House Savilli enters into no assassination pacts with foreigners. And I've no wish to traffic with you, ambassador, no matter how fine your kitchen or how lovely your harlots. I take my leave."

Assassination pact!

"'Tis your late father's signature, Lorenz," said the crow-like woman with a sour chuckle. "Every one of us recognizes it. Some of us likely signed this thing to please the old fool. A fine legacy he's left you, *grand duc*!"

"I'd advise you consider well before departing, Segnoré di Savilli," said Egerik, quite cheerfully. "The consequences of this document falling into the wrong hands—my tyrant Mistress's hands in particular—would be dreadful; she is a firm believer in the *vendetta omnia*. But there is no need for your children, cousins, retainers, and villagers to suffer Balbina's wrath. I have brought this list forward merely as a means to gather together a group of determined, powerful people—noble men and women who would be pleased to see the world change in certain ways that could enrich their houses and enhance their influence in the world. I seek mutual support, segnori, commitment that can clear away impediments to *your* advancement, as well as my own."

"What kind of support?" said the powerful-looking woman. "Why would you expect backing for your Tyrant Whore from those who've signed this pledge to eliminate her?"

Egerik acknowledged her with a sketchy bow. "As I said, the document simply demonstrates your willingness to commit to those sentiments you've just voiced—sentiments that *many of my own countrymen* share. But rather than pursuing the specific action you've agreed to in this document, a faction of most respectable Mercediarans wishes me to present a different plan. One more personally fulfilling to you all."

Savilli sat down. The others shifted and glanced at each other. The crowlike woman murmured to the curly-locked man, Malavesi, who bit his lip and shook his head vigorously. He was very unhappy. Most of the others appeared to be intrigued. As was I. An assassination pact with none other than the Protector of Mercediare as its target. Egerik must be a brave man even to hold such a document . . . and clever, too, to use it for his own ends. Perhaps he was trying to save the Protector's life!

"If anyone wishes to leave . . ." he said, drawing out the offer.

So was he sincere or laying some kind of trap? I couldn't tell. The Lady's concern swirled inside me like the floodwaters of the Venia in the Great Deluge that drowned Cantagna during my childhood.

No one left.

Egerik's enthusiasm grew. "I take it you are willing to hear more, yes?"

The seven rattled answers all at once. Some eager. Some grudging. Some skeptical. "Aye . . . Yes, let's hear it . . . What do you know of our grievances or ambitions? Assassination is simple; what is this different plan?"

Egerik settled to the elegant chair just beside me and leaned forward, forearms pressed to its carved arms. "Let me speak in metaphor," he said. "Rather than cutting the mast and figure-head from the pirate ship that is Mercediare, my associates and I prefer to create a fleet of strong, swift, smaller ships that will force the pirates to see the error of their ways. With such a solid bulwark, the pirates might then see fit to accept a new captain who would lead them to honorable prosperity . . ."

As he continued his persuasion, the meaning of his meta-phor sank in. A sworn pledge to assassinate the Protector . . . but now an alternative plan . . . shared ambitions . . . a new cap-tain. Not assassination, yet still a new Protector? An overthrow, then, but perhaps not deadly, though even a lowborn woman knew of Mercediare's bloody history.

Surely this was the stuff of history. The kind of knowledge that got eavesdroppers dead. How was it that the daughter of a swindler was allowed to witness it? Certain, anyone here could end my life with a fingersnap.

Only one answer came to mind. Ambassador Egerik, a true believer, wanted me to hear these things so I could weave them into my divination. He wished the Lady to guide his enterprise—which was exactly what she had called me to do. If I was to guide significant events, the risks would never be small.

". . . your houses have robust treasuries and substantial mil-itary cohorts that we could use to outfit the first ship in our mythic fleet. Segnoré di Taglino, as Governor of the Sestorale Prison, controls an especially large and competent brigade, and Segnoré di Berlinguer over here controls barge traffic on the Venia." Egerik waved the scroll. "In return for this group's cooperation, I shall destroy this list and remove the most serious obstacles to your personal ambitions. In other words, this first and most important ship in the fleet would be named the *Cantagna*, and you seven would be its officers."

For a moment there was silence, and then growing murmurs of appreciation and approval. But the Lady's elation had cooled.

"Let us be clear, ambassador." The strong bass timbre that sliced through this swell of interest belonged to the hugely fat man. His sonorous voice was as direct as his gaze. "Our signatures pledged us to fund an assassin, not to supply some sort of martyrs' brigade to goad Mercediarans into rebellion against Protector Vizio."

Egerik nodded seriously, yet enjoyment danced about his finely drawn lips and thin nose. His pale blue eyes gleamed. These seven powerful people sat firmly in his thrall.

"Rest easy, Segnoré di Berlinguer," he said. "No martyrdom is required. Only my own cohorts shall be sent to the southland, not yours or Navilli's or those of your compatriots here. But I need a safe place for my brothers and sisters in this fight to build strength out of the Protector's sight. Training from your estimable Gardia, perhaps. Free passage of your docks and roads. Nothing you cannot easily afford."

The crow woman wagged a finger at the ambassador. "Perhaps a Mercediaran does not realize that we are but seven of twenty-one—not even a majority of the Sestorale."

"I am well aware of Cantagna's governance, grand segnora. But you are not just seven individuals, but a consortium of power that has no need of any other. Years of careful observation have revealed the essential leaders amidst your one-and-twenty—as well as those who might be considered . . . obstacles. Together we can persuade the rest to join this happy arrangement, lest they too become obstacles. Once we've supped, I shall demonstrate my personal commitment to this agreement, but before that . . ."

He stood and offered me his hand. His entire person, body and spirit, voice and manner, changed in that moment. All his hidden glee, all dancing amusement, all pride in his audacity to bring these people into his grand design had vanished. He stood sober. Eager, yes. Greedy, even. But for the Lady's words. This was how he had appeared yesterday, when my fingers' blood signaled my Mistress's intervention. This was Egerik di Sinterolla, the true believer, who had brought me to seek the Lady's insight into his venture.

"I realize this is unusual for either a feast among friends or a gathering of unexpected allies," he said. "You may think me childish. But I am a devout man, and when engaging in grand alliances, I do not proceed lightly—a quality prospective partners should appreciate. Thus, I beg your indulgence. Yesterday, Lady Fortune, in an entirely random circumstance, warned me of a specific danger arriving with this evening's guests. The augury rang so true, parts of it so clearly enmeshed with my plan for this occasion, I could not ignore it. Thus before I divulge the whole of my grand design, I choose to hear a new augury in the presence of those very guests. Before us all, the Lady's handmaiden—Mistress Viviana of the Nine Mysteries—will cast her needles asking for guidance. Lady Fortune might suggest some adjustment to our plan—or our company."

"I think we're all intrigued enough to indulge you, Egerik," said Savilli, stretching his long legs in front of him. "Whether we are believers in such foolery or not. If you have a true notion of our current *obstacles*, then you'll understand that Fortune's involvement is a necessity to cure them."

"My servants shall refill your wine and prepare the room. Then we shall begin."

The guests shuffled and murmured.

With new-lit fire in his pale eyes, Egerik released my hand. "Take your place, Viviana."

I knelt inside the circle of candles and sat back on my heels, breathing deep and slow to settle my mind.

My master crossed to the great windows, now showing a few scattered lights in the lengthening shadows. He rang the brass handbell from the shelf under the windows. As he returned the bell to the shelf, his hand stopped in mid-motion as if a demon sorcerer had turned him to stone. Only a moment passed until he snatched up something from between the enamelware box and the precisely arranged candle lamps and spun around to face his guests again, his hands tucked away behind his back. Only a person with my perspective—eyes fixed to him from my position near the floor—could have noticed the tremors in those hands, the lack of color in his complexion, or the quick return of discipline to mask . . . terror?

I quickly averted my gaze. Such a man as my master would not thank me for noticing. But my mind whirled with curiosity. What small thing sitting on a shelf could have caused him such fear?

Mella came in and poured wine. Before she could withdraw, Egerik grabbed her arm and cornered her behind his chattering guests. He showed her whatever he had snatched from the shelf, and she shook her head vigorously. Their postures were so strained, I was surprised he didn't strike her. When he released her at last, she almost ran from the room. None of the guests noticed.

Meanwhile Cei had doused all but a few of the lamps. Beyond the window glass was moonless evening. He brought me a lit taper and white towel, and then withdrew to his place beside the outer door.

Egerik's hard gaze followed Cei.

Curious. I'd never seen him give this beautiful servant the smallest glance.

Egerik returned to the circle of guests. "I ask for your consideration as we begin, grand segnori," he said, as the swollen murmurs died away. His voice had risen a note, as when a string on a vielle is stretched tighter. "Mistress Viviana is not accustomed to such a large audience as she communes with the Lady Espe."

A snort or two intruded as Egerik gave a brief description of the rite. Non-believers. There were many in the world. Many of these seven would be Academie educated, and philosophists disdained all who approached the Twins with reverence and ritual. They claimed some of us dabbled in sorcery. That was another reason for one like me to seek the protection of a powerful patron. Wealth could add legitimacy to endeavors that powerless poverty would endanger.

As Egerik spoke, Mella returned with ropes of sea lavender and quickly laid them across the latches of the window shutters and over the shelf where Egerik had found whatever disturbed him so. Sea lavender . . . to protect against malignant spirits . . .

"Now, Viviana." Egerik's command startled me. "Take what time you need to prepare. Let me know when you are ready to begin."

I acknowledged his command.

To seek my Lady's voice, I lit the nine candles one by one, shoving concerns of guests and mysteries aside. I pulled the nine slim lengths of bronze from the red silk at my belt. Fingering each needle, I contemplated the Mysteries in turn: Presence, Judgment, Mysticism . . . all nine of them and their varied manifestations.

"The divine Espe, Lady Fortune, guides my fingers, petitioner. By her hand alone will this casting be done. Humble in the face of her will, serene in the surety of my calling, and steeped in her lore will I venture interpretation." As I spoke the ritual words, the Lady's serenity and confidence steadied my soul.

Eager as a beggar at palace door, Egerik knelt facing me across a bare expanse of floor sufficient for a casting. The candles pooled their light between us. Beyond their bright ring the chamber had vanished into darkness. Stillness.

All was ready. I closed my eyes and began.

27

First, the invocation: "Sweet Espe, Lady Fortune, daughter of the Unseeable divinities, lay the needles I cast in patterns that speak of this man's enterprise. Show me your truth and let my tongue provide faithful report of your guidance."

Next, the invitation: "Petitioner, what do you ask of my Lady?"

"Insight," said Egerik, solid and sure. "As I embark upon this great venture, pledging life and fortune to the redemption of my beloved Mercediare and a healthy future for this noble city of Cantagna, and seeking the partnership of these noble women and men, I ask for Lady Fortune's guidance and the blessings of augury in answer to a single question."

Though trained to refrain from personal judgment, I was pleased to hear such noble purpose. I held my needles ready. "Speak your question."

"Does anyone in this house pose a threat to our joint enterprise?"

Closing my eyes, I twined my fingers around the needles,

detecting their embossed rings and symbols as I considered my master's request. Then, with all the will I could muster, I yielded my hands and my will to the Lady's spirit. She filled me like a flagon of mead—heady and sharp—until I lost all sense of myself and existed in some half life that was the both of us. Then I raised the twined needles in the air between my master and me and let them slip one by one from my fingers.

They clicked pleasingly upon each other and the candlelit floor. I bent over and examined the lay, seeking first the obverse end of the Mystery of Jeopardy—the sharp bronze tip that stood for *danger*. That's where his answer would lie.

The Lady's hand could not be more clear. Every other needle centered there.

"See the placement of *danger* here as a foundation," I said, showing him.

His head moved to acknowledge me.

Then I touched the intersection of Judgment and Reason. Judgment's needle—signifying the span between *rightness* or *wrongness*—lay centered on the obverse tip of Reason—the *impossibility of knowing*.

"Among your guests are some who doubt," I said. "Doubt is ever a danger to bold enterprise and must be soothed or eliminated."

Next, I showed him where the steeply tilted needle of Relationship—indicating a most significant relationship—rested halfway between Order's extremes of *chaos* and *structure*, while also touching the center of Presence.

"Among your guests—those present in body, as well as those held so deeply in mind that their presence hangs over this gathering, are some with whom you share a strong bond of kinship or fealty or contracted agreement. Yet this bond wavers, for it rests upon this confusion of *structure* and *chaos*." I pointed to the opposing ends of Order's needle. "To mitigate such a danger—the struggle for commitment between what is sworn and what is needful—requires careful steps."

One more tangle of needles gave me pause. Unsure of whether I should report it, I glanced up at my master. Behind him the candles wavered as if caught in the breeze of a spirit's passing. As the light danced, the notion occurred that someone had strayed between the candles and the window. A blink proved it naught but shadows and reflections.

"Have you more to report, Viviana?"

I shook off my distraction. "Nothing else in this casting speaks to a *specific* threat to this enterprise by anyone in this house."

Egerik examined my face as if to penetrate my very thoughts. Understanding smoothed the crease in his brow. "Well done. We shall explore your mistress's deeper advisements later. Snuff the candles and return to your place."

Cei's white tunic ghosted through the room, lighting lamps. Lost in my Lady's work, I had almost forgotten about the men and women in the half circle of chairs. The curly-locked young man squirmed uneasily, the crow-woman sneered in disdain, others gazed, fascinated, at Egerik and me.

As I gathered my needles, blew out the candles, and returned to the lowly footstool, Egerik jumped to his feet with the lightness of a youth. "Do you see why this woman inspires me to draw her under my wing? This group I've gathered is ordained by Lady Fortune, bringing no danger to our enterprise, save the most natural. Doubt is to be expected, thus I ask that any of you overly troubled by doubt to consider my offer to be excused without prejudice."

He extended his hand to the twin bronze outer doors, where Cei waited—hands at his back, elbows wide, eyes down.

"As to uncertain commitment among the oathsworn"—Egerik sobered for the moment—"that is my own trial of conscience. My sworn fealty to Protector Vizio vies with my duty to Mercediare, my ancestral home. I would guess this conflict is reflected in everyone here to some extent. Partnerships, childhood friendships, vows you've sworn or inherited vie with your concerns for your own beloved Cantagna. Thus the divination guides me for the evening. I promise that by this gathering's end, your conflicts shall be resolved and all uncertainty dismissed. If not, we shall call on Viviana again, and you may voice your own questions."

With a jerk that attracted everyone's notice, Segnoré di Malavesi of the long curls brushed the broad-shouldered woman's hand from his arm and rose. "My late father signed this document you wave in our faces, Ambassador di Sinterolla. But as segnoré of House Malavesi, I cannot support it. Who would not prefer Mercediare to be less threatening to our interests? But I cannot be a part of what you offer in exchange for opening our purses and barracks to your plots. To perdition with your tyrant Mistress's threats. I do not commit my house to dangerous enterprises in response to extortion. I take my leave and encourage the rest of you to the same."

Though none cheered his words, two others nodded and frowned.

"Vitalo, wait," drawled the other youngish man of the group, who rose and joined Malavesi. Though his nose was pinched between protruding eyes, his legs were especially long and elegant. "Ambassador, I wish to speak to your diviner. Is that permitted? I've wide experience with fortunetellers—from back alleys to courtly houses. I've developed a nose for frauds."

"Certainly, Segnoré di Secchi. Here, Viviana . . ."

Heart pounding, I rose and joined the two segnori. What did he know of the Lady's devotions? The powerful so often lived by whim. What if he named me a fraud?

My master remained close by, arms folded across his chest as if watching children at play. The other guests quieted, listening.

"Mistress Viviana." Secchi's bow was no more than a twitch. Every one of his fingers was ringed with bands of small gemstones. One of those sparkling fingers lifted my chin.

"You serve Lady Fortune, Mistress?" he said, drawing his narrow lips into a pout. "You feel her power within you? Perhaps in your purse, a little heavier for this refined performance? Or is it your family benefits most—a husband or auntie or father who encourages your grand mockery so as to curry favors with this Mercediaran?" A tweak of his jeweled finger set my sapphire earring dancing. "Perhaps it is Lady Greed you serve."

Though a believer himself, Egerik made no move to defend me or my Lady from these insults. I must do it myself—but within his rules. So I turned to him and raised my brows in question.

Pleasure graced his pale eyes. "Answer the gentleman, Viviana. Truthfully."

I returned my attention to the smirking Secchi. "I am a true servant of divine Espe," I said proudly. "Years of study and preparation have led me to this day, though even when her presence fills my spirit, I am laid bare by astonishment at the blessing of it. My father, the only person in the world who truly cares for me, tried to *prevent* me heeding her call, fearing the hardships and insults that face one committed to the divine. But I would not forsake my calling, even for him, even for fear of these weighty matters I cannot comprehend. Your slights, grand segnoré, are no more than *I* deserve for presuming to this life. But I would not recommend that anyone, even one so high-placed as you, insult my Lady mistress."

The young man's expression, grown sober as I spoke, now blossomed with good cheer. His flopping hands fanned himself as if he'd overheated, setting his gem-laden fingers sparkling. "Mother Gione's precious daughters, Vitalo, she is true. Belief so strong cannot be scorned. If Lady Fortune is with us—"

"I am determined, Arrigo," said the curly-haired Malavesi, his long features withered in distress. "Papa was wrong. You are wrong. All of you are wrong. My ambitions do not countenance assassination of friends—or onetime friends—even if we disagree on important matters."

My chest felt banded in iron at the young man's declaration. Egerik had offered to remove *obstacles* to his guests prosperity. It came as no shock to hear that, in such circles as these, some might approve assassination as a part of great enterprise. Protector Vizio was Cantagna's enemy and perhaps there were other such enemies. Why should Malavesi's anguish affect me so terribly?

Serious discussion among the Cantagnans grew in volume. Berlinguer, the big man, expressed his own doubts.

"Honorable segnori!" Egerik raised his palms in a plea for concord. "I wish my guests to be comfortable and my business partners secure in our joint ventures. Segnoré di Malavesi, I am grieved to lose your support, but I can ask no more than the hearing you've already given and a modicum of discretion going forward, as you promised when you accepted my invitation. In return, I shall protect the document containing your signature."

"That's not enough, ambassador. I wish to remove my name from this document. *Prove* that any of us may walk away."

"Naturally, segnoré. It shall be done," said my master.

And so it was. Cei brought a cup of ink, a brush, and a small bag of sand to one of the small tables, where the astonished young segnoré obliterated his signature.

"Are you satisfied, segnoré?" Without waiting for an answer—for what could the man say?—Egerik snapped a summoning finger at Cei. "My servant shall show you out, with all respect and good wishes for Fortune's benefice upon your undertakings."

"Virtue's grace grant you all a smat of wisdom." Bitterness flavored Malavesi's politeness.

With only a last disturbed glance at Secchi, the curly-headed man headed for the bronze doors. Secchi was already deep in conversation the crow-faced segnora.

The fiery band about my chest tightened when Cei opened the door and followed the troubled gentleman through. I wasn't sure why. It seemed a fair move to allow the gentleman to choose his course, and only polite to send such a favorite as Cei to escort him on his way.

My master pointed at the footstool, and I returned to my lowly seat. My properly downcast eyes strayed occasionally to the guests. Everyone else in the room seemed to have breathed a great sigh. They were all standing now, conversing with each other or with Egerik. Comfortable interactions, it seemed. Even burly Berlinguer seemed satisfied.

I gave thanks to Lady Espe for her grace and asked her, if

possible, to loosen the unnamable fear that yet constricted my breathing. But as if to tell me that the fear was proper, she led my roving eye to the shelf beside the window, where sat the glass candle lamps, the enamelware box, the brass summoning bell . . . and one thing that did not belong. A fist-sized ball of worn, stitched leather. A child's ball.

How had it come there? Logic dismissed the shadowy reflection I'd seen during the divination. The only servant in the room at the time had been Cei, and his white tunic and shaven head would have been instantly recognizable. The guests all wore enough jewels to sparkle in the candlelight.

Feathers teased my spine.

As if drawn by my observation, Egerik crossed to the shelf. For a moment he stood paralyzed, then snatched up the bell and rang three short bursts. Whirling about, cheeks rosy as the lamplight, he scoured the chamber with a glance. One hand held the leather ball at his back.

At the far end of the chamber, between the statue of Mercediare's hero queen and the marble plinth that held the odd display of rose and knife, a footman opened the painted doors. One of Egerik's shaven-headed retainers brought in wine and fresh cups. A second perfectly groomed man carried a tray holding a porcelain basin, a steaming pitcher, and a stack of small towels for hand-washing. On the other side of the room, Mistress Mella hurried in from Egerik's private chambers.

"Allow my servants to provide refreshment according to Mercediaran custom," said Egerik with all graciousness. "I'll return shortly and lead you into our feast to join two latecomers to our celebration."

Beyond the painted doors, a grand hall, all gilt frescoes

and brasswork chandeliers ablaze with candles, was set for feasting. Two men still in traveling cloaks were greeting each other, wine goblets already in hand. One was an older, dapper gentleman with an patch over one eye. A jeweled baldric adorned his luxurious attire. His companion, a younger man of modest height and fine, but unextravagant, garb, bore himself with an assurance that marked him every bit the first man's equal. When the dapper gentleman genially slapped him on the shoulder, the self-assured young man burst into exuberant laughter. A footman closed the door carefully, even as that hearty cheer snagged my spirit, leaving me short of breath . . .

"Viviana, attention."

A scowling Egerik summoned me to his side. As I crossed the room to join him, he shook sand off the scroll that had concerned his guests so sorely, rolled the curled document, and inserted it in a tooled leather scroll case.

"I need a word with Viviana," he snapped quietly when Mistress Mella reached for my arm. He thrust the scroll case into her hand. "See to my guests. When Cei returns, usher them to the seats I've designated, and put this on the table with the other documents ready for review after the meal. You and Cei will keep it in sight for every moment until I take my seat."

Mella dipped her knee, and before I knew it my master and I were back in his dressing chamber. I expected a scolding for allowing my attention to wander from him.

But he'd other things on his mind. Hands atremble, he threw the leather ball on the floor, ridding himself of the thing as if it carried plague. A small bundle yanked from his doublet dropped beside the ball. It was a straw doll with black yarn hair. Someone had painted delicate features on its canvas head. He crushed the doll with his boot.

If it was the Lady's concerns that fueled the fires of terror at the back of my mind, then something in this sight must have satisfied her. No hour in my life had erupted in such contradictory emotions as this one. Surely madness felt like this.

I lowered my eyes as Egerik spun back to me.

"You saw something else in the pattern of the *ascoltaré*," he said. "Another risk?"

His voice was tight, his shaking hands clenched at his back. Were I not careful, my own hands would shake as well.

"Indeed so, Master. I hope I've not displeased you. The danger revealed was for you alone. Though any threat to you as the principal of this enterprise is a threat to the enterprise itself, I hesitated to report it in front of your guests. What is spoken cannot be unspoken. What is heard cannot be unheard."

"You did right. I commend you. Now show me."

Kneeling on the floor, near the discarded playthings. I laid out the needles of Presence and Relationship exactly as they had related in my cast. "The obverse ends of these two needles, representing *spirit* and *enmity*, cross each other. The relative position of these two others"—I added the needles of Power and Mysticism to the pattern—"provide elements of *strength* and the *unexplainable*. The tilt, the strong angular positioning . . . Master, among your guests in this house is a spirit who bears you a powerful, longstanding malice. When I add the fifth needle of Judgment, as it lay within the cast, that malice demands atonement. As the entirety of this pattern rested atop the sign of danger to your enterprise—"

"Damnation! I should never have told her!" Egerik's rant, though forceful, remained quiet.

A quick glance showed his tremulous fists crushing his temples. I fixed my gaze to the floor, knowing his words were not meant for me. A mad night for certain. How could playthings cause terror in such a man? Why did a nameless stranger's laughter cause such breathless horror inside me?

"The moment has come for action at long last," Egerik murmured as he paced to one end of the dressing room and back again. "I cannot delay. Now that we've launched this enterprise . . . taken irrevocable steps . . . no guilt from the past must get in the way. But these cursed things appearing out of nowhere . . . Are knives next? Or poisoned wine?"

He kicked at the ball and the crushed doll. "Did you see someone place these things on the shelf, girl? If she has a human instrument, I'll give her *that* one's blood."

Give her blood . . . knives . . . poison? *Sweet Espe!*

"No, Master." I dared not mention my foolish notion that someone neither guest nor servant had been present during the casting. And yet . . . I breathed deep and centered myself on the Lady's presence.

"Master, do you know who the malignant spirit Lady Fortune warns of might be? If so, we could petition divine Espe to reveal what's needed for atonement. If it is a child and you know the burial place, the price might be small. Sweets. Music on every First Day. New playthings. A bit of blood now and then . . ."

I dared not meet his gaze after such bold questioning.

"I know exactly who it is," he said, his words dropping on

my head like iron pellets. "And why. And I know exactly the atonement she wants. But she cannot have him. Not yet."

He crouched in front of me. I dared not breathe as he touched the lacewing pendant at my breast, then moved his fingers to my brow and then my lips, tracing their shape.

"You are everything I hoped, Viviana. Humble in your position. Bold in your certainties. A beauty to shame the stars. Exquisite."

The air quivered with fearful promise—like the gleaming beauty of a keen blade. This could be what I had waited for since hearing the Lady's call. Eyes yet lowered, I parted my lips and sighed, demonstrating my pleasure even as the knot in my stomach tightened.

"Three years gone." The back of his curled fingers stroked my cheek. "Wrenched with grief as she prepared an exquisite ending to her pain, I tried to make amends. Swore to be chaste. To pursue only the perfections we shared. To work tirelessly for the future we chose on the day we met our liege lord and he offered us true power.

"'Confess your sin, Egerik,' she told me as she lay in her tomb, prepared. 'Your spirit abandoned me after Ligo died, and it never came back. I thought little Cei might take his place in your heart, but instead you took the boy deeper into the dark. Even when he avenged me and the unborn one, you did not relent.'"

Such a terrible story! I dared not interrupt.

Egerik hissed. "She was right, of course. There at the end, with only hours left, she demanded to know why, and like any besotted, grieving fool, I told her how my plan for the boy had rebounded when his jealous rage sent our Ligo to his death. I thought she would make peace with it. Instead, she swore eternal vengeance unless she drank his blood before she died."

His spread hand slipped into my hair and tugged, tilting my head up. His ferocity locked my gaze, scaring me a little. "But like you, my lovely, he is perfect and irreplaceable. Only when I'm finished with him may she have him. Then, my debt paid and my position secure, I will most assuredly have you. All of you."

Passion fueled that kiss, none of it for me. I doubted he cared about my own trembling, or even knew I'd listened to his tale. Defiant, he was, gripping my hair with his clenched fingers, spreading more dry kisses along my jaw and down my neck. This was show for the one who'd sworn him to chastity. His wife. The malignant spirit who wanted Cei's blood.

My future was here if I was bold enough to claim it. No more trailing around behind Papa selling lies. No more striving for one more illicit coin to buy a book or seek proper teaching. No arrogant segnori treating me like a harlot. Egerik valued me. Desired me. I had no wish to live as his possession, but he had already approved my boldness. And this tale—this fear he battled— could give me influence in the world far more significant than choosing my own garments or my own name. Lady Fortune had laid this opportunity in my hand. Only a fool would refuse.

Thus, I allowed my lips to melt into his, accepting what he demanded. *My* pleasure would come as my power grew to match his.

"Unseeable deities, I must go before my guests think too much," said Egerik, leaping to his feet. "We've almost got them in line."

He left me on the floor. "Return immediately to your bedchamber. I've no need of you until feasting yields to the climax of the evening's business. Mella will burn these hellish tokens. Then she'll tidy you and bring you to the hall. Before the night is out, you'll be able to pledge fealty to our new lord. Till then, you speak to *no one*. Better that you think on my requirements. Don't imagine I didn't notice your wandering eyes. My rules—"

"—are my law, Master." I bowed my head. "I shall beg Lady Espe for enlightenment in ways we might appease this unholy spirit until you can yield her what she wants."

"Good. Yes, do that." A touch of my hair and he hurried back down the passage we'd taken to and from the reception room.

Blade-sharp terror at my boldness pricked at me as I gathered my scattered needles and retraced the route back to my apartment. To my disappointment Papa was no longer in the hall. It would be good to hear his ideas about what Egerik's great enterprise might be. Despite his burlesque of serious commerce, Papa had sensible estimates of current affairs. Prospects of my attachment to a wealthy man of such broad influence should certainly please him. If my future unfolded as I planned, perhaps I could persuade Papa to pursue a more respectable profession. I tried to think what that might be, but not a single notion came.

So where had they put him? The mess of his drunkenness had been cleaned up. I doubted snobbish Mella would have put him in a householder's apartment. When she came, I'd ask. For now I'd best do as I was told. She would enjoy finding me disobedient, adding to whatever penalty I'd already reaped for my wandering eyes.

A lamp had been lit in the flowered chamber, and a flask of wine and a cup awaited me on the table. I poured the wine and settled on the bed, hoping for enough time to consider all I'd heard. *Fealty to our new lord,* for example. A lord of Mercediare? We had no *lords* in Cantagna, just these very rich segnori. *Il Padroné* himself was no duc or conte, but a rich banker and grand segnoré of House Gallanos. Was I a Mercediaran citizen now that Egerik had taken me into his household? I'd not considered that or that Egerik might ever return to the south. That would be a long way from Papa.

And then there was the matter of the angry spirit, his wife, who wanted Cei's blood. Cei had served Egerik as a *child* . . . and done something . . . Was Ligo their own child? And the *unborn one*. That could explain natalés everywhere. But what had Cei—?

A whisper of oiled hinges heralded a slight movement of the door.

I sprang from the bed, expecting sour Mella had arrived to "tidy" me. But the door moved ever so slowly.

"Housekeeper?" I said.

A head poked through the gap. Not wearing Mella's cap, but a healthy crop of black curls and a featureless gray mask. A whisper came from behind the mask. "Are you alone?"

"Why would I answer a man who won't show his face?" I sidled over to the dressing table and scooped up the long pick Mella had used to primp my hair. I gripped it as if it were a stiletto.

A skinny fellow in scuffed leather and dusty canvas stepped inside. He closed the door softly behind him, and then yanked down the mask, revealing dark eyes and the flash of a grin.

"Because you're one's always got to know everything," he said. "Guess you're wondering who I am, eh?"

"Yes. Be sure that if I don't like your answer, I'll scream and guards will come running." I spoke softly, like he did, without the least notion that any guards were close enough to hear.

"Please don't scream, Monette," he said, instantly sober. He spread his hands wide—empty, although a fine dagger hung at his belt. "There's bad doings around here. I've brought a message from your da."

"From Papa!" I said, lowering the pick slightly. "Where is the damnable sot? Is he all right?"

"Says he's got a wicked headache from that wine. Can I tell you his message? We've got to be quick. I can't get caught here."

"Yes, yes, tell me." Maddening, indefinable urgency clawed at my patience.

"He says I've got to whisper the message, as it's something mustn't be heard in this house. And I'm to give you this." He pulled a little bag from his shirt. "Knucklebones and such."

"All right, but not too close. And leave the bag on the bed."

Halting just beyond arm's reach, he tossed the bag on the bed. I waved the bronze hair pick.

"Nervy, you are. Don't blame you. I overheard a bit what's going down there. Not enough to understand but you almost had me convinced you're a diviner."

"I am Lady Fortune's voice. Doesn't matter what my father tells rapscallions like you. Now, stay there and whisper his message. My hearing's fine."

"All right, all right. Easy." He tapped his chest. "You and I, we've met before."

"I don't recall that." Though there was a familiarity . . .

"Name's Neri. And you're"—he lunged and caught my wrist just as I struck—"Romy. Ouch!"

28

THE DAY OF THE PRISONER TRANSFER

EVENING

The shivers gripped me like a mother wolf's teeth—as always when I left magic behind.

I gripped Neri with similar ferocity. "Gracious Mother, little b-brother."

My eyes blinked rapidly as if staring at two worlds at once. Events sloshed and swirled inside my head—battling each other, aligning with each other, creating a deadly landscape. Monette and Romy . . . Egerik and the segnori . . . Rossi and the Assassins List. And Sandro, here.

"Cripes! Didn't have to stab me!" Neri sucked on his hand that was bleeding freely. The bronze hair-pick had fallen to the floor, leaving a splotch of blood.

"Ssshhh. Ssshhh. So much to tell. But first . . . Is Placidio truly all right?"

"Aye. They locked him up in the cellar, just up the passage from the lady's tomb. Told him 'the master wanted him out of the way.' Dumond and I were patrolling the tunnels, making sure they stayed clear. Heard this caterwauling up near the palazzo cellars where there's enough of a dungeon to house three or four prisoners. He's the one told me I might find you here."

"Excellent. Excellent." There was no measure for my relief.

"He says he whistled and sang for two hours, hoping we'd come before the guards drowned him. They kept giving him more wine to shut him up. He's still there, but we unlocked his manacles and broke the cell's lock so he can get out when he wants. They took his boot and sleeve knives, but I fetched his main gauche for if they come after him serious. And his sword's hid outside the cell where he can find it."

"Now listen, but be ready to hide . . . or vanish. The house-keeper could come any moment."

I grabbed the blanket from the bed and wrapped up in it to quiet my chattering teeth. Neri sat cross-legged on the floor behind the bed, where he'd not be visible from the outer door.

"The Assassins List is here," I said.

"You got it!"

"Not in my hand. It's sitting on Egerik's feasting table, where the guests who know what it is can be intimidated by it. But even if you could snatch it right now, it wouldn't stop what's playing out here. Egerik's used the list to draw seven grand segnori—names from the list—into a conspiracy to overthrow the Sestorale."

I squeezed my eyes shut and the fragments of Egerik's offer came together, fitting like a Bettini mosaic. A *new captain* for Mercediare. Rossi, of course, the *new lord* who would command our fealty. And *persuade the rest to join this happy arrangement, lest they too become obstacles*—obstacles Egerik promised to elimi-nate. *Cantagna the first ship in a fleet. Fernand Empire Builder.*

"He says that if they support a *faction* planning to install a new ruler in Mercediare, he'll give them Cantagna to govern as they please."

"Give them Cantagna!" Neri puzzled at it. "Why would they believe him?"

"He's played to their vanities, offered them a bribe they can't pass over. Egerik is offering to assassinate *anyone* who opposes their ascendency in the city—including *il Padroné*."

"Demonscat! We've got to get you and the list out of here right now. You can warn him."

"Too late. He's already here."

The shivers of waning magic yielded to perfect terror. There was no misunderstanding my certainty as the mosaic took on life and color. Why in all the universe had Sandro accepted an invitation to a feast in this house?

"He's in company with Rossi," I said. "Egerik and the other damnable traitors are to join them at supper. No matter what else happens tonight, remember these six names. Navilli, our aspiring grand duc. Longello, whose House controls the city gates. Berlinguer, dock access. Secchi, horse farms and stables. Gavonti, market land. Taglino, the Gardia and Sestorale prison—which explains why Rossi got such comfortable prisoning."

They were Cantagna's elite, their great Houses onetime allies of Sandro's grandfather, father, and uncle. All of them filled with resentment at how *il Padroné*'s reforms intruded on their privileges. Secchi and Malavesi had been Sandro's boyhood friends.

Another chill shuddered my bones. Careful as Egerik was, he'd never risk Malavesi spreading word of their plan. The young segnoré with a smattering of honor would never make it home alive any more than Sandro would.

". . . Berlinguer, docks . . . Secchi, horses . . ." Neri repeated them all.

"Do you see?" I said. "These families control Cantagna's life-blood. They have fat purses, and together control more fighting men than the other Houses combined—resources Egerik's faction can use to bring down the Protector. But that's not all he wants."

Egerik had promised to send only his own cohorts southward, not Berlinguer's or Navilli's or the others'.

"By doing murder tonight, Egerik will be the true power in Cantagna tomorrow. He will control these six traitors through the Assassins List and the tale of their treason, and through them he will control Cantagna's docks, the gates, the markets, even the Gardia itself. Because his objective is not simply to overthrow Protector Vizio. Egerik and Rossi are going to conquer Cantagna first, not with Mercediaran legions, but using our own people."

It was damnably clever. The six would think their ancestral rights restored, their grievances satisfied. And after such a sudden overthrow, they'd think it only sensible to eliminate disgruntled rivals and any lingering support for *il Padroné*, especially if they didn't have to dirty their own hands. Egerik would do it for them, putting them more in his debt. Meanwhile Egerik would use their wealth to hire mercenaries, choose his own officers from theirs, drill their family cohorts together with the mercenaries and Taglino's Gardia, luring the fighters to his cause with arms and his bounty. Once Cantagna sat firmly in his grasp, our city would become the war engine that gave Rossi his throne.

"You're saying six?" said Neri. "Thought it was seven."

I told him of Malavesi, brought here by his dead father's signature on the Assassins List. "Egerik sent *Cei* to escort Malavesi out."

"The perfect assassin." Neri grasped the situation right away. "Where would he do it? In the streets? Away from this house for certain."

"But not *far* away. He expects Cei back before they begin supper. And they would have to get rid of Malavesi's servants. . . . I don't know how it was managed."

"Maybe we can stop it."

"Maybe. Though it's likely too late for Malavesi," I said. "It's Cantagna we have to save."

"So we kill Egerik and Rossi and the six traitors."

Possibilities, strategies, and consequences charged through my blood like chariot horses. "We're only four, while Egerik has a houseful of guards and servants. Even if we could kill all eight, and wanted to do so, assassinating the heads of six Houses is not going to preserve the peace. If the Shadow Lord is the only person who leaves this feast alive, his life won't be worth a spoonful of spit in the desert. Seven Houses would be certain that he arranged the murders. Add in that Egerik's tyrant Protector would take it very ill if her ambassador was assassinated in our city. And Rossi has friends everywhere, who will never believe he is Cinque the spy, much less a serious claimant to the lost throne of Mercediare."

Three times I had insisted that assassination was not the Chimera's weapon. I still believed that. Our armory held trickery, diversion, impersonation, magic . . .

"No," I said, a glimmer of an idea sparking my imagination. "No murder. We have to break the *conspiracy*. Expose this little gathering to the light like a festering sore. Make it so these six quislings would never in the farthest reaches of reason associate themselves with Egerik di Sinterolla. The only way I can think of to do that is to summon the law to this house before any more murders can be done."

"Makes sense," said Neri, downing the remainder of the wine in my pitcher. "But if Egerik's got Governor Taglino in his pocket, we can't count on the Gardia. And no regular constable would dare barge into a palazzo—much less a foreign nob's palazzo—without a magistrate giving them warrant. What crime would a magistrate believe? Even for treason or murder like is happening, Monette di Fabroni's witnessing wouldn't be enough to make him move.

"There's only one arm of the law that pays no mind to palazzo gates, diplomatic protocols, Mercediaran tyrants, or heads of great Houses," I said. "To attract them here—and have any chance of getting *il Padroné*, the segnori, and ourselves out of here alive—we will need chaos, confusion . . . and the crime of magic."

Neri's complexion turned an unattractive shade of yellow. "Demonscat," he said. "You want to call in sniffers."

. . .

The brass latticework, mounted across an open doorway high on the wall of Egerik's Great Hall, made a perfect squint. The finely wrought metal strips were variously angled so that every tile of the Hall floor was visible, from the tall painted doors of the reception chamber to the gated archway that opened into the palazzo's inner courtyard.

Egerik sat at one end of a sumptuously laid table. The ermine-trimmed bonnete at his right identified Navilli, the aspiring grand duc. Scar-faced Taglino, who would bring him the Gardia, sat on his left. The other segnori were distributed along the sides. Short, tight black curls and glinting gold earrings put Rossi near the foot of the table, his back to me, and beside him the man I would recognize in any circumstance. *Il Padroné* . . . the Shadow Lord . . . Sandro. I looked down on the very image of an exquisite coup d'état.

Relaxed, Sandro leaned across the table to converse with the stolid Segnora di Gavonti. Did he suspect his mortal danger? Had he any idea that the leather scroll case, obscured by several other rolled documents at the center of the table, contained the Assassins List—the worrisome article he so desperately wanted found? Did he see the wolf behind Cei's eyes?

I'd near chewed my lips raw over the past two hours. Watching. Waiting.

My principal task in the scheme Neri and I had devised was a critical one: Prevent the Shadow Lord of Cantagna from getting murdered before my partners of the Chimera laid down enough magic to spark a sniffer invasion of Palazzo Ignazio. The implication that magic was involved with Egerik and his scheme in any way should send the rats scurrying from the ship. We hoped.

In a far corner, a troupe of musicians sawing at vielles made it near impossible to make out the conversation. A servant carried a tray of refreshments through the arch to the courtyard where Sandro's white-haired bodyguard Gigo waited with other private retainers.

Once Neri had vanished through the walls of my bedchamber, I'd scurried back to the public rooms of the house, evading Mistress Mella, Egerik's guards standing post in dark corners, and an endless parade of footmen and serving women carrying bowls of scented water, trays of heaped fruit, and troughs of meat. The savory aroma of roasted pig had me near fainting—not that the cramps in my stomach could have allowed me to eat anything.

When I reached the reception chamber, I'd had to hide behind the statue of Gratiana while a maidservant wiped up spilled wine, moved chairs, set burnt candles aside. When she left, I'd raced to the stair closet beside the brass grate. The unexplored passage at the top of the stair led to this squint as well as the one in what Neri called the *chamber of momentary magnificence.*

For two interminable hours I'd sat here trying to pretend that our hasty plan was not lunacy. Trying not to move so much that someone below would notice me. Trying to will Egerik to forget about Viviana until my partners had everything in place.

They needed time. I'd left them to decide whether Neri or Placidio would work the trail of magic to lure the sniffers. Dumond would stay in the tunnels to maintain his portals. I could not allow my thoughts to dwell on their danger, lest I be paralyzed when my own time came.

Cei glided gracefully among the other table servants, fetching cheeses from the laden sideboard, pouring wine, offering finger bowls or towels. Tonight he was dressed in the same blue tunic and leggings as the rest, but whereas the other servants tended all the guests, Cei served only *il Padroné*. The food on Sandro's plate appeared untouched; he rarely ate or drank anything at tables other than his own. But Cei might carry a garrote or a poisoned needle. Or did he kill with his bare hands?

Spirits, how could I know when he would strike? I needed to be closer, yet I needed to see without being seen.

Better if I were devout like Monette. Then I could pray Lady Virtue to bless the Chimera's endeavors and Lady Fortune to advise how we might do what was needed and stay alive.

The burr of conversation, music, laughter, clinking glass, and the wafting scents of food, spices, and wine poured through the slim openings in the lattice. The remains of the pig floated in a pool of grease on the side table. For the fiftieth time I patted the needle bag, reminding myself that Dumond's knucklebones and the thorn rattle were there. More fuel for Egerik's fears.

The conversation faded. The music fell silent.

Skin chilled, nerves aflame, I knelt up and peered through the lattice.

Egerik had left his seat and joined Mistress Mella a few steps from the table. Her arms were spread helplessly as she spoke. Egerik's complexion flamed so red I could almost feel its heat. A last exchange of words and she dipped her knee and fled, gathering four of the servants to her as she bolted from the room. They knew I was missing.

The world went out of focus, as when the droplets of ice on a window pane began to melt. Whispers of failure and death filled my head like smoke. But I tightened my jaw and peered through the squint, not at the Shadow Lord, not at Sandro, but at *il Padroné*, who embodied the hopes of Cantagna. This conspiracy must not succeed.

Egerik returned to his guests, gesturing to the table servants to clear away plates and empty the sideboard. Cei passed along dishes and crumpled towels to other servants, but when all was cleared, he alone did not leave. Rather he took up his waiting posture behind Egerik. In the courtyard beyond the arch, Gigo and the other bodyguards were no longer visible.

The time had come.

I'd not told my brother exactly what kind of distraction I planned. In truth, I'd hoped to come up with something better. Alas, I had not. I knew what Egerik feared.

I stripped off one of the sapphire earrings and the silver ornament from my hair and stuffed them in a dusty corner, then pulled out the knife Neri had left me. With a few swift strokes, I shredded the beautiful skirt, slashed the silver-threaded bodice, ripped one sleeve, and left my mantle hanging from only one shoulder. Then, gratified that Neri kept his weapons well honed, I clamped my lips hard and zipped the blade across one temple. Scalp wounds always bled a lot—as did knees and knuckles.

Five shallow cuts should be enough. Though scarce breaking skin, each was more difficult to accomplish than the last. My skin was on fire. But Monette had to be convinced—and convincing.

As I hurried through the dark to the downward stair, I smeared blood all over myself. Across my forehead, in my hair, on my arms and the ruined gown, especially around the rips and slashes, suggesting deeper wounds.

When I reached the stair closet, I tripped the latch of the

reception room door. If I allowed myself to think or question, I'd never go through with this. Wishing I had Teo's talents, I whispered to Neri, Placidio, and Dumond: *Create a fine chaos, my friends. Don't get dead. And remember your promise.*

Then I considered a story of malignant spirits, assassins, and traitorous enterprises, reached deep for magic, and became Monette once again.

29

I burst from the Night Eternal into a mid-world of smoke and perfume. Vague shapes appeared . . . chairs, candlesticks, but no human souls. So little light. She could return at any moment . . . the luminous being with claws of honed steel. My skin yet burned from her touch.

"Divine Lady Espe, protect me!"

Wild with terror, I ran toward the last place I'd seen my master. I had to give warning. For greed, for arrogance, I had submitted to him. To ensnare his favor, I had reached too deep and waked a demon.

I slammed my palms into the painted doors of the feasting hall.

"Master! Beware, beware, beware! The danger Lady Fortune warned of . . . the malignant spirit . . . she's come. She's in your house!"

They were all present—Egerik, the guests, the two latecomers—sitting around the long table, cups raised in formal salute. Cei, wickedly beautiful like the demon, glided from behind my master to a place behind one of the guests. One of his hands, tucked properly behind his back, held a bright little blade . . . or was it a claw, extended? Could no one else see it?

"Master, help me!" I cried.

Egerik twisted around and burst from his chair, taking in my bloody disarray. "Viviana! What is this?"

"She desires *your* blood, as well as . . . his. The one you told me of." My shaking finger pointed in Cei's direction. I dared not speak his name, lest the word summon the demon spirit.

"Boy!" Egerik whipped his hand from Cei to me. "Take her out! Find out what's going on."

Cei retracted his claw and glared at me full on. I near fainted. *Demon.* Why did no one else recognize it?

Several of the guests had bolted from their seats, chattering as one. "What is this blood on her, Ambassador? Have we been attacked? Summon our bodyguards."

My resolve wavered. If I stayed to give warning, the spirit would surely destroy me. Jealous of Egerik's kisses, she hated me as well as him. But Lady Fortune's displeasure with my desire for wealth and acclaim brooked no cowardly retreat. She demanded I make amends.

"The poisonous spirit from the divination . . . she is *here,* Master."

"What say?" snapped crow-like Segnora Longello. "Are you dabbling in the occult?"

"Hysteria." Egerik's sympathy was cold. "It often afflicts weak minds that are gifted with divine talent."

Hateful words, though I knew he believed and was deeply

afraid. I had seen it in his dressing closet before the dead woman came tapping at my door.

"Be at ease, friends. My residence is well guarded. My servant will remove poor Viviana, and my housekeeper tend her gently. If someone has tried to take advantage of her fragile state, that one shall be discovered and punished."

"'Tis the malignant spirit has bled me," I said, hoarse with terror. "She says it is only the first expression of her wrath!"

Cei drifted slowly around the far end of the table as if I wouldn't notice him.

"She appeared in my bedchamber. She said"—I swallowed a wail at the memory of it—"she commanded I give you these things, else she would rip out my throat."

With bloody fingers, I held out a child's thorn rattle and five knucklebones. Egerik stared at them, color abandoning his cheeks in a rush.

As if playing a macabre game, I backed away from the approaching Cei and circled round toward the side of the table he had abandoned.

"Get your house in order, ambassador," snapped the crow-woman, disgusted. "We must settle this business tonight."

No, no, no. This *business*, built on my guilt of greed and arrogance—on my master's lies—must end. The Lady demanded it.

Cei glided silently around behind Egerik, closing the distance between us.

Take away the foundation of this evil plot, said my Lady's voice. *Then run. Yield to me and I'll guide you.*

I threw the bloody playthings at Egerik and dashed toward

the table. But before I could reach for the leather scroll case at rest in the wood cradle, one of the guests stepped up and blocked my way. It was the younger man who'd come too late to share the divination, the one whose laughter had near stopped my heart.

"Who is she, Egerik?" he said, looking on me in puzzled concern. "Is it Mercediaran custom to have bleeding women wander into your feasting hall, warning of malignant spirits?"

My soul shriveled. I lowered my gaze. This was the man Cei's claws had threatened. Was he an ally or yet another spider weaving this web of deviltry and murder?

My feet took a step backward all on their own . . . just as Cei locked iron fingers around my arm. Trapped between the demon and his prey, I moaned with fear and failure.

"The lovely Viviana is my household diviner, Segnoré di Gallanos," said Egerik. "Most talented in Lady Fortune's service, but new to public attention and household discipline. Your friends here can attest to the astonishing efficacy of her interpretations."

"A diviner?" Gallanos, startled, peered at me closely.

With a curt bow to the man, Cei marched me toward the high arch that opened to the palazzo's inner courtyard. His vicious grip drew me so close, his sweet breath brushed my ear.

"Espe might forgive interference, but Master won't." So cool and pleasant a voice, as if offering wine. "Your blood will be a poor substitute for *il Padroné*'s, damizella. But I shall be pleasured to lick it from your tender flesh."

Il Padroné! I craned my neck to look back at the man. But my feet stumbled and Cei wrenched me up and onward.

Before we could leave the chamber, Mistress Mella, red-faced, her cap all askew, darted past us, while two house guards took up a defensive posture in the archway, their backs blocking our passage. They leveled their spears in the direction of the courtyard.

"Has my household gone entirely mad?" snapped Egerik.

The panting housekeeper dipped her knee to Egerik. "Another grand segnoré has arrived with his full cohort, demanding entry. He says *vendetta* has brought him here to slay one of your guests! Vigilio refused him entry. But his men threw Vigilio into the slough and are even now—"

"Where is he?" bellowed a giant of a man, from the courtyard. He was armored with cuirass, mail skirt, and a steel cap planted atop a rat's nest of red hair. At least a dozen men and women, all with wild red hair and variously armored, clustered behind him. Bristling with blades of every kind, they made quick work of disarming the two guards and setting their own backside defense.

The big man strode through the arch and halted, his gaze raking the hall and the company. "We've word that Placidio di Vasil lurks here amongst Mercediaran scum. My scouts saw him enter. Give him over, and we'll leave you to . . . whatever this sterile gathering is."

My master stepped up to confront him. "You trespass on soil claimed by Her Eminence Cerelia Balbina Andreana di Vizio, Protector of Mercediare, and so acknowledged by the Sestorale of Cantagna. Leave now or you'll be hanged by sunrise— segnoré or guttersnipe as you may be."

"Won't leave till Vasil's carcass stops twitching. The *stronzo* murdered four of my house. Give him over, or we shall raise vendetta against *this* house and all within. Her Bulbousness, too, if she protects him."

My master ground his teeth. "There is no one here by that name. I've no notion who he is or what liar puts him here, but I'll give you my word—"

The painted doors from the reception room crashed open.

"Do not perjure yourself, my good ambassador," announced the newcomer. "Your offer of sanctuary was well meant."

A tall, broad-shouldered man wearing a Mercediaran tabard over a mail shirt sauntered through the open doors, a feather flying jauntily from his conical helm. An ash-colored cloak swirled about his knees, and a black mask covered his face.

"Sanctuary!" spluttered Egerik. "I never—"

"Alas that our partnership was short-lived, my friend," bellowed the masked man. "Though Digo di Pizotti is a fool, as you've said so often, he is not fool enough to accept a Mercediaran's word. And to be fair, I did fail to mention the vendetta when I sought work in your employ."

He drew his sword. A shorter blade appeared in his left hand. "Good even, Digo, and Vesci, Tartuno, and the rest of the lunatic House Pizotti. Shall we dance?"

Dance? Fight? One against twelve?

"I know nothing of this person! Nothing of any vendetta!" Egerik gaped at the masked man and the growling red-haired mob pushing through his courtyard arch. An instant's pause swelled larger, as when an archer draws his bowstring tighter . . . tighter.

"Remove your slobbering dogs from the ambassador's house, Pizotti!" taunted the masked man. "He's got half the Sestorale here as witness to your trespass."

But the red-haired giant simply lifted his chin and emitted

a throaty warbling cry that rattled my bones. A whirl of his sword, and the red-haired cohort echoed their leader's bawling and raced forward to meet their prey. The feasting hall dissolved into chaos, as more of Egerik's house guards arrived and gave chase, engaging those at the rear of the mob with spears and swords.

Surrounded by flailing blades, Egerik and several of his guests drew daggers and pressed their backs to the table. The rest of them and Mistress Mella took refuge under the table.

The mob surged and swirled around them, interested in no one save their quarry. How was the masked man not dead already?

My arm jerked. Cei dragged me away from the fighting. I could scarce think amid the noise, the stinging of my wounded skin, the unexpected battle erupting in the middle of conspiracy. The malignant spirit had promised chaos.

A red-haired ruffian with a scabrous complexion and sores on his mouth slid to a stop mid-charge and blocked our path. He clutched my ripped bodice and snatched my hair, drawing my head to his seeping lips.

"Already had your way with this little sweetmeat, pretty boy? Let Tartuno have a turn."

"Take her." To my horror, Cei shoved me at the leering man. But then he quickly stepped behind my assailant, twining his arm under the fellow's shoulder and around the back of his head. In a single deadly motion, he pressed the man's head forward and plunged a thumb-length knife into the base of his victim's skull.

Tartuno's arms fell slack and he slumped to the floor, causing me to stumble.

Nauseated, I staggered back toward the table. The Lady had commanded me to fetch the scroll.

Cei snagged me again. His expression had not changed in the slightest. "You are Master's possession, else I'd sever your spine as well."

He dragged me to Egerik and spoke not a word.

"Find Gallanos," said Egerik, red-faced and sweating. "He must not leave here."

Cei pivoted on his toes, scanning the crowd.

"There!" shouted the whining Segnoré Navilli from under the table. He pointed toward the reception room doors, where the masked man was battling three of the red-haired crazies at once.

Behind them, a slighter man, also in mail-shirt, Mercediaran tabard, feathered helm, and mask, fought off a leather-armored woman who warbled gleefully at every stroke, hers or his. Tucked away behind the slender fighter was Gallanos— Alessandro di Gallanos, *il Padroné*.

The slender swordsman gained advantage on the woman and slammed his fist into her chin. She plummeted like a stone. The swordsman waved *il Padroné* into the reception room and backed through the door protectively, turning only at the last moment to follow him through.

Cei dodged through the melee toward them, knife in hand.

No! The Lady's voice threatened to crack my skull.

I ran, ducking and weaving between a Mercediaran guard battling one of the crazed Pizottis and the grunting Vasil trading blows with the red-haired giant. I threw myself at Cei just as one of the panel-wall doors closed behind Gallanos and his defender. We crashed to the floor.

A fast runner I might be, but even with the Lady's strength, I was no match in a grapple. Cei kicked me in the side, leaving me heaving. When he pulled open the door to the stair closet, the two men had vanished. *Two lives saved.* I wanted to weep.

Cold and expressionless, Cei grabbed my hair, dragged me to my feet, and propelled me back into the feasting hall. My flailing hands and elbows had no more effect than feathers. We passed the masked Vasil, who glanced up from the floor where he had pinned the red-haired giant.

"Chaos!" he called, grinning through his mask.

I hissed at him. "Demon. *She* brought you here! The devil spirit."

Cei yanked hard. My scalp felt like to rip.

A backward glance showed the giant Pizotti writhing on the floor alone and the reception room doors falling shut. Piercing terror rose inside me, as if I teetered on the brink of a lightless chasm. Unable to contain a whimper, unable to get free, I stumbled after Cei.

A few skirmishes were still ongoing. Several Pizottis lay bleeding and moaning. More had fled. Cei's victim and two of the household guards lay dead. Egerik's guests were slowly emerging from under the table.

Cei shoved me to the floor at Egerik's feet, his fingers yet entwined in my hair.

"Where is Gallanos?" Egerik hissed.

"He had help," said Cei. "Another man garbed like Vasil—or whoever he was."

"Who has also vanished. Damnation." Egerik growled through his teeth where none but us three could hear. "I want

Gallanos's entrails smeared across the Piazza Livello before dawn."

Cei released his grip on me, bowed curtly, and pelted away. The remaining guests mumbled to one another, while Egerik snapped orders. To servants to clean up the mess. To his guard captain to seal the palace gates and provide a detachment of guards for the Mirror Room.

The guests gathered close, debating whether or not to continue with their plan. I crawled under the table, praying all would forget me. They had refused to heed Lady Espe's warnings. I had to take the scroll—the *foundation*, she had called it—and escape from here. *Please, goddess, let Papa be waiting for me at home.*

"Come friends," said Egerik, as the captain hurried away. "Let us retire to a secure room where I can reveal the rest of our strategy."

"No," said the stolid Segnora di Gavonti, dusting off her sleeves with trembling hands. "Summon my bodyguards, Egerik, assuming they're not slaughtered. I knew it was a mistake to trust a Mercediaran. 'No need for personal servants,' you said. 'My house is impregnable; my servants are perfection.' Pssh."

"On the contrary, segnora and the rest of you," said Egerik, clear and confident, now his guards had ended the last skirmish. "This is but proof of the rightness of our course. Who but the Shadow Lord of Cantagna could have orchestrated such an invasion? My promises hold. Alessandro di Gallanos will be dead before sunrise."

Blaming the man he'd ordered Cei to kill? The Lady was right. Ambition had blinded me.

The segnori did not flinch at the declaration of murder. Nor did the dapper man in the jeweled baldric who had crawled out last.

"This is the lawlessness the Sestorale's indulgence promotes," he said. "The Pizottis are a blight. *Il Padroné* may have schemed to bring them to his rescue, but they've no loyalty but to their own foolery. If Egerik's servant performs as he has in the past, we shall at last be free of the Shadow Lord's dominance. All will be well."

"I still don't know what interest you have here, Rossi," said the slab-sided woman.

"Nothing happens in the Costa Drago without my knowing," he said, laughing, "and I'm interested in all of it. How else will I earn my next meal?"

"I don't like this," said one of the segnori. "To take down Gallanos while we were here was a stupid plan. His bodyguards knew he was in this house. He's likely told a hundred people. And I don't like Rossi here blabbing about this meeting at every supper table in Cantagna. You promised complete discretion."

I wished they would go. I needed to be gone from here. If only I knew where they'd put Papa. *Don't be dead, Papa.*

"Our agreement is a mutual bond, Segnoré di Berlinguer," said Egerik. "Just like the original agreement that bears your signature. My lord . . . Rossi has a great deal to contribute to our plans."

"My lord? *Rossi?*" Several people burst out laughing. "Have we elevated a scrounger?"

Do you hear me, friend?

Startled by the whisper, I looked behind and to either side, expecting that one of the segnori remained under the table with me. But I was alone. My fist pressed my stinging temple.

I need you to listen carefully. With all of yourself, what is outside, what is inside.

This was not Lady Espe. Not a womanly voice at all. It was a voice of the air, a sea breeze brushing my skin. Clear as morning. Yet those standing around the table took no note. They were still arguing about their plan to seize control of Cantagna.

Take a full breath, my friend. I mean you no harm. Trust me. Heed me. Believe. Feel my presence inside you. Open your heart as is your nature.

Perhaps it was some other divinity. One of the Unseeable . . .

Your name is Romy. And you need to get out of there right now.

30

Romy I was.

And the voice ... Teo. The power of that voice, the mystery of how it was possible he could pull me from Monette, I had no time to consider. The arguments of rattled guests and the clatter of servants as they cleaned up blood and wounded fighters had fallen quiet. And from the direction of the main gates and the residence wing came wordless howling and the clank of chains. Sniffers!

"By the Unseeable, Ambassador, what have you done?" yelled Navilli. "Have you ensorcelled us?"

Somehow my partners had managed to instigate not only the chaotic assault of the Pizottis, but the sniffer invasion Neri and I had planned. At least three screeching hunters sounded near enough to be in the house—and I was stuck under this confounded table with my teeth clattering. I needed to be out of here.

"Impossible," said Egerik. "No magic has been done here. See to this, Taglino."

Taglino, the scar-faced prison governor, jogged toward the courtyard arch. Egerik followed with more dignity, only to be waylaid by one of his servants. "Master, one of your guests is killed! Over by the windows. Dead from a knife to the neck like that Pizotti devil . . ."

"Everlasting curses! Get him out of here before anyone sees."

But it was too late. The remaining guests could hear as well as I did. As Egerik hurried after Taglino to stave off the sniffers, five Cantagnans followed the guard in the opposite direction.

Seizing my opportunity, I scrambled out from under the table and reached for the abandoned scroll case only to find Rossi with the same idea. As his eyes widened in surprise, I grabbed a porcelain wine pitcher and smashed it into his face.

Rossi crumpled. I rounded the table and scooped up the leather scroll case fallen from his hand.

"Malavesi!" The cry came from the group beside the windows. "Murdered! I'll see that Mercediaran devil dead!"

Spirits, Neri, you found him! And he'd brought the young man's body here to bear witness.

The rattle of chains and baying screeches from the courtyard shot frissons of terror up my spine. Of all things I wanted to put distance between me and the sniffers. But if the Chimera's mission was to preserve Cantagna's peace, I had to delay once more.

I darted across the feasting hall to the windows, where Arrigo di Secchi bellowed in rage and grief as he knelt beside Vitalo di Malavesi's corpse. Secchi, Malavesi, and Sandro had once been closer than brothers.

Egerik already had these men and women believing that the Pizotti assault was *il Padroné*'s work. Just as I'd told Neri, if Sandro emerged from this house unscathed, while these five were tainted with scandal or worse, the resulting upheaval would boil over into unending strife. Whether or not his own plan succeeded, Egerik would leave Cantagna ripe for Mercediare's plucking.

"Please, excellencies," I said, dropping to my knees behind them, head bowed, hands over my face, and drawing up what sobs I could muster. "Heed Lady Fortune's word."

When I felt their attention heavy on my head, I continued, "My master has done this terrible murder and used magic to raise a malignant spirit. Lady Fortune augurs he'll have all of you dead or captive of sniffers before the night is out, because you're witness to his crime. Such was his intent all along—to blackmail you into yielding *him* control of the city through your ports, your gates, your wealth and lands. Likewise he used me. Used my Lady Espe. If you value your families and your honor, you must leave the Mercediarans and the traitor Taglino to the sniffers. Lady Espe has shown me a way we might escape unseen, if you will but trust her messenger and follow. Whichever you choose, may she ever bless you and Cantagna."

Clutching the scroll case under the remnants of my mantle, I darted into the reception room. Ensnared by their own greed, trapped by treason, murder, and magic, they had little choice but to find a way out. Evidently Viviana the Diviner would do well enough. The five venal fools scuttled after me like scorpions.

I unlatched the door to the stair closet. When the scorpions arrived, I sent them down the stair. "Hide in the cellars, and I'll fetch your bodyguards."

Five of the most powerful leaders of Cantagna did not argue—a true measure of their befuddlement. Not one of them so much as asked about the Assassins List, much less noticed the case. Certain, I did not want to be alone with them if or when they came to their senses and realized what I carried. Dumond, Placidio, and Neri would be on the alert in the tunnels, waiting for me. They'd sort the ladies and gentlemen out.

Just as I slammed the stair closet door behind the five, one of Egerik's guards appeared from the feasting hall. He pointed at me and yelled over his shoulder, "She's in here, Master."

Urgency bade me vanish and let the consequences rain down on those who had planned to overthrow my city. But I had to make sure.

From outside the bronze doors that separated the reception room from the *chamber of momentary magnificence* came a sniffer's spirit-freezing howl, closer every moment. I waited. Waited. Waited. Until Egerik arrived from the feasting hall.

"Viviana! On your knees. Here." He pointed to the floor at his feet.

I flung open the bronze door to brawny nullifier and his green-clad slave. Not twenty paces from me.

I slumped to a crouch and pointed my shaking, bloody finger at Egerik. "Your honor," I cried. "Please sir, my master's witched me with sorcery, as he does all his servants, as he did his beauteous wife. He's buried her in his cellar in rites of perversion and says he'll do the same with me!"

The nullifier, perhaps sensing bigger prey than a bloody courtier, dragged his screeching sniffer past me. I looked over my shoulder, straight into Egerik's horrified countenance, and smiled. Then lurched to my feet and ran.

I threaded the household passages where I'd met the parade of kitchen servants. Followed the lingering aroma of roast pig to a downward stair. Into the torchlit kitchen yard. Thirty paces left of the kitchen house was a well house, and behind it—

Boots thumped down the stair behind me. Chains clinked on the flagstone terrace that overlooked the gardens. Heavy boots. A hiss from a sniffer.

Mouselike, I scuttered around the shadowed periphery, scarce breathing.

The door of the kitchen house flew open, flooding the yard with gold light from the great ovens. Three servants trudged across the yard toward the suddenly noisy kennels, carrying pails of scraps. I dashed across the pool of light behind them and into the darkness behind the well house.

"Ayee!" The bone-chilling screech originated not a hundred paces away.

I fell to my knees behind the well house, half blind in the dark, frantically patting the matted grass and tangled vines as chains clinked on stone behind me. "Be there. Be there. And be ready."

My fingers found a squarish slab of wood. When they touched a metal ring and not just a flat, painted surface, I blessed the universe. A tug at the ring drew the trapdoor open, and I grinned at the dusty grizzled face looking up at me from the dimly lit hole. I scrambled through and jumped, trusting that my friend Dumond would catch me.

"Quickly now," he said, once he unwrapped my arms that were near choking him. "Got to get out of the tunnels before your fish man's trail of magic leads the sniffers down here."

"*Teo's* led them here?" I said, trying to sort out who I was, where I'd been, and everything we had yet to accomplish.

Dumond drew a stack of splintered crates under the trap door. The stack must have been sturdier than it looked, as the individual crates did not shift a finger's breadth as he climbed.

"Here and gone. He's been on the run near two hours now, laying down a trail of magic as this city has never seen. Atladu defend us all if he pauses to take a breath."

As faint howls grew louder above us, he tugged at the trapdoor and threw the latch.

"He's already wound the trace through here to the palazzo cellars to ensure they find the arms cache and the lady's burial chamber. Now he's off to the river. He says the water erases his connection to the demons?" He looked down at me from his perch with brows upraised. "Sniffers?"

"Yes . . . yes, that seemed to have worked before."

Dumond laid his hands on the trap door and whispered, *"Sigillaré."*

The close-fitted, hinged, and latched trapdoor fitted between the wood supports of the ceiling dulled and shifted—and became naught but a square of wood holding up the ceiling. In the garden above, an unpainted square of wood would lie amid the matted vines. Magic. Glorious!

"So we're the last and need to go. Down that way." His head bobbed toward a trail of cheery torches marking a way through the dark, and then he doused the rusty lamp that hung from the wall a few paces away. The wall with the narrow slot that led to the arms cache . . . and Oriana's burial chamber . . . and the cells where Placidio had been held . . . and the palazzo cellars.

"No, wait!" I said, slapping my hands to my head. "Where does the stair from the reception room closet come out?"

"Between the lady's tomb and the palazzo cellars. Are you worried about the five very angry lordlings who crept down that stair, cursing Egerik's diviner and every other person in this benighted house? Because we locked them up in a cell and said that if they made a sound we'd not send anyone to find them. Figured the sniffers would put a righteous scare into 'em."

"Better we get them away. There'll be no peace in Cantagna if they're caught. Do you have more of those masks?"

The smith wearily rubbed his balding head and pulled a mask and a thin gray cloak out of the pack on his shoulder. "Was hoping I wouldn't need these."

He had a mask for me as well.

In a quarter of an hour, Dumond had given each of the angry men and women a torn strip of gray to tie over their eyes, as "the sights down here are too terrible for the virtuous to lay eyes on."

One by one, I gave each of the five a hand to get them past the tight slot in the tunnel wall. I infused that touch with magic, replacing the name *Placidio di Vasil* with an impression of a mysterious, heroic masked swordsman who had rescued them from the machinations of Egerik di Sinterolla. I kept it simple, hoping to leave few broken threads to confuse them.

Though I'd met them all, they gave no hint they associated the ragged, blood-streaked Viviana with *il Padroné*'s onetime mistress. Rather, for every step of the way through the sad remainders of the plague, they cursed the day we were born, the day Egerik was born, and the day the monster Dragonis shattered the tip of the Costa Drago into what would become Mercediare.

At the end, Dumond and I remained in the tunnel, watching

as they angrily stripped off their masks and climbed the short steep path through the Cat's Eye rift. Happy to be shed of them, we hurried back toward the rubble heap and the side passage that would take us to Dumond's portal to the Merchants Ring. We'd not gotten halfway when the screeching of sniffers filled the tunnels from ahead and behind.

We ran. By the time we reached the turning, torches blazed not fifty paces ahead of us and less than that behind.

Sobbing for breath, I scrambled up the rubble heap. Once into the side tunnel, Dumond used a broken plank to knock each lamp and torch from the wall to mask our trail.

Nerves stretched beyond bearing, I almost screamed when I reached a plank wall and the last light went out behind me, leaving me in the tarry, airless dark. Druda's empty soul could be no blacker. But a callused hand squeezed mine and set me still against a wall. Surely the sniffers heard my thumping heart as I waited for Dumond to say the word.

Blue flames sparked in the darkness illuminating Dumond's calm face. "*Cederé.*"

The sniffers' howling swelled, threatening to split my skull. But the air shifted, releasing the scent of old earth and ancient mould.

"Now run." Dumond's steady hand took mine, as my eyes picked out a narrow rectangular glimmer of light far ahead of us. The lantern hung in the familiar brick passage that led from the Via Mortua in the Merchants Ring to the Piazza Livello. Halfway across the Heights.

We crossed the distance in moments. There standing watch, swords drawn, were Neri and Placidio, bloody and bandaged but upright.

Neri shoved the simple plank door shut, and Dumond slammed his hands on it.

"Sigillarré!"

The door vanished. Dumond pressed his back to the spot where it had been and sagged to the dirt. Though we needed to be away from the tunnel and whatever residue of Dumond's magic yet lingered, exhaustion settled over us like a blanket of lead. None of us spoke a word.

Placidio tossed me his flask with the green frog stopper. I relished a swallow of the nasty salt, lemon, and ginger tea and passed it to Dumond. He wrinkled his nose, swallowed no more than a teaspoon's worth, and passed it to Neri, who drained it.

Momentarily invigorated, I tossed the leather scroll case into the space between us. "The Assassins List. In and out. Simple."

With a burst of laughter, we gathered our remaining will and got back to our feet. We split up, each taking our own path to home and cautious sleep.

31

Cantagna woke that morning with rumors flying about like an invasion of overexcited sparrows. They spoke of a sorcerous assault on Cantagna's great Houses, of sniffers scouring the streets of the Heights, of grand segnori abducted by the *daemoni discordia* and dragged through the Great Abyss before their virtue triumphed and they found their way home again. The Philosophic Confraternity was investigating the event which seemed to be concentrated in the Quartiere di Fiori. Notably absent was any mention of *il Padroné*'s entrails being spread across the Piazza Livello. To my relief.

Events had left my mind in fragments. I needed an anchor. And I needed answers. Too many loose ends still dangled: Egerik, Rossi, the cache of arms, Cei.

After sleeping for most of a day, I spent a morning dispatching messages to my current clients apologizing for a bout of the grippe that had prevented me completing their documents. I set a new schedule and went to work. A few mundane hours of pen, ink, parchment, and meticulous copying soothed some of the ragged edges in my head. The Assassins List remained hidden beneath the floor of my house.

Neri slept for most of *two* days, waking only long enough to eat whatever he could find on our shelves. On the third day he was up with the dawn, gone to the woolhouse to run and practice, hoping Placidio might be there for a lesson. Placidio did not come, but when Neri went to work an evening shift at the Duck's Bone, they said Placidio had been in twice that day to eat soup. He'd said he was recovering from a bout of *goat stomach*—usually associated with excess mead. No one deemed it unusual.

Neri and I agreed to go about our normal business, waiting until we four were all together again to fill in the details of our experiences. He did tell me that he and Placidio had taken *il Padrone* through the tunnels, allowing him to see Egerik's caches but not themselves before delivering him to the Cat's Eyes rift. "He didn't ask who we were. Didn't try to look at us. Just said he'd never forget what we did to save the most arrogant *stronzo* in Cantagna. He also said, 'Do *not* destroy it.'"

"I'll have to think about that," I said. What good could ever come from the Assassins List?

When we lay in the dark that night ready to sleep, I said, "One thing more. Whose idea was it to ask Teo to draw the sniffers?"

"Dumond's," he said, "but only after Placidio insisted we should bring in Teo to help. Placidio said Teo could likely bring you out of your magic without touching your skin. How was that possible?"

As I'd suspected since they met at the woolhouse, Placidio

knew more of Teo's talents than he let on. Like it or not, he was going to tell me.

Visiting my lawyer clients to deliver or pick up documents for copying gave me opportunities for gossip the Beggars Ring markets could not provide. Segnoré di Navilli had taken to his bed with an attack of spleen. Segnora di Gavonti had moved her whole household to Ricci-by-the-sea for the summer.

Fernand di Rossi had been attacked in the streets after leaving a dinner party. *Il Padroné* had kindly sent him to Villa Collina, his house in the countryside, with his own physician. It was not known if Rossi would recover.

Did the Shadow Lord suspect Rossi's heritage or his role in Egerik's plot? He'd not care about a pretender reinstating Mercediare's throne. But he would look very dimly on the notion of overthrowing Cantagna or any other independency to create a base for revolution. I trusted he would find out what else he needed to know. Rossi's *recovery* might be a very difficult one.

Digo di Pizotti had been summoned before the city's High Magistrate for pursuing a vendetta, a practice outlawed by the Sestorale only two years since, and for violating the residence of a foreign ambassador. Found guilty on the first charge, Pizotti was fined heavily and warned that any further pursuit of vendetta would result in forfeiture of his house and land.

The second charge had been dismissed as Ambassador di Sinterolla had failed to appear in court for three days running and could not be found.

Curiosity near drove me mad, especially when I heard that the grand processional to celebrate the birthday of *il Padroné*'s wife would include the distribution of a *bounty of food* in the Beggars Ring. No mention was made of any distribution of armaments.

Had Vizio got wind of Egerik's plotting or had the Shadow Lord taken Egerik's fate into his own hands?

But later that same day, I received a note in box number one. It read:

> *My brothers and sisters believe the use of magic at the*
> *site of an exquisite death is most unsubtle.*

> *Nuccio*

The note bore a sketch of a rose and a knife with a curved tip, and a single dot of red ink.

This could not be coincidence. Nuccio had said it was *lack of subtlety* had gotten Lodovico di Gallanos expelled from the Brotherhood of the Exquisite, just before he died of poisoning—a murder yet unsolved. I suspected that the Brotherhood had dealt likewise with Egerik.

I did not rejoice at that, but neither did I feel any guilt. The few hours I'd spent as Egerik's exquisite possession were the only part of that fraught night at Palazzo Ignazio that haunted my dreams. The triumphant glitter in his eyes as he directed me to the stool at his feet—dressed as he commanded, my eyes to be focused on him alone, sworn to accept his will as my law. Dreaming of that moment caused me to bolt awake with a case of the shudders.

Egerik's plan would have cost thousands of lives, and we had stopped it. Yet I doubted that one of his worst crimes could ever be undone. What had become of Cei, a child who had killed Egerik's eldest son in a fit of jealous rage? Cei, the boy whom Egerik had taken *into the dark* and groomed into a perfect assassin?

A tantalizing—horrifying—notion came to mind. Rossi had told me the ambassador would likely know what had become of Vizio's son. Had Balbina bargained a beautiful boy child for Egerik's support in her ascent? Had Egerik groomed Cei to assassinate Vizio? Egerik would call that an exquisite bargain.

That same afternoon another note arrived in box number six. Terse. To the point.

> *To the Chimera: If the object of our contract is in your possession, leave it at our exchange location this evening at sunset. If it is not, leave a message with your best assessment of the object's location. Your contracted payment will be there.*

The note was unsigned, but I would recognize the hand anywhere. I was of a mind to destroy the Assassins List and tell him it was lost. But he trusted me—and through me, the Chimera, and I would not lie to him.

Late that afternoon, as the afterglow painted the sky and river red-gold, I strolled along the riverside to the Avanci Bridge. Two men sat fishing under the bridge. A youth dug for mussels in a sandy sleugh. I sat on the steep embankment upriver and waited.

As the bells rang the evening anthem, the fishermen pulled in their lines and hurried away, and the youth moved his digging downstream. Cross with myself for the disappointment that washed over me like a cold splash of river water, I stomped over to the mold-blackened abutment and unlatched the tricky lock to a hidden stair.

Sandro was waiting, sitting on a step and twiddling the ties of a leather bag that sat between his feet. He shot a quick glance up. Just long enough to see that it was me.

"Would you walk with me, Romy of Lizard's Alley? On the bridge?" He motioned to the tight-spiraled stair behind him. "I've arranged— No one will bother us. No one will see."

No matter the concerns and questions circling in my head like vultures, words would not come.

"No. Certain, it's a terrible idea," he said, waving his hands dismissively while I stood voiceless. He kept his eyes averted. "I had no intention of coming. It's foolish and entirely violates our agreement. But I needed to apologize to your friends. The Chimera. I knew the Assassins List was dangerous, but by every bright spirit in this universe, I had no idea of Rossi and this Egerik and their lunatic scheme. When I received Egerik's invitation to join him on the day of the prison transfer, I was so curious. Honestly, I didn't trust your friends enough, being so new at this kind of work. Decided I'd best see what was what myself. You know how I am; no one else could possibly do it right."

Certain, I did. But I'd never heard him apologize for it.

"My arrogance nearly laid Cantagna in his lap and endangered all of you and so many others. So I thought you should know . . . so you could tell them . . . I'll be much more careful in the future."

"The *future*?"

And then he glanced at me full on with the smile that had melted my bones for nine years and endeared him to the citizens who loved and honored *il Padroné*, even as they feared his shadow self.

"Naturally. After such brilliant scheming as I've learned of these last few days, I'd be an even greater fool to ignore such talent. When a particular kind of need comes up that my usual retainers can't resolve, I will call on the Chimera again. For Cantagna. Would that be acceptable?"

"I can't speak for the Chimera." My voice sounded much more composed than I believed possible. "But I'll pass on your comments. I'm sure it would depend on the particular case."

"Certain," he said, and proffered the leather bag.

I passed him the scroll case, but before accepting our payment, I considered a piece of unfinished business. When I touched the heavy little bag, I made sure my finger touched his hand.

Relieved, I looped the bag's ties over my shoulder and under my cloak.

"I should go," he said. "Gigo will be apoplectic." He rose and started up the steps to the bridge.

"Two more things," I said, my wits returning before the stair took him out of sight. "The ambassador's bodyservant . . . Cei . . ."

"The odd, silent one with bare feet. The favorite."

"He is a meticulously trained assassin. Skilled. Savage. Unaccounted for. Egerik ordered him to kill you. So I was told."

His eyes grew wide. "I'll keep watch."

"I was also told that when Vitalo di Malavesi realized the price of Egerik's scheme, he refused to be a part of it. He died for that."

"I wondered." His suddenly grim demeanor told me I was no longer in the presence of Sandro or *il Padroné*, but only the Shadow Lord. "Be sure I'll not forget."

As it should be.

And then there was nothing more to say. "Fortune's benefice, *il Padroné*."

"Virtue's grace, *l'Scrittóre*."

The shadows under the bridge were deep when I slipped out of the door, and I was glad for the torchlight of the River Gate and the evening noise and crowds of the Beggars Ring. Uneasy shadows yet danced behind the light.

A brief stop at home to pick up a bundle of scraps and then I hurried around the Ring Road to Dumond's house. I had notified my partners of the coming payment and suggested we meet there to share it out.

• • •

Vashti greeted me at her door. "Welcome, welcome, Romy-zha! I thought I would never get to hear the full tale of your adventures. Basha is a poor storyteller."

She rolled her eyes and I laughed in agreement. "I've brought replacements for the costume I lost at Palazzo Ignazio," I said, offering her one sapphire earring and the scraps of silk and brocade from the garments Egerik had prescribed for me.

"We have tea that has no salt in it, and supper noodles if they've left any." She pointed me to the low round table where a pot of tea sat steeping and Placidio, Neri, and Dumond were stuffing themselves.

"Hoped you'd bring a goose," said Neri without pausing his spoon. "At least a wheel of cheese."

"You must get him back to lessons," I said, laying a grateful hand on Placidio's shoulder as I claimed a vacant floor cushion between the two of them. "He'll go to fat and drive me back to penury with his appetite."

"'Tis the magic does it," said Placidio, shoveling in his own hefty serving. "He was in and out of that palazzo—"

"—and up and down that warren of tunnels—" Dumond interjected.

"—so many times, he was naught but a phantom for most of a day."

"I've never been so proud," I said. "It was the playthings cracked Egerik. Indeed, all of you were exceptional. No matter if this bag was filled with gold instead of silver, it would not be enough to repay the risks you took."

"What of *you*, sister witch?" said Neri. "Going ahead with the impersonation while believing Placidio was out of reach. After Bawds Field? Don't know as I'd have had balls enough for that."

We each laid out our pieces of the story as we devoured Vashti's noodles and tea and the supply of mead Placidio had brought to wash it down. Placidio said he'd heard that Falco di Taglino had abruptly retired as head of the Gardia Sestorale. Like Rossi's sojourn in the country, we felt the Shadow Lord's hand in that. Then I showed them Nuccio's message and, though Neri would have preferred a more public punishment, we all agreed it was likely for the best.

"No rumor of Cei?" asked Placidio.

"I warned *il Padroné*," I said, "but we all should take care. He never saw Romy, only Monette, but you, Placidio, he heard your name, and saw both you and Neri, despite the masks—"

"We should all of us lay low with our magics. Cautious, yes, boy?"

Though Neri's mouth was full of almond biscuits, he agreed. Without rolling his eyes.

Despite Cei and the inevitable increase of sniffer patrols, we concluded this was an even more satisfying venture than our first.

"It seems our employer agrees." I opened the bag I'd collected, and spilled out at least a thousand silver solets. My tale of Sandro's apology entertained them almost as much.

"When I collected this, I made sure that the Shadow Lord will not recall the name of the swordsman the Pizottis came hunting."

Their shocked silence surprised me. As it did me, as well, when I thought what I had just confessed. I'd used my hateful bit of magic on Sandro. Without hesitation.

Vashti brought four small bags to divide our pay.

"Maybe a fifth?" I said.

"He won't take it," said Placidio. "Promise you that. He said he'd sworn to do whatever you needed forever."

"When he says forever, it sounds like he means it," said Neri. "He seems a cheerful fellow, considering he was near dead a sevenday ago."

"Say the silver is from the rest of us, Romy-zha," said Vashti. "He could have saved *you* by merely speaking your name. Putting himself in front of sniffers saved us all."

"I'll persuade him," I said.

"So *il Padroné* didn't say what our next venture might be?" said Neri, carrying in yet another bowl of noodles from Vashti's kitchen. The rest of us groaned and flung cushions and spoons at him.

After a while Vashti and Dumond walked out to fetch their children from their friend Meki's house, and Neri raced off to the Duck's Bone. Placidio and I strolled around the eastern arc of the Beggars Ring that would take us past the docks. We stayed alert.

"We did a good thing," said Placidio. "Hearing the actual detail of the plan . . . It could have succeeded."

"I believe that, too. I erased your name from memories of the five quislings as well. Couldn't get to Taglino. Will that come back to haunt you?"

"I'll stay clear of him. Without the Gardia or the other five to back him, I'm not thinking he'll ever admit he was there. And it doesn't seem like Egerik or Rossi will be after me. The Pizottis likely won't back down, but they're chastened; certain, there's fewer of them in fighting trim. Cei's the worry."

"What does such a man do when the person who's owned him since childhood is gone?"

"Break into pieces. Run. Hire out, maybe. I've seen all those happen with young soldiers who've lost a strict commander."

We didn't talk much more. The night air was as soft on the skin as silk pillows, as only summer in Cantagna could be. I was lost in Dumond's report of Neri popping in and out of the palazzo all that terrible night because he didn't like thinking of me alone, and Neri telling of Placidio going out into the streets and deliberately taunting Digo di Pizotti's favorite son so as to draw the entire clan to come after him. And Dumond, painting for hours. Waiting. Ready to catch me if I fell. No confidential agent ever had such partners.

As we neared the South Gate, where I would turn down to the docks to give Teo his share of our fee, I summoned the daring to ask my question. "Back at the woolhouse when we questioned Teo, you weren't surprised that he could speak in my mind. And you immediately asked if I could speak back to him. Why?"

"It's none—"

"Don't you dare say it's none of my business." Having just enjoyed the camaraderie of the evening, I wasn't harsh. Just determined. "I'm the one who endured the three of you telling me how stupid I was for rescuing him. I'm the one who's felt the guilt for it. But when this stranger worked a most astonishing feat of magic, you believed it *instantly*? And you *bowed* to him. I've honored your boundaries, swordmaster, but *magic* is not your private fiefdom. Can you not trust me in this one thing?"

We walked on toward the gate. By the time he opened his mouth, I was at the point of bursting.

"In the past—long past—I lived near the sea. I heard of—I met a woman from Lesh. The Isles. She had the skin markings and this magic, both to speak and to hear. Neither did she lie. Talk *around* things, yes, but not lie. Their people have—a way of life that is worthy of respect. But they also have strict . . . absolute . . . privacies, so I can't—I just can't. If he could remember these things, Teo would thank me for honoring that."

"But you won't tell him what you know about his people?"

"No. They have their ways. Reasons."

In this tortuous telling, Placidio was clearly filtering the secrets from truth like a sieve filters rocks from a slurry. My own perverse logic recognized it as his attempt to acknowledge the rightness of my anger without breaching whatever stricture forbade him say more. It was not whim or pique or selfish hiding, but honor.

"And the five candles?"

"That was a guess. A test. Call it an insult. With all he's forgotten, he likely couldn't tell you why it bothered him so. Now, please . . ."

"Fair enough." I'd no wish to torture him. "So I'll tell you a conclusion I've come to. I know what Teo's searching for."

That stopped him in his tracks. "And?"

"The Antigonean bronze. The statue we so carefully ensured would go to the grand duc of Riccia-by-the-sea. Every place Teo felt the presence of his mysterious quarry, the statue had been. The woolhouse. Dumond's workshop. My house. Sandro's house. When Teo lay so ill, I had a dream of a sad, fracturing city—*his* dream, I believe. It was very like the visions Dumond and I saw when we touched the statue with magic. Dumond agreed. Am I mad to think Teo's hunting the statue? Should we tell him?"

"Not mad. And not yet." The answer came so quickly, I knew he'd guessed the same. "There's naught to be done about it right now. It's too far away. Until he remembers more of his purposes, what would he do with the knowledge? Let me think about how to approach . . . the problem." The problem of Teo and Eduardo di Corradini, two people Placidio respected, laying claim to something of importance for reasons I could not fathom.

"All right," I said. "In the future, it might be well if you would share your thoughts about such topics right away. I promise that when you say *no more,* I won't press. But it might prevent me combusting, which would be better for everyone involved. And maybe someday, you might be able to shift the boundary a bit."

"I'll consider it." We arrived at the turn for the gate. "But likely won't. You'll have a care going home? Keep aware of your surroundings?"

"I will. But remember it's you and Neri that Cei saw. Fortune's benefice this night, swordmaster."

"Virtue's hand, lady scribe."

I watched him go. Placidio, the rootless man. Deliberately so. Having lived with Sandro whose roots were so deeply entwined with Cantagna as to be inseparable, the contrast was very clear. Someday Placidio di Vasil was going to walk away and never be found in Cantagna again. That would be a terrible day.

The evening was still young down at the docks. Fishermen were mending nets, coiling ropes, and sloshing buckets of water through bloody fish troughs. Cats' eyes gleamed from the shadows, as their owners pounced on unlucky rats or glided through the clutter to find tasty tidbits from the day's catch. Human gleaners crept through the shadows, too. I heeded Placidio and stayed alert. I held tight to my bags of silver.

Frenetti's pilchard house sat at the less favored upriver end of the docks. But I didn't have to venture the warren of drying racks, emptied casks, ropes, nets, and brine ponds in Frenetti's yard to find my friend from the Isles of Lesh. It was easy to guess where he'd be this time of night. Indeed, as I walked to the far end of the nearest open pier, I spied a lanky silhouette dangling his feet in the water.

"Watching the stars come out, are you?" I said, joining him on the plank decking before he could jump up. "They seem to multiply as the city goes to sleep."

"Aye, they do. But never so many—"

"—as would be visible in the Isles of Lesh."

I could feel his smile, even if I couldn't make it out in the dark.

"Someday I'd like to see your home. My whole life has been spent in this city, with only a few short journeys around the northlands. I can't imagine what it's like to live surrounded by the sea."

"Very different." He scooted around to face me, folding his legs and peering through the dark. "Is all well now? Such a dangerous venture. So courageous of you and your friends to do it for the good of your people . . . your city."

"With your help, we had as good an outcome as we could hope. Which is why you must share in our fee." I set his bag on the damp planks between us.

"No, I didn't help for coin. I told you—"

"And I'll be ever grateful for your willingness to believe our purpose was worthy and for trusting us enough to put yourself at such risk. But you also spent time of your own—work time, perhaps, or time you could have been resting so as to work the next day. It's only fair that your time be paid for, if not your risk or your magic. Use it to get yourself a good pair of boots. Maybe a wool cloak and blanket for winter; ours are not so mild as in the southlands." I shoved it toward him. "I won't accept a refusal."

"All right. I'll find something worthy to do with it. But until then . . . would you keep it for me? Down here, I've no place for it." He pushed it into my hand.

"If you wish."

I tied the bag to my belt alongside my own. "Perhaps you can use it to find your mother's friend. Have you remembered any more about her?"

"Yes! As I was running around the city that night. Domenika is her name, and she is one who studies events of the past."

"A historian."

"In Lesh, we would name her as *one who unravels the winds of time*."

The nape of my neck prickled at his words. I scraped my fingers through my hair and laughed. "Someday, Teo, we are going to talk about what that means. The way you put words together sends my head spinning. But my head has experienced enough stretching over this tenday. I should go home."

"Weary, yes, I hear it in you. Anxious, too. I am, also, ever since you dragged me from the river. Do you know what gives me peace?"

"Besides watching the stars come out?"

"Together with it. Take off your shoes."

"But I need to—"

"I promise it will help with the overstretching."

In moments we were sitting shoulder to shoulder, bathing our bare feet in the cool urgency of the Venia, as the silken night air bathed our faces. The quiet power of the river infused my tired spirit—or perhaps it was some magic of Teo's that soothed. Sounds of the city receded. The flow eddied about the pilings with a soft slurp. Distant pinpoints of light swirled in the deeps . . . and shadows . . .

"Beware!" Teo twisted his torso away from me and flattened himself to the pier. The blade that had just missed Teo's spine raked a gouge in his shoulder. The wound gouted blood as he swept his arms behind his head, grasping furiously at scrabbling feet. Cei's bare feet. Training brought my dagger from sheath to hand faster than I could think it.

Off balance from the miss, Cei scuttled backward to avoid Teo's entanglement, then raised up for another strike.

"No!" I screamed. The blade slashed at my neck. My dagger blocked the blow, near cracking my arm. The weapon fell from my numb fingers.

A great splash of water near blinded me, and for a terrifying moment I thought Teo had gone into the river. But instead, faster than an eyeblink, he had rolled over backward and planted two wet feet in Cei's midsection with such power as to explode the air from the assassin's lungs. As Cei staggered, I pivoted onto my knees, stayed low, and lunged for his ankles. I missed. Teo didn't. Cei went down hard on his back.

Teo scrambled on top of him, pinning him to the planks, clamping Cei's wrist so tightly his fingers opened. I snatched up his dagger, slick with blood, and threw it into the river.

Cei snarled and writhed, but Teo's hold . . . hands and feet and knees . . . immobilized him.

"Who is this?" said Teo, cold as I'd never heard him.

"Egerik's favored assassin," I said. "Trained from childhood. Did at least two murders on that fraught night. Others in the past. But why he's after you . . ."

"Me?"

"No, no, of course not."

All became clear as I recalled the youthful gleaner down at the Avanci Bridge. Cei had been stalking Sandro. But Sandro had left our meeting by the stair and the bridge, while I was the one who came out the door.

"I was in the wrong place at the wrong time. Evidently he doesn't stop killing, even when his master has vanished and their plot crumbled."

"What shall we do with him?"

Cei's limbs were taut, murderous rage quivering the air.

What else was there besides the choice I'd sworn the Chimera would not make? Cei had seen Placidio and Neri and now me and Teo. What else did he know to do but murder?

"He cannot go free," I said. "I should summon the Gardia." Though it could take all night to get a warden down here. And how would I answer their questions?

"Fetch some rope if you would, while we consider. That skiff just up there is Frenetti's. I'll pay him for the rope."

When I got back with the rope, Teo was sitting beside Cei, not on him. The beautiful young man lay perfectly still. A hand on his chest testified that he was breathing.

"What did you do?"

"I didn't kill him. I just . . . forced him to turn inward for a while."

He uncoiled the rope and bound Cei securely. I cut the length with my own dagger, retrieved from the edge of the pier.

"I'm guessing you can't explain exactly how you did the forcing."

"There are ways to deal with evil that are not death," he said, which was not at all a satisfying answer.

"He's dangerous. Skilled," I said. As Teo was. The speed and power of Teo's reactions made Placidio look slow. And Teo had magic I did not yet comprehend.

"You've brought me funds enough to buy a small boat, yes? I'll take him away from your city for a while. Someplace he can do no harm."

"Teo, why would you do this?"

"I killed three bargemen from fear and weakness," he said.

"I need to make amends. I swear I'll not let him hurt anyone else. I think that's what I do . . . when I'm at home." The tilt of his head told me he was smiling. "It's very late. You'll be mindful on the way to *your* home?"

"Indeed so. Fortune's benefice, Teo. Do come back."

"No doubt of it. I've much more to learn here. *Theía Mitéra* embrace you, Romy of Lizard's Alley."

I strolled up the dock, racking my brain to figure out where Teo might be taking Cei. My hand strayed to the heavy little bags chinking at my belt. Silly. I'd not left him coin enough to buy a sausage, much less a boat.

"Teo!" I reversed course, only to halt halfway down the dock.

Teo . . . At the end of the dock my tall, slender friend stood naked, his pale flesh marked with coils and spirals and sinuous lines in the hue of midnight. Throwing his head back, he lifted his spread arms to the starry sky in supplication. Or exaltation. Perhaps both. Then he rolled Cei's bound body into the flowing Venia. He made a graceful arc as he dove into the flood after it.

I raced to the end of the dock and found his slops and shirt folded neatly and left atop a bollard. There was no sign of either man in the dark river.

For an hour I sat beside that bollard.

I did not believe Cei was drowned. And vicious as he was, I was happy we hadn't killed him. Foolish, perhaps, for a woman who approved the Brotherhood exacting mortal penalties on Egerik and Lodovico di Gallanos.

Maybe it was the night. Maybe it was the wonder of Teo's gifts. Or just that my head was so tired from housing two souls. But fragments of conversations flitted through me along with facts and observations like snowflakes swirling on the wind, settling into odd and marvelous patterns that would have no hold in the daylight.

Teo's love for the sea. His declaration that he would not let Cei hurt anyone else. What had he said? *I think that's what I do. When I'm at home.* He prevented monsters from hurting others.

Teo who did not lie. Whose language and markings came from another millennium.

Another fragment—my dream of ruination, a dream I believed Teo shared. An apology had drifted through that dream: *Your time has come early.* Time for what?

On the night before we met Egerik, Vashti had teased Placidio, "Leviathan is with us. A fighter, yes? Dormant, waiting for the world's need. Is that not your Costa Drago legend?"

It was. But it was not Placidio who brought that legend to my mind this night. It was Teo.

Placidio claimed to have seen Leviathan portrayed as a human, naked like Atladu.

Atladu. *Theíko Patéra*—the divine Father. And Placidio had bowed to Teo and said his people and their secrets and their customs were worthy of respect.

Not least, there was the Antigonean bronze. The statue, depicting Atladu and Dragonis and a missing companion, not in combat with each other, but on a hunt or in a footrace, sat in the grand duc of Riccia's castle. I believed—and Placidio believed— that statue to be the object of Teo's searching. Teo who bore the sign of the wind on his swift feet. Was it possible that the missing companion—the piece of bronze broken off and lost—was *Leviathan*? And that somehow, in some way, Teo . . .

Well, I could not say it, even to myself. But certain, there were mysteries beyond the things we knew. When I finally accepted that my friend was not returning from the river that night, I tucked all those bits and pieces away, promising myself to look at them another day.

I strolled homeward on the Ring Road, paying careful attention to my surroundings, as all my male friends advised as if I wouldn't think of it myself. Indeed the night market was still lively. People bargained with bootsellers and candlemakers, and crowded the noodle stalls. Cheery music of pipes and tabors drifted through the market alongside the aromas of biscuits and rosemary and garlic sausage.

Though bone weary, I chose not to go straight to bed, but to stop into the Duck's Bone and eat sausage and drink wine and tell a basketmaker that I would meet her on the morrow to write a letter to her son in Tibernia, and that yes, it should get to him before the winter solstice. Neri was there, tossing out drunkards and stopping fights. Later, I could tell him of Teo and Cei and the snowflake pattern that had come to me. Then I would sleep.

Cantagna was my home, and for tonight, she was safe.

The Needles of the Ascoltaré

Mystery	Primary	Obverse	Symbol
Order	Structure	Chaos	Sun/Starburst
Jeopardy	Safety	Danger	X
Presence	Existence/ Arrival	Absence/ Departure	Arrow
Power	Strength	Weakness	Flail
Judgment	Justice/ Rightness	Error/Crime	Balance
Substance	Flesh	Spirit	Barred crescent
Reason	Knowledge	Faith/ Impossibility	Crescent moon
Mysticism	Enlightenment/ Faith	Mundanity/ Reason	Egg
Relationship	Friend	Enemy	Heart

Acknowledgments

Unending appreciation to my ever-faithful critiquing crew—Susan, Saytchyn, Curt, and the two most excellent Brians—for saying what needs to be said and sharing the journey of words. To the Writers of the Hand for the focus, encouragement, and the consistent reminder that membership in the community of writers is the one of the greatest rewards of this strange profession. I must also give a shout-out to Markus the Fighter Guy for timely consultation, to Lucienne the Agent for her steady hand, to Lindsey the Editor for her careful reading, and to my faithful readers for your companionship in adventure. And thanks, always and ever, to the Exceptional Spouse for everything.

About the Author

Cate Glass is a writer of fantasy adventure novels. She also dabbles from time to time in epic fantasy and short fiction. For more information, check out categlass.com or follow her on Twitter @Cbergwriter.